Rock with You

USA TODAY Bestselling Author
Nora Flite

This was originally published as the Body Rock Series 1-4, but has been re-released in this updated format to better tell a fuller, richer story. There's also a sexy bonus short story in the back about Brenda and her crush!

ROMANCE THAT PUSHES
THE LIMITS

- Chapter 1 -
Drezden

The cigarette hung from my lips, red-tip preparing to fall to the earth. If I moved, the ash would spill. It would take so very, very little to break that perfect, gravity defying cylinder.

My shoulder swung, carrying my knuckles straight into Johnny's mouth. The end of my cigarette dissipated, falling away with my abrupt movement.

Johnny tumbled backwards, spilling onto the hard floor and taking a few other chairs with him. Around me, I heard gasps, especially the sweet cries of the groupies who'd been on him like flies just seconds ago. "What the *fuck,* man!" he shouted, sprawled there in shock and pain.

I planned to give him more of the latter.

"Whoa, man, hold up!" The voice came from my left, a familiar, high-pitched rattle; Colt, the drummer for my band. He was a good guy. That meant there was no way was he going to lay a hand on me.

Glancing sideways, I saw how he stood there with his fingers spread.

No. Colt wouldn't stop me.

Turning, I realized Johnny was backpedaling across the floor. We were in a private room in an otherwise hardly-private bar, the only shabby environment available after our show.

Johnny kept moving on hands and knees. He wouldn't get far doing that, not with my long legs striding over the toppled chairs.

"Yo, man!" he shouted, grappling with my wrists as I lifted him from the ground. He wanted to escape, who wouldn't? "Drez, man, fucking stop! What's your problem?"

He was light, I was strong. It made bringing him up to eye-level a simple matter. Our noses nearly touched, the blood on his teeth smelling like rust. "You know what my fucking problem is, Johnny. You better *fucking* know."

The centers of his eyes were tiny pin-holes. He struggled once more, the crimson stain dribbling on his shirt growing when I gave him a hard shake in response. "I—what the hell are you talking about?" He was already on his way to being piss-full of beer, his breath reeking.

"You were a damn mess out there tonight," I snapped. Just thinking about how he'd dropped his guitar in the middle of our opening song made my neck cramp up.

"Oh, come on," he laughed, eyeing the room of gawking people like they might agree with him. "I hit a few wrong notes, that's nothing to get so—"

He didn't finish his sentence; the thud of him hitting the floor did it for him. Johnny coughed, then wheezed as I pressed my shoe onto his chest. "You fucked up every song, Johnny. You've been a wreck for weeks. I'm done with it."

I pulled away, ignoring how he grabbed for my ankle. "Wait! What the hell does that mean?" The hard lines of his mouth twisted into a nervous smile. "It sounds like you're kicking me out of the band, man, but you can't do that. You *know* you can't do that." Johnny pulled himself to his knees, laughing at my back, laughing at the people who still just stared. "You can't do that, you couldn't—it's not even an option!"

Digging into my pocket, I slid a new cigarette between my lips. Everyone kept telling me to quit; it was an awful idea for a singer to smoke. *I only do it when I'm pissed or stressed. Too bad that's all the fucking time lately.*

"Hey!" Johnny wasn't laughing anymore. I heard people mumbling, then a scream. It was sharp, mixing with the explosion of glass near my face. The bottle left a wet stain on the edge of the door, some of it trickling onto my cheekbone. "Get back here you fucking asshole, you can't do this!"

Pulling the cancer-stick from my mouth, I glanced behind me. I was going to say something about how I *could* kick him out, I'd just done it, in fact. Instead, I saw Johnny with

9

his arm wrenched back. He had another beer, preparing to launch it at my defenseless face.

There was a second where I wondered if my fans would dig my new scars.

A large man, larger than me, hooked his arm around Johnny's throat. I hadn't noticed Porter before now. The bassist for my band wasn't much for dank drinking holes, he usually just made time for the swankier after-parties.

He had our—former—singer on the floor in a simple swing of his thick arms. Johnny had been choked into submission a few times in our career together, but this was nothing like that.

"Two fucking years!" Johnny bellowed. "Two fucking years together! *Fuck you, fuck you Drez!*"

His ragged shouts broke the anxious silence like it was a fragile egg. The groupies, the waitresses, everyone began to move. Some helped Porter with subduing Johnny, but mostly, everyone wanted to take a picture of the conflict. I was sure I saw seven girls on their phones.

Maybe some of them are calling the cops.

Who the fuck was I kidding? All they cared about was getting the most likes or upvotes or whatever the hell it was these days on their social media accounts.

Breaking into the night air, I closed the backdoor and leaned on the building's cold wall. My jacket sounded like aluminum foil when I slid down, sitting on the asphalt with a grunt. It was dark, the only light coming from a single flickering street lamp. The dying orange reminded me of my unlit cigarette.

Patting myself in search of my lighter, I glanced up as the door cracked open beside me. "Near death by a flying bottle sure makes you wanna rush out and get some of that tasty lung cancer, huh?" Porter asked.

Chuckling, I spoke out of the side of my mouth, still looking for my lighter. "I'll take tobacco over a concussion any day."

He crouched beside me, his own lighter flicking to life. Leaning in, I let him turn the tip of my smoke cherry-red. "Funny," he mused, "I didn't know there were only two options here."

Inhaling deeply, I shut my eyes while smoke floated around us both. "Tragedy just likes to rub elbows with me, that's all."

The thick man pulled his knee to his chest, frowning up at the foggy sky. The stars were nowhere to be seen. "You're serious about getting rid of Johnny."

Flicking ash, I stared at the bloody smudges on my knuckles. "Yup."

"Guess that means we need a new guitarist, huh?"

"Yup."

Porter scratched at his head, fingers not putting a dent in his blonde faux-hawk. "Well, fuck. You know Brenda is going to be pissed over this."

He was right, and I *did* know it. Our manager was going to lose her shit when she heard I'd kicked Johnny out. Chances were, she'd already heard it through the tweets and blogs of our fans.

She'd already dealt with a number of things on this tour, but I'd be insane to think that would make her take this news any better. It would have been nice if any of the other bands playing with us as we went city to city could have caused a bit of havoc.

Just a *little* bit, anyway.

Porter moved his hands in front of him, pantomiming outlining a headline for a newspaper. "Four and a Half Headstones becomes Three and a Half Headstones! Singer is a maniac, kills their guitar player!"

I waved smoke away from my eyes. "I didn't *kill* Johnny."

"But you sure looked like you wanted to."

"I did want to," I said, sticking my smoke into the corner of my mouth.

That made him laugh, which got me to smile in spite of everything. My hand was burning from the sucker-punch, my mood dark as I imagined hunting for a new guitarist. "Whoever we get," I mumbled, "We'll need them fast. We've got two days before the next show."

"That's a fucking slim-shot."

Crushing the cigarette on the ground, I eyed Porter thoughtfully. "He'll need to be reliable, and not a damn joke like our last guy."

"Our last guy who's probably not going to just vanish contentedly while we replace him."

The back of my head tapped the wall. "Good point. So, he'll need to be tough, reliable, talented, and not mind that there's a good chance Johnny will take a swing at him someday."

Porter reached out, clasping my shoulder grimly. "Like I said earlier, Brenda is going to be *pissed* at you. No way we'll find someone like that, not out here, man. We're on fucking *tour!*" I moved to brush him off, but he just squeezed harder. The way his thin, near-white eyebrows lowered made me hesitate. "Drez, do you honestly think replacing someone like Johnny is possible at this stage in the game?"

Gently, I pried his fingers off of me. Standing to my full height, I brushed dirt from my jeans and gave Porter the most serious look I could. My voice was flat, all steel. "Yup."

The answer was simple.

If only the situation could have been, too.

- Chapter Two -
Lola

"Easy with that," I growled, reaching up to steady a speaker that had been tossed into the back of the van. "This is expensive equipment!"

The kid—he had to be younger than me, and I was only nineteen—just rolled his eyes. Like everyone else so far on this tour, he wasn't going to give me an iota of respect.

Biting my tongue was my only solution. *I'm beginning to second guess this whole trip,* I thought bitterly. Hoisting another case into the van, I wiped my forehead and sighed. Each time we packed up, preparing to move to the next location, I wondered if my muscles would give out.

The tour had only been going on for four days, but I'd assembled and disassembled the set for my brother's band three times. I wasn't very big, but I put my heart into helping—my everything, honestly.

Shooting a look at the guys loitering nearby, I thought, *We'd be done much faster if anyone else put in even half of my effort.* Most of the team consisted of groupie guys who were tagging along in the hopes of snagging second-hand pussy.

They hunted after each show, scooping up the girls who'd been denied private time with the bands. A few had even tried it with me... until I'd decked a guy so hard his jaw swelled up like a grapefruit.

They'd mostly stopped flirting after that. Mostly.

Shutting the van doors, I felt some relief in knowing that we wouldn't need to unpack everything for another two days. The driving time to the next location, the gorgeous mountains of Colorado, would be my time to relax.

I should go make sure Sean doesn't need anything else from me before we get on the road. Walking along the asphalt, past the cars, the buses, I tried to catch a glimpse of any of the other bands.

If I was honest with myself, I wasn't acting much better than the groupies I mocked. There was a chance I'd spot a member from one of the bigger bands, like the Silver Sideways, Backwater Till Sunday, or maybe even Four and a Half Headstones.

That had me excited.

Especially Four and a Half Headstones.

The news about the fight last night had spread through the caravan of vehicles. Websites were exploding with rumors about it all, making claims that famous singer Drezden Halifax had beaten Johnny Muse to a bloody pulp.

I'd heard things ranging from him being charged with manslaughter to Drezden being the one who had actually gotten beaten up. There'd been no solid proof about any of it— which sucked, because who knew what it meant for the rest of the bands.

Four and a Half Headstones were headlining everything. If they had a fallout and had to cancel... it could be disastrous. *Will my brother's band have to pull out?* It was an awful possibility. Barbed Fire had been ecstatic to be invited on the tour. Sean had scared me with the phone call, he kept screaming without making sense—I'd thought he was in trouble.

The memory of his excitement made me smile. It hadn't taken much for convince me to come along. I was eager for my brother to finally get the big break he deserved.

Who knows. Maybe I'll meet an agent or someone who'll get me started in the right direction while I'm here. I wasn't as good as my brother when it came to playing guitar, but that was fine; everyone had to start somewhere. It could happen. *Anything* could happen.

I spotted Barbed Fire's tour bus ahead on the side of the road. The paint job was a shoddy red that had gone mostly brown, a hastily painted swirl of orange fire peeling on one side. It was nowhere near as fancy as the other buses, barely big enough to fit the members, which was why we needed the shoddy van to cart the equipment around.

16

Rapping my knuckles on the door, I tugged it open and peeked up the steps. "Hey, Sean! You in here?"

He was hunched in one of the seats, surrounded by the rest of the band. I'd known he was inside—of course he'd be here—it was just the most casual way for me to ask if it was alright if I came in. I was awful at being direct.

Sean lifted his head, his pierced eyebrow crawling high. Everyone said we had the same blue eyes, except I always felt like my brother just had *something* in his stare that I didn't. A kind of razor steel that could cut you into pieces.

I rarely saw him look at me that way, luckily.

"Lola," he said, "I was just about to go look for you."

"Yeah?" Shutting the door, enjoying the air-conditioning, I put my hands on two seats and swung my legs forward. I landed in front of the group with a big smile. "I was coming to see if you wanted me to do anything else before we got on the road."

My older brother cast a look at the rest of the band, their silence suddenly uncomfortable. I wondered what I had walked in on. He said, "Did you hear about what happened last night, about the singer from Headstones and his guitarist?"

"Yeah, of course I did," I laughed. "People won't shut up about it, but no one has

17

anything real to say. I'm starting to think it's a big joke." No one else was smiling; my lips quickly drifted into a thin line. "Okay, I get the feeling you're about to tell me something important. Something bad." *Shit, were the rumors true, did someone get beaten to death?*

Sean pushed his thick bangs from his eyes, slumping back into the seat. "It's actually potentially good news."

It was hard for me to pull my gaze from my brother's face. "Tell me what's going on."

He waved at me to sit, so I dropped down on the edge of the leathery cushion diagonal from him. "Lola, Drezden kicked out Johnny Muse."

"Kicked him out," I repeated in disbelief. "Kicked him out *of the band?*" The idea blew my mind. I was glad I was already sitting. "Why would he—that's insane!"

The heavy-set drummer, Shark, flashed me a wide grin. In spite of his name, his teeth were actually nice and straight. "Right? It's crazy! I was in the place, though, I saw the whole thing! Dude went nuts, just pummeled Johnny to the ground."

My mind conjured up an image of Drezden, of how the muscles in his arms would flex when he was screaming on stage. He looked like the type who could tear a guy's face up with ease. "Jeez," I whispered.

Sean slid deeper into his seat, kicking Shark in the knee. "Chill, it wasn't as bad as that. I saw Johnny last night, too, before they dragged him off to keep him from throwing more bottles at folks. He was in one piece. Drezden didn't 'pummel' him. He *did* kick him out though, yeah."

I folded my hands in my lap, crossing my knees. One pink and black sneaker tapped nervously in the air. "That's still insane. If Four and a Half Headstones doesn't have a guitarist, what are they going to do?"

"They're going to need to find a new one, and fast," my brother said.

"Yeah, fast." I smoothed my messy dark hair. The humidity had turned it into a wild mane. "Real fast. Where are they going to find a guitarist before the next show?"

No one said anything. Baffled, I raised my eyes, looking from each member to the next. Sean was smiling, it made my stomach twist. "Oh no," I said, my back going straight as a rod. "I can't, I'm not anywhere *near* good enough to be in their band!"

Sean slid out of his seat, shoving Shark aside as he did so. "Lola, come on. You're the sister of the lead guitarist in Barbed Fire! I taught you everything you know." He came to stand over me, grasping my shoulders like it'd calm me down.

I wasn't ready to be calm.

"Shit," I said to no one. "Holy shit." He wasn't kidding when he said he'd taught me everything I knew. The advantage to being the younger sister of a talented guitarist was you could learn a lot. The downside?

Well, we couldn't *both* be the lead guitarist in the same band.

I'd never get to play with Barbed Fire. The closest I'd ever come was carting their equipment onto the stage at their shows. And now my brother was trying to get me to go and try out for the guitarist in fucking Four and a Half Headstones?

"Shit," I said again. I was saying it a lot.

Giving me one more squeeze, he patted me so roughly it shook my skull. "The auditions are going on today. I already went and talked to their manager when I heard what was going on. You've got a great chance here, Lola."

A great chance? I wiped my clammy palms on my ripped jeans. *He's right, it's an amazing chance. I know all their songs by heart, but... there's no way I'm good enough, there's so much more than being able to repeat back a song. If I audition, I'll look like an asshole.*

"—an hour," he was saying, my brain so fogged I missed the start of his sentence. "I know you brought your guitar, grab it and take it with you."

"Sorry, what?"

"You've got an hour to get ready, they're doing it before we all drive out to the next pit stop."

"Sean," I blurted, climbing to my feet in a hurry. "Listen, wait, I can't do this."

His eyebrow piercing glinted as he wrinkled his forehead. "What? Why?"

"I just—come on!" I said, giggling uncomfortably. "It's *me*, I'm not a rock star!"

"You've played in bands before," he said.

"Garage bands, joke bands, nothing serious."

"And I've seen you listening to Four and a Half Headstones since they launched."

I couldn't stop shaking my head.

Sean opened his mouth, then halted. Eyeing the other members, he jerked his head at the door. "Give us a minute, guys."

They trundled out, leaving me alone with my brother. The air in the bus felt sticky.

"Sean—"

"Lola," he cut me off, burying his hands in his pockets. "Do you not get it? This is a huge opportunity, why are you sabotaging yourself?"

I let my hands fall to my hips. "I'm not, I'm just..." *I'm just scared.* "There's someone else here who'll get the position, someone better."

"I don't get it," he muttered, looking everywhere but at me. "I thought you wanted to make music, to become a star. I figured that was the fucking point of all of this."

"I do want to! Sean, I really do, I'm just not ready for it. Not right now."

21

Tightening his jaw, my brother brushed past me. "You're right," he said, tongue coated in acid. "I guess you're not." He left me alone on the bus, not once looking back.

For some time, I stared after him. My mind was as messy as my stomach. Gripping the seat, I crushed the slippery material until it squeaked. *Great job,* I told myself. *You wanted him to quit pushing you to do this, and you got your way.* Kicking my heel into the side of the small table between the seats, I grit my molars.

Fucking dammit.

He claimed I was giving up an opportunity—sabotaging myself. Was he right? *Sean can't really think I'd pass this audition.* But then, why tell me about it if he didn't? My brother knew me deeply and truly. If I ever questioned my skills, he was there to correct me. To boost me.

He believed in me.

So why didn't I?

Being in the bus was too much, the air was thick in my lungs. Clawing at the already torn seats, I tripped out the door and into the air. Gripping my knees, I hung my chin and took a deep breath—then another. I did that until my ribs ached.

Around me, I heard people laughing, talking casually as they prepared for the drive ahead. It was warm, and I was sweaty, but I wasn't thinking about the weather.

I have one hour, he said. One hour to decide if I'm going to take a shot at becoming the guitarist for freaking Four and a Half Headstones.

A band I'd been obsessed with since their first song.

Maybe I do have a chance. This isn't like a world-wide announcement with applicants coming all over to audition. We're in the middle of a tour, slim pickings. I could... I could actually have a chance here!

Wiping my hair from my eyes, I began the trek back towards Barbed Fire's van.

If I was going to do anything...

I would need my guitar.

****

They'd rented out the back room of a nearby gas station. The line of people coming out of the door was like a trail of bread crumbs.

On the one hand, I thought to myself, *I don't need to go ask Sean for directions to where the audition is happening. But it looks like every single person who can hold a guitar showed up. And some who can't.* Rubbing my neck, I hooked my case over my shoulder, attempting to act casual as I got in line.

Everyone was talking, the vibe excited and hyped. I heard snippets about the fight last night, or comments from people who admitted they were only auditioning so they could meet the band.

With the sun beating down on my shoulders, I started to second guess my decision. *At this rate, I'll pass out before I get inside. There's no way they'll get through all these people!*

A movement up ahead at the gas station door drew my eyes. There was a woman, her hair all wild red curls that made her skin ghostly in comparison. Most of her was hidden under a giant sun hat, sunglasses gleaming where they perched on her elegant nose.

She was inching down the line in a pair of ankle-breaking heels, whispering into the ears of the gathered people. Leaning in, she'd either scribble on a clipboard in her arms, or wave the person away.

The murmurs grew as the line shortened. Disgruntled men and women melted to the sidelines as the mystery red-head cut through.

What's happening, what is she saying? Why are people leaving? The closer she got to me, the tighter my stomach became. The unease was turning my knuckles white, I had to drop my guitar to my hip just to keep a hold on it.

Fuck, don't come here, don't talk to me. Somehow, I was sure if she spoke to me, she'd tell me to leave.

She'd ruin my chance.

The woman whispered to the guy in

front of me, a lanky dude who listened... then whispered back. A single word, I thought, but I didn't catch it.

The woman straightened, nodded, asked him his name and scribbled something down. He remained where he was, and then she set those giant mirrored glasses on me. I could see myself in the reflection, I looked paler than she even did. *Calm down, just chill out.*

Her lips, perfect rubies, spread in a tiny smile. I always wondered how some women managed to look so put together during tours in spite of all the traveling and time on the road. Bending low, her heels making her taller than me, I felt her breath tickle my ear. "Hey there," she whispered, "I need to ask you something. Real quick. 'Kay?"

Swallowing, I gave a sharp nod. "Uh, sure, ask me anything." I didn't know who she was, but she was obviously working for the band in some capacity. Could she be their manager? I was familiar with the band's music, not their business details.

"Right," she said, pen tapping her clipboard. "This is just so we can weed down to the people Drezden wants to listen to. Answer honestly, one word if you can. What do *you* think is the most important thing you need to be a good guitarist?"

Oh, shit, I thought quickly. *Why didn't I eavesdrop on the guy in front of me? Fuck fuck fuck... what's the most important thing you need to be a good guitarist? What kind of question is that?*

She was staring at me, no longer smiling. Impatience was written on her soft features, gravel crunching under her fidgeting heels. I needed to say *something*, and I needed to do it soon.

But what could she want to hear?

No, what could Drezden want to hear?

My skull felt swollen, too many worries bubbling up. The answer I'd give would wreck me or reward me. I didn't know much about Drezden beyond how he sounded when he was singing. *Well, I know he beat up Johnny Muse last night. That doesn't help me much.* My mind was blank. I couldn't plot out anything worth saying.

Staring at the red-head, I licked my lips with my dry tongue. The word that left me had a mind of its own, escaping from my subconscious before I could try and stop it. "Honesty."

The way she twisted her mouth, leaning away from me, it sank my heart. That was not the look of someone who was happy with my answer. "Sorry, what do you mean?"

Sweat crept down my spine. It was even collecting uncomfortably under my breasts. What *did* I mean? It had just come out, but... *But it's true,* I thought to myself. *It's actually kind of true.* "Uh, well. I think a good guitar player is someone who is honest with themselves, with the music. If that makes sense?”

Her frown said it didn't. “Hm. Drezden asked me to look for something else.”

My skin was cold. Defeat was worming into my core; I'd fucked my answer up, destroyed my chance. “Can I answer again?”

She hesitated, pen twisting between her elegant fingers. “What's your name?”

“Lola Cooper.”

“Cooper,” she said, lifting her glasses to squint at me. “You're Sean's sister, aren't you?”

Hoisting my guitar, I nodded. “Yeah, that's right.” *Didn't he say he talked to the band's manager earlier? This must be her!*

Considering me in a new light, one I wasn't sure I liked, she slid her sunglasses back onto my nose. The pen was loud as she wrote something down. “Stay here, it'll take maybe twenty minutes before you get in.”

My jaw slid open as I understood. I wanted to thank her, but she was moving down the line that had formed behind me. Many more people would be kicked out before she was done.

I'm actually going to get in there, I'm doing this, I thought in amazement. A laugh sprung free, making me cover my mouth to stifle it. *Holy shit. This is really going down.*

I'd been so nervous, so unsure about trying out. It was funny, thinking about arguing with my brother over even bothering to try. But when that woman had appeared, when my opportunity looked like it would be crushed to bits, I'd felt genuine sadness.

Even if it meant standing in the boiling sun for a bit longer, I'd do it.

I'd stand here until I was burnt to a crisp and my fingers fell off from how hard I was squeezing my guitar. This was it. This was the chance I'd always been waiting for.

How could I have almost let it slip by?

- Chapter Three -
Drezden

I drummed my fingers on the table, studying the bandage wrapped around the skinned markings from the night before. *Maybe I should just wrap the other hand, too. People are already acting like I boxed Johnny, might as well roll with it.*

"Drez?"

Looking up, I met Porter's eyes. He was peering at me, reminding me of what I was supposed to be doing. In the middle of this filthy backroom stood a kid whose name I'd already forgotten. He was standing there wearing a stupid grin, eager to hear what I had to say about his playing. He'd strummed for a few minutes, but I'd formed my opinion about his skill on the first pluck.

Still, I'd let him keep going. Maybe that had been cruel.

"Drez," Porter said again, prompting me. "What did you think about Renold's playing?"

Renold. Huh. I'd already forgotten his name the second he'd mentioned it. He just wasn't worth remembering. With a quick scan of the room, I said, "Next."

The guitarist's face morphed, falling low. I wondered if he was going to argue with me— he wouldn't have been the first. In the end, he just limped out the door and didn't look back.

The moment we were alone again, my band was on me. "What the hell, man?" Colt asked, his fist slamming down on the table. "That guy was good!"

"Seriously," Porter sighed, bare arms flexing as he folded them tight. Even with the tattoos crossing his dark skin, he looked like a pouting child. "We need to get on the road, pick a damn guitarist already!"

"None of them have been right," I said, reaching into my pocket for my smokes. A glare from Porter stopped me. "Look, sorry, but I already said I wouldn't replace Johnny with just any fucking kid who can tug some strings."

Colt snorted, pointedly turning his head so I could see the bandage stuck by his ear. Someone had managed to tear one of the drummer's gauges in the brawl last night; just another casualty from my decision to banish Johnny. "You need to find someone, Drez. I'm not exactly keen on letting a new scar be all I gain from this tour."

Wrinkling my nose, I went to argue, but a knock on the door interrupted us. We'd been auditioning people for over an hour. I knew we needed to get back on the road, and I also wondered if we were hitting the end of the pack. *Is Brenda even weeding out the time wasters?*

What if she was, and this was really the best the roadie and groupie riffraff had to offer?

"Come in," I grunted.

Her fingers came first, curling around the edge of the door. Then it was her too-big and too-blue eyes that joined the party. She was lean in all the right places, round in the rest. There was a hint of pink on her bare shoulders from an abundance of sun.

On impulse, my gaze fixated on the way her jeans fit her tightly. They were torn in places, a sign of someone who was used to working hard. They also hinted at the perfect curve of her ass.

But ultimately?

I was busy staring at her guitar case.

"Uh, hey," she said, wide pupils flicking between all of us one by one. "I'm here to audition—I guess that's obvious, though." Pointedly, she tugged the strap of her instrument's case.

Porter shot me a glance, then leaned forward over the table where we were all seated. The room was small enough that the woman wasn't more than four or five arms away. "What's your name?"

"Lola," she said, unclasping the case on the floor. The guitar inside was violet, a Fender Stratocaster that she slipped out, and on, with casual familiarity. For a second she looked around like she was lost.

Colt read her movements, standing up and plugging the guitar into the nearby amp. "You been playing a while?" he asked.

31

She shrugged, fingers gliding over the guitar pegs, tweaking them easily. I'd been slouching since this fiasco began; her first strum as she tuned made me sit up straighter. "I guess so. I've been playing since I was little, my brother taught me a lot."

"Yeah?" Colt asked, dropping back beside me. His face was indulgent; wistful. "I learned from my brother, too. Alright, you must know a song or two of ours. Or I hope so, if you're planning to join us on stage. You have a preference on what you wanna play?"

The young woman looked my way, fixing me with a nervous smile. "Actually," Lola said, "I know *all* of your songs. Do you guys want to pick?"

I felt everyone looking at me, but I was busy staring Lola down. It was a bold claim, saying she knew all our songs. *Encouraging, but big talk doesn't cut it here.*

"Alright," Colt said, eyes narrowing into slits. I suspected he was becoming as curious as me about the girl. "Guess that makes it easy. How about you play the start of Black Grit—"

"Tuesday Left Behind." It was with brisk intensity that I cut my drummer off. Linking my fingers, I leaned across the table. The blue in Lola's eyes swelled like a river that planned to drown me. "Play that one."

Her lips curled, winding down into a cheeky grin. I had the funniest idea that she was toying with me—or that she knew something I didn't. "That's one of your early ones," she said.

I nodded, a scant movement. "You said you know all of them." *Is she bluffing? Coming in here and trying to impress us with some bullshit about knowing all our music?*

I hated arrogant people who couldn't back up their claims. If Lola was fucking with me, I'd—what? Be disappointed? *In a way, yeah,* I thought with sudden confusion. *There's something about her... something that I want to be real.*

Lola grazed her thumb over her guitar strings. I expected her to admit she didn't know the song. It wouldn't have surprised me; it was from the first CD we'd released as a band. It was unknown, relatively unpopular. I'd given her a challenge I hadn't bothered to give anyone else.

I expected her to fail.

Her pick came down, fingers spinning over the wires to produce the first note from Tuesday Left Behind. It was clear, hanging in the air with the perfect amount of anticipation.

Then, Lola began to play.

Her eyes were closed, hiding away her deep sapphires from my seeking gaze. With perfect ease, she played the song that I had asked for. She played it as good as Johnny ever had. Far better than he'd been playing lately, really.

Lola's hands embraced her guitar's neck,

gliding along to coerce it into making bits of music that sank into my ears. They burrowed inside, grinding through my skin and down to my very bones.

She was good. She was damn good.

I realized I was squeezing my thighs under the table. Shifting in place, I saw Colt and Porter both staring at me. Those were pointed looks, looks that said 'Holy shit, are you hearing this?'

I am, I'm hearing it, but I want more than just a mimic. Waving at her to stop hurt me in a funny way. I could have listened to her for hours. "That's enough, alright."

She faltered, concern showing like a shadow on her soft jaw. The song still reverberated in my flesh. "Sorry, did I do something wrong?" she asked.

The rest of the band was eyeballing me. They were pissed I'd cut her off, but I didn't care. There was more that I wanted here. I was desperate to know if Lola was what I'd been hoping for—what I *needed*. Impatience clawed at me to find out fast. "You know our music, good. I want you to play something else."

"I—something else?"

Porter pushed his lower jaw out. Him, Colt, they had already decided this girl was perfect. It wasn't so simple, though. Not to me. "I want you to play anything you want. Just go for it, show me what makes you want to create music in the first place."

It made me sound fucking insane, I was sure of that. I was ready for Lola to open her mouth and fumble. Maybe she'd even turn and walk out the door.

I had my reasons, though. This was what would separate those who played from those who *played*. Johnny had been good, I'd never say otherwise. He just never had the drive; it was what kept him from performing as best as he could at every single show. He didn't care about creating music.

Fucker just wanted to be famous. Let's see if this girl is different.

Lola was watching me. Not with the deer in headlights look I expected, no. Her eyes were shining like new frost, the face of a woman who was excited.

It was contagious.

Before she started, I noticed I was hunching forward and holding my breath.

Her fingers came down, tickling the strings. It was a sharp movement, sound bursting in my brain like a fresh orange. Just as I was feeling my pulse quicken, adjusting to the intensity of her strums, Lola came to life.

The song she played tugged at the very roots of my hair. Lower and lower it went, drilling so hard into my body that I had to shift on my chair.

She was good. So fucking good, I was falling into the trap of her music. It wrapped me tight, tempting me to sink in and let her keep going.

Lola's eyes were closed, lower lip tucked just slightly in her teeth. She was living in that moment like it was her last. I *knew* that look; the body language of someone in their own creative trance.

Every small movement she made was intentional. She traveled across the guitar, a land she'd been living in all her life. There was no part of the instrument, the song, that was a mystery to her.

Who is this girl? I wondered, noting I was gripping the edge of the table hard enough to turn my fingertips white. Her poise was distracting, back arched into a high speed curve. The muscles on her lower arms flexed deliciously with each note.

I was fantasizing about how her limbs would flex in other situations. Perhaps the dark corner of an alley, her head tilted back and breath steaming in the night air.

Fuck, calm down, I told myself. Shaking my head, I snapped my fingers and broke the spell Lola had put on all of us. Porter and Colt were openly gawking, and worse, they clapped when her last twang faded.

"Holy shit!" Porter shouted, jumping up with his hands by his head. "Lady, you're fucking awesome! You're in, you're seriously in —"

"Porter," I snapped.

"—the band, I don't care what Drez has

36

to say over there, you're—"

"Porter!" But he was ignoring me, and so was Colt. They were too busy sucking up to the kid, patting her on the back and laughing.

To her credit, Lola only had eyes for me. She hadn't said a thing to the other two.

"What did you think?" she asked me, imploring.

Kicking my chair back, I stood smoothly. "You're good. Colt, go tell Brenda to send everyone away."

He didn't waste time. I'd made my decision, something he and Porter had both doubted I would ever do. The wiry drummer vanished out the door, leaving the three of us behind.

Lola looked one step from the edge of panic. "Wait. Wait, holy hell. Does this mean what I think it does?"

"Brenda will get the papers squared away. Get ready for two days of exhausting band practice," Porter chuckled.

Rounding the table, I extended my hand, giving the girl a sideways smile. "You do *want* to be in the band, right?"

"Of course!" Her astonishment was... pure. Even the way she shook my hand, muscles jittering, was genuine. The heat in her skin sent a quick thrill up my spine. Before I could stop myself, I gripped her palm hard.

The flash of confusion in her eyes morphed into something raw—something hot and eager for more. It happened too fast, leaving me unsure if I should push further or back away. I didn't know if I liked how fast she was making my heart dance.

Quickly, I released her. It wasn't normal for anyone to throw me for such a loop. I made myself speak flatly, fighting for indifference. "Good. It'll be hard work, but if you don't mind that, you'll be fine."

"Of course I don't mind!" Her exuberance stunned us both. Scrubbing the nape of her neck, she darted shy eyes away. "This is crazy. I never expected you'd pick me. Wait until Sean hears."

A bitter thing wormed through me. I didn't know what it was, but it was hot and burned like acid. "Who's Sean?" *And why do I fucking care?*

Lola bent down, fiddling with her guitar and packing it away. "My brother, he was the one pushing me to come do this."

That was comforting. Shit, *why* was that comforting? Because it meant she was single? *Fuck. Get a grip.* Clearing my throat, I went to speak again. The door slammed open, ruining my chance.

Brenda shoved inside on her deathly sharp heels, angry voices thrumming outside. She gave me a smile that didn't reach her eyes. "Okay, you win. You said you'd get someone to replace Johnny, and you did. I owe you a drink, but *you* still owe me an apology."

38

My fingers went in search of my cigarette pack, touching, but not freeing it. "Not now. Just give the kid the papers, I want to get going."

Rolling her eyes, my manager approached Lola with her sparkling porcelain teeth. She was striking in her immaculately perfect red lipstick. Her business-like demeanor never really fit with the vibe of the grungy rock tour, but Brenda didn't care. She was like me, she did things her own way.

It was why we always clashed.

"First, congratulations," she said, manicured nails pressing on the girl's shoulder, leading her to the cheap plastic table.

Grinning politely—or was she still excited from the news? —Lola went with her. She had one hand buried in her pocket, the other digging into her thick hair. Was Brenda making her nervous? Was Lola just shy?

It doesn't fucking matter, who cares? Inhaling sharply when I caught Brenda tracing Lola's forearm, commenting on her tattoo, I wrenched my gaze away. I *loved* ink on a woman. It didn't just enhance the flesh; the right tattoos usually told a story.

What was Lola's story?

Don't get wrapped up in a new face just because it belongs to a skilled body.

A gorgeous, hot body.

Shit.

"Sign here," Brenda instructed, pointing

down at the stack of papers.

"Shouldn't I read it first?" she asked, the unease in her tone drawing my eyes back. She was squinting, flipping the pages over.

Brenda folded her arms, impatience turning her comments into thin razors. "It's all standard. I know this can't be the first time you've seen a performer's contract."

What the hell does that mean?

Lola's blush was like champagne, tantalizing. I needed a cigarette badly. Bending over the table, she laughed nervously. The sound of the pen scribbling over the paperwork sent my blood flying in my veins.

She'd signed the contract. It was done, Lola belonged in my band.

"Well," she said, meeting Brenda's eyes and offering her the contract, "To be fair, Sean never really shared that side of things with me."

My manager reached out, winding elegant fingers on Lola's and giving her a firm handshake. "Not everyone is so open, I guess. It doesn't matter, you get to show him yours, now." That made Lola grin, her eyes flicking to mine over Brenda's shoulder. "Welcome to Four and a Half Headstones, Lola Cooper."

Cooper. Adrenaline and cold anxiety flooded into my guts. *Cooper. Holy fuck, she's Sean Cooper's little sister.*

The realization shook around in my skull. It brought with it a memory several years old. Impossibly, Lola wasn't the first Cooper to try and get into my band.

But unlike her brother...

Lola hadn't failed the audition.

Did Lola know about that? She had to, certainly she had to.

Lola watched me with such genuine delight that it turned my heart into a drum roll. But I was suspicious. I didn't want to be, but I knew too well the terror of betrayal. What was I supposed to do, though?

Turning back won't solve anything. I need her, there's no one else that's so perfect for this band. For *my* band. Mine.

I didn't know if Lola was here to sabotage me or fuck me over.

But I did know that... for now...

She was the only chance we had at surviving this damn tour.

- Chapter Four -
Lola

I couldn't believe it. I could not fucking believe it.

I was the new guitarist for Four and a Half Headstones. Holy shit. How could I be so lucky?

The look on Sean's face when I held the papers up to him was proof, but my dopey smile gave it all away long before that.

"Son of a bitch," he breathed out, snagging the contract. Squinting at it, then me, he waved the papers like they were a flag. "You actually did it!"

Together we laughed, and for the first time in... forever? Sean grabbed me in a rib crushing hug. We were standing just inside the tour bus, the engines rumbling. Everyone was about to take off, we needed to hurry to get on the road.

Rubbing my nose, I folded the contract up and shoved it in my back pocket. "Impressed?"

"Hell yes," he said, muscles flexing over folded arms. "How was it? How was Drezden and the rest?"

The reminder of the tall singer, his piercing green eyes, warmed my cheeks. *How was it?* I could never explain. Drezden had both scared me and intrigued me. Being near him was like daring a tornado to roll closer.

I said, "He was—*it* was fine. They asked me to play one of their songs, and they apparently thought I was good." I tried to shrug casually, but I was glowing too much to get away with being indifferent. "Sean, I'm in their band. I'm in the tour!"

"I know, I know." Chuckling, he looked towards the front of the bus. "You should grab your stuff and hurry over there. They'll leave without you."

The memory of Brenda telling me I'd be traveling with Four and Half Headstones, to help use every minute to prepare, was sobering. "I... yeah. Jeez. I'm really doing this."

Sean nodded deeply, his eyes glittering with something I couldn't identify. "You are. Make them proud, but more importantly, make *me* proud. Don't slack, and when we stop next, I want you to tell me everything about practice. Okay?"

The request didn't feel weird, just the intensity in how he asked me. "Yeah. No problem."

His hug, the second one, was lighter. "Okay, now get the fuck out of here, rock star." He was teasing, but it sounded almost like an insult. Had I done something to upset him?

Burning with strange trepidation, I gave him one more quick hug. Then I hoisted my bag and guitar, jumping down the bus steps. *Is something going on with Sean?* I couldn't explain it, but my intuition was screaming. I'd known Sean my whole life.

I knew when he was being strange.

I'll worry about it later, I decided. The bounce in my walk was pronounced; I had more to think about than my brother. I was in a *real* fucking band, I was headlining on a tour! I'd woken up today hoping that I wouldn't end up with a busted neck from doing all the manual labor for Barbed Fire again.

How had I gotten *here?*

Some people stared at me as I strolled towards the giant, black behemoth that was the Four and a Half Headstone's tour bus. Word that I, unimpressive Lola Cooper, was the new guitarist had traveled fast. It was hard not to grin at the adoring looks. Even the angry ones made me swell.

The stairwell opened before me, glass doors sliding apart. The driver was an older man, his squishy body struggling to fit into the seat. He offered me an impatient glare, jerking his chin over his shoulder. "Hurry up, lady, we need to move."

"Sorry, I had to get my stuff," I said with a wince. His flat stare said he didn't care. Ascending the steps, my mood crumbled ever so slightly from this sour man's attitude.

Then I saw the inside of the bus, and everything was good again.

Velvet, leather, and no doubt some silk, too... the inside of the bus was a treasure trove of expensive material. Every seat was huge, made to sink into and never bother climbing out of. I spotted not one mini bar, but three, all of them stacked with bottles.

Unlike how hot the Barbed Fire bus got when the air conditioning failed, this vehicle was comfortably chilled. The burning sun outside couldn't hope to break in.

Wow, I thought in wonder, staring without blinking. *This is the perk of being a real rock star. Sean would be so jealous if he saw all of this.* It occurred to me that he might actually know already.

There was a large curtain hanging at the back of the aisle. Through it, I heard a familiar laugh. The skinny, pale guy that passed through the thick material was speaking to someone behind him that I couldn't see.

That's Colt, the drummer, I realized. I'd know him from any distance; almost as easily as I'd know Drezden.

He spotted me, a smile warming his gaunt features. "Hey! Lola! We were waiting on you, I even joked that you'd run off."

As if that was what he was waiting for, the driver jerked the bus forward and onto the road. I was violently jostled; I grabbed a seat, partially falling into it with my bags on top of me. "Sorry!" I said, struggling to get my balance. "I just needed my things. Should I put them somewhere?"

Shrugging, he jerked his head towards

45

the curtain, where he'd come from. "Probably back here. Come pick a bunk."

A bunk? My chest thrummed at the idea. *Do they have real beds here? No sleeping with my neck crushed at an angle on a window?* Carefully I stood, rocking down the aisle after Colt.

The black curtain revealed that the rear of the vehicle was just as startling as the rest. There were alcoves along the aisle, most covered by more curtains. Small rooms, but certainly grand when compared to where I'd been sleeping.

"Drop your bag there, but keep your guitar," he said. Nodding, I abandoned my stuff on the mattress of the nearest empty room. Colt motioned with his fingers, so I followed him deeper into the bus.

What I found next blew my mind.

The entire back of the bus was set up like a studio. There were speakers, wires, and a thick padding all over the walls to soften the noise. It was a little bit cramped, but it was also a fucking *mobile studio.* I couldn't judge the space too hard.

Drezden and Porter were lounging, toying with their gear. At my arrival, all eyes flipped up to stare at me. Unsure what else to do, I wiggled my fingers in a weak wave. "Hi guys."

Porter strummed his bass, blonde faux-hawk glowing from the sunlight streaming in through the tiny window above. "Welcome to the party," he grunted.

Drezden said nothing, twisting a bottle of water in his palms. Across his knee I saw a wire, the microphone dangling like a ripe piece of fruit from a vine. The intensity around him, even with the others so near, made my throat tight.

He has eyes like a killer, I realized. It called to mind the talk about Johnny Muse, how Drez had beaten him into a bloody mess. *Stop it, brain. I never saw that, don't give me creepy imaginary images.* Even so, red blood filled my mind's eye.

"You want something to drink?" Colt asked, sliding around me towards a cooler. At my nod, he tossed me a bottle. I fumbled, clutching it to my chest. He dropped down by his drums, expert hands going for the smooth sticks. "We should be blunt with you, Lola."

They were quiet, waiting for my response. Blinking, I sat down on a bench against the wall, furthest from Drez as I could get. "Sure. Okay, go ahead, be blunt."

Colt parted his lips, but it was Drezden who spoke first. He was soft, brisk; an autumn breeze. "We've got two days until the next tour stop. We need you ready, or we're going to look like assholes up on stage. Get me?"

"Yeah," I squeaked, then tried again. "Yeah. I get it, don't worry. I'm ready to do whatever it takes to impress the world."

47

The drummer rolled his neck, the giant gauges in his ears rattling. "You say that now. Wait until you survive this practice, *then* we'll see how eager you are."

His doubt rattled me, a sourness etching into my voice. "I'll be fine," I said, breaking out my guitar to tune it. I squeezed the pegs too hard, my skin aching. *Do they think I'm some pathetic newbie?*

Rustling noises made me look up. Drezden was there, standing over me so I was level with his waist. He crouched, offering me some papers, enveloping me in the warm scent of tobacco and oranges.

Fuck, he smelled good.

"Here," he said, waving the pages. For the first time I noticed the bandage over his knuckles. "Music notes for our songs. You'll want to follow along, even if you think you know them already. We'll start with Black Grit."

I was blushing, why was I blushing? He had a vibe that was overwhelming. It suffocated me, dared me to inhale more of his existence or to let myself pass out in a daze. *Focus, take the papers.*

My fingers shook when I did.

Calm the fuck down! I screamed in my head, fighting with my warring emotions. I was acting like a fan girl, but why? *Because he's Drezden, that's why. You've been a literal fan of his for years. You've listened to his music, danced to it, cried to it, fallen asleep to it. You know how talented he is. How powerful.*

That had to be it.

That had to be all it was.

He moved away, languid on his long legs. Not sitting that time, he scooped up the microphone and stood tall. "The volume will be lower in here to keep our ears from exploding. Keep that in mind."

Nodding, I adjusted on the bench, music sheets on my knees. The papers moved slightly from my trembles; I forced my feet flat to stop them.

Colt tapped his sticks, Porter strummed briefly, and Drez took a swig of water.

Then they began. It was my own private show with Four and a Half Headstones.

A show I was part of.

"You fight me," Drezden began, his words all wet sand. "Backed into a corner with your hands, and I can't keep my feet beneath me!" He crooned in low vibrations, his voice soaking me from scalp to belly.

I almost forgot to strum my notes.

He's so good, I thought in awe. *He was born to sing.*

Drezden had closed his eyes, the texture of his voice gliding over my throat, into my ears, like it belonged. "Fight me, hate me, kill me!"

Colt emphasized the cries with his cymbals, my world becoming an ancient war of

49

metal and smoke.

I'd never fought so hard to keep myself together. To just *breathe.*

"Fight me," Drezden growled. "One more night until we fall. Fight me with curled nails and wicked teeth." His eyes opened, fixing on me, their green depths a sea of hot desire. "You fight me, and I can't keep my feet beneath."

I fumbled, the off chord sickening in my ears. With my face in flames, I ducked my head and kept going. *The way he sings, I can't concentrate.* If Drezden had put his hands on my shoulders, he couldn't have gotten any closer.

What was wrong with me?

The heat in my stomach warned me this was more than admiration or star-struck nerves. I was feeling a pull towards Drezden that I'd only ever felt while indulging in my private fantasies.

The one boyfriend I'd had was brief, and we'd broken up just after graduation. Harold, his name had been. Horny Harold, I'd teased him, because he'd always wanted to fuck me... but I'd always been too scared.

One time, he'd convinced me to go down on him, and that— *I shouldn't be thinking like this,* I thought desperately. *I need to make this work, it's a huge opportunity.*

Maybe the only one I'll ever get.

There was shame in me, and when

50

merged with my baffling excitement, I was losing ground. I couldn't play like I usually did.

And everyone sensed it.

"Stop!" Drezden's shout made me startle, fingers striking the wrong strings again. The brittle screech of music turned my hairs into rusty needles. He was glaring at me, eyebrows narrowing low enough to create a sea of lines on his perfect skin. "Fucking stop, everyone. You," he snapped at me, "What the fuck was that?"

"I—what—it just—"

"Shut up," he growled, crushing the microphone until his knuckles lost blood. I imagined he wished it was my throat. "Are you messing with us?"

"No!"

"Then get your head in place and try again," he said, swiping his hair back. Porter jumped when Drezden pointed at him. "Play No More Stars."

The bassist scowled, challenging Drezden with a glare. "Sure man, calm down."

No one said anything else, the silence punctuated by Colt tapping his sticks together uneasily.

Where before there had been anticipation, now there grew a sticky tension. These guys had been impressed with me when I'd auditioned. Their admiration was melting away.

It galled me to imagine the version I'd

presented to them, a crafted piece of myself that had looked like a prodigy. Now, I'd become a disappointing accident.

I'm not an accident, I know how to play, I reminded myself.

I'll remind them, too.

The stiff pick in my fingers snapped along my guitar strings. No More Stars was a song that began with a warning. Brooding notes, building with foreboding that came faster, louder, spreading to give space for the words that would soar between.

Deep, hollow punches erupted from the drums. The three of us, we were there to herald the birth of Drezden's lyrics.

That time, when he sang, I scrunched my eyes closed. I wouldn't fuck up again. No matter how good his voice was, or how it slipped into my ribs and tickled a piece of me it never should have, I wouldn't falter.

He parted his lips, but I didn't look. "In the black, you walk with me. In the black," he croaked, "You never see. Walk away and you won't bleed, walk away and I am... I am freed."

I slammed my hand down, hard music striking the brief silence. Together, we all crashed in unison.

"No more stars!" Drez screamed, pure power that stabbed at my core. It was a demand, he forced my eyes open. Drezden was an accident I needed to witness, even when I knew it would bring me nothing but horror.

Wild green centers found me, his face flushed, lips proud across bared teeth. The face of a man who wanted to fight, or to flee, or to fuck.

Pure energy.

He didn't even get to the second part of the chorus before I missed my notes. The sharp explosion, so off key, made Porter shout.

Drezden froze, mic hovering in front of his clenched jaw. I wasn't confused by his expression anymore. That face said 'fight' in every crease of furrowed skin.

Fucking fuck, was all I could think. I was glad I didn't accidentally blurt the words.

The last painful note faded away. Drez let his arm fall, and for a terrible second, I thought he'd just drop the mic entirely.

He strode forward, the small gap between us erasing. I didn't see his hand, I just felt him lift me. We were nose to nose, his tang of sweat filling my head. "Are you doing that on purpose?" he growled.

"No!" I coughed, scrabbling at his wrist. My toes were the only thing on the ground. Was he really that much taller than me? "No, I'm sorry! I'm just—"

"Just what?" he snapped, giving me a shake. I wished that his rage would help the flutter in my heart dissipate. Instead, I just felt a flicker of heat. The cords of his arms flexed under my nervous touch.

He's making it so hard to think! I need

to get away from this, from him, I...

"Drez." It was Colt who'd spoke, forcing himself between us. He was strong, too; all sinew and bone. The body of a swimmer, he even had a smooth scalp free of hair. I saw him glance at me, pushing me back. I fell onto the bench like I was made of wet noodles. "Leave the kid alone. She's just nervous, this is a lot of pressure."

I'm not a fucking kid, I thought in a moment of clear rage, *I'm not much younger than the rest of you!* I was a bundle of tremors. Never, *ever*, had a man dared to do to me what Drezden had. I'd been in actual bloody fights, but they'd never left me as drained as this.

The way the singer snorted, sneering at me in derision, turned my belly to ice. "Nerves? That's no problem, then! It isn't like she'll have to perform in front of a giant fucking crowd in a day or anything!"

"Calm down," Porter said from the corner. Looking up, I saw how the bigger man was staring at me. Dark brown eyes, full of pity.

I hated that.

Rubbing my forehead, then my neck, I made myself stand. I hoped they didn't see my knees shaking. "I'm fine. Colt is right, it's just nerves. I'll get over it, I just need to keep practicing."

"Yeah, you're going to keep practicing," Drez said. He showed me his wide back, hands digging something from his pocket. "I'm going to go have a smoke. Play without me."

"Drez—" Porter started, but it was too late. We all watched the singer push from the room, stomping further into the tour bus. Sighing, Porter looked at me again. The pity was gone. The sympathy wasn't much better. "Sorry about that. Drez isn't the most patient guy."

I shook my head, touching my chest gently. *My heart is easing up, finally. Why the hell was I so worked up that I couldn't play?* It had to be the nearness of someone as famous as Drezden, it had to be. "It's alright. He's not wrong, I need to keep practicing. Can we try No More Stars again?"

I wanted to do something with my hands. They itched to feel something.

Or someone.

"Yeah," Colt said, moving back to his drums. "Fuck Drez, we'll play without him for now."

My smile was weak, but it was there. Hearing their casual rebuking of their leader made things feel less professional. It reminded me of playing with smaller bands, of being around guys who didn't have the pressure of a giant tour over their heads.

When we played the song a second time, my fingers didn't trip once.

It was obvious they were pleased. They became actually impressed when I made it through the second piece. By the third, perfect performance, there was a quiet unease stretching between us all.

Setting his bass down, Porter came my way at a frightening speed. Giant arms coiled around, crushing me and nearly my guitar in a hug. "Holy shit! *Were* you fucking with Drezden?"

"No. Of course not," I said. Slipping free, I adjusted my shirt. Porter could break ribs if he wanted to.

"Then why were you so much better this time?" Colt asked, chugging some water. He was gleaming from working the drums over.

My mouth opened, yet I shut it quickly. *How do I explain it? Can I even explain it?* I was spared the attempt when Drez shoved his way back inside.

Glancing at me, setting my neck and cheeks on fire, he crossed his arms. The scent of cigarettes was heavier than usual on him. Sharply, he said, "I could hear everything." Amazingly, I felt a flicker of guilt. Drez stared me down, his eyes hard with... something. Distrust? Pride? "Nerves or not," he said, "You were playing much better."

My heart swelled. "Thank you." I didn't know what else to say.

He cocked his head, looking from me to the other band members. "Let's give it one more go."

There was some uneasy shuffling. Some of it was on my part. "You sure? Maybe we should all take a break," Porter mumbled.

Drez already had the mic in hand, fingers curling around it solidly. "One more song. Then we'll break."

"Easy for you," Porter said softly, "You already took a smoke break."

Settling on the bench, I waited on the razor's edge that was my nerves. Was I going to fuck up again? Or could I reel in whatever part of me was turning to mush when Drez sang so close by?

There was little time to wonder.

"No More Stars," Drez demanded, eyes raking over the three of us. In response, Colt tapped his sticks, and Porter hit a belly-grinding low note on his bass.

I was slick with sweat when I strummed. Even the air conditioning couldn't solve the issue of the heat inside of me. But I wasn't fumbling, not yet. Even with Drez staring me down, expecting—was he expecting it?—my failure, I was controlling myself.

I could handle this.

My guts wriggled like snakes as Drezden licked his lips. His first whisper slid into my ribs, tangling up and choking my heart. "In the black, you walk with me. In the black, you never see..."

That whisper went lower, brushing my core until my inner thighs were hot and sticky. The air in my lungs fled. I was glad I wasn't the one who had to sing.

My mouth was somehow dry and liquid at once. Pushing my tongue on the back of my teeth, I went one step further and bit down. The pain gave me focus, though I wasn't proud of the method.

It hit too close to home, too near a memory of my rough teenage years where inflicting pain solved every problem.

It's solving this one, I realized. Honing in on the sharp taste of copper, I listened in wonder to my own music. Against the forefront of Drezden's lyrics, I was shaping a background that was flawless.

The air in the room was heavy. Glancing up, I saw how Drez was eating me with his eyes. He didn't blink, like watching me was all he ever wanted to do. All he *could* do.

Flushing hotly, I dug my teeth into my tongue.

"No more stars!" Drez screamed, shattering the hanging note. We all scraped down on our instruments, creating a tune that was wild, ambitious.

This was the sound of Four and a Half Headstones. A sound I was now a part of.

The end of the song rolled over the room. Drez had two hands on the mic, cradling it close to his curling lips. "Walk away and you won't bleed, walk away and I am... I am freed." He had shut his eyes, I didn't know when. I only knew when he was looking at me again, making me flinch.

The last of the beautiful music flitted away; ghosts in our ears.

"Well, fuck," Porter said eloquently. Setting his bass down, he stared around at our faces. The grin was slow to grow, but when it was done, his teeth were showing. "The kid can do it. Convinced now, Drez?"

Placing the microphone aside, he cracked another bottle of water and chugged all of it. Wiping his mouth with his arm, he shrugged. "Guess it was nerves after all."

Squirming, I gripped the neck of my guitar. The squint Drezden shot my way said he wasn't as convinced as he claimed.

"Break time. I need some air," Colt said, shoving out from behind the drum set. He smiled at me as he passed. "You hungry, Lola?"

Clutching my stomach, I stood. "Yeah, actually I—oh!" Saliva and blood slid from my mouth. Clasping a palm over my jaw, I swallowed. I wanted to hide the evidence of my brutal tongue gnawing.

Lifting my eyes, my paranoia revealed only Drez looking my way. Porter and Colt were both brushing past the curtain, laughing together about something else.

Did he see? He wasn't moving, just standing there with his arms folded. *Fuck. How bad did I bite my tongue? But I needed to, it worked! I played the song perfectly.* My heart was hammering in my throat.

"How bad is it?" he asked me.

I shook my head, voice muffled on my own hand.

Lowering his eyebrows, Drez leaned in close. That froze me on the spot. I didn't fight when he grabbed my wrist, pulling my hand away. He looked me over, but not like a doctor would. It was more like a coroner examining a corpse. He studied me, but there wasn't a level of caring anywhere. "Open up," he said flatly.

To my amazement, I hesitated. Drez was stunned too, his eyes glimmering as they went wide. That was replaced by a grim set of teeth. "I said open up, kid." Without waiting, he squeezed my cheeks, thumb digging in one side and fingers the others. It *hurt*, my lips parting with my gasp of pain.

"Back off!" I said, pulling away, flushing with too many sensations at once. My tongue burned, but my cheeks rivaled it. What was Drez thinking, touching me like that? He had no right to get so close to me. It made me angry...

And it made me dizzy.

"You bit the hell out of your tongue." It was a casual observation, his hands releasing me and squeezing his hips. "What were you thinking?"

Wiping at my lips, I saw the smear of pink on my arm. "I was thinking I would finish a song, that's all."

Snorting, Drez gave me a once over. "There are better ways than chewing yourself

60

up."

His eyes said he wanted to chew me up, himself. I didn't comment on it, but my wavering stare must have hinted at what I suspected; I saw it reflected in his eyes.

He smoothed his hair back, looking away and breaking the moment. There was no fake flattery in his voice when he spoke. "You're good on the guitar, but your decisions are insane. That injury has to hurt."

It throbbed, in fact. I kept rubbing it on my teeth like it was an itch to scratch and making it worse. *The bleeding is slowing, I think.* "It hurts a little, but I've had worse."

That got him to arch an eyebrow at me. "What the hell is acting tough supposed to do? Impress me?"

The wind vanished from my sails. I *was* trying to impress him. More so, I was trying to get him to leave me alone. I was embarrassed about the decision to hurt myself. It wasn't anything to be proud of, but I couldn't explain that.

Not to him. Not to anyone.

"Come on," he said, digging something from his pocket. His phone was black, glossy like a beetle. "I'll call Brenda, she can take a look at you."

Now I was humiliated. "No!" Drez paused, looking at me expectantly. "Don't... just don't call her. This isn't a big deal."

He held the phone like a gun. "You don't

want me to call her? Fine. Let me take a look at how bad you bit yourself, and I won't."

"That's blackmail," I spat. Drezden ignored me, stalking my way and erasing the gap between us. Our chests were a breath from rubbing together, I could see the flecks of gold in his smoky green eyes.

"Open," he whispered.

I didn't think about it; I just did it.

Drezden cupped my chin, keeping me still. Hilariously, I began worrying if my breath reeked. *What a stupid thing to think about,* I chided myself. I had more things to concern me. Things like how his fingers felt so firm, and how he smelled so wonderful it made my brain struggle to think.

The blood in my veins was rumbling so hard, I was sure he could hear it sloshing. "It's not as bad as I thought," he said. The tip of his thumb ran over my lower lip, then grazed my teeth. It was so sudden that I convinced myself it was an accident.

Drez's skin was saltier than my blood.

He let me go, pulling away and leaving me to lean on the wall. I was already ashamed, I didn't need to crumble and make it worse. My own fingers brushed my lips, then further, prodding the side of my tongue. I grimaced, but the pain was dull. "It's really not bad?"

"You should know, it's your own tongue." Drez scratched his neck, the strange pull between us turning into a cool wall. He was looking at the exit. "I'm hungry. Let's go."

And just like that, he closes off. Why couldn't he do that when he was singing? I wouldn't have needed to bite my tongue if he'd been as distant and detached then.

Following him through the bus, we found the boys draped in the seats, beers dripping condensation onto their laps. Porter waved me over, offering me a bottle. "Here, before Colt drinks it all."

"I couldn't if I tried," he laughed. Finishing his drink, he grabbed another. The two men were seated across from each other in the middle of the big bus.

Drezden draped himself in a seat opposite them, reaching for a beer wordlessly. It reminded me of my brother and his band. The thought was comforting, though it caused me to look out one of the tinted windows sadly, imagining them in their busted up vehicle further down the caravan.

"You alright?" Porter asked.

His words startled me. "Yeah, yeah." My smile was weak, I tried to cover it with a swig from the beer. The fire burned on my wound and made me grimace.

Colt chuckled, waving his beer in the air. "It can't taste that bad, kid."

It tastes fine, I thought silently. *Better he think I was making a face over the flavor, though, and not an injury.* Settling down on one of the seats behind the pair, but furthest away from Drez, I made myself grin. "You'd think you guys would have better stuff, seeing as you're headlining."

"She joined us because she hoped we had fancy beer!" Porter shouted, his false anger quickly vanishing. "I knew it all along."

"I wonder if she's even old enough to drink," Colt teased, looking me up and down. I wasn't, but underage drinking was so common on tours, I didn't expect to have to defend myself. "Either way, she isn't getting it all," he declared, finishing his bottle to prove a point. "I'll get it first!"

We all laughed, the tightness in my neck smoothing out. Looking over, I caught Drez wearing a sideways smile. His eyes flicked to mine, holding them a moment. "You should eat something," he said.

My mouth went dry, the beer forgotten. The word 'eat' from Drez's lips had too many dirty connotations.

"In fact," he sighed, shooting a glare at the two men, "You all should. Don't get drunk before dinner, I'm not dealing with that again."

Colt rolled his eyes, setting his bottle down loudly. "Shit, you never had to babysit me, Drez. We all know it was Johnny getting sloppy, and he's gone now, so calm down."

Drez's silence was stifling. I *felt* how he studied Colt, watched the drummer wither under that look.

"Dammit," Colt said under his breath.

"Sorry, didn't mean to bring him up. It isn't some dirty secret or something, though."

They all gave me a meaningful look. Clearing my throat, I spoke carefully around my swollen tongue. "Everyone knows about the fight with Johnny. Sort of, anyway. Can I... can I ask what really happened? The stories are pretty wild." Shark's version of the incident rippled in my memory.

Drezden sank into his chair, feet kicking up onto the small table. "It's not much of a story. Johnny just fucked up too many times. I wanted him gone, he didn't like that. Not exactly shocking."

"He tried to murder Drez with a bottle," Porter said, pushing his empty one away like it was the actual weapon being discussed.

Drez made tiny circles with the base of his beer on the table, wet smudges that went round and round as he spoke. "He didn't try to murder me. That's how these shitty rumors start, Porter."

The bigger man tilted his chin down. "Sorry. Johnny was pretty pissed, though. I think he would have messed you up if he'd had the chance."

I hadn't realized I'd begun leaning forward. Half off my seat, I spoke with unbridled curiosity. "So what actually happened to him?"

Drez continued to twirl his beer. "He got dragged off by security."

"Not before that asshole ripped my gauge, though," Colt muttered. He pointed to his ear for emphasis.

"Honestly," Drezden said, "I don't know *where* the fuck he is now. I don't care, either."

"You're not worried he'll come back and cause more trouble?" I asked. "If I'd been kicked out of my band, I think I'd be furious."

The singer lifted his eyes, showing me a hint of the fierce animal living in his head. The beer didn't slow its perfect circles, his voice was a low, dry mutter. "Johnny knows if he ever shows his face to me again, I'll break his fucking jaw."

And I believed him. Down to my gut, I didn't think he'd made an idle threat.

Porter started to say something. A hard, meaningful glare from Drez stopped whatever it was. I had the terrible idea that they knew something and didn't want to tell me.

"So," Drez went on. Lifting the beer, ending the endless circles, he took a deep drink. "No. I'm not worried about him."

My breath came in, sharp and loud. I'd been so wrapped up in Drezden's words and tangible emotions I'd forgotten that I needed oxygen. A thrill went up my spine, tickling the back of my brain and throat. His passion turned my insides to butter. That worried me.

Colt broke the serious mood. "About that food. Should we call Brenda, see where we can stop?"

Yawning, Porter stretched his beefy arms over his head. "As long as it isn't pizza again. I'm so sick of pizza."

Drezden pushed his phone to his ear. "We need to stop and refuel soon. I'll tell her we want to stretch our legs and get a bite." His attention shot to me, and instantly, I squeezed my beer too hard. "What do you want to eat? Any preference?"

"Uh," I managed to say. "I don't really care. I'll eat anything."

The green in his eyes went wild, a forest that was eager to sweep me up and let me get lost. Whatever flicker of heat between us that was there vanished when he stood, speaking into the phone. "Hey, we're hungry. When's the next stop?" He waited, listening. "No, no more damn pizza. Uh huh. Then pick a place where we can get a private room and not get mobbed. That's what you get paid for."

Smiling, I imagined the put-together woman arguing with Drez on the end of the line. I was getting the impression she got frustrated with him a lot.

I was starting to know the feeling.

"Yeah, fine. Yes, it's fine! Brenda, just— yeah." He rolled his gaze to me, thoughtful. "She's fine, we'll be fine. Even better if we can eat something before we all starve. Then you'll have no band at all." He winked at me, which of all the things so far, set my hair on end the most.

Is he trying to be friendly? Is it an act?

Showing us his back, Drez nodded his head as if Brenda could see. "Alright. Sounds good. See you soon." Shoving the phone in his pocket, he gave us all a tiny shrug. "Private room at some place called the Griffin Bar and Grill. An hour away or so. Best I could do."

Colt stood up, making the table and bottles shake. "An actual restaurant? Hell yeah!"

"Brenda didn't like the idea, did she?" Porter rubbed his nose, matching the amusement on Drez's face.

The singer just shrugged again, shooting me a look from the corner of his eye. "She never likes my ideas. Hope you're ready. You're about to get a taste of what it means to be famous."

If it's anything like being close to you, I thought, smiling like some plastic doll in his direction—a plastic doll full of heat and icy nerves who was barely keeping it together.

Then it just might kill me.

- Chapter Five -
Drezden

This kid.

This fucking kid.

How could one girl throw me for such an endless loop?

First she blew me away with her talent, then her innocent fucking little smiles and genuine reactions to everything around her. Next, she's dropping notes and sweating herself into a mess like it's her first time performing. And we weren't even *on* a stage with thousands watching us!

Rubbing my inner arm, I watched Lola from the corner of my eye. After telling her we'd be stopping to get food, she'd gone off to use the showers on the bus. My lip ticked at the memory of how high her eyebrows had shot up when we'd told her the showers weren't a joke, they really existed.

Now, the young guitarist was stretched out on one of the long couch style seats. Her hair was ruffled, that wet just-out-of-bed look that made my cock firm up in seconds. The racer-back grey top she'd had on was replaced by a long sleeved black sweater, too thin to bring much warmth, and sleek enough to reveal the swells of her breasts.

I couldn't break away from eating up her sexy body. Up and down, I scanned her from head to toe, as if I could scribe her image into my mind for later. Like she sensed me, Lola flicked her blue eyes up. They met mine and stayed there.

I was the first to look away.

Shit, I thought angrily. *I need to get it together, but it's a challenge when this damn woman with legs all the way up to her asshole is inches away from me. Yeah. It's just about sex, that's all.*

Just sex.

Nothing else.

On the couch, she absently toyed with her hair. Right away, I thought about how her hands moved like birds through a storm when she played guitar. Lola was fucking *good;* I had to admit that. *Talented... and with a mouth made for kissing.*

I thought about how I'd held her cheeks as I checked out her injury in the back of the bus. *She bit the shit out of her tongue,* I reminded myself. That was both dumb and disturbing. If I told myself that Lola was messed in the head, would that turn me off?

No, you're fucked up, too.

My fingers dug into my knee cap. I wanted to push the image of her wet mouth and wide eyes from my skull. My attempts to stop thinking about Lola were backfiring.

I'm a smart enough guy to know this is a bad road to go down. The last thing I need is fucking drama because of where I stick my dick. I'd seen bands torn apart because of members fighting with each other. Relationships didn't belong in a band. One bad breakup, and boom.

The show was over with.

Literally.

Porter said something; I missed it, but whatever it was, it made Lola laugh. The sound was like sugar in my mouth. My tongue tingled as I looked back at her, stuck staring at her long throat and sparkling eyes.

She looked at me again. Once more, I broke my stare. It wasn't that I was nervous, no. I just knew that this *thing* in me, this fierce hunger that wanted to jump on Lola and taste her moans or her sweet pussy, rose to the surface every time she looked into my eyes.

This was a dangerous game. I needed to end it.

"We're here!" Gerald grunted. Our bus driver was a cantankerous man, easily unlikable and often in a sour mood. All I cared about was that he was the most reliable driver I'd ever seen.

Rocking from my chair, I adjusted the hoodie I'd thrown over my tank-top. I'd left it open, the zipper teeth grating across the thin, white cloth beneath. "Come on, let's get some food." I needed to dig my teeth into *something*.

A hot meal would have to do.

The air outside was crisp. It was a far cry from the earlier heat in the day, but I was still amazed that the weather had shifted so fast. We were still a day and half out from Colorado, could the warmth flee so easily as the time vanished?

Craning my neck, I saw the line of cars parking behind us and across the street. The restaurant was about to get slammed by the groupies trailing the tour. I felt a glimmer of pride over knowing we could hide in our private room and avoid most of it.

"Wow," a soft voice whispered at my elbow. Lola had come up beside me, hands shoved deep in her pockets. "I'm so used to being near the end of this caravan. Look at all those headlights." Her attention darted up to me, making me aware of her nearness, how thick her lashes were. "It's kind of intimidating, huh?"

My heart jabbed into my ribs. *Intimidating? No, what's fucking intimidating is how much I need to rely on someone like you to make sure the rest of my shows even happen.* That knowledge was making me anxious.

"If you think that's scary," I said in a low tone, "You'll piss yourself when we play in front of them all later." Brushing past her, I made a beeline for the front door of the building. I didn't look back to see if my words had hurt Lola. I didn't care. I couldn't fucking care.

Dressed in a tight, dark jacket and matching leggings, I almost didn't see Brenda.

She had arrived ahead of us, a security guard for the Griffin Bar and Grill at her side. "Drezden, hey!" Her arm snapped side to side.

I said, "Hey. Everything okay for us to go inside?"

"It was such short notice," she groaned, juggling her phone up to her ear for emphasis. "Couldn't you just let me order you some catering and have it delivered to the bus?"

The familiarity of her exasperation brought a smile to my lips. It was comforting, a status quo returned in my recently turbulent emotions. "Sorry, we were all sick of stale pizza and sandwiches."

"Whatever, whatever." Her sigh was dramatic, her heavy-makeup coated lashes swishing at the guard. "Can you show them to the room in the back?"

Something bumped into me. For a second, I'd hoped it was Lola, but no; Porter had squeezed past, impatiently walking in front of the security guard. "Yeah! Show us. I'm starving, let's go."

We formed a sloppy line through the restaurant. To our sides, I saw and heard the flashes from camera phones. We were probably the biggest stars the building had had in some time.

Wanting to see Lola's reaction, I glanced backwards. The young guitarist was walking next to Brenda, the two of them speaking with their heads close. My manager had swept her long arm around Lola's sharp shoulder blades like they were old friends.

If I knew Brenda, she was probably getting a kick out of feeling important, informing Lola about this or that as we moved through a sea of excited people. It was the ease in which they were touching and talking that was making my neck throb.

My attention stuck on Brenda's nails digging into Lola's side. *I* wanted to be the one bending my lips near her ear and making her grin. I ached to swallow Lola in my arms and smell her hair, to feel her shiver.

It took all my strength to rip my eyes away and look ahead.

The guard led us into a side room, a door blocking it off entirely from the restaurant. There was a game area attached with some pool tables and flat screen TVs. Along one wall was a series of tables that had been pushed end to end.

Porter dropped into a chair, snagging a menu from the middle. Someone, probably the owner, had placed a bottle of champagne in a bucket for us. The very-pink label winked at me as I got closer.

I didn't bite back my snort. "Who thought we'd drink this?"

"It's champagne," Brenda said, sliding around and freeing Lola from her grasp. She touched the neck of the green bottle. *"Fancy* champagne, even. I'll keep it if it doesn't get touched."

Colt slid the bucket away from her, sitting across from Porter with it in his grasp. "Oh no, I'll take it. It'll make a great dessert."

"Or we could all *share* it," Porter said, snatching the champagne back. He ignored Colt's pout. "We've got an excuse to celebrate."

I suppose we do, I thought silently. As a group, we all turned to watch Lola.

She shifted from one foot to the next. "What, because of me? Come on, don't make me blush."

A chunk of me lurched forward at the simple idea of making her cheeks glow pink. It was close to the itch I got for tobacco when things were stressing me out. Striding forward, I pulled the bottle from Porter. In my other hand I snagged an empty champagne flute. "Everyone," I said, "take a glass."

Lola twitched as I approached. "I'm not technically allowed to drink," she said, laughing. "Maybe I should have said that sooner? Before all the beers?" The tilt of her lips at the corners sent electric pricks over my spine. She reacted to me so openly. Was *that* what was drawing me to her? How she projected her emotions on her lovely face?

"No one is going to say anything to you, not in this group," Colt chuckled.

"Here, take this." I pushed the glass at Lola until she took hold.

"Seriously," she said, sourness dancing

on her tongue, "We don't need to do this."

With ease, I gripped the bottle. The sound of the cork popping made her flinch. I said, "Yes, we do." Lifting an eyebrow, daring her to stop me, I filled her glass.

Like we were in some unbreakable bubble, the rest of the group hovered nearby, not getting too close.

Staring Lola down, the champagne fizzing in her glass, I waited. I didn't know what I was waiting for.

"Hey," Colt said, nudging me and shattering the moment—whatever that moment really was. "Share the stuff, Drez."

After I filled their glasses, grabbing one for myself, I abandoned the bottle on the table. There was no need to explain; I lifted my drink, they all copied me.

Even Lola.

Looking her dead in the eye, I said my piece. "Cheers to a new guitarist who won't be found with her cock buried in some random girl in the bathroom while we're *supposed* to be playing on stage."

They all laughed. Well, everyone but Lola. She just looked away, a delicious red heat crawling up her neck. There. That was what I'd wanted.

Why the fuck did I need that so badly?

We finished our toast, which seemed to give the two waitresses hovering by the door enough courage to sway the rest of the way inside. The one with long, onyx hair spoke first. "Can we get you boys anything to drink?"

Brenda's scowl had us all smiling again. "This *boy* will take a vodka tonic," she said with false, sugary sweetness.

Tugging a chair out, I sat towards the end, furthest from Colt and Porter. The way the girls were staring at me was familiar. They knew who I was, they smelled money and fame. Beyond that, they were ogling my chest as it peeked through my open hoodie.

I said, "I'll take whatever beer is on tap."

The scrape of another chair, right across from me, made me look up. Lola settled in with her eyes lowered. I wanted to see into her head, to know what she was thinking. *Is she being shy, or is she nervous she'll get carded in spite of what Colt said?* I doubted anyone would bother. The restaurant was happy we were here, if they said a peep about Lola not being twenty-one, they risked us leaving.

They wanted our business more than they feared a single underage drinker in a private room.

Corruption is a funny thing.

"I guess I'll have what he's having," Lola said, glancing up at me, then to the dark haired waitress. She only relaxed when the other woman nodded, scribbling the order down in her tiny notebook.

The girls moved down the line, talking to the other two men. The chair under me creaked as I leaned towards Lola. "I figured Brenda had done her research, making sure you could legally sign that contract, but please tell me you're not secretly a preschooler," I teased.

"I'm nineteen," she laughed, pure blue eyes landing on my greens. Then, like water on oil, she her eyes back to the menu on the table. "I'll be twenty in four months."

Nineteen. She's getting her break pretty early. I was twenty-one now, but I was only seventeen when I'd started foraying into the music world seriously. A chance meeting at eighteen had been the start of my rise to fame.

Squinting at Lola, I studied the top of her head. She had her nose near touching to the menu. Not sure what to say next, or if there even was anything to say to her, I took her cue and looked at my menu.

By the time the waitresses returned with our drinks, I hadn't figured out what I wanted.

No, that wasn't right. I *knew* what I wanted.

She just wasn't an option.

Flicking the plastic sheet up so the dark-haired girl could take it, I met her smoldering stare. "Just give me what you like best."

"I—what I like?"

Taking hold of the chilly glass of caramel colored beer that she'd handed me, I put on a half smile. "Yeah. Your favorite food, whatever you'd eat here. Get me that."

Tossing her hair back, clearly enjoying

the envious glare of her fellow waitress, the girl giggled. "Alright, I can do that. I'm Scarlett, by the way."

"Scarlett," I repeated back. The name sounded fake, but who was I to judge? "I guess I should introduce myself, I'm—"

"Drezden!" she blurted, her smile wide as the moon. "You're Drezden Halifax. Yeah. I know."

Of course she knew.

I hid my smile behind the beer, the crisp and bitter liquid refreshing on my throat. I caught Lola watching me covertly from behind her menu. "You going to take her order?" I asked Scarlett.

She realized she was ignoring the rest of the table. Casting me a final, flirty smile, she moved over to the young brunette. "Sorry about that. What can I get you?"

"Just some tenders and fries," Lola said. She watched Scarlett nod, then stared after her as she bobbed out of the room, hips swinging. I was sure she was doing that for me. I peered at Lola curiously. What did she think about such over the top behavior?

"She's cute," I said flatly, gauging her reaction.

"Yeah. Beautiful, even." Her fingertips went white on her glass of beer. It told me nothing.

Is she envious of the flirting or not? Why can't that information just be stamped on her—

"Fuck!" Lola coughed, covering her mouth and holding the beer at a distance. "That's strong!"

The laugh escaped me. I couldn't have stopped it if I'd wanted to. But, fuck. It felt *good.* "It does have a kick. Don't tell me that weak beer on the bus was your first?"

Narrowing her eyes, Lola slid the drink closer to herself. "Please. I'm surrounded by rock stars, how could that beer be my first."

"Oh, sorry." Lifting my palms in mock defense, I gave her a cocky grin. "You were the one saying you shouldn't be drinking. I thought that meant this was all new."

"It's just *this* beer, that's all." Fidgeting, she watched me warily. "It's just strong."

"I know," I said. Angling my chin up, I took a long, deep drought from my glass. It was a stupid move, entirely too braggart. Why was I acting like a show off? Setting the mostly empty drink down heavily, I arched an eyebrow at Lola's stunned expression.

Perhaps she wanted to prove something. I couldn't be sure. All I knew was that she proceeded to emulate me, chugging back half of her huge glass. I gawked at her jugular as it pulsed.

She managed not to cough, watery eyes challenging me after she slammed the drink down harder than I even had. "Well," I murmured, gliding my fingers over the top of my damp drink, "Guess you showed me."

Lola went red from chin to hairline. It was a sweet treat after the beer.

"Stop teasing her." Brenda draped herself into the chair beside Lola. The vodka tonic in her slender fingers was already halfway gone. As professional as she was, I'd never known her to curb her love of booze. She knew too well that she had a whole day to sober up before the next show.

The red-head reached out, lifting Lola's beer and taking a quick sip. I gave her a pointed look. "She's right. It's pretty strong," she said, ignoring my frown.

"I believed her." The beer had warmed my blood. That was good, it helped melt the crisp shard of irritation caused by Brenda breaking into my moment. "You don't need to protect her, that won't really help her 'blossoming rock star' image."

Brenda rolled her eyes, but it was Lola who spoke first. "Drez is right, I'm fine. Besides, I'm sick enough of my brother acting like he always needs to protect me. I can handle myself."

Right, her brother. I fixed my attention on Brenda. She just perched her plump lips on the rim of her drink. "About that," I said slowly. "Sean Cooper, he's *really* your older brother?"

"Sure." Lola hesitated, glancing between me and my manager. "Why, is that a problem?"

It could be. "No," I said, taking a pull

81

from my glass. "If Brenda didn't think it was, then no." *She knew, there was no way she didn't realize when she took her name down.*

The ice clinked in Brenda's suddenly empty glass. She pushed it aside, making it obvious for the waitress that she needed a refill. "I didn't think it was, and I still don't." She leaned towards Lola. "Drez is just being paranoid."

"About what? What's wrong with my brother?"

"Nothing," Brenda said quickly. She scrunched her nose at me, and I knew she hated that the topic was coming up at all.

But it had to.

Looking over at Porter and Colt, I made sure they weren't listening. They were busy laughing over something or other, deep in their own glasses. "Lola," I started, wondering how much she did or didn't know, "Your brother doesn't have the best history with me."

"I didn't think he had *any* history." Lola craned forward, confusion twisting her features. "The most Sean ever said about you to me was telling me to lower your music when I was blasting it."

That made me smile. "He really never told you about how he auditioned for my band two years back?"

Lola's fingers were wet from clutching her glass. "He what? I—why wouldn't he tell me that?"

It was Brenda who spoke first. "Drez, stop. You said if I thought it was fine, then it was fine. It doesn't matter what Sean did, he's not holding some grudge against you."

My mind tickled, recalling how Sean had knocked over one of my amps after I'd told him the bad news. I knew what hatred looked like. I'd dealt with it my whole life. *Could a guy like that let a grudge go so easily?* Johnny's face swam behind my eyeballs. "Why are you so sure?" I asked.

She propped her cheek on her fist. "Because he came to me this morning, asking me to consider our friend Lola here for the open slot. Why would he send us help if he was still mad?"

My fingers slid to my jeans, seeking the shape of my cigarette pack for comfort. "He came to fucking see you this morning?" The hard ball that was my guts only got worse when I saw Lola biting her lower lip. An awful idea hit me. "Did *you* tell him to do that for you, Lola?"

She shook her head quickly, sensing the distrust wafting off of me. I was sure she had to feel it. I was boiling with a sensation of betrayal. Had this all been orchestrated without my knowledge somehow?

Lola said, "I didn't know about the audition until Sean told me. He did mention he'd talked to your manager, though." Those lovely blue eyes fixed on Brenda.

"Drezden, calm down." Brenda had no patience for my moods, she never had. "You're getting that look in your eyes."

"What look?" I growled, drinking from my beer. It was empty somehow. When had I finished it? The warm buzz in my skull had no answers.

Reaching over, she slid her manicured nails onto Lola's shoulder. "The look that says you're about to say or do something stupid. Lola didn't trick you, Sean didn't do anything. Even *if* they somehow had arranged things, it was still on you to choose her for the band. How could they force your hand? What would they gain?"

She's right, I thought sullenly. *I'm looking at this the wrong way. The kid didn't do anything, how could there be a conspiracy at all?* Staring at Lola's face, I felt a tug in my belly. *She's innocent, it isn't her fault her older brother was an asshole. Two years ago, even. I'm being paranoid.*

"Listen," the guitarist said, her voice soft and frail. "I don't know about you and Sean, or why he never told me about—well. The thing is, if it wasn't for him, I wouldn't even be here." Her shrug was pleading, her gaze more so. It took everything I had to face down her blue depths and the gentle curls at the edges of her frown.

Rubbing my neck, hating how much I was sweating, I grunted. "It's fine. Don't worry about it. I'm probably being the real asshole here. The thing with your brother was long ago, I bet he didn't mention it to you because he forgot." My smile wasn't really sincere, neither were my words.

There was no way Sean had forgotten about that day. But, the chances of him plotting against me were on the level of evil scheming that only happened in movies.

Lola's smile bloomed. It froze me stiff, worse than my angry shock had. She was so fucking *real*. I'd never known someone who could smile so honestly. It touched her eyes, turned them into a calm sea.

I wanted to drown in it.

"Yeah," she said, sipping from her beer. "Besides, he's got other things to worry about. He *is* the lead guitar in Barbed Fire, you know?"

Of course I knew. "Right. Glad he's doing well for himself." Truthfully, I didn't give a shit. But Lola did, and if my comments could make her beam like she was, what was the harm?

Plus, I thought privately, *I'm getting a kick out of seeing her smile.* My mouth twitched to match hers. I caught Brenda peering at me. Turning away, spotting the waitresses and the food, I let relief wash over me. Dinner was an instant subject changer. "That looks great," I said, blessing Scarlett with a wink.

She nearly dropped the tray. "Oh! Uh, thanks! It's our Paradise Chicken." Her cheeks were glowing when she put it in front of me. "It's my favorite, like you asked for."

Inhaling the scent of pineapples and the tang of spices, I nodded. "Glad I did. Thanks for your expertise."

The young waitress looked lost. Her friend nudged her, reminding Scarlett that we all needed utensils. The girls set the table, and with the sounds of Porter and Colt cheering in my ears, I felt myself relaxing.

Chewing on the sweet chicken, my eyes flicked over to Lola. She was working on her second beer. With her lips touching the rim, she leveled her attention on me.

There was a river of fire slowly crawling through my veins. The tides were rising, I was keen to blame the alcohol. It took a lot to get me drunk, but the strong beer was doing its job.

She set the glass down slowly, fingers shaking. "What? What is it?" she asked.

Brushing fingers over my scalp, I reclined in my chair. "Just wondering how your food is."

Lola nudged the plate towards me. "It's just fries and chicken, try it."

Grabbing up a tender, I took a bite off the end. The batter crunched, the sound of snapping branches. The flavor spread over my tongue. "Not bad at all. A little salty, maybe."

Her smile was muted. "I like things salty." In spite of her words, her plate was still mostly full.

Why would she be eating so little if she —Oh, I thought, *right. Her tongue. I bet the salt hurts on that wound she gave herself.* Thinking of that moment on the bus, my fingers holding her cheeks so she was trapped near me, had my pants tightening.

Nostrils flaring, I started to cut into my chicken. "Here, try some of mine." Offering the fork to her, the bit of white meat and pineapple glinted between us. I expected her to take the utensil from me.

Lola swayed over the table, teeth plucking the food right off the end of my fork. My jaw dropped, and it was a miracle the fork didn't, too.

The fact she had taken it as she had, that she was chewing now with a tiny half-smile, it was sending tremors into my cells. *Is she fucking with me now?* She'd done something meant for lovers, not brand new band acquaintances.

Clearing my throat, I shifted on the chair. Her pink lips and pinker cheeks had made my cock swell. The inside of my zipper, even with my boxers, was becoming a cruel enemy. "Well. Do you like it?"

Lola nodded, wiping her mouth with the back of her hand. "A little too sugary, but still good."

My plate slid her way. "Here, just have mine then."

"I—what?"

Her barely eaten food was still warming the air around it. Pulling it to me, I slapped away her hand when she reached to steal it back. "Just trade with me." Cocking an eyebrow, I gave her a meaningful look. The corner of my eye warned me that Brenda was peering at us both. "That sugary stuff will go down *easier*, got it?"

Personally, I didn't care if Brenda found out about how she'd chewed her tongue up. She'd dealt with worse. There was a good chance she'd roll her eyes and think Lola did it accidentally, if she didn't just shake her head to signal it wasn't her problem.

But Lola cares. One look at her pale face made that obvious.

Swallowing loudly, she started chopping at the meal with deliberate motions. "Thanks, Drezden."

In answer, I crunched down on a fry.

Most of the evening went as expected. We ate, we drank, and there was even some laughter. Most was from Porter and Colt, but it still counted.

Scarlett kept my beer topped off, long after I stopped gulping it down. My skull was tingling with the warm tickles of alcohol. I enjoyed a good buzz, but on tour, I liked to keep it together. That plan was falling by the wayside.

The dark-haired waitress said something, bending towards me as she did so. "What was that?" I asked. Her smell was like grease and cloying lavender. No doubt she'd been on shift for hours.

"I said," she whispered, crouching down to blow on my ear, "I get off in thirty minutes. What are you doing after this? I'd *kill* to see your tour bus. Seriously, just to get inside, I'd do anything." Scarlett's meaning was as obvious as a kick to the face.

My smile was brittle. Across from me, I spotted Lola staring intently. Brenda was babbling at her, yet she wasn't listening. Lola was stuck on me like frost to a metal pole in the dead of winter.

Was she jealous?

Scarlett's fingers glided down, touching my knee. I clasped her thin wrist before she dared to go further. "Listen." My voice wasn't even strained; I'd been down this road before. Fighting off hungry fans after a show was old news. "I can't."

"You can't?" She stiffened, gaze flicking from my face, to my grip, then back.

Letting the waitress go, I leaned in just enough so only she could hear me. "Sorry. I meant I won't." Grinding the chair back, I got to my feet. "Colt, want to shoot some pool?"

"Fuck yes," the drummer laughed, nearly falling from his seat. "I'll beat you this time, too!"

"One of these days, maybe." Strolling towards the green-felt table in the room, I couldn't stop myself from looking back. Just one small, scant look.

There were two pairs of eyes watching me; the dark pits of a girl who'd been scorned. And the other...

Lola's deep sapphires were starkly relieved. It sent a thrill to my core, one that was all too soon replaced by tense muscles. I wanted so much to believe she was happy that I'd denied the girl.

No, I told myself, yanking a pool stick off the wall. I could have broken it in my ripple of confused emotions. *Stop getting excited over the prospect. You're making up signs that she likes you, when you should be spending your energy resisting the very concept.*

Crushing too much chalk onto the tip of the stick, I stared at the back of Lola's head. Sometimes, even if it was the right decision, choosing music over other things made me feel hollow.

I couldn't risk the band over a fucking pair of pretty blue eyes that turned my blood to liquid silver. It was too reckless.

For them.

And for her.

- Chapter Six -
Lola

There was too much alcohol in my blood. But even worse... there was starting to be too much of something else. I didn't have a name for it. I only knew that it flared up when *he* was close.

When Drezden Halifax got near me, something clawed up from my very center and clutched around my middle. It turned everything into pressure and heat. It made me long for *release*.

Brenda was giggling, tangled up on my arm and saying something about me looking like my older brother. Nearby, Porter and Colt were having an argument over who had actually won at pool.

With four—or was it five—beers in me, I'd lost track of Drez in the fading hours of the evening. He'd been playing with the other guys, ignoring the wistful stares from the two waitresses each time they entered the room.

At some point, he'd vanished. I was too swept up in my conflicting desires to think about searching for him. Hell, if I found him, who knew what I'd do?

After such a long day, I just wanted to sleep.

"Excuse me," I said, pulling away from

Brenda. The red of her lips reminded me too much of fake, Halloween wax candy.

She let me go, her hand hovering in the air. "Wait, where are you going?"

"Just to get some air." The migraine that pulsed behind my eyeballs needed more than fresh air, but I'd take that over the stifling backroom of the restaurant.

Brenda frowned, not moving to stop me. "If you need to go out, use that door there." Pointing, she drew my eyes to an exit in the far corner. It was meant for escaping fires, but it was hot enough in here that it seemed appropriate.

I wondered why we hadn't entered that way. If we'd wanted to avoid the insanity of the fans swarming the place, it would have been logical. *Unless everyone wanted that attention. Was that it?* It hurt too much to think about. Instead, I gave a brief nod and stumbled out of the heavy door.

The sky was purple and black. It reminded me of Drezden, of the centers of his eyes when he got angry...

Or passionate.

Stop, stop thinking about him like that.

There were no clouds. Overhead, the stars guided me—called to me. Inhaling till my ribs threatened to break, I held my breath. Could I just float up, vanish forever into that void and not have to deal with the insanity growing in my heart?

Closing my eyelids, I endured a memory; Drez, offering me a forkful of food. And me, as I imagined myself from the outside, leaning in to take it like some pathetic dog.

What made me do that?

I couldn't make sense of anything anymore.

My lungs burned, I breathed out quickly. There was a gentle buzzing of people just around the edges of the building. I could see some of them, and the closer I got, the more their shadowy bodies stood out on the horizon.

On shaking legs, I walked until I was among the throngs of groupies and roadies, everyone that couldn't fit inside the restaurant. Would the recognize me and rush at me, like I was Drez or Porter or Colt? *They won't,* I realized. *No one knows me as a member of Four and a Half Headstones. Not yet.*

To these people, in the dark of evening lit only by some lamps and small tin-can fires, I would be a blank face in the crowd.

Maybe, after they see me on stage...

Did I want that kind of attention? Part of me was thrilled by the idea. *If—when—I get on stage, if I fuck up like I was doing earlier, these people will remember me for all the wrong reasons.*

My teeth hurt from clenching my jaw.

Tonight was so weird. Drez was cold, then he was a magnet, then he was off of me again. Flirting with that girl, talking about

Sean like they had some awful history or something.

Reaching for my pocket, I felt for my phone. Sean had told me to talk to him after practice. I was sure he was somewhere nearby, possibly even in the restaurant, hoping to run into me.

Clutching the cold device wasn't comforting. I was tired, a bit drunk, and not sure what to even tell him. *Yes, Sean. I fucked up today at my first practice. Why? Because I turned into a sloppy mess around Drezden. I really fucked up. Oh don't worry, I got better. How? I just chewed up my own tongue!*

Sean would be pissed, or worse, disappointed if he found out I'd hurt myself just to get some control. After everything I'd worked so hard to get over in the past, I couldn't handle seeing his face scrunch up in shame.

Tomorrow. I'll talk to him tomorrow.

Weaving through the laughing, drunken crowd, I headed towards the tour bus. There were a few men standing near the front door, men I hadn't seen before. They took one look at me, arms folding to transform them into standing walls of muscle. "What is it, little lady?" one of them asked.

Little lady? I almost told him to eat a dick. The edges of my lips felt dry, licking them did little. My near-to-drunk state made my brain muddled. "I need to get inside."

Their laughter cut deep. "Yeah? Sure you do. Get lost. Unless you want to have some fun with me?" The guard who'd asked that had a jack-o-lantern smile.

Shaking my head, I fought down a wave of frustration. "Let me the fuck inside," I growled, pushing forward. "I just want to go to sleep!"

I didn't see anyone move, but my back hit the hard cement, all of the wind fleeing my lungs. The spray of starlight overhead felt like I could reach it if I just stretched my arm up. Everything was echoing as if I was underwater. *What the hell? Did someone just push me down?*

Sitting up on my elbows, ignoring the dull burning on my raw skin, I stared at the guards. "What the hell?" I coughed, forcing in delicious air. Rocking on my side, I stumbled to my feet. "What was that for?"

No sympathy existed in the eyes of those men. Behind me, the sea of people was a background of emotionless ignorance. No one cared about what was happening to me, no one gave a single shit.

Swaying forward, I went to shove one of the guards. I didn't have a plan; I was just bursting with rage that had nowhere to go and enough alcohol to smother my good sense. But I wanted to get even with them—they'd actually pushed me down! This was *my* tour bus, too. Didn't they understand?

Easily, the guard dodged me. Another pair of hands grabbed me and yanked me sideways. All around me the men roared with laughter. It felt too much like I was being spun on a roller coaster with no end in sight.

Then it *did* end; I hit the ground, grunting. The motion jolted into my guts. Hunched over with my palms splayed wide, I wasn't proud when I threw up. On hands and knees, shivering in shame, I stared down at my puke and coughed.

My brain itched, recalling a time when I was in middle school. I'd been in a fight with some kids, and I'd ended up just like this; broken, a weak mess.

Pathetic.

Back then, the only person who cared was... was Sean. Lifting my eyes, I fought through my daze and expected to see the face of my older brother. It was a poor wish that went nowhere.

I was alone.

Well, not alone—the guards were a hellish kind of company. One of their hands came down, curling in my scalp. Ripped to my feet, I jabbed an elbow into one of them and shouted, "Let me *go!*"

"Little bitch actually hit me!" the man growled. My head was yanked back. I couldn't see the sky that time, my vision was spinning too much, but it didn't matter. Behind my eyelids, stars of color bloomed.

I fell again, crumbling in a heap on the asphalt. Bile slid down my chin; I was relieved it wasn't blood. Over me, the voices were loud, the men laughing at me where I was crouched.

They're going to throw me aside, now. And no one will do a thing about it.

The metallic sound of the bus doors opening cut the laughter apart. "What the fuck is going on out here?"

I gazed up at the silhouette of a man who was crafted from sharp edges and wicked shadows. A man who, in just a tank-top and jeans, was more intimidating than the group of guards surrounding me.

Drezden's eyes scalded like acid.

My stomach tightened, I nearly retched again. Drezden seeing me sitting over my own vomit was just what I needed. My shame was complete.

"Sorry, sir," a gravelly voice said. Hard fingers gripped my upper arm, yanking me to my feet. In spite of my desire to be strong, I gave a pained cry. "Just another drunken whore starting trouble. She was trying to get inside. We'll get her out of the way for you."

My chin swung, I caught a glimpse of the black clouds that had started to roll in and cover the twinkles of starlight. *Walk away and you won't bleed, walk away and I am freed. No more stars,* I thought bitterly.

Someone was grabbing me around the middle, hoisting me against their chest. Musk and tobacco filled my world. "You damn idiots," Drez said over me. "Are you blind? This is Lola Cooper, our new guitarist. Fucking hell, what did you do to her?"

Soft cloth pressed on my cheek. *I'm leaning against Drezden's chest.* It was a stunning realization. *No, even better, he's holding me against him.* Looking up, I saw the slightly rough stubble on his lower jaw. I couldn't see his expression, but the raw disgust in his voice said enough.

The guards stammered, speaking over each other. "But she—"

"Shut up, just stop," Drez snapped. Gently, he guided me to follow him up the steps into the bus. "I'll have Brenda talk to your boss. I should have guessed some a bunch of wanna-be cops wouldn't have a clue who to keep out and who to let inside."

My shin scraped the top step of the bus as I stumbled. Drezden coaxed me on, helping me into the vehicle. The soft 'whoosh' of the doors shutting behind us was comforting.

Jostled, I let myself be set on one of the seats. My eyesight was blurry, not focusing on anything. Drez's hand took my jaw, forcing me still. Green eyes bore into mine.

Then, I felt clarity.

"Are you alright?" he asked, his forehead crinkling with worry.

I blinked. Then, I blinked again. *Am I alright?* I wasn't actually sure. My skull felt like someone had used it to play kickball, my insides were painfully empty.

Remembering how I'd vomited outside the bus, I blushed hotly. My mouth still wore the sour taste. "I need a glass of water," I said, moving to stand.

He pushed me back, not rough, but without any room for question. "Sit. I'll get it for you."

The singer left me, freeing me from his intoxicating aura. Looking after him, my alcohol-soaked brain began to work. Studying the burning sensation on my arms revealed that the fall I'd taken at the hands of the security had torn the elbows off my shirt. The skin there was red, exposed.

Drez returned, offering me a cold glass. I took it, the both of us clearly seeing my fingers trembling. Drinking hurt my throat, it made me worry I might vomit again as the cold water hit my empty stomach. Flinching, I wiped at my mouth.

Ultimately, I was fine—a few scrapes at most. The only other damage was to my pride.

That couldn't be fixed with a glass of water.

He sat across from me, squinting so fiercely I couldn't stop myself from squirming. "You're really okay?"

"Yes," I said softly, eyeing the scrapes on my palms. It was all minor stuff. *So why do I feel so awful?* Glancing at Drezden, I sipped my water. *I was being bullied out there. That must be why I feel so rotten. I was getting assaulted and no one gave a shit.*

My fingers squeezed the glass. *No, that's not true.* Peeking through my eyelashes at Drez, I felt blood surge to my cheeks. *Someone did care.*

Shaking my head, I looked at the singer, keeping my voice steady. It still sounded like I'd been eating rocks. "Listen, I need to thank you."

"They'll be fired for this," he said, showing me his profile; that sharp nose and strong jaw. It was as if he hadn't heard me, he was busy talking to himself. "Bunch of fucking idiots. I've told Brenda, if we're going to hire freelance security, prep them so they don't do shit like this!"

In my chest, my heart slammed against my ribs. "Did you hear—I said thank you. Thank you for saving me out there."

Turning back, Drez considered me for a long moment. "It was nothing."

"You could have easily not bothered."

His palm hit the table, startling me. "Do you honestly think I could have *easily* ignored what was happening? Fuck, the sound of you throwing up alone was..."

Biting my tongue, the bloom of pain contorted my face.

Drezden's frown created deep rows in his skin. "Stop doing that—hurting yourself.

Anyway, forget about what I did. Maybe next time, though, drink a little less."

Pointedly, I banged the empty glass onto the table. "Thanks! Hey, while we're giving advice, maybe next time don't *force* me into a drinking contest with you."

"I didn't force you to do anything," he snorted.

"You were trying to get under my skin all night! Challenging me with your 'tough' beer chugging, forcing me to take that champagne. You're not blameless."

Drez looked away; I regretted my accusation. I was the one telling everyone to stop treating me like I was a fucking child. I was on control of my choices—*I'd* ordered the damn beer.

I just wanted this night to end.

We sat in tense silence. I would have gone outside if I wasn't worried about facing anyone who'd witnessed me falling apart out there. *New guitarist of Headstones vomits on tour!* I really prayed no one had gotten a photo. *Funny, earlier I was angrier that no one noticed what was happening to me. Now, I want that to be true.*

"So," I started, "You're going to tell Brenda?"

"In the morning. She'll be useless tonight." Reaching out, he grabbed my forearm. I was too surprised to fight him as he turned my limb over, spotting the blazing crimson scrape and torn fabric. "Shit, let me get something so this doesn't get infected."

I yanked my arm back, but the damage was done. His touch had my veins pumping. "It's nothing. They're just scrapes."

"They?" he asked, looking pointedly at my other arm. "You've got more? Come on, come with me to the bathroom."

I squeezed the edge of the table like it could keep me from having to stand ever again. "Calm down, it's nothing."

Drezden was not a man to argue with. Reaching out, he tangled his long fingers in the neck of my shirt and pulled. "Get up. Now."

The cloth stretched, pressing into my skin and coming close to tearing. My gut said to fight, but one look at the heat in his eyes melted my resistance. I was lightheaded when I stood. "There," I said. "Happy?"

Rolling his eyes, Drez didn't let go. His strength demanded that I follow him as he led me down the aisle like I was on a leash. If the sweater hadn't been ruined by holes already, Drez had now wrecked it by stretching the neck out.

The bathroom was just up the hall from the studio room we'd practiced in. Thinking of our session made me fight him even less; it was a reminder of my failures, of my slow evaporation in Drez's presence.

Who was I anymore?

He pushed me into the bathroom, finally

releasing me. "Lift your arms," he said.

Unsure what else to do, I held up my hands. Grabbing the cuffs, Drezden tore my sweater and my shirt right off of me in one go. My hair fluffed from the motion, brain dazzled by the sudden exposure. In only my white bra, I gaped at his bold action.

Drezden didn't seem to be as amazed. Digging into a cabinet, he set some cotton and bandages on the edge of the sink. "Sit down for a minute."

That was an easy request. Nearly dropping onto the toilet lid, I shivered in the pallid light from the basic white bulbs. I'd been shirtless around other people before, but this felt... different.

There, sitting under Drezden's shadow, I was vulnerable. His eyes studied me casually, not seeming affected by the same baffling emotions I was. Could that be possible? Was I alone in fighting this back and forth temptation that screamed 'Kiss this man, touch him, just do it!'

I'd had a shower earlier... I felt like a needed another one.

A cold one.

Water ran briefly in the sink. He crouched in front of me, a damp rag in one hand. "Hold still," he said, so brisk he clearly didn't expect me to argue.

Like a deer in front of a car that was about to smash it to bits, I froze. His strong fingers lifted my arm, dabbing the cloth on my raw flesh. Pain jolted into my nerves, searing and making me hiss.

"Hurts, right?" he asked.

"No," I said over my numb tongue. "Not at all."

His sideways smile grew a bud of heat in my blood. "Always acting so tough."

I watched the way his jugular pulse along his long neck. When he rubbed my wound, I inhaled—and his pulse quickened visibly. "It isn't an act," I said.

"No?" Meeting my gaze, not blinking, he dug the hot cloth into my other arm. It wasn't hard, just enough to make me yelp and give up my act. His throaty chuckle was worse than the pain.

He whispered, "People who put on an act piss me off."

But I need to be tough. Leaving it unsaid, I watched him bandage my elbows. A*round you, I need to be... Callous. Strong.*

Without fronting some kind of a wall, who knew what would happen between me and Drezden? I certainly had no clue. That was why I was so fucking nervous. This *thing* between us, whether it was fanatical adoration or idolization or... or something else I didn't want to name...

I just had no plan on how to deal with it.

My only option was to put up a barrier and hide.

Drezden still held my forearm. Leaning near, the long fibers of muscle in his shoulders flexed. It reminded me of his strength, how easily he had helped me inside of the bus. How he'd saved me from the guards, faced them without a fragment of fear.

The thrum in my heart was distracting. It threatened to climb right up my throat and out of my mouth. I thought, if I spoke, I'd just stutter.

"This tattoo," he said abruptly, "What does it mean?"

Focusing on my own arm, I scrutinized the beautiful and intricate design he was referencing. It was a castle, a single stone tower wrapped in veins of ivy. Stark black and grey, I'd had to sit for a few hour long sessions to finish it. "Nothing."

Drezden barely moved. His tiny smirk was a road map to his doubt. I was never a great liar. "It clearly means *something.*"

Of course it did. It meant everything about my life, about that space of time where I'd let everyone hurt me. When school had been filled with cruel bullies and crueler teachers.

The depression that had made a razor my best friend.

I'd been a hollow chunk of myself. This tattoo, though... it represented my restoration. It was the walls that I'd built to keep me from feeling fragile, the ivy a symbol of the music that had brought me back and kept me together.

But I could never explain all that to Drezden.

"You don't look well," he murmured. His words moved a strand of hair on my forehead. Then, he straight up placed his palm on my skin. He was warm, I was a broiler.

Sucking my teeth, we both heard my throttled whistle. "I'm—I'm fine!" I blurted, twisting away in a panic. *Shit, he touched me. Fuck fuck fuck I felt that between my thighs!* It had been like he'd reached right inside of me and stroked my center. Except... except more pleasant.

More raw and wild.

I was worked up, sweating and pale. I saw myself in the mirror; my skin was the color of milk. Drezden went to hold me down, saying something about not moving so fast, not to panic. How could I listen to him with my ears thumping?

I wrenched upwards, shoving at his chest and swaying off balance. One of us kicked the other in the ankle; it didn't matter who was to blame. I went from fighting him to grappling with his arms, my world flipping under me as I lost my balance.

"Look out!" he cried, grabbing out for something to stabilize us. Together we tumbled, my legs over my head almost comically. The porcelain of the nearby bathtub rattled as we landed inside, stunning me.

106

Drezden crashed down on me like a landslide. I coughed, coughing in pained shock, the sickening thud of a skull hitting the wall beside me demanding I focus. "Shit," I groaned, "Drezden? You okay?"

Fluttering my eyes, I stared into the peaceful face of the singer of Four and a Half Headstones. His weight was heavy, but somehow comforting on me. The red mark on his temple showed where he'd banged his head.

I was too nervous to move or breathe. There was a chance Drezden was hurt. Yet, for me, it was the first time we'd been so close without him paralyzing me with those intense green eyes of his. He wasn't yelling or growling, he wasn't sending iron burrs into my limbs.

Pressed under his warmth, I wasn't... scared of him.

But I was scared *for* him.

One of my arms was trapped between us. The pulse of Drezden's heart trickled up my skin. Reaching out with my fingers, I hovered just in front of his jaw. *I need to see if he's okay.* "Drezden?" I whispered, voice scratchy. "Drez, wake up."

The singer didn't budge.

My mouth tasted like batteries. The ends of my fingers quivered, desperately wanting to alight on his cheek. If I did, I'd risk breaking everything; that moment that could go on forever. A slice of time that allowed me to bask in the intensity that was Drezden Halifax, his beauty and heat, without turning into dribbling and useless chunks.

He might really be hurt, I realized. All at once, the tranquility vanished. With just the one free hand, I dropped it, clasping his bare shoulder. It was tepid, smooth as glass. "Drezden! Drezden, wake up! Are you alright? Talk to me!"

Breathing suddenly through his nose, the man cracked his eyes and looked at me. He might as well have been Medusa for how I stopped moving. "Why the hell are you touching me?" he asked softly.

Opening my lips, I found... nothing. No words. The situation had transformed and he was once more a fucking god of rock who spun perverse thoughts to life inside of me just by being near.

Just by being alive.

He shifted, hissing as he gripped his skull. His weight ground against me, rubbing jeans on my pelvis. The sensation was wonderfully awful. My lower belly danced, my tongue knotted.

Watching me, Drezden paused. The look in his eyes went from surprised to accusatory. I preferred the first expression by far.

I felt it, didn't I? I'd noticed it soon after he'd fallen on me. Distracting myself with his injury had served somewhat, but now... under the loaded gun of his hot gaze, his strong scent and moving body, I was all too aware of what was happening.

Drezden's cock was hard as a rock, and it was pushing into my hip.

My thighs tensed from holding the position I had for so long. I didn't dare move, though. The result of everything I'd been trying to deny was pinned between me and Drezden.

He adjusted again, slowly that time. The pressure of his hard-on rolling over me was torture. It was almost enough to make me want to find those guards again, just to let them beat me senseless.

To make me forget that Drezden Halifax...

Wanted *me*.

Tingles rose through my sternum. My nipples firmed in my bra, betraying me with their reaction. The small tents were obvious through the thin material. Sensing his attraction was doing things to me I wasn't ready for.

Oh fuck, what do I do? I thought wildly. Turning my chin, I stared at the wall where Drezden had hit his temple. I ripped my hand off of him, leaving it floating in the air uselessly. "Are—are you alright?" I choked out.

"I'm fine," he said, knees spreading outside of my calves as he sat up. I still couldn't bring myself to look at him. His shade fell over me in the small space. "But I asked you something. Why the hell were you touching me?"

His question reminded me too pointedly of our tangled bodies. "I was worried you were really hurt. I—fuck, I'm sorry that I knocked us down."

Hard, callused fingers suddenly dug into my chin. Drezden twisted me, forcing me to look at him straight on. In his emerald depths, I saw my own lust-filled expression reflected. "You could have broken your fucking neck," he hissed. "Let alone mine! Why do you always fight me so hard?"

A million reasons danced on the tip of my aching tongue. *Because you turn my legs to mush, because you make me forget my name, because you scare the shit out of me with how you make me feel.*

I could say none of them. "Because," I croaked, "You keep treating me like I'm weak."

Considering me, Drezden finally let me go. My jaw throbbed where he'd held me. "You'd prefer I treat you like something else?"

"Of course!" Disbelief flared in me. "I'm not your kid sister, okay? I get enough of that already in my life."

His weight settling on me. Gasping, I writhed in spite of my situation. Was he intentionally grinding himself in between my legs? No, he couldn't be. He wouldn't. "You want me to start acting like we're the same?"

Only my still sputtering anger allowed me to speak so flatly. "Yeah, that'd be a nice start."

Something threatening slid across his face, a hint beneath the surface at a part of Drezden I'd only glimpsed when he sang. "You couldn't handle that."

Tension crawled up my spine. He was too serious, and it made my goosebumps stiff. With both my arms free, I grabbed at the wall and edge of the tub. The forewarning in Drez's tone, his words, advised me to escape

Easily, he pressed down on me. The back of my head bounced off the porcelain. It didn't hurt, but it left me stunned. His tank-top crushed against my bra, along the tops of my breasts. "What the fuck are *you* doing?" I gasped.

"You wanted me to stop coddling you like you might break," he growled. "I'll do just that. And if you're as tough as you keep claiming, you'll be just fine. Because Lola, when I go all out?" His hands squeezed my shoulders like a vice, his breath brushing over my puckered lips. "Only the strong ones survive me."

My world was swimming. Even if I hadn't banged my head, I'd have been dazed. *What is he saying? This is too much, too intimate.* Being trapped under the firm, smoldering body of Drezden Halifax wasn't something I'd ever expected to encounter. *I wish my heart would stop pounding!* Licking my lips nervously, I said, "Drez, hey. I don't— you shouldn't be doing this."

His eyebrow crawled upwards. "I haven't done anything yet."

Yet, I thought, fighting down a wave of desire. Every second I spent with this man brought me closer to giving in. I was more excited than I'd been with anyone else in my life, but his threat stayed with me.

He was a sexual monster who was warning me what he could do.

And I was a virgin.

"Lola," he whispered, and the sheer hunger in his voice made me clench my jaw and close my eyes. "What the hell is this, what are you doing to me?"

Doing to HIM? All I could do was shake my head. I moved so slow, trapped in a world of thick syrup. It was Drezden who was making this happen. There was no way I was causing it.

His expert fingers glided down my arms, as much as they could in our cramped confines. Lying across me, he rocked his hips; a single movement that made my pussy twitch.

I couldn't think, couldn't talk. Everything around me was made of Drezden. My ears sought him out, my nostrils drowned in his scent. I might have vanished entirely in that tub if he hadn't stiffened, then sat up.

Confused, I opened my eyes to see him looking at the door, straining as he listened. I understood why when a voice called out. "Drez? You in here?"

Porter, I realized.

In a whirlwind of limbs, the singer flew off of me. He didn't even look back, just darted out the door and shut it softly behind him. Our private world of wicked heat vanished. I was alone, it could have all been a drunken dream.

Blinking, I shifted my gaze up to the white ceiling. It was a perfect canvas for my mind; blank, featureless.

What just happened?

With my ear to the tub, I heard the metallic echoes of people speaking in the distance. The familiar rumble of Drezden, the baritone of Porter. I listened for some time, unsure what I should do next.

He was going to... to what? Recalling his fit body straddling me, I touched my fingers to my chest. The places he'd pressed against *felt* the same; that frustrated me, because I knew I'd changed somehow. Deep in my gut, a part of me had spread open, seeking what Drezden could bring.

And what's that? I asked myself cynically. *A gigantic erection?* I wanted to laugh, but remembering how obvious his arousal had been made my insides go electric.

Trailing my hand down my stomach, I scratched the junction of my thighs where his cock had been rubbing through his jeans on me. The reality was too much for me; gingerly, I sat up and climbed from the tub.

I found my shirt, tugging it over my head. The mirror showed my pink face, my

113

messy hair. Touching my lips, I wondered if he'd been thinking about kissing me. He'd forced me down, talked about testing if I could handle him and twisting my demand to be treated as an equal.

My whole neck burned as an idea occurred to me. *How many women has he been with? He's twenty-one, it could be a lot.* Thinking of the famous singer rolling around with tons of faceless women didn't help my mood.

Cracking the door open, I peered into the hall. The voices were still speaking, a friendly murmur towards the front of the bus. On unsteady legs, I darted out of the bathroom and dove through the curtain into the room I'd chosen. As alone as I could be on the bus, I dropped heavily onto my bed. My hands coiled in my hair, chin falling to my collar bone.

In a tight ball, I wedged myself into the corner where the frame met the wall. I wanted to shrink down, and at the same time, I wanted to go find Drez and press him to continue. I was itching to know what he would have done if we'd been left alone.

How could my life transform so much in one day? I asked myself. When I'd joined Four and a Half Headstones, I was sure it would be the biggest change in my life.

Now, with the musky flavor of Drezden Halifax in my nose, and the imprint of how his hands had felt on my naked skin...

114

I realized I couldn't have guessed how big a change it would be.

- Chapter Seven -
Drezden

I'm such a fucking idiot.

Though I smiled and nodded, leaning on the bus seat so casually while I listened to Porter ramble, my mind was elsewhere. It rested in a porcelain bathtub, trapped by the amazingly stupid decisions I'd made.

I really am a giant fucking idiot, I thought, watching Porter grin and pretending to chuckle at what he'd said. *How could I have let it go so far?* Lola had been challenging me in the bathroom. Then we'd ended up tangled together, her warm body searing against mine.

Tenderly, I touched the spot on my temple. I hoped it didn't bruise.

"Hey, hello?" Porter leaned in, waving his hand at me. "You alright Drez? You look out of it."

You have no idea. But I just gave him an apologetic frown. "Sorry, been a long day." I felt like I'd lived a whole year in Lola's presence. One long, torturous year. How could I wake up and do it all again?

"You're right, it's been stretching." Standing with a yawn, he cracked his back with several loud pops. "I might just go hit the sack, myself. You seen Lola at all? She left, and I didn't see her when I was outside with Colt."

Thinking of Lola's nearly exposed breasts, I balled my fists in my lap. "She came back a while ago. I think she's sleeping already."

Porter's forehead ran with wrinkles. "Huh. Alright then. She's probably more exhausted than all of us. It's been a crazy day for her."

My chin barely moved as I nodded. Porter was more right than he even knew. It turned a knife in me, guilt flooding my senses. Lola had experienced a day full of things she never imagined, and for some of those, I was to blame.

Glancing out the window, I squinted through the tinted glass. The guards were still there, the party only beginning to die down. I spotted the glow of garbage-can fires and wondered if the police would swing by to force the crowd to disburse.

The walk to my small room was short. I'd picked the one furthest down the hall, closest to the practice room. Passing by Lola's bed, unable to see inside, I struggled with my raging desire to shove through and finish what I'd begun.

Shoving aside my heavy, charcoal curtain, I let myself drop onto my mattress instead.

It was dark, I'd covered the small window in the wall with a slice of thick foam. My insomnia was bad enough as is, I hated the idea of the sun seeping through the glass before I was ready to wake up.

Sliding my shirt over my head, I dropped it carelessly. My belt would have come next, but when I touched the cold metal, I was assaulted by the memory of her heat.

In spite of myself, I sucked air through my teeth. Lola had squirmed under me, so warm and tender and soft all at once. *Mostly soft,* I mused. The hard-on I'd sported could have cut through my jeans.

At the time, when I'd found myself strewn across her, I'd stopped thinking about all the reasons I'd crafted to stay away. Her chest had thrummed against mine, heart stampeding. Feeling her, seeing her reactions and knowing I had to be the cause, I'd just... I'd started to give in.

Lola had made it too easy. Grinding under me, her blue eyes so wide and unsure, I'd sensed her hunger as clearly as she'd felt my massive erection.

I'd wanted to crush my mouth on hers until she either begged me to keep going or pleaded with me to stop. *Which one did I want from her?* I gave my head a shake. That porcelain tub had been so perfect.

It had doomed me.

I told myself to stay away from her. The danger of sleeping with Lola is obvious! Scowling, I ripped my jeans down to my ankles. The engorged bulge in my boxers was a constant reminder that my rational thought didn't exactly agree with the rest of me.

Lying back on my bed, I stared at the ceiling. There would be no key there to crack this puzzle. Still, I stared, unblinking. *If I wondered about her wanting me, now I know the truth.* My cock gave a sympathetic throb.

The way she clung to me when I saved her from the guards... and the way she touched me when she thought I was hurt... It shouldn't have been insignificant. Instead, it all cemented my desire to get closer to Lola Cooper.

Shutting my eyes, I recalled again how she had trouble meeting my gaze. How she'd turned so red, writhing beneath me, my erection grinding on her belly.

Fuck, I'd wanted to kiss her so bad. Reaching up, I dragged my fingertips over my lips. *If Porter hadn't shown up, making me worry about getting caught, I don't think I would have stopped. I would've given in, dropped the walls and taken a bite out of Lola Cooper.*

My fingers crushed against my mouth violently. *I'm awful, a fucking monster. I'd risk ruining my future—the band's future—by taking what I want from her.*

If I let myself give in and had my way with Lola, she'd probably hate me after. Every woman I slept with eventually did. I couldn't balance sex and my career before, why would now be different?

She'd probably quit the band.

My muscles turned to lead at the idea. Inhaling deeply, I thought I could still smell her in my nose—and I wanted that. I longed for more of her, every single inch she had to give me.

I was selfish.

And I knew it.

Tracing my stomach, the crevices of abdominals, I cupped the shape of my raging hard-on. *Fine, I'm selfish. I'm greedy and terrible and all I want is to taste Lola's sweet pussy. To hear her gasp and fucking scream because my cock is stretching her to the brink.*

Squeezing the head of my cock through my boxers, I moaned. It was true. All of it was true.

But if I gave in to my desire for this blue-eyed woman, everything would crumble. Not just the band, though that was a real issue. Not just my relationship with Lola; but my ability to hold back.

Once I went after Lola, there *was* no stopping. I didn't do things in half-measures. When I wanted something, I took it. It became *mine*.

If I'd just kept things professional, it would have been fine. I could have controlled myself. Then she'd yanked me down into the tub, and everything had changed.

A thick growl rose in my throat. Dipping my hand under my boxers, I traced the hot skin of my prick. It was painfully erect, as tense and strained as my mind was.

Lola was all I could see in my head. Her stunned face, her exquisite fingers. My ears flooded with the memory of the music she played. I was desperate to make her create a new song for me. A song made from the notes of her breathing, punctuated by her sobs and passionate moans.

I wanted to make Lola Cooper into a part of me. And I could have *fucking* resisted that, if I hadn't landed on her in that bathroom tub. If she hadn't caressed my head in worry.

If she hadn't cared.

Panting softly, I pumped my fist over my cock. The strokes weren't slow, they lacked the control I felt represented me. Lola was seeping into everything I was. Even now, in private, my composure was wrecked due to her.

My teeth barely bit off a grunt. *If I'd just stayed away, not saved her, not helped or touched or seen or smelled or... or... or...* A quiver of electric delight danced in my lower belly. It mixed with the last bit of my resolve.

If I had just never met Lola Cooper...
I wouldn't need to have her so badly.

Shuddering, the pressure built in my balls. My tight fist coerced me, demanding I crash over the edge of release. My muscles twitched, a spasm so strong it left me dazzled.

121

As I sprawled there, sweat coating my flesh and sin tainting my thoughts, I had one final burst of clarity before toppling over into the tingling realm of orgasm.

I'm such a fucking idiot.

Crying out, muffling the sound with my pillow, I came all over my pumping fingers. The explosion was so violent I had to use my other palm to keep my sheets clean. Hot flashes thumped in my temples. The release was glorious, but it was missing something important.

Her.

In the backs of my eyelids, colors danced. Among the dots, I saw Lola's perfect face. She might not know what was in store for her, but I didn't care. Not anymore. All I wanted was her.

And I knew she wanted me.

I would do everything I could to make her mine. As long as she was in my band, there was security in knowing I had plenty of time to make it all happen.

Opening my eyes, I looked at the ceiling again. I imagined Lola, and I wondered if she was doing the same. Was I haunting her tonight, too?

When I fell asleep, I dreamed of sapphire eyes, bandaged elbows, and the first notes of No More Stars when played by someone who understood what the song really meant.

It was a song that began with a warning. If I'd done anything to Lola, any favor at all... I'd tried to warn her away from me. In every glare, in every brisk word, I'd shown her what was under my surface. What I was.

But it hadn't been enough. She'd gotten close to me whether she'd planned it or not.

Lola Cooper was going to be mine.

I just hoped she was ready.

- Chapter Eight -
Lola

I didn't remember falling asleep.

I barely remembered waking up.

The voices outside my room were hushed but frantic, making it clear they were trying to keep their volume low. Cracking my eyes open, I regretted my decision instantly. "Fuck," I hissed, rolling onto my side. Had someone been punching my skull all night?

Tenderly feeling my way up my neck, I pushed my face into the sweaty blankets. *No, not punched. I was tossed around by those asshole security guards.*

Digging through the slowly clearing fog in my head was torturous. Alcohol and sneering dickheads were bad enough, but it was something else that invaded my brain.

Drezden.

Even when I first wake up, he's haunting me. Grimacing, I pushed my face into the pillow harder. *Is that what I'm dealing with now? Instantly remembering his eyes, his smell, as soon as I regain consciousness?*

Could I get no peace from that man?

Someone was shouting. Tugging the pillow off of my eyes, I dared to look around my tiny bunk. Light was struggling to break through the tinted window on the wall beside me. Through it I could see static buildings. *It must be early, we haven't started driving yet.* I was glad for that. Especially when I sat up and everything spun in my stomach.

Groaning, I held my forehead tight. My whole head felt like it was stuffed with bees. Hanging it between my knees, I traced the bandages on my elbows when they touched my bare thighs.

They reminded me of Drezden's fingers; callused and firm. How he'd held me still while he'd administered the burning medicine to my shallow cuts.

He was so tender, so insistent when he fixed me up. Blushing furiously, my eyes darted to the curtain over my door. I recognized one of the angry voices out there as Drezden himself.

His throaty tone riddled me with goosebumps. *Demanding is more fitting word for him than tender. Like when he was on top of me in the bathtub, that...* Shaking my head cleared the cobwebs. *Stop. Don't think about that right now.*

Maybe never.

As if I could help it.

Who could erase a moment like that? His heavy scent in my nose, his hard chest and wicked smile turning my insides into cotton candy—*No! Ugh, stop it Lola. Just stop.* Scowling at my weakness, I filled my chest with air. It took everything I had to get on my feet and not vomit.

Brittle as an elderly woman, I slid

carefully into a tight blue shirt and the same jeans from yesterday. I hadn't packed much for the tour, but I hadn't expected to have to worry about it.

As a sweaty grunt moving gear for my brother's band, my clothes didn't matter.

As the new guitarist for the famous Four and a Half Headstones, well... *Maybe I can get Brenda to pick me up something*. Borrowing from her would be no joke; the manager wore things I'd never think about trying on. Her heels could murder me.

Sliding the curtain aside, I strained to listen to the still ongoing argument. It was hard to see much from my angle. Crisp and clean, Brenda's voice rang like a bell. "—it's the easiest way!" she cried, sounding like she was stomping in place. "Last night wouldn't have happened if they knew who she was, let me put her face out there!"

"The problem," Drezden growled, "Is you hiring assholes who don't know how to do their job. Even if she *had* been some drunken fangirl, they roughed her up! That's not fucking acceptable!"

The rawness in his voice was decadent. It hit at a place inside of me so primal that I shut my eyes and bit my lip. There was no time to argue with myself over my inappropriate reactions. They were talking about last night. About *me*.

Shoving into the hall, I stared at the

front of the tour bus. Sunlight streamed through the open roof window, turning Brenda's hair into fiery gold. She was sitting on a leather seat, one heel occasionally kicking the base of the table. Her eyes, thick with makeup, jumped to me.

With his arms in a tight pretzel, Drezden's gaze widened. I didn't know what was glinting in his green depths, only that it set my skin aflame. Quickly he hid behind his indifferent squint. The sun highlighted every muscle on his bare shoulders, the black tank-top exposing him deliciously.

They both watched me, but Brenda spoke first. "Lola! You're awake, good. You can answer this for yourself—"

"She isn't doing it!" Drezden snapped, nostrils flaring.

"I'm not doing what?" My voice was scratchy. Clearing it, wishing for some water—and a toothbrush—I eyed them both warily. "Tell me what's going on."

Brenda smoothed her long crimson hair. "Drez told me about last night." My cheeks went pink as I wondered how much the singer had actually admitted to. "Don't worry," she said suddenly, mistaking the source of my flash of panic. "No one got any photos or anything. Plus, I fired the assholes involved. We'll have new guys for the next stop, but..."

Leaning off the wall, Drezden took a step my way. "She wants you to do a photo shoot

127

before the next show."

"Oh!" Blinking at his sour frown, I looked to Brenda for an explanation. "And why is that a bad thing?" I'd never done a photo shoot before. Certainly it couldn't be that hard, let alone worth arguing over.

With a smug look at Drez, the red-head motioned me towards her. Wordlessly, I sat down on the other seat. "Lola, it's not a bad thing at all. It'll get your name out there, your face, and hype you up to the fans of the band. Clarifying that Johnny Muse is gone, you're in, it's all important. Plus, things like last night won't be an issue anymore."

Drezden's palm came down, slapping the table between us. Jumping, I grabbed at my chest, willing my heart to calm down. "It's not the photo shoot that's the problem! It's the time it will take away from practice! Brenda, we have one fucking day before the show in Colorado, we need every minute we have to make sure Lola is ready."

"And I *told* you," she huffed, "That I can call ahead and squeeze in a chunk of time tonight! Schedule around it, it'll just be an hour at most."

"An hour to take photos, yeah. What about the hour to set up the location, then the hour to prep her?"

Brenda rolled her eyes, lips going white.

Though my heart was still struggling to climb into my mouth, I looked up at Drezden.

"Why can't we just do the shoot here on the bus? Then we won't lose all the time stopping and setting up or whatever."

Reaching across the table, Brenda clasped my hands in hers. "Yes! That's perfect! I can have the photographer climb on our bus, along with the makeup and wardrobe, then you won't even need to stop practicing until they're ready for you! When we're done, you can go right back to the music while they pack up and hop out into the car that will follow us! Lola, you're a genius!"

I didn't miss the wink she gave Drezden, nor the harsh scowl he answered with. His eyes, normally so green, were dark as a storm when he glared at me. "Fine. Just do whatever you have to but make sure last night never happens again."

"Of course I will." She wrinkled her nose. "Give me some credit, I've kept things going for you this far." Rising out of the seat, she brushed past the tall singer and dug her phone out. "I'll make some calls. We'll be on the road in thirty."

The moment Brenda left the bus, Drezden became a black hole. Alone with him, my world shrank to a pinprick. His palms touched the table; mine twitched underneath on my thighs. "You shouldn't encourage her. Brenda gets off on every little win over me. She's ruthless."

My tongue felt heavy when I spoke.

"She's right, though. Last night happened because the security had no clue who I was."

Studying me under lowered eyebrows, Drezden didn't move an inch. "Last night happened because we gave weak people a taste of power. They ran with it, it controlled them."

He was losing me. "What does that—"

"Think about it!" His voice was as good as a slap; I flinched. "Just because they thought you were some drunken slut looking for a ride —" My throat tightened painfully. "—doesn't excuse what they did! Those assholes should have escorted you away. Why did they need to go as far as they did?"

Nail marks formed in my palms. It took a concentrated effort to calm the muscles in my forearms. "You're partly right." Drezden tucked his chin, confusion blooming. "They went too far, yeah. My cuts and pride will have to agree. But honestly? If they had just tried to escort me away, it would have turned into a fight anyway. I wouldn't have just gone away, I wanted to get inside."

Drezden considered me, then cracked a smile that melted the strength from my body. "You'd have fought them instead of just going and finding Colt or Porter or even Brenda?"

His honest surprise told me how little he really knew me. *How could he know? My life isn't written on a CD like his is. There's no way for him to understand what I've had done to me... and what I've done.* Memories of the asphalt behind my middle school surfaced. Fists that pummeled, my mouth full of blood.

"It doesn't matter," I said. Scrunching my shoulders to my ears, I started to slide from the seat. "You said you wanted to practice. Let's begin."

"You should eat first." Sighing in exasperation, he twisted to face the line of cupboards high on the bus wall. "I wish we had more, we haven't stocked up in a while. I'll remind Brenda. Think you can stomach some plain bagels?"

In the filtered sunlight through the open roof, I watched the back of his head. Then without meaning to, my eyes drifted down his spine. The rows of muscles barely hidden by his tight shirt were like train tracks on a course to my destruction. He was... beautiful. Why did someone so intimidating have to be so easy on the eyes?

I said, "Bagels are fine, sure."

Together we sat at the small table, eating our stale breakfast. It was oddly normal. I didn't remember the last time I'd eaten so casually with anyone, not even my brother. Life was always so busy.

Picking apart the bagel, I stared at Drezden from the corner of my eye. It was a face I'd seen so many times in magazines or on blogs, but in person, it served to remind me of where I was. I hadn't gotten over how, just yesterday morning, I'd woken up with a tight

131

neck on the hard seat of my brother's busted up tour bus.

And now I was riding in luxury.

The bite of bagel was dry in my mouth. I'd inevitably found my mind wandering to last night. Drezden, the bathroom, the tub... I reached over, itching at the bandage on my elbow.

Craning his neck, his hard green eyes locked onto what I'd just done. "Do they hurt today?"

Tingles rolled up my face, causing me to flush. Taking a swig from the bottle of water he'd found for me, I wiped my mouth, stalling. "No, they're—I'm fine. Don't worry about it. I'm tougher than you think."

"I think," he whispered, "That we went over that last night." His slow smirk was as tangible as fingers running over my thighs.

Squeezing my knees together, I fought down a wave of—what? *Lust, fear, why can't I tell the difference?* "Could we not talk about that?"

"Which part?"

"*All* the parts," I muttered. Tossing the rest of my bagel in the trash, I glanced towards the back of the bus.

Drezden said, "If you're worried about the band finding out about you throwing up outside, don't be. Brenda won't say anything to them."

Sucking in a slow breath hardly calmed

132

me at all. "I know. I'm not worried about that. I'm thinking about... the aftermath." Even bringing up the incident in the tub was making my skull throb.

Other parts of me, too.

Something touched my ankle under the table. It took me a second to realize the hard material was Drezden's boot. "What about the aftermath?" he asked.

My poker face was the worst. Widening my eyes 'til they ached, I watched him without blinking. How could he look so smug? Did he not care if anyone found out about us rubbing our junk together? I'd been around enough band drama to know that shit like last night never ended well. It only took one rumor—or one reality—to tarnish a name.

This band is my opportunity. No way I'll risk that. I don't even fucking know what I'd be risking it for—a night with Drez, or more?

His eyes were a slithering world of dark promises. "Listen," I started to say.

He pulled his foot away. It left me emptier somehow. "Lola, I'm not a fucking moron." There, that was the harsh side of the singer I was used to. It wasn't comforting, but it left me feeling less of a mushy mess. "I'm not going to say anything to Porter or Colt, or anyone."

The flutter in my heart died. His words were supposed to reassure me. Instead, they

133

left me stiff and aching with a frustration I couldn't express. *He thinks that what happened is something that needs to be hidden. He's right. Why does that hurt to hear?*

Squeezing my water bottle, I jumped into the aisle. "Then we're on the same page. Fine. I need to call my brother." Not giving him a chance to argue, I trotted down the bus steps and into the early morning air.

I *did* need to talk to Sean, but I hadn't been planning on doing it now. I just needed to escape from Drezden and his cloying existence.

The parking lot of the Griffin was packed with cars. Finding Barbed Fire's bus didn't take me that long. Debating calling him first, I instead just clomped up to the door and pushed. It opened easily, revealing Shark slumped over at the wheel. He was startled at the sight of me. "Lola! You scared me, shit!"

"Sorry." His genuine shock made me smile. A tug of sad nostalgia hit me. *No, it's too soon for that.* "Is my brother in here?"

"Actually," a voice said behind me. Spinning, I found myself eye to eye with Sean. He wore a gentle smile, a tray of coffee cups in his hands. "I went to get drinks for the guys. I got an extra, want it?"

Taking the cup, I felt the heat sinking through the cardboard sleeve. "Thanks. I thought we'd catch up before everyone takes off for the day."

Sean lifted the tray, shoving it at Shark. He took it with confusion. "Hand those out," he explained. "I'm going for a walk with Lola."

****

We strolled along the parking lot, then up the road. It was reckless to go too far. We could be left behind-as unlikely as that was. In wordless agreement, we walked in circles, repeating the same steps around the area. "So you're enjoying it?" he asked, sipping from his cup.

I held my coffee close, sniffing the bitter scent. "Well, most of it." Sean slowed, lifting an eyebrow. I went on at his silent prompt. "The music is coming along. They seem to trust I can perform tomorrow. It's just..." How did I phrase this? "Drezden is sort of intense."

That was putting it mildly.

"Intense how?"

My insides rocked and rolled. "I don't know. When we play together, his singing is overwhelming." I thought about his fingers on me, his rough jeans grinding, and I shivered.

Sean kicked a rock, watching it skid over the road. "Don't be afraid of Drezden Halifax. He's the kind of guy you should try to get closer to. He can take you places, tell you things, teach you things."

My feet froze. I stopped walking, staring at Sean. "How do you mean?"

His smile was tight. "A guy like him has a poet's heart. It's why he's so good at what he does. You should go ahead and try to steal some of that."

Steal some of Drezden Halifax. It was an absurd thought.

He was the guy who was trying to fucking steal parts of *me.*

It was impossible to tell Sean that, though. "Alright. I'll keep that in mind."

"You sure you're alright, Lola?" Turning, my brother studied me with new eyes.

I pushed my shoulders into my ears. *Just trying to handle a guy who scares me while also turning my insides into Jello,* I thought sarcastically. Rubbing my elbows self-consciously, I was glad my injuries were hidden. "I'm fine. I should get back though, Brenda said—" I trailed off. Mentioning Brenda had forced something else up. A piece I'd left drowning in alcohol last night. "Hey. Sean?"

He tilted his head, waiting.

In my hands, the coffee felt colder. "How come you never told me that you auditioned for Drez's band years ago?"

I knew my brother very well. The instant his face fell, I was sure something was wrong. "Oh. That."

"Sean, talk to me. Why hide that from me?

Fiddling with his neck, he eyed the sky. "Lola, that was a long time ago. You had...

136

other things to worry about. It was a dumb audition."

A dumb audition that I nailed yesterday. What he'd said, though, it made me think. He was right that two years ago I was busy with some important things. Helplessly, my fingers wandered to the inside of my right arm. Nails itched at where the tattoo hid. "You didn't tell me because you... what? Didn't want to worry me?"

"I didn't want to depress you more, yeah." His tongue held an edge. "Fucking— Lola, listen. Two years ago things were hectic. But you're fine now, and I'm fine now. We've both dealt with our demons. The only thing that matters right now is *literally* right now."

Inside, I wanted to agree. No one wants to be suspicious of their own sibling. "Okay. Okay, don't worry. It's not important anymore."

His face smoothed with relief. "Good. Now, what were you going to say before that?"

"Brenda scheduled a photo shoot today. I guess she'll try to make me look *fancy.*"

"Oh la la," he chuckled.

Grinning, I walked backwards towards the bus with a wave. "I should go, we'll talk later!" Cradling my coffee, I jogged back to the bus. I'd hoped that speaking with Sean would clear my head, but it had only left me more lost.

He was hiding something.

137

But what... and why?

I jumped up the stairs and into the bus. Inside, I found Drezden and Porter standing in the aisle. The bassist grinned, showing every tooth in his mouth. "You look like you're ready for some practice!"

Chugging my coffee, I nodded. "I'm definitely ready." Music would heal my soul, if anything could.

"Fantastic!" Porter laughed. "Colt drank enough that there's no way he doesn't have a huge fucking hangover." His arm draped over my shoulders, pulling me close. "How about," he chuckled in my ear, "We wake him up in style?"

The camaraderie was welcome, and I was grateful for Porter. Gripping his hand, I put on my biggest smile, but it didn't come close to his. "I think I like the sound of that."

"Great," he said, clapping his palms. "Because Colt sure won't."

- Chapter Nine -
Drezden

By the time the bus rolled out, we were all awake and in the practice room. Lola had tuned her guitar, then at Porter's suggestion, strummed with the amp turned up until Colt stormed in clutching his skull. It was what they needed; a moment that broke the tension.

I wished it worked for me.

My night had been plagued with visions of Lola. Her pouting lips, the curve of her neck, the way her dark hair fell wildly over her shoulders. Even her smell had been in my dreams. When I awoke, it was clinging in my very pores.

Then it faded, and I'd actually longed for it.

Seeing her that morning had soothed me briefly. Wrapped up in my fight with Brenda had made dealing with Lola's appearance easier, if only because I'd been forced to behave myself.

I didn't think I was dangerous. But now, with a horny beast coming to life inside of me, I had to wonder. If I was left alone with Lola, no one around to judge me or stop me... what would I do to her?

The thought of her mewling mouth sent my blood careened through me chaotically.

I was chaotic.

Fuck.

Leaning on the wall, I wrapped the wire from my mic around my fingers. I pretended it was her hair; my tugging became firmer.

"Yo," Colt said, downing another palm full of pain meds for his headache. "We doing this or what? Pick a fucking song, maestro."

In a burst of speed, I stepped into the dead center of the room. I was positive I saw Lola flinch, leaning away from me on her bench. Everything she did made my damn cock twinge with desire. How could one girl drive me so insane?

"Let's play Velvet Lost," I grunted, acid coating my words. Hiding my hunger for Lola was so fucking hard. The only way to even try was to embrace my voracious anger.

"Fine, whatever," Colt grumbled. His mood was bleak, but he only had himself to blame. He never should have gotten so drunk. But unlike Johnny, I'd never known Colt to let me down. When he started drumming, my confidence in him remained solid.

Together we began our mixture of sounds. Porter let the bass punctuate, making Lola's sweet licks of strings sound so clean.

Chugging from my water, I dropped the empty bottle aside. It fell, forgotten. "Sticky sweetness, burning fast. My love, my dear, this will be your last..." I whispered into the mic, letting the lyrics flow from my guts. Every song

I ever wrote had a meaning. It was something the band had fought with me over.

I would tell them a lyric couldn't be changed. I'd fold my arms and stand my ground at Brenda's laments. It was my music, my fucking heart and core and blood.

No one was allowed to change it.

Looking straight at Lola, I gauged her playing. She wasn't struggling like yesterday. That was good. We didn't have the luxury of time for her mistakes. Softly I sang, "If I take you from the grave, you'll be mine... you'll be mine."

Her eyes glimmered, sticking to me, then my lips. I spread them; a kiss across the room.

A promise I would taste her as soon as I found a way.

"Lost in time," I hissed, all rocks and leather. "Your end is mine. My love will be your last."

Just like that, Lola missed her mark. Dead air, a wrong note, she was stammering as much as if she'd forgotten her words during a public speech. To give her credit, she recovered and kept going. The knots in her neck and shoulders were pronounced.

Yesterday, when she'd kept making mistakes, I'd been attacked by disgust. Staring at her red skin, the sweaty sheen on her throat... I knew what was happening.

I finally understood.

When I sing at her, and she feels it, she can't control herself.

It was me that kept fucking her up.

Me.

The realization was awful and astounding all at once. What fucking power I had over her. I could make her so weak that she'd forget every bit of talent she had. She'd become as flawed as someone who'd never touched a guitar before.

I could break Lola.

That shouldn't have excited me so much.

Everyone was still playing. I'd always demanded perfection and hard work. Inside of me, a tempting wall of sin was tearing me in two. Lola *needed* to perform up to par. The band relied on her doing her best.

But the idea of seeing her crumbling because of *me*, to have that direct of a connection into her mind and body...

Fuck, it made me shiver.

When I sang my lines, my mouth was salivating. "Velvet lost on the skin of your bones, velvet rugs that lead to just stones." With every fiber of intensity, I channeled the heat from my core to my voice. My jeans were tight from my excitement. I needed Lola's reactions. I needed them so bad it made my molars throb. "Sweet love, last love, you'll burn for me..."

There; the twang of failure. Her misstep sang at my heart, soared through me like a bird with a promise. No one saw it, but I trembled with need.

Was I so fucked up that I'd find such joy in touching her the only way I could?

Caressing her with my song until she shattered?

I am that sick, yes. I really am. Clutching the mic, I let the music fade on the unfinished song. Watching Lola, my forehead was smooth. Everything inside of me, the hidden pieces, were slithering in my dark lust.

Calmly I said, "This is why I told Brenda we needed all the time we had." *Why I need every damn second with you I can get, Lola Cooper.*

"Sorry," she whispered, fingers running nervously through her hair. Over and over she toyed with the long strands. It did little to subdue their waves. "Can we try again?"

My eyebrows made a tight fist. "You sure it won't be wasting everyone's time?"

"Drezden!" Porter snapped. "Fuck, man. Just chill out, you know she can do it."

"I don't know shit." *That's a lie. She can do it when I'm not trying to sing right into her cells. I'm making her fumble intentionally. Fuck fuck fuck, I'm so hard over this.* Ducking down, I grabbed a new water bottle, secretly adjusting my erection. "Again, let's go again."

I could keep doing this forever.

Any question about my promise last night fled. I'd told myself I'd make Lola mine, that I'd do whatever it took to claim her. If I had to start with her skill, with controlling how she performed, then I would. I was a monster.

And I didn't care.

The next song was Black Grit. Lola knew this one well. She held up smoothly as I sang. Once, she even managed to look me in the eye without dropping a note.

She had no idea I'd figured her out.

I wished I could see into her head.

Swelling with energy, I belted out the wild chorus to the song. It could bring the house down on stage, I'd sung it for crowds so big you'd get lost for days. Now I aimed that surge at one single girl. Lola had no chance.

If it weren't for the strap around her neck, she would have dropped her guitar entirely.

The rest of the band voiced their frustration. Inside, I cheered with rapture.

"Shit," Colt sighed. Holding a water bottle to his forehead, he squinted across at me. "Look, at this rate, I've got to say... maybe we shouldn't have kicked Johnny out."

My stomach coiled like a cobra. A twinge of pain slid through my neck; I'd twisted that fast to look from my drummer, to Lola. *Holy shit, what am I doing?*

The clarity was colder than the deep ocean; I was sabotaging my own band. *But I need her, and this is the only way I can reach inside of her in a way no one else has a right to, or could even dream to.*

But was it worth it?

Warring with the rancid chunk of me that wanted to affect Lola, I gazed at Porter and Colt. These two had stood by me for years. They knew me at my best and at my worst. Well, not entirely my worst.

It was Lola that was learning what that really meant.

If I keep this up, we all lose. Observing the dark haired girl, I licked my lower lip. I knew what I had to do. "I made the right choice. She can do it." Lola sat up, gawking at my compliment. "One more time. Play it again."

That round, I reined myself in. I didn't try to make her flounder. It took everything in me to control my need to brush that part of her brain... but I did it. With the last of the chords capering around the room, I looked over my band.

Their relief, their excitement, was contagious.

"See?" I said, gracing Lola with a subtle smile. "I knew she could do it."

I need her to be able to do it.
And I need to affect her.

Fuck, how could I have both?

Rolling his eyes, Porter plucked his bass. "Yeah yeah, you're clairvoyant. Let's do another one."

As a solid unit, we played. Four and a

145

Half Headstones came alive. My ears rang with our sound, telling me we were as good now as we'd been at our peak; before Johnny had started dipping into his fuck-up habits.

He'd never been as good as he'd been the day he auditioned, the same day we'd told Sean Cooper no. *Lola's brother. I wonder what they talked about this morning.* Had she said anything about me to him? Had the guy even asked?

It wasn't my business, yet at the same time, anything that had to do with Lola tugged at my curiosity; my need for her. Even now, just a few feet away, I wanted her. My skin boiled with my starvation, tongue tasting like delirium.

I actually almost missed a lyric. No one noticed, just me.

That was plenty.

Winding down an hour into practice, I kicked the pile of plastic bottles around the floor. Lola was sweating, the front of her shirt stained. The dark patch drew my eye to her heaving breasts.

Leaning on the bench, head tilted to the ceiling, her throat bobbed. The way she panted summoned filth from the base of my skull. Instantly, I recalled how she'd looked beneath me in the tub. Her parted lips, wide-eyes and hazy scent.

I'd heard her heart, her very blood, and still pressed harder against her.

Ruffling my hair, I fought down a wave of static-charged lust. I didn't have to work hard to sober myself, though, because Brenda pushed through the curtain. She looked at all of us but focused on Lola. "Good, perfect timing."

"What's perfect timing?" I asked.

Lifting her brown eyes, my manager brushed past me. She still wore her ridiculously tall heels, the sharp bottoms tearing at the floor. "Come on, Lola, we're pulling the bus over for a minute."

The guitarist lifted her eyebrows. "What? Why?"

"Our photographer is up ahead, he's with his crew in the parking lot of a furniture store." Gripping her curved hips, Brenda tapped her toe. "Come on, be quick!"

Lola's sapphire eyes jumped to me. That expression was pleading. *Is she asking my permission to leave?* "Go, make it fast," I grumbled.

Brenda fluffed her hair. "Relax. We're doing it right on the bus. They just need to clean her up first, then they'll take some shots as we drive. Easy."

Saying nothing, I folded my arms and watched them leave the room. When their footsteps faded, Porter gave a sharp cough. "So. First time we've all been alone together since Lola joined."

"Yup." Colt rubbed his chin with a stick.

They were waiting for me to talk. I could

see it in their eyes. Setting the mic on the stand, I dropped onto a bench. "Say whatever you need to."

Poking at his bass, Porter watched the floor like it had words there to read. "She's good. I think she's gotten a handle on her nerves."

Nerves. My lips twisted. Nerves wasn't the right word, but they didn't need to know that. I was entirely convinced that Lola was caught up in *me*. Her awkward moments were crafted from her blooming arousal.

"Forget about that," Colt mumbled. "What's this photo shoot thing all about? Did I miss something, do we all need new head shots or some shit?"

Leaning forward, I gripped my knees. "Brenda says Lola needs some photos. Stuff for social media, that sort of junk."

The two men nodded, happy to accept that answer. It was close enough to the full truth to be believable. "In that case," the bassist yawned, "I'm going to grab some coffee. Pretty sure we got some instant stuff left in the cupboard, but we're running low. Papa needs his java."

"I'll remind Brenda we need supplies." My legs creaked when I stood. I was young, but lately, my stress and lack of sleep made me feel ancient.

Porter and I wandered towards the front of the bus. I don't know what I expected to see out there. Maybe a camera guy or someone doing Lola's makeup. Instead, a tall umbrella-light was parked in the aisle, blocking most of the path.

Porter paced in front of it, his hands held high. "Hey, come on, let me through!"

"One second," Brenda snapped. She appeared beside me, dragging Lola by the arm out of the bathroom. Irritation had started to swim in my veins...

And then I saw *her*.

Someone, no doubt Brenda, had forced the guitarist out of her ratty pants and fitted top. In black jeans that revealed chunks of her skin all the way up the backs of her thighs, Lola was a sexual vision.

A white and black spaghetti top, the back shredded to display her shoulder blades, and knee high vinyl boots completed her ensemble.

It wasn't the Lola I knew, but I could see myself liking this version just fine.

Her cheeks were on fire. Blue eyes sparkled, casting my way in another silent cry for help. *She hates this already,* I realized. Brenda guided her past us, our bodies brushing in the tight aisle. The sweet scent of Lola sank into my lungs.

Porter made room for the girls, then scowled as the umbrella light was pushed back into his face. "Hey! Come on, I don't want to break this, but I need some fucking coffee."

"Chill," Brenda said, grabbing a carton off of a table. Steaming, bitter smelling liquid was poured into a tall cup which she hastily thrust at Porter. Someone from the photo team had brought us fresh coffee.

Lola was handed over to the group. Two woman and one man quickly surrounded her like hungry wolves.

I could hardly see the girl. Anxiety jumped through me like grasshoppers on cocaine. It shouldn't have been so uncomfortable for me, she was just getting her makeup done. *You know it's more than that. She's going to be showing herself to the world now.*

I shook my head vigorously. Lola was going to be on stage tomorrow anyway. Hadn't I realized what that meant?

I didn't fucking think about it until now. Gripping the seat next to me, I listened to the group titter around Lola like little birds. *She's going to be famous like the rest of us. That means fans, stalkers, obsessive people who will try to take pictures of her—with her.*

Lola was going to become a star.

I wanted her to be mine, but she would belong to the world before that would happen.

Porter moved beside me, sipping his coffee. "They never put as much effort into *my* makeup for these shoots."

My mood was too black for his humor. "She's going to look like a different person."

"No more than the rest of us," he snorted.

But Porter was wrong. Eventually the group cleared, another umbrella-light added into the aisle. Lola was a queen, her black hair winding down her shoulders in lazy, smooth curls of liquid-looking smoke. They'd turned her eyes into lands of coal, lashes so heavy I was amazed she could blink.

And her fucking lips... they'd made them plumper, shiny and crimson. It was a frown made of rubies begging to be kissed. Lola looked absolutely miserable.

My bassist whistled, low and private for us. Jerking my glare at him, I witnessed the stare of appreciation on his face. He was seeing Lola in a way he never had. It was a sliver compared to what *I* saw in her from the start. "Wow, she's kind of hot, isn't she?" he said. "Damn."

Biting my tongue, I went back to watching the girl I hungered for. They were coaxing her into posing. Stiff as wood, Lola let them adjust her until she was draped in a seat. Cameras flashed, blinding her pretty blue eyes.

Though I didn't enjoy seeing her so uneasy at the hands of the photographers, I had to admit, she looked stunning. My jeans were crying out, begging me to give my cock more room. Scratching at my skull did little to chase the degenerate thoughts away.

Someone shoved Lola's guitar at her.

She took it happily, transforming before my eyes. The instrument was a lifeline. It completed the picture, made her whole. Lola was lost without her music; it hurt me how similar we were.

Now the photos would make sense. They'd show a girl who was a masterpiece of talent, not a half-finished plastic replica.

My heart throbbed in empathy.

The shoot was over as fast as Brenda had promised. We'd driven a few miles with the van for the photographers following us. Tires squeaked, stopping the bus so the group could clamber off. They were efficient. I appreciated that.

"So!" Brenda whirled to face me, not stumbling on her spread feet when the bus took off violently again. "That went well, didn't it?"

"It went fast," I said. Eyeing Lola, I noticed she wasn't looking at me. "You ready for a break?"

Peeking upwards through her rain-gutter of lashes, she hesitated. "Do we have time for that?"

She's worried about the show. I was, too, but no longer for the same reasons. Lola was ready to play. As long as I held back from aiming my carnal need-to-fuck-her-raw-energy right at her, she wouldn't mess up.

She'd be amazing. Everyone would know her, and they would love her.

I was fucking terrified.

"We've got time," I said. "You won't do us any good if you pass out from hunger." I glanced at Brenda. "We need more supplies. There's literally nothing here but alcohol."

"I know, I know." Messing with her hair, she pouted. "Think you guys can handle pizza today? I promise after the show tomorrow I'll pack this place full of goodies for the next hike."

Porter stole more coffee from the box on the table. "I can eat more pizza if you promise to add some fruit to the next stock up." Noting Brenda's squint, he bobbed his shoulders. "We can't live on sugar and fat alone. You want this band to make it another few years?"

"Actually, I don't know if I'll make it to tomorrow," Colt groaned. He stumbled down the hall, his face looking like wet cheese. "Fuck, I really did drink too much."

The sweet, shocking sound of Lola's laugh lit my ears up. She was sitting in the chair, one knee hugged to her chest. The blue in her eyes was glowing. "Sorry," she said quickly, covering her grin. "You guys are hilarious sometimes."

Tugging at the hem of my shirt, I sat across from Lola. "Pizza's fine with you?"

"Anything is fine right now." She toyed with the ends of her hair, her smile fading. "Whatever they used made my hair super soft. I'll never replicate this."

The tip of my fingers itched to touch the

silky strands; to touch any part of her. "Wait till we get backstage at the show. You'll see some real crews for hair and makeup then."

The bus seat opposite us creaked as Ported fell into it. "Yeah," he chuckled. "And if you thought last night was crazy, the afterparty will destroy you."

I didn't like his phrasing. My lips made a bloodless line. *The afterparties, where guys will be fawning all over the new guitarist of Four and a Half Headstones.* Now my fingers were aching to choke the throats of those imaginary men.

"I've been to afterparties." She folded her legs, the tip of her boots almost brushing my knee. I felt the kiss of air like it was a lightning bolt. "I *was* following and helping Barbed Fire, remember? On the first leg of this tour, we ended up at this random girl's house. It was insane."

Colt's chuckle was patronizing. "Right right. Like Porter said, wait till you experience a *real* afterparty."

Her delicious mouth became an electric eel. "Fuck you, the parties I went to were great."

"But you weren't famous," Colt said. He folded his arms behind his head, leaning on a window nearby. "After tomorrow, you will be. Then you'll see."

Then she'll see.

Looking up, I spotted Brenda on her

154

phone. She had her back to us, standing near the front of the bus. *Ordering us some food. Good.* The longer I sat near Lola, the more I needed to put something between my gnashing teeth.

I worried I'd grind my molars down before this tour was done.

- Chapter Ten -
Lola

The pizza fueled me enough for the next four hours of practice. That was good, I needed something in my stomach; it kept doing flips and pretzels the closer we got to the concert location.

I was relieved that I'd been able to make my hands listen to me as we played. Something had happened that morning. *It was like Drezden hid himself behind a curtain.* He still sounded the same, it was just the fuel in his emerald eyes had burned out. Whatever the change, not being on the end of his assassin style demeanor let me play to my fullest.

I had to admit, we sounded fucking great.

Porter and Colt squeezed out into the hallway, arguing over who was taking a shower first. When the curtain dropped, I became acutely aware that I was alone with Drez. *Relax, he isn't going to bite you.* I wasn't sure about that.

Tying my hair off of my sweating neck, I rolled my head. "Starting to get a muscle cramp," I mumbled. Rubbing at the gap between neck and shoulder, I winced.

A shadow fell over me. "Is it bad?" he asked.

The inside of my throat was made from sand and ash. *Remember how he said to stop pretending to be tough. Just tell him!* "It's super tight, yeah," I admitted.

Drezden settled next to me on the bench, straddling it so he could face me. He twirled a finger in the air, motioning for me to turn around. "Let me massage it out. You'll be stiff and useless for the show tomorrow if I don't."

Is he right about that? I'd never practiced so much in such a short time. If he was right, then all of this work would be pointless if I didn't let him help me. Flipping one leg over the bench, I gripped it between my thighs. "Fine, if you think it's necessary."

He was a wall of heat against my spine, a volcanic explosion I couldn't run away from. I braced myself for the first touch of his hands.

Firm palms came down, clasping not just one, but both sides of my neck. Drezden used precision, rolling his fingers over the knots I didn't even know I had. The tension in me went beyond just my shoulders and neck.

Lowering my chin, I hid behind the curtain of my hair. He couldn't see my face from where he was, I wanted any bit of protection I could find. The last time Drez had touched me, things had gotten crazy.

Far too crazy.

A shiver jolted down to my core as he rolled a thumb along my jugular. "You're tight

157

as a rusty spring," he murmured. I wasn't prepared for his breath to tickle the shell of my ear. Hot pin pricks danced everywhere, the hairs on my body becoming unbreakable needles.

Right away, I knew the inside of my panties were damp.

He's like a beacon of living sex. Trembling harder, I dug my nails into the tops of my thighs. His motions were amazing, which made it even scarier. Drezden knew how to touch me. He rubbed away the soreness from playing, all the while leaving a new tension in its place.

Soon, my body rocked along with his rhythm. The ball of air in my chest threatened to shred my lungs. Solid steel touched my shoulder blades; his chest, he was leaning into me.

That alone would have been too much.

When the stiff, hot bulge of his erection bumped my lower back, I was done.

Gasping, I jumped off the bench. I thought he'd try to stop me, but he made no such effort. Breathing heavily, I stared at the singer with disbelief. The fervor in his eyes, the passion he'd been restraining while singing, was back.

"What are you doing?" I hated how breathy my voice sounded.

"Massaging you," he said softly. The way he shrugged pissed me off. He wasn't *just* massaging me, he knew that.

I thought about what my brother had said to me that morning: *A guy like him has a poet's heart. It's why he's so good at what he does.*

You should go ahead and try to steal some of that.

Blushing furiously, I looked away. "You were doing more than massaging me. Way more."

The bench moaned, abandoned by Drezden's weight. His long legs carried him to me in a blink. Impossibly, his scent filled my nostrils all over again. "I don't know what you mean," he said.

How could my heart handle this? The blood in my body was certainly magma by now. Lifting my eyes, I tried to stare at just his chin. Maybe then I could concentrate. *No, now all I see are his lips. His fucking smirking lips.* I spoke to them anyway. "You're going too far with me. I'm not a fucking idiot. I don't know what your game is, but..."

In a blur, he gripped my upper arms, pushing me into the wall and leaving me stunned. Vibrations rolled through my head, but nothing could muffle his words. "I don't know what game I'm playing either," he whispered. "I only know the prize."

My vision was constrained on his face. The hard edges of his teeth, the part of his smile that wanted to cut me open. Drezden had made his goal so overtly clear, it left me wondering why I'd thought to ask. He was a man with no fear. Nothing held him back.

And he wanted to have me.

I was the fucking prize.

"Wait." My single word was fragile. I tried again, bolder. "Hold on, I'm not yours."

"No," he agreed. Strong fingers slid down the insides of my arms, taking my strength as they crawled. "Not yet."

I couldn't handle this. There were many things I considered myself; smart, capable.

Strong.

No one had ever walked into my world and toppled me so easily. Why was Drezden so good at it? What made him invade my mind and body with rapid speed? Cotton swaddled my brain. My tongue was useless, it held no arguments.

I found myself on the verge of collapsing, or running, or slipping away mentally. It felt like I'd been cornered by a rabid tiger. He was going to consume me, he'd said himself that he wanted me. Didn't he realize I wasn't able to cope with that?

Maybe I wasn't as tough as I thought. Maybe my act was backfiring. *He thinks I'm tough enough to take him on. That's my own fault for calling him out in the damn tub last night.*

Drezden Halifax was a passionate being full of fire and acid and pure stars. He *was* a star. A fucking poet, as Sean had said.

And I was no one.

Not just no one, I'm a fucking virgin. Rock stars aren't virgins. Holy shit, he'll leave me in pieces. We're on entirely different levels. Different worlds!

He bent down, all lips and smoky smirks. The seconds slowed. I knew he was going to kiss me. Instinct kicked in—fight or flight. In a great flex of muscles, I kicked a leg upwards. My knee landed solidly in his stomach, thudding on his sculpted abs.

Grunting, he let me go and backed up. His eyes were as wide as they could get. "What the fuck was that for?" he growled.

Suddenly I felt... really stupid. "You were —the look in your eyes, I just..."

"Just say *no* next time! Or stop! Jamming a knee into my guts is kind of over the top. Fuck." Rubbing his shirt, he looked me up and down. I caught the humor in his sideways sneer. I hadn't injured him, he wasn't even upset. "You really don't want me near you, do you?"

Guilt dug in with its sharp fangs. "It's not that! I actually think you're—" *Stop, stop talking!* "This just isn't a good idea, for either of us."

"Why isn't it a good idea for me?"

My lips parted, hesitating. I didn't know why it was bad for him at all. "Fine. I'm being selfish, okay? This is a bad idea for *me,* for my

161

career." His grimace was brief, but I saw it. "If it goes bad between us... the band might not recover."

I was the newest member. If push came to shove, they'd cast me aside and get someone to replace me. I needed this too much.

Sean's face commanding me to realize what an opportunity this was filled my head until my skull twinged. My brother knew how important this was. He'd encouraged me for a reason.

I couldn't bear letting him down when things inevitably went sideways.

Drezden filled my world again. He slid upwards, chest grinding on mine. I gasped, then clenched my jaw. His hands crept down to hold my hips possessively. "So you *have* thought about us hooking up."

"No!" *Yes.* "Never!" *Since I listened to you sing during practice yesterday.*

That wasn't right—my interest had a longer tooth. I'd had a crush on Drezden Halifax since the first time I'd played his CD. He'd kept me company before he knew my name or my face.

Now, that very man was so close I could rub my nose on his if I just bent forward. "Tell me, Lola," he sighed, claiming my waist, pulling up the shirt I still wore from the photo shoot and showing off my navel. "Why are you fighting this? I could tell last night that you wanted me."

Images of his hard body holding me down in the porcelain tub flooded me. "I just told you!" My voice was rising, gaining volume with my confused energy. "I don't want to fuck up the band!"

"But you do want to fuck me," he chuckled darkly.

Ignoring the pulse between my thighs, I said, "I figured you'd care about the band, too."

He didn't shout over me. He didn't need to. "You think I'm not worried about the band?" The texture in his throat was raw and wet and it begged me to hear him say *anything*. I was addicted to his voice. "You think I don't *care?* Lola, it's not about that! It's about being willing enough, strong enough, to take a damn risk!"

Barely standing, his hands were all that kept me on my feet. *Take a risk?* I knew what it meant to take risks. *Sean accused me of not being ready for this band. He goaded me into going to the audition, made me see I was going to miss an opportunity otherwise.*

But this wasn't the same thing.

There was noise in the hallway. Drezden released me, backing up and heading for his microphone. I stayed against the wall, my fingers half-bent, my lips hanging partially open in shock. If my mind could have been pulled out, put on display, it would have looked even more disheveled.

Colt swung into the room, a cup pressed

to his lips. The sound of Porter's grumbling followed him into the room. "I don't care if it was the last of the coffee," the drummer said. "You had three fucking cups, I deserve one—" He halted, spotting me where I stood.

Oh, shit.

Licking my lips slowly, I searched for the ability to speak. I knew I looked conspicuous with my glittering eyes, red cheeks and heavy breathing. Firm nipples cut into my bra, blessedly hidden.

"Lola," Colt said carefully, "You alright?"

I didn't answer in time. Porter bumped into the drummer, the two stumbling as coffee splashed onto their clothes and floor. "Dammit, Colt! Why would you stand right behind the curtain?"

"Why would you walk into me!" he shouted back, wiping at his shirt.

In the fray, I freed myself from the wall that I'd been glued to. I hoped no one touched it; the surface had to feel like lava from my body heat. Threading around the edge of the room, I burst through the curtain and escaped before anyone dared to stop me.

Drezden's green eyes followed me; I saw them in my brief glance. They marked me like they were carving a tattoo into my skin. *I need air, I just need air.* In the aisle, I was alone. Brenda had joined up with the crew in their own van after we'd picked up the pizza.

The driver had slid a flimsy plastic sheet

164

between the front seats of the bus, giving himself some privacy as he played the radio.

Taking a seat next to the plastic, I cracked one of the tinted windows. Crisp air poured in, stinging my face wonderfully. The world outside flew by like a painting on rails; mountains, cerulean skies and clouds so thick you could have held them.

We'd crossed into Colorado.

That means we'll be arriving at the venue by... I dug my phone out, looking at the time. Was it already six in the evening? *Tomorrow morning. I can't believe it.* Everything with Drezden was fading in the wake of my reality.

Soon, I was going to see the place I'd be playing my first show. My first very real, very actual show. Holding my phone close, I started to type a message to Sean. *He's the only person I can talk to about this.* He'd understand the elation and sickness burrowing deep into my flesh.

'Hey,' I typed to him. 'We'll be arriving soon. I might piss myself.'

Pressing the button to send it, I waited impatiently. My heart beat once, twice, then fifteen times before the device buzzed. Sean's words displayed themselves on my blinking screen.

'Get used to that feeling.'

Smiling helplessly, I tucked my phone away. I liked to think he was right. I wanted him to be. *Could this really be happening? Me, Lola Cooper, going to play on stage for thousands of people.*

Drezden's face entered my head. He was in my heart, too; that smile and how pained he'd sounded when we'd talked. *He wants me to take a risk and hook up with him—to give in to the primal ache haunting us both. But...*

Not every risk can be worth it.

Watching the beautiful landscape roll by wasn't enough to erase my shame. Drezden had grown something inside of me. A piece that throbbed and cried and begged for him. A piece that wanted me to take the fucking risk he'd asked me to.

My hand traced the shape of my phone.

How could he ask me to risk everything when I'd barely gotten a taste of it?

- Chapter Eleven -
Drezden

The sky outside was pale blue, but I'd been awake since it had been a melting tie-dye of sherbet orange. Sleeping was harder than ever. Lola plagued the sparse dreams when I managed to find them. In them, she'd always dangle out of my reach. Then I'd grab for her, only to wake up in a sweaty mess.

We'd driven through the night. I'd abandoned my bed hours ago, dressing for the day in broken-in jeans and a long sleeved white sweater. Now, I was settled on a bus seat and just... watching. Denver trickled by in all its glory.

I'd never played in Colorado before. Once, when I was younger, I saw the Wingless Harpies play at the Fillmore. I'd gone with my father, back when he'd been drinking himself to death but before he'd started using me as a target for his impotent rage.

I cupped my lower back, phantom pain burning.

Now I'm here again. This time, I'm playing on the stage. It should have filled me with pride. Instead I was wrapped up in my usual antsy energy. I wouldn't allow myself to feel happy with anything until the show went on without a hitch. Only then I could allow myself some joy.

In a great stretch of arms over her head, Lola pushed through the curtains and into the main bus aisle. I peered at her as she approached; she hadn't seen me yet.

Everything has to go perfectly. And if it does, she'll get everything she could ever want.

And I'll start to lose her even quicker.

She saw me, looking up like I was a ghost. Rubbing the corner of my nose, I turned away. It was a mistake to let Lola into the band. *No,* I admonished myself. *She's perfect for the band.*

The mistake was letting her close to me.

Lola's success would send her away from me like dandelion puffs on the wind. *Unless I can get to her first.* If I could curl my palm around her, then I'd catch her before she floated right into the arms of someone else.

Remembering her flash of distress when I'd cornered her yesterday sent rickets down my body. I'd been so close to kissing her. I'd only resisted when I'd heard her argument. She was worried about the band?

No, she's worried about herself.

I wished for a way to make her see that taking this risk, diving into the deep pit of desire and decadence with me, was worth it.

There might not be a way. The seat beneath me suffered my clawed fingers. *I'll find one.*

"Alright," our driver shouted, "I'm pulling into the parking lot behind the Fillmore. Security should keep people out of the area, but it's pretty open, so just be aware."

Being mobbed didn't scare me. Twisting, I found Lola watching me. In a ripple of black hair, she stared out the window again. *I don't want the fans or media to scare her.* The rational part of me knew she needed to see it, to handle it on her own. *Welcome to being a rock star,* I thought cynically.

Colt and Porter joined us as the bus parked. It was early enough that I didn't expect many people to be crowding the venue. Eagerly I climbed from the bus, inhaling the fresh air.

There were cars and tour buses all around; other bands and crew for the show tonight. Small carts owned by the Fillmore were parked in the lot, the scent of coffee and grease hitting me hard. Before I could follow after Porter and Colt to get something to eat, Brenda appeared to block us. "Hey! You're awake, good. I need to go over everything for tonight."

"After." Brushing by her, I stalked towards a muffin that had my name on it. "I need some breakfast." Her hand grabbed my shoulder. For a second, I thought about shoving her aside. Instead, my feet paused on the cement. One eye looked her way. "Can I eat *and* talk? I'm pretty talented."

Brenda jammed a paper bag in my face.

"I took the liberty of grabbing you guys some donuts. Now, will you come with me?"

The rest of my band—including Lola—crowded in, eager for the food. Colt snuffled and snorted, pretending to be an animal. "Tell me what you want from me," he said. "I'm all ears. And mouth. Fuck, just give me a donut, please."

Squeezing the bridge of my nose did little for my growing migraine. "Okay, okay. Lead on, Brenda."

She took us through a backdoor of the Fillmore. Traversing a tight hallway, she guided us into an area plastered with 'staff only' signs. There were people running all over, some with clipboards, others with headsets that they spoke into softly.

The show wasn't until five, but everyone was getting prepared.

Once we were in a quieter room Brenda put the bag on a table. Porter and Colt ripped it open immediately. "Have a seat, guys," she said. "I've got details to give out and I need you all to listen."

Reaching for a fat, glossy Boston cream, I settled into a swivel chair and kicked up my feet. The baked good was fucking delicious, sweet filling coating my tongue. I had it half finished before Lola picked up a simple glazed one for herself.

We ate while Brenda covered the table in paperwork, finger jabbing as she spoke. "I've put you all up in the Ramada tonight. Here are your keycards, room info, the whole lot." Passing out the hard chunks of plastic, she looked me in the eye. "We roll out tomorrow morning, the bus will stay here to keep the fans from mobbing the hotel. I'll send a car. If you need anything, just call."

The meaning in her voice wasn't lost on me. Glancing at Lola, I finished my donut. *There won't be an encore of shitty security guards attacking her this time.*

Porter grabbed another pastry, crumbs spilling over his chin. "What time do we need to be back here?"

"You're on at seven, so be here by four at the latest for sound check." Her smile spread, fixing on Lola. "Here, take a look. These are being plastered all over the Fillmore website, as well as in our newsletter and every social media outlet we have our claws in." She slid a thick folder across the table.

Lola eyed it, uncertainty turning her pretty mouth into a knot. It only got worse when she opened the folder, revealing the glossy prints inside. "Oh, holy shit."

Holy shit indeed.

The photos from yesterday were stunning. Lola was a vision, the blue of her eyes made even crisper by saturation. She was poised in front of the bus window, lashes lowered to create a canopy. Lola's smile contained too many secrets.

171

I knew I'd need to taste her so I could start to understand.

Shifting in my chair, I fought down the surge of arousal. I'd have to get a copy of those pictures.

"Well," Brenda prompted, "What do you think? Good, right?"

Sliding her hand over the prints, Lola said, "These don't look anything like me."

Brenda rolled her eyes, pulling the folder back. "Sure they do! They're just doctored up some. That's normal, everyone does it."

Doubtful, Lola poked at the other half of her donut. "If you say so."

The rest of the meeting was a blur, I was too busy staring at the girl I was so addicted to. Letting Brenda ramble, I tuned out for the first time in my years of singing professionally. Normally, I was keen on these meetings. They kept problems from happening.

I hated problems.

Now, I was twitching one boot over my opposite crossed ankle. Each movement matched my heart, thumping to a tune—a song —that had been forming for two days now. Lola was a single lyric. I wanted to say her name over and over until I owned her like I did all of my music.

When Brenda waved at us to leave, I shrugged out of my daze like it was a heavy jacket I could shed. Our group started to head for the exit. Lola was dragging her feet, lost in thought.

She's getting overwhelmed. Those photos really bothered her.

Wishing I could erase her gloom, an idea hit me. My fingers snapped out, curling firmly around her wrist. "I want to show you something."

Under my touch, her goosebumps prickled. She froze on the spot. "What?"

Porter and Colt turned back, expecting us to be following. I gave them a tiny nod. "Go on ahead. I want to give Lola a look inside."

Understanding spread between them. "Sure," Porter said. "We'll meet you at the hotel."

Free of their stares, I tugged Lola further into the hall. She came reluctantly, tension in her steps. "A look inside? But why?"

Because I want to see you smile. Of course, I said no such thing. Setting my jaw, I led her deeper into the Fillmore. The halls were tunnels, we were explorers, and I knew where the treasure was.

Together, we broke out into the main room of the building. I'd seen the stage before; when I was a child, my dad had slipped us into the upper levels to view the band from above.

This time, I gazed around a wide room full of people organizing wires and lights. The vast size of the space was enhanced with all of the empty seats. Next to me, Lola gasped. The

173

sound danced right to my center.

I still held her wrist, and for a heartbeat, I almost linked our fingers. Releasing her, I gestured with my head. "How's it look?"

Her answer was pure, her lips showing off her perfect teeth. "Beautiful."

No. It's your smile that's beautiful, I thought.

She whispered, "I'm actually standing here." She felt the moment in its entirety; how heavy it was, like a piece of fruit ready to fall to the earth and explode. "I'll be playing music in front of thousands of people tonight."

Peering at her hip, I watched her hands clench. "Does that scare you?" I asked.

Lola met my gaze with one of her own. The severity boiling deep inside of her eyes halted my breathing. "Of course it does. Aren't you scared?"

Thinking to myself, I considered my reply. I was only scared of one thing lately, but it wasn't something I was ready to admit to her.

Not yet.

"When I first played on a big stage," I said slowly, "I was extremely afraid. That's normal."

"I'm sorry, did you just try to call yourself *normal?"* The smile she wore was made from innocence and mystery. It took a concentrated effort not to curl my fingers into her thick hair, right there in front of the massive stage we'd soon perform on.

Perform.

This fucking girl made me want to create an entirely new meaning for that word. It would be glorious to bend her over and witness what we could do together. Lola's nearness made it a chore to stop thinking about wet sex.

Breaking the gravity between us, she looked at the large lights overhead. "It'll be packed in here, won't it?"

My fingers hooked into my pockets. "The concert sold out the day it was announced."

"I wonder if Sean will watch me?" She spoke wistfully, like her question didn't need an answer.

I'd love to watch you from the crowd, too. "Barbed Fire is opening tonight. He should be able to see you from backstage if he hangs around." The thought was a squirming maggot in my belly. Though Lola and Brenda had done their best to convince me that Sean Cooper held no resentment for me, I didn't want to see him up close.

The guy was as unwelcome in my presence as Johnny would be.

Rubber scuffed on wood; the toe of her converse sneaker digging into the floor. "Lot of pressure on me tonight. He'll be watching to make sure I don't make a mistake."

Crinkling my nose, I tilted my head. "If it'd help, I can make sure he *isn't* backstage."

Cold distress filled her voice. "No no! I

175

want him there. I just meant, you know, it's a big deal. Performing tonight is... fuck." She clasped the side of her throat. "It means everything to me."

My chest ached with a yearning to pull her against me. Not so long ago, I'd have said the same thing she just had. Lola's existence, the way she'd come crashing into my life, had changed things. *The music doesn't mean everything to me. She does, now.*

I wanted to take her away and hide her from the world. I didn't want the crowd to see her like I did; talented, astounding... perfect.

Had I always been so greedy?

"Can I ask you something?" At my quick nod, she pushed on. "Did any of your family come to your first show?"

I hadn't expected that question. "My mother did," I said softly. "She came to all of them for a while." *And if that bastard hadn't hurt her, maybe she could still—no.* I had no intention of cutting my heart open here. Being vulnerable had its time and place. "Are you asking because you want to have your parents here? I'm sure Brenda could find a way to fly them out by tonight, if we tell her right now."

Lola was shaking her head before I'd finished. "Don't worry about it. They wouldn't want—" Closing her mouth, she stopped herself.

"What?" Hunching closer brought us to eye level. "They wouldn't want to what?"

176

Her eyes became frosted glass. "They wouldn't want to fly. They hate airplanes, that's all. Can we go to the hotel? I'd like to clean up."

The change of subject wasn't lost on me. Lola was hiding something. "Sure. Follow me." Straightening, I led her back down the hall. It was a silent walk; heavy dread hung off of Lola like thick lace. *What's wrong with her?*

My plan had been to cheer the girl up by showing her the stage.

Now, glancing at her as we broke into the early daylight, I had the feeling I'd lifted her up just to drag her back down.

I just wished I knew what I'd done.

****

We rode in a simple black car, tinted windows hiding us from the world. I'd even slid on a pair of shades to help protect my identity. It was a fast trip, the Ramada was right up the street.

Lola said nothing as we drove, her hands wrapped on her guitar case and bag. Each tap of her nail on the solid wood sent ripples up my neck. *She's miserable, and I just want to nibble her pouting lower lip.* Wiping my mouth didn't remove the thought.

Our car slowed in front of the hotel entrance. Sensing a chance to escape the claustrophobic depressing bubble, I kicked my

177

door open—the driver slammed his brakes. Lola jerked against her seat belt, eyeing me like I'd lost my mind.

Grinning, I said, "Come on, let's see how expensive our rooms are."

Her tiny smile was encouraging. "I don't remember the last time I even slept in a hotel."

"You traveled with your brother," I said, reaching my hand out to help her from the car. "Where did you sleep when you were on the road?"

Her laugh was sharp and short. "Bus seats are comfortable enough in a pinch."

I started to chuckle—the sensation of her fingers wrapping in mine stopped me. A river of energy flowed from her hot skin into mine. I'd meant to steady her next to the car, but instead, we both stumbled.

Lola's face came close to mine; I could see the tiny diamonds in her blue irises, fragments that broke up the rich color. My lips were magnetized to hers, and it was only thanks to the driver coming around, trying to yank my bag and be 'helpful' that I was stopped from tasting her.

"Here you go," the guy said, beaming up at me.

My fierce glare made him drop my bag; I caught it before it hit the pavement. "Thanks," I mumbled, "But I can take it from here."

Lola exhaled, it came out in a great whistle that she had no control over. Her cheeks were glowing. When she spun to face the hotel, I suspected she was trying to hide her reaction from me. "This place is gigantic," she said.

Her comment made me scan the building again. I'd grown so used to staying in a hotel that they all blurred together now. Unlike Lola, I'd never had to crash on a bus seat. When I'd started Four and a Half Headstones, we'd gone from driving our cars to local shows, to getting picked up by an agent in a mere few months.

Realizing how blessed I'd been was a cold eye opener.

I would never call myself entitled, but what would I do if Brenda ever suggested we sleep on a hard bus seat? *And Lola's been doing that for... I don't even know how long.*

Strolling up to the front desk of the Ramada, I fought with a drilling sensation of guilt. This honest woman had, unintentionally, made me reevaluate my privilege. I was torn between appreciating that... and hating it.

Lola stood beside me, her head level with my shoulder. From the tip of her nose to the curve of her mouth, she was beautiful. Like she felt me weighing her worth, Lola peeked upwards.

Those fucking eyes reassured me of one thing: A similarity existed between us. The ancient pain boiling in her eyes reflected my own. I didn't need details to recognize her scars

—but I still wanted them. I needed to understand Lola Cooper.

"Can I help you?"

Turning, I smiled at the woman behind the counter. She was cute, though exhaustion and a too-tight hair bun were doing her no favors. Digging out my keycard, I flashed it like it was money. "You can, in fact, help us. We have rooms here. I'm—"

"Drezden Halifax," she blurted, fingers covering her mouth. I smirked at her struggling to find the line between being a fan and acting professional. "Right! Your room is on the seventh floor. If you have your card, you can go right up." Gesturing at the elevator, her cheeks went pink. It was endearing, but Lola's blush was far more enticing. "Um, do you need help with your luggage? I can—I mean, someone can —"

Waving my hand, I gripped my bag. "Thanks, but I think we can handle these." Facing my companion, a wave of surprise careened along my spine. Lola's elegant fingers were crushing the handle of her guitar case, turning them the color of ivory. Every line in her forehead told me a story.

Jealousy.

Lola was *jealous.*

That fact pleased me so much, I could have hugged her right there. I'd sensed it the other night when we were at the Griffin, too; how she'd fidgeted over my flirting with the

180

waitress, a girl whose name I'd already forgotten.

Standing tall, I slathered my best smile onto the girl behind the front desk. Her hazel eyes were glazed over. "Actually,"I said, "I *could* use help with something." I squinted at her name tag. "Amy. If it isn't too much?"

"Of course not!" Beaming wide, she smoothed her already too-smooth scalp. "Just ask! I'd *love* to be of assistance."

I pointed at Lola's bag. "Could you carry up her luggage?" Amy's eyes followed my finger, excitement deflating. "She's tired from practicing all night on the bus. We've got a *big* show tonight, so I'd like to have her as rested as possible."

Her uncertainty melded into disbelief, then it became recognition. In an act of blunt unprofessionalism, Amy whipped her phone out took a photo of Lola. "Oh my gosh! She's the new guitarist, isn't she?" Amy stared from Lola, to me, then back again. "You're Lola Cooper, the one replacing Johnny Muse! I'm so sorry—I should have noticed!"

Now Lola squirmed, shuffling her feet at the attention. "Oh, uh, it's fine. Don't worry about—"

"I saw all the photos last night," Amy rambled, the flash on her phone blinding us a second time. "Everyone was talking about it, it was all over twitter and everything! I can't believe I'm meeting you before you play for the

181

first time!" Her eyes bugged from her skull. "Can I get your autograph?"

It was hard not to laugh. Lola was gawking at me, mentally begging me for help. *If you lose it here, you'll faint tonight,* I thought in amusement. *If I don't step in, she'll have a heart attack.* But before I could explain that Lola couldn't sign anything without permission from our manager, the guitarist blurted out, "Sure, what would you like me to sign?"

"Here," Amy gushed, handing over a pamphlet about the Fillmore. "Just sign this, it's that or an information packet for this hotel."

My scheme to save Lola from embarrassment at the hands of a hotel receptionist crumbled under their mutual giggles. With a messy, unpracticed hand, Lola signed the paper. Amy held it high triumphantly. "This is so great!" Grinning at me, she offered it my way along with the pen. "Um, could you sign it too?"

Bending over the pamphlet, I studied Lola's name. It looked like swirling flowers on a breeze. *Is this her first signature ever?* It was certainly the first as a member of my band. Amy had a piece of gold here—I was about to make it even shinier.

Taking the pen, I signed my name with my usual sharp angles. The letters twisted near each other, not quite touching. It was fitting, when I thought about it.

Kissing the back of the paper, Amy did a full body shiver. "Oh my gosh. Thank you! Okay, let me get that bag up to your room."

Reaching down, I pulled Lola's luggage from her unprepared fingers. "Actually, on second thought, I've got it. Thanks, though."

"Oh." Blinking, Amy tugged anxiously at the hem of her blouse. "Okay. Alright. Um, call down if you need anything. Anything at all, okay?"

My nod was faint. Hoisting everything with a soft grunt, I hurried towards the elevator. Lola said something softly to Amy, her sneakers clomping as she caught up to me. Ducking through, she set her guitar case on the floor while the doors closed behind us.

In the tiny box, mirrors flashing our images all around, she spoke over the repetitive elevator music. "Are you alright? You hurried out of there really quick."

With my hands tied up in the bags, I could only shrug. "It's nothing, just thought you might want to get to your room and chill out before tonight."

Messing with her hair, Lola squinted up at me. "It feels like something else is going on. What's wrong, Drez?"

Everything is wrong. I can't decide what I want from you, from this, and it's giving me a fucking ulcer. Normally I wanted to gaze on her sweet face and intoxicating eyes.

Now, I regretted that no matter where I turned, her reflection waited for me in the elevator.

I asked, "What if something *is* wrong? In fact, I think you know what's on my mind."

Her sigh cut into my ears. "Drezden, look. All of that stuff with us yesterday…"

Stuff. She calls it stuff, like it's so meaningless.

"…And the stuff from the night before that…"

My fingers choked the handles of the bags.

"It can't happen, *we* can't happen. I was serious when I said I won't risk this chance. I want to make a name for myself, being in this band is a once in a lifetime thing for me." I saw her look at her feet in the mirrors. "Seeing that stage today, I just—I knew I had to stay firm, to focus. I'm sorry."

Having her apologize to me was worse than being stabbed. My insides balled up, knotting until they overwhelmed my mind. *She's right. Hooking up with me—getting close to me—will put her career in danger.*

Why don't I care about that?

Like a man hanging below the surface, inches from the air he needed not to drown, I lifted my head high. In the mirror, I saw my eyes; the green was the color of acid, but it was my mouth that was ready to dissolve.

All around me was *Lola*. The molecules in the air were crafted from her energy, her scent. I felt her on me even though we weren't touching. My lips ached to crash onto hers. In that elevator ride that never seemed to end, I made my choice.

I couldn't hold back any longer.

So I wouldn't try.

Lola wasn't looking at me, not at first. The sound of me dropping the bags changed that. For a second, I saw her wide blue eyes focus on me. I glimpsed her fear—I spotted the lust she kept trying to hide from me.

Then I was on her, my long fingers trapping her against the hard wall. Dizzy with the need that had haunted me since the night we'd rubbed together in the tub, I let myself go. My lips turned her mouth into a landing zone; she was ground zero for me.

Lola tasted like caramel and salt and nightshade. I'd let her poison me if it came to that. If she wouldn't let me into her life, death was on my horizon, anyway. She filled my lungs with her high pitched whimper—how could a man breathe when he was denied such sweet air?

My nostrils flared to claim her scent. In my ears, her moan was a mixture of surprise and delight. She wanted this. *Wanted it.* She'd called being with me a risk. *I'm no more a risk than she is.*

I lost my hands in her thick brunette locks. My ribs screamed, telling me I needed oxygen. Ignoring them, my mouth pressed on her even harder. Lola wrapped her perfect hands, her fucking perfectly magical hands, around my waist. It was an aphrodisiac.

The 'ding' of the elevator ended the moment.

Lola's seeking touch become rough; a shove, aiming to push me away. I gasped when our lip-lock shattered. Her creamy cheeks were hot as fire. So was her voice. "Get off of me, Drezden."

It took everything I had to step backwards. My hands slid through her hair, the strands silken and buttery. We were both breathing hard. I saw the hint of her nipples straining through her shirt. Each heave of her lungs taunted me.

Lola's gaze darted down. I knew she'd spotted my raging hard-on. I'd never been so stiff, so *thick*. My cock desperately needed to be inside of her. She moved towards me; I inhaled sharply.

When she just grabbed her bag and guitar, fleeing out into the hall, I felt the first cold prickles of disappointment.

Lola was running away from me.

Giving into my burst of desire hadn't changed a fucking thing between us. She stumbled down the hall, stopping in front of a door, and I did nothing. When she fumbled for her keycard, dropping it then picking it up again, I still did nothing.

It wasn't until she vanished from my

sight that I acted.

Lifting my bags, I stomped out of the elevator. That mirrored box was cloying with her scent. I wanted to laugh until my throat was ruined. *Fuck, did I mess that up.*

My erratic behavior had been something a teenager would have done. *She's the nineteen-year-old. I should fucking know better.* Lola had resisted me—she was stronger than I thought. But I had a bigger problem: I'd given up my cards and shown her my hand.

Lola now knew I'd put her career at risk just to be with her.

Digging into my pocket, I revealed my keycard. It said room 504. Looking up, I stared blankly at the door Lola had entered: 505.

We were right next to each other.

- Chapter Twelve -
Lola

I couldn't get my breathing under control.

Leaning on the inside of my hotel room door, I buried my palm on my chest and hyperventilated.

Holy shit holy shit holy shit holy shit.

Drezden had kissed me. Kissed *me*.

Holy fucking shit.

Reaching up, I dragged my fingers over my lips. His taste remained; cinnamon and tobacco. I should have hated it, but it was exotic and it made my head foggy.

He fucking kissed me. Now what was I supposed to do?

Every inch of my body was vibrating. Even the backs of my ears felt like someone had run a static roller over them. Waves of heat ricocheted from head to toe, settling into my lower belly until I had to scissor my thighs helplessly.

Each time Drezden had gotten close to me, fate had intervened before he could act. The tub, the practice room, outside the car... But this time, he'd gotten a taste in before the elevator could reach our floor and interrupt us.

He kissed me!

I couldn't get that image out of my head. At my feet, my bag and case lay in a heap. I'd dropped them unceremoniously as soon as I'd escaped Drezden's molten stare. The way he'd looked at me when I shoved him off had cut into my soul.

He didn't expect me to stop him. Running my fingers over my eyebrows, I smoothed them repetitively; nervously. *Well, too fucking bad! I told him we couldn't, we shouldn't, and he fucking has the balls to try anyway.*

I hated that he'd pushed himself onto me.

I loved it, too.

What do I even want anymore? I was supposed to be thinking about how I'd be playing in front of thousands of people tonight. Instead, I was getting swept up in my growing obsession with Drezden Halifax.

Drezden and his velvety mouth.

Drezden and his dexterous fingers and searing heat and fuck could he kiss.

I banged the back of my skull on the door. *Out, thoughts! Out!* They remained like ticks, burrowed and bloated in my flesh.

I wanted Drezden. Wanted him in a way I'd never known was possible. Being a virgin became increasingly more frightening to me. Was it normal to be so hot, so hungry for someone?

A guy couldn't kiss like that, hold me

like that, if he wasn't experienced. The wildfire in his eyes had turned my strength into ash. If the elevator hadn't opened, ruining the spell, I might have let him go all the way.

I didn't need that. What I needed was a shower.

Preferably a cold one.

****

Sweet and blacker than pitch. Whatever I was hearing pulled me from my dream. It was a sound I'd heard before, during a time when I needed to feel like someone understood me. At the tender age of seventeen, it's impossible to feel anyone does.

In my case, with bullies and the tantalizing kiss of a blade, even harder.

Cracking open my eyes showed me a white wall. *Right, my hotel room.* The shower had stolen all the strength from my muscles. With my thick, wet hair wrapped in a towel, I'd crashed onto my bed and promptly passed out.

The sound came again; words through the walls. I caught snippets and clung to them.

"You fight me," the familiar voice sang.

Drezden. It was Drezden singing through the plaster.

"Backed into a corner with your hands, and I can't keep my feet beneath me..." He wasn't screaming the lyrics. It was a low rumble, baritone and shaking with constraint.

He's singing to me, was my initial, throat gripping thought. *No. Impossible. He's just practicing for tonight.* Sitting up, the towel fell from my head. Damp strands tickled my bare shoulders while I ripped my cell phone off the side-table. It was already three in the afternoon.

I slept that long? Shit. Tugging at the snarls in my hair, I tuned into Drezden's soft murmur. Even with a wall between us, his music filled my soul. He was connected to me in a way he could never know.

My arm throbbed sympathetically. I rubbed my tattoo, soothing the phantom wounds.

He sang, "One more night until we fall. Fight me with curled nails and wicked teeth..."

Closing my eyes, I let myself drift under his trance. There was comfort there among the passion, the fear. In my room, I was safe. Drezden couldn't see or hear my reactions.

It was like I was seventeen again, chasing his lyrics down into the soft belly of my mind. Back then, I'd never imagined I'd talk to Drezden Halifax in person.

I'd dreamed about playing on a big stage, but that was pretty optimistic. I knew I was good. Being good wasn't enough for breaking out in this industry. If I'd needed proof of that, I only had to look at my older brother.

Sean had struggled for years to get to where he was, and I knew it still paled next to what he desired. Even so, if I could have gotten into a position as glorious as my brother's, that would have been enough.

And now I'm soaring above him.

Opening my eyes, I stared down at my bare feet. *He'll see me tonight. He'll cheer me on, be so proud of me.* Remembering standing in the Fillmore with Drezden, my mouth twisted into a bitter frown. *Too bad my parents will never come. Drez actually offered to fly them out.*

It was sweet, but a useless effort. My parents couldn't be coaxed to believe in what I was doing. They'd hated it from the start.

Only Sean has been there for me. Clasping my phone, I called him. It rang several times, each one dampening my mood. His voice mail beeped. "Hey," I whispered, afraid Drez would hear me in his room. "Uh, just calling to say I can't wait to see you tonight." I wanted to say so much more. *Thanks for everything, thank you for pushing me.*

Thanks for being more of a parent than either of them.

"Okay. Bye." That was all I had left in me. Hanging up, I hid my face in my waterfall of hair. *He's probably getting ready right now. He goes on at five, it makes sense that he wouldn't answer his phone.* Logic wasn't the best for quelling my frustration. I needed to talk to someone.

"You fight me…" Drezden sang, tormenting me. "And I can't keep my feet beneath."

Vigorously I scrubbed at my cheeks. *Two can play this game.* My guitar case thunked, clasps snapping open from my quick fingers. I spent the barest time tuning, one ear aware of the next song Drezden was prepping for.

"Sticky sweetness," he crooned. My pulse jolted, the stiff pick between my fingers tickling my strings. Behind the cloak of my strums, I heard him falter.

He hadn't expected me to reply like this.

"Burning fast." He was louder; stronger. Had he moved closer to my wall? "My love, my dear, this will be your last."

Standing smoothly, I didn't miss a note while I walked towards the painted barrier. With everything and nothing between us, Drezden and I played together. We were perfection. Without needing to see, we *sensed* the tempo and followed the trail. As we sped up, my heart did, too.

There was an echo in his lyrics; like his cheek was pressed against the wall's surface. "If I take you from the grave, you'll be mine."

Clenching my molars, a tremble boiled through my cells. Before, he'd been singing for himself. A shift had happened.

He was singing for me.

"You'll be mine..."

Swallowing over my swollen tongue, I pressed my knees together. The heat was back. It clawed at me, steam that needed to be vented. I was fucking ready for Drezden. That was what this feeling was. An emotion that bent me to his will, held me prisoner as much as my dark singer's voice did.

I wondered what it would be like to kiss him again.

Groaning, I endured a hot ripple in my pussy. Just the memory was making me wet. *He was so insistent, so primal. He smelled so good, too. If I got close to him again...* Before I realized what I was doing, I placed my puckered lips on the wall. It was stupid; I knew that. If someone saw me they'd think I was insane.

There was no one to spy on me. Right then, with our music mixing, there might as well have been no wall at all. I was kissing cold paint, but his gritty tone vibrated through the material. It numbed my mouth, brushed my lungs, my spine, and beyond.

With my eyes closed, I played the ending of Velvet Lost. The last of the music melted like snowflakes on my scalding skin.

I thought of his honey tongue, his magnetic gaze. When I looked up, the blank wall left me dejected. Fighting Drezden was too hard. Everything was too fucking hard.

Just like him. Everything about him is hard, too. Several times I'd seen his massive erection in his pants. He was brazen about it; he had no shame. Drez wanted me to see how much he wanted to fuck me.

I turned beet red, grateful again that no one could see.

"Lola."

Startled, I jumped back from the wall. *Oh, shit.* What else had I expected but for Drez to speak to me? "Hey," I said lamely, hearing the cracks in my voice.

Something slid over the wall. I didn't know if it was his hand or something else. My eyes went to where I'd kissed, imagining him copying me. "Lola," he said again, metallic. "We should get the guys and head to the Fillmore."

I was nodding, knowing it was invisible to him. "Alright. Let me get changed."

"They'll have clothes for you there."

Crinkling my mouth, I laughed. "Seriously? Fine. Most of my stuff is dirty anyway."

He said no more, so I scrambled to my feet and slid on the cleanest things I had left— some jeans and a plain black t-shirt.

Tying my hair back in a tail, I let my neck breathe. I was sweltering from our private jam session, and not because of the effort. *When he sings, I feel like he's sliding through my skull and into my heart.* Thinking about

195

Drezden sliding himself into *any* part of me was making me wilt.

For a long moment, I stood with my hand on the brass handle of my door. I was counting the seconds. Each one was a bit of existence where a solid barrier stood between Drezden and me. I needed that protection; willing my body to calm the fuck down wasn't working.

Okay, I told myself. *I'm ready. I can do this.*

Tensing my jaw, I pushed out into the hall. Drezden was waiting for me.

His ankles were crossed where he leaned on the far wall, his fingers in his pockets. He reminded me of a cowboy from an old western; he even had an unlit cigarette in his teeth. The heavy cloak of tobacco was hanging all over him. *Was he smoking in his room?*

Drez pushed the cigarette to the corner of his mouth with his tongue. "I need a quick smoke before we head out. That alright?"

Shrugging, I propped my case on my hip. "It's whatever you want."

He crooked an eyebrow but made no comment. I actually hesitated when he entered the elevator. The mirrored surface threw my bloodless face back at me. "You coming?" he asked nonchalantly.

Is he pretending nothing happened in here? Biting my tongue, I dragged myself inside. *I guess that's the best way to handle*

196

this. I did reject him, it's only fair. If it was fair, why were my palms so clammy?

I knew the answer.

I told him to get off of me, told him this couldn't happen between us, and here I am lamenting his aloof fucking attitude. My head was throbbing. I started wishing for some Advil just to get through the next few hours.

When we landed in the lobby after our tense ride, Drezden marched through the doors. It was hard to keep up with him, his long legs gave him an advantage. We'd barely made it outside, his hands cupping around his lit cigarette, when a car pulled up in front of us. In the back seat, Porter and Colt waved.

"Hey!" The bassist looked quite proud. "Perfect! We were going to head out and send the car back for you two, but you're here, so just pile in."

The end of Drez's cigarette smoldered; smoke billowed from his lips. "I need to finish this, first."

Colt stretched over Porter, scowling wildly. "Man! Don't fucking smoke before you sing! I keep telling you this."

It was a good point. For a man so obsessed with how the band sounded, it was out of place to see him openly indulging in his lung-ruining addiction. "Can't you just smoke after?" I asked softly.

His glare was so sharp I stepped backwards. "Are you giving me fucking advice

197

on singing?"

"I'm only saying—"

"She's only saying what we're *all* saying," Porter growled. Leaning out of the car, he took a swipe at Drezden's cigarette. Sidestepping, Drez avoided the attempt with ease. "Come on! Just get in the car!"

He faced away from all of us, inhaling deeply; his response was flat. "Send the car back for me." Then he was gone, strolling around the building without looking back.

I took a single step after him before Porter reached out, grabbing me gently. I wasn't as slick as Drez; I couldn't avoid him. "Forget it, Lola. Let's just go."

I asked, "Shouldn't we make sure he's okay? That he's coming?"

"He'll come." Colt rubbed his shaved head roughly. "That guy just gets into a black fucking mood sometimes."

In the evening sun, Porter's eyes looked like melting chocolate. "It's fine," he said. "Remember who we're talking about. Drezden won't abandon a show. Not ever."

That word—abandon. It made my stomach contort like I'd swallowed rotten milk. Once, I would have believed Porter. The Drezden I thought I knew wouldn't walk away from a show, it wasn't in his blood.

But he wasn't the same man any longer.

Somewhere along the way, something had changed him. Something that had allowed him to think risking Four and a Half Headstones was worth it.

      Me, I thought, climbing into the car with great effort.

      I was the one who'd changed him.

- Chapter Thirteen -
Drezden

When the car came back for me twenty minutes later, my anger had faded into something less volatile. Dropping the last of my third cigarette to the ground, I crushed it under my heel. I had no idea when the last time I'd smoked so much was.

The sidewalks leading up to the Fillmore were packed with wandering people. The show would be starting soon, the place was about to get swarmed. *And all because of me,* I mused silently.

Normally I'd be getting amped up right now—thinking about the energy of the crowd, the way my teeth would vibrate as the speakers roared with my voice. But I couldn't focus; my mind was elsewhere.

Pushing my cheek onto the window, my breath fogged up the glass. Idly, I pressed my finger there and dragged it to create a single letter:

L.

Lola Cooper.

I'd been miserable back in my hotel room. Knowing that Lola was right nearby, right in the opposite room, had been maddening. I'd paced in a circle, finally deciding to try and shake off my unspent energy by warming up my vocals for the shows.

And then I'd heard her guitar.

That sound had taken away my ability to sing; just for a second, but that was ages to me. Lola could have stayed silent. Instead, she'd joined me with her music, our song entwining into one with only a simple wall between us.

Always a wall of some kind.

I wanted to tear every fucking wall down with my bare hands.

Shaking off the memory, I stepped out of the parked car. The crowds outside of the blocked off lot screamed at the sight of me. Bending my head low, I followed the throng of gigantic men in Security shirts through the back of the building.

Drums thumped in the halls, a bass rocking the air with its low ripples—Porter and Colt were doing sound check. The trail of music guided me behind a dark curtain, bodies murmuring and stomping as they ran around to get everything ready backstage.

Then I saw her.

Lola was poking her guitar, not noticing my arrival. Her hair swept over part of her temple; I buzzed with my desire to close our distance and brush those strands behind her ear.

A hand came down on my shoulder. "Drezden! There you are!" Brenda huffed, blowing her bangs from her eyes. "You almost missed sound check."

"Almost," I agreed. My brief moment of invisibility was over, everyone had noticed me. There were several other bands prepping in the area, as well as some fans sporting special VIP passes. I flashed a lazy smile at all of them. "Sorry for the wait. I'm here, let's get this done."

Lola shot me a quick look—was she relieved? —before she went back to tweaking at her guitar. Porter nodded knowingly, while Colt flipped a drum-stick and rolled his eyes. He was probably thinking that, even now, I was stealing the show.

The girls with their special passes giggled at me, doing their best to look both casual and interested. Scanning the group, I started towards my mic stand—then I stopped. Someone else was here that I should have expected, but in my distracted state, hadn't. He was standing off to the side, his intense eyes pulling me in among the sea of faces.

Sean Cooper.

He was hovering near some guys that I assumed were from Barbed Fire. I didn't know for sure, I didn't give a lot of thought to the other bands on the tour. As it was, I'd rarely seen any of them backstage before a show. In a set up like ours, with my band headlining, it was rare for anyone but us to get a chance to do sound check.

I guess they got a chance tonight because of how late I was.

Ignoring him, I scooped up my microphone. Glancing upwards, I spotted the guy who would help test the speakers and make sure that I—that we—sounded perfect. He dipped his chin, wordlessly understanding that I was ready.

From the corner of my eye, I saw Lola watching me again. There were so many things I wanted to say to her. A thousand words that would never explain the conflict inside of me.

So I said nothing.

And neither did she.

****

The Fillmore was a mosaic of faces and bodies. They shoved and shouted and begged for the show to go on. Barbed Fire had finished their first song, they were opening for us and they were *killing* it.

I watched from backstage as Sean Cooper scratched his guitar. He tore it to pieces, like it was an enemy he wanted to maim. The guy was good—better than he'd been two years ago. Hearing his sound, his style, I knew Lola had learned from him.

My mouth twisted perversely at one fact: Lola was better.

I wonder if he knows. Staring at his broad back, shoulders rippling with effort, I fought down a wicked grin. If he didn't know yet, he'd learn tonight.

I gave the band credit, though. They'd warmed the crowd up for us. Their singer, a guy named Thomas, stopped their set long enough to welcome everyone to the Fillmore. He said what he was contracted to, mentioning all the bands that were playing on the tour. And, especially, highlighting Four and a Half Headstones.

There were still plenty of people rushing around backstage. Standing off to the side, I didn't think anyone would notice me. A gentle cough proved me wrong.

Lola was wearing dark, ripped skinny jeans and a top that strained over her chest. It was similar to the outfit she'd worn in the promo photos. No question, Brenda had dressed her intentionally. My manager was doing her best to burn Lola into everyone's heads.

"Hey," she mouthed, the music drowning her out. Her extra-tall boot kicked at the floor. Could she walk in those? Before I could say anything back, her blue eyes abandoned me, leaving a hole in me as they did.

She stared out at the brightly lit stage, absorbing her brother's performance as intensely as I had been doing. Leaning down, I spoke right in her ear; the way she gasped gave me a thrill. "They're playing really good."

Lola's nose nearly touched mine when

she twisted towards me. "They *always* play really good! You've been on the tour with them, haven't you heard them before?"

A hot flash crept up my neck. Normally I did sound check, then vanished until it was time for me to play. The other bands were just blurry noise in the background. *I should have paid more attention.* It didn't matter.

The only band that I needed to focus on was mine.

"Sure," I said quickly. "Listen. We go on after the next group, come get some air with me."

Brushing back her thick curls, she peeked longingly out at the stage. Barbed Fire had one more song left. I knew her answer before she spoke. "Not yet."

Drums crashed, muffling my words. "You've heard them a million times. Why do you need to be here for this, too?"

A crisp frost inched along her lips. It stuck them into an immovable frown. "Because I want to be."

Without a counter argument in my pocket, I just shrugged. "Fine." My fingers touched my empty pack of cigarettes. "That's fine. I'll just—fine." Even the small denials from Lola drove me insane.

Shoving around her, I hurried towards the side door that led to a small, walled off patio outside, a place for the crew to take their breaks. With a band on stage, the area was empty.

Slumping to the cold ground, I pursed my lips. My breath swirled, the closest thing to smoke that I had. *I should have saved one damn cigarette. Fuck. I'm smoking too much.* It was so hard to hold back. Lola was my new addiction, but when she wouldn't allow me to have a hit, tobacco was all that remained. It paled next to her.

Scratching my hair vigorously, I sighed. I'd told Lola that I didn't get scared before shows anymore. I wished I *was* scared, though. Feeling anything but starvation for a woman who kept resisting me would have been easier to handle.

Palming my forehead, I gazed up at the burning orange sky. An early moon dangled in the corner. The laugh that escaped me was unsettling. *What the hell is this? What do I do with this fucking itch?*

I'd have ripped my flesh from my bones if it allowed me to feel normal again.

Through the thick walls, the music died. Cheers replaced it; Barbed Fire had finished. It meant Lola would be celebrating with her brother. *We'll be playing in front of that audience soon.* In a short time, everyone would see Lola. Really see her. They'd bask in her fucking music, longing to celebrate with her when it was all done. I was going to lose her in a sea of eager fans.

Shutting my eyes, I thought about the

elevator. Her lips had been so eager—I hadn't expected her to stop me. Buzzing with energy, I'd started to sing in my room afterwards. Together, we'd played a private show blindly through our hotel walls.

The music was one thing, but knowing she was there... I'd called out to her. I'd placed my forehead on the cool plaster, imagined touching her, grinding the wall down and holding her close.

Crushing my head in my hands, I hung it between my knees and laughed again. *I kicked Johnny out of the band so he wouldn't drag us all down. I brought Lola on to save us. Now, I'll be dragged into hell by her instead.*

Lola had wrecked me. There was no coming back from this. The only way to get some control was to sate this damn *need* I had for her. I knew that if I couldn't taste her—hold her... *Fuck her...* I'd go insane. I couldn't take being so close to her all the time. How could my band survive if I was busy losing my mind?

"Drez!" Brenda shouted, both before and after she kicked the patio door open. "There you are! I knew you'd be out here getting a smoke. Come on, the show is about to start!" When she looked at my face, she stopped. "Are you okay?"

Nope, I thought dryly. Filling my chest, I climbed to my feet. "I'm ready. Let's do this."

I wasn't ready. I'd never be ready for Lola.

But she was about to debut in front of the entire world.

I wouldn't miss being part of that for anything.

****

The crowd was screaming for blood.

Luckily, I was ready to empty my veins.

Everyone in the Fillmore was at peak levels. They'd been waiting for us: Four and a Half Headstones. We walked onto the stage one by one, and each time, the screams grew wilder.

Looking out over the ocean of blurry faces, I glimpsed signs toting our names... even Lola's. Some of the giant pieces of cardboard demanded we bring back Johnny. Our fans were ready to judge our decision. To judge *her*.

A flicker of worry stalled my heart.

If Lola played poorly they would not be kind. She stood to the side, purple Stratocaster at the ready. It was her armor. Lola looked at me, a silent cry for help or strength or maybe that I just wake her up from this dream.

All I could do was smile and hope it inspired confidence in her.

I wanted us to please our fans. I also didn't want to lose Lola to them. It was a conflicting knot of emotions. I grabbed the microphone, throttled it like it was my wandering brain. "Hey there, Denver." My voice was sugar and velvet. As I expected, the crowd exploded in a roar. It was unadulterated energy, a drug that ruled me.

I needed more.

"You know," I said, walking across the wide stage. "This is our first time playing at the Fillmore." More noise, I waited for them to calm down. "But it isn't the first time I've been here." Curiosity and excitement rolled over the sea of people.

It was exactly what I wanted.

Turning, I found Lola watching me. I'd never seen her eyes so big. "I came when I was a kid. And you know, back then? All I could think about was that *someday*, maybe I'd make it here." My stare wandered over the arena. "Maybe I'd get to play." *One, two, let them breathe.* The strained patience was overwhelming, but this wasn't my first rodeo.

Timing was everything.

I shook my head and said, "Well. Here I am. Guess it's time to do what I wished to back then..." With a giant smile that flashed all my teeth, I winked. "Bring this place to its fucking knees."

That was it. The crowd was done.

In the canvas of the stage—*my stage*— clean drum taps signaled the beginning of our set. Colt primed the air for our art, silencing the audience to a low rumble. My mouth tasted like adrenaline mixed with cotton candy;

everything tingled.

This was my first love: music. Lola stood at the ready, stroking her strings. *This. This will replace the void she's created.*

She smiled at me, and I knew that wasn't true.

Into the mic, I roared as only a man falling to pieces could. I was held together by determination; fragile and ghastly at the same time. Caught in my blast, the world would be destroyed. I'd revel and dance in the hot ashes.

Singing the words of Tuesday Left Behind, I showed the crowd who we were. Four and a Half Headstones had changed when we lost Johnny Muse. But not in a bad way. We sounded better than we had in months.

I should have kicked him out sooner.

If I had, would I have ever met Lola Cooper?

She clawed her guitar, eliciting notes that turned me inside out. The people felt it, too; they became nothing but tooth-filled mouths that begged for more. They wouldn't lynch her. They couldn't, not when they'd just learned what I recently had.

Lola was beyond amazing.

Every song merged together for me. They made a map that took the audience through a world of smoke, charcoal and rust. They tasted our enthusiasm, reveled in every lyric like I'd written it just for them. By our last song, I was panting. Sweat turned my skin bronze; shiny and new.

The back of my shirt was soaked through. The front, well... *The eyes of every girl in the first row says it all.* "Listen up," I whispered into the mic. "This is our last song." I let the cries of sadness die out. "It's my favorite. Maybe yours, too."

Porter and Colt summoned the first notes that heralded No More Stars.

Bathing in the cheers, I stalked across the stage. Lola met my eyes. She was glowing, lips puckered. Everything in her face, her aura, made me think of sex. I wanted to grab her, kiss her harder than I had in the elevator.

The gravity between us tugged. I *saw* it, how her joy stumbled. She wasn't angry. It wasn't the cold wall of rejection. With the heat of our momentum—the music—sinking into both our souls...

Lola shivered with lust.

Fuck. Fucking hell.

Pouring that voracious need into my voice, I belted out the words to No More Stars. She followed me down, rampaging over her strings. Nothing could stop us; none of us.

Four and a Half Headstones was whole. Once I had Lola...

I would be whole, too.

- Chapter Fourteen -
Lola

I'd never felt more alive.

Perspiration ran down my sternum, the backs of my knees were taut as elastics. I thought, if I tried, I could have jumped straight up and never come down.

This was what playing music was all about.

Laughing, crying, none of it mattered; none of it would have helped. I was a bundle of nerves ready to explode. Or, perhaps I *had* exploded. My ears were ringing, the powder keg of my mind leaving fragments that coated one word across the inside my skull.

Rock star.

I was a fucking rock star.

When I used to stand backstage or in a crowd during shows, I thought I knew what it would be like to play in front of so many people. I thought I understood.

I didn't have a clue.

Drezden pranced for them, he stormed and kicked and screamed. Veins stood out on his throat. The insides of his forearms became trails, his tattoos rippling while he strangled the microphone. In his element, he was more beautiful than ever.

I'd been worried I'd fumble, but something had changed; the concentrated

212

essence of his voice wasn't aimed at me. Standing back where I was, I was spared his attack.

It was the crowd that took every hit.

The ending notes of No More Stars faded in my ears. *No, not yet. I'm not done yet.* On a whim, I tangled up my strings and extended the music. It was spontaneous, but the fans wailed for more. Next to me, Porter and Colt went silent. Abruptly, I was performing a guitar solo.

I met Drezden's gaze. Like that day, when I'd auditioned, I felt the pull from him. This was the man who turned me inside out. He felt his way into me with just his eyes. Drezden didn't need anything else to touch that place deep down in my core.

Quaking in my vinyl boots, I let my guitar go; it swung from its strap like a pendulum.

The dead silence was brief, swallowed up by the black hole of the Fillmore's crowd. It was as if every single person in there was making as much noise as they could.

They crowed for an encore, but someone was leading me off stage. Without thinking, I ripped my arm away. I didn't want to go anywhere! This was my home, my life, and every nerve begged to keep me standing in the worship of—

"Lola," Sean said, teeth glinting. "Lola! Holy shit! You were amazing!"

I shoved him backwards with my hug. Together, we stumbled backstage, away from the blinding lights. "Sean! Sean, oh my gosh! Did you see? Did you see that?"

We were jumping, a mess of shouts that kept building with our excitement. What we said didn't matter. Only our feelings counted.

Gripping my shoulders, he gave me a shake that rattled my teeth. "How did you get so *good?*"

Feeling cocky, I let myself smirk. "I was always that good."

Sean's forehead wrinkled. My gut said I'd gone too far, until I noticed he was looking just past me. Turning, I stepped aside and found Drezden within arm's reach. "She is really good," the singer said. Reaching out, he offered his hand to my brother. "Long time no see."

"Well," Sean said, accepting the handshake. "Not exactly. I've seen *you* a bunch."

The tightness in Drez's smile unnerved me. "These tours get busy for me, sorry I didn't come over before now."

I didn't have time to get anxious from their tension. A crowd was forming, Brenda leading Porter and Colt our way. "Great job tonight, guys," she said. She beamed at me, then spotted my brother. "You especially, Lola. Sean! Hey, good opening act."

"Thanks." Thumbing his ear, he looked

over us all. "Getting packed back here. Lola, me and the guys are going to be partying at a place down the street. I'll text you if you want to show up for the afterparty, okay?"

I said, "Sure. Sounds good." I was smiling again. I couldn't keep my exuberance in check. "And thanks, Sean."

He walked backwards, wiggling his fingers. "For what?"

For being there for me, for pushing me. "Just... everything." He rolled his eyes before hurrying away.

Brenda grabbed her hips, hair bouncing. "Afterparties, about that. You guys better be ready to climb on the bus tomorrow morning."

"I'll be fine," Porter said, elbowing me firmly. "Can't speak for the newbie, though."

I gave the bigger man a light shove, laughing. "And I told *you*, this isn't my first afterparty."

"With us, it is." The drummer hooked his arm in mine, while Porter pushed me forward. The two of them had no trouble forcing me towards a back exit. "Come on! Our driver will take us to the club, it's supposed to be awesome!"

Drezden was following, a bloodhound who had my scent. "Wait," I said. I dug my heels in, the floor screeching under me. "Wait, wait! We're not going to the same place as Sean and the rest of his band?"

They let me go, none of them meeting

my eyes. All the fun had evaporated. "He might show up," Porter mumbled. "Who knows?"

"Might?" Wrinkles crawled over the bridge of my nose. "They're not allowed into this club, are they?" I didn't wait for anyone to speak, their eyes were darting around, gliding off of me like I was made of oil. "If he or any of his band show up, they better be let inside."

A hand clapped onto the top of my head; Drezden. "Calm down. I'll let the security know they can get in. Sound fair, kid?"

Kid. My heart swelled at the name he'd stopped calling me so quickly. *I told him not to, that's why. I said I wasn't a damn kid.* Pin-pricks crawled up my arms. *Then he asked me... he asked me what I was doing to him.* Every inch of me heated up, reliving the memory of being in the tub.

Unable to handle his nearness, I pushed away. I kept going, being the first to step out into the open air. The world was full of screams, flashing lights, and men in black holding an army at bay. These were the fans of Four and a Half Headstones.

My fans, I thought in wonderment. Looking over my shoulder, I challenged the rest of the band with my eyes. "You guys said you wanted to show me a 'real' afterparty. Then come on, show me what it means to be a member of Four and a Half Headstones."

****

Inside the club, there was no air. It was a place built from human heat and purple lights. No one cared; everyone was eager to suffocate if it meant they could be near the stars.

Near us.

Near *me*.

Thumping music pumped into my muscle fibers. It made me dance, but the alcohol was what made me feel free. No one cared I was underage, they didn't dare turn me away. I'd told the guys I'd been to afterparties before. It galled me how right they'd been, though.

This was nothing like the parties Barbed Fire ended up at.

Packed to capacity, the club was sweltering. Bodies without faces ground against me, turned me to hamburger with their rough motions. Tossing back my third—fourth? —rum and coke, I closed my eyes and rolled into the sea.

Thump. Thump. Thump. The rhythm rocked my heart.

It was fun to have time eaten away like this, I didn't need to think about Drezden and how his presence was making me fall apart. My temples were expanding with pressure from the noise. *Alcohol, I've had too much alcohol.* Something bumped me; a hip or a thigh. *I should stop, get some air. I need to breathe!*

Foreign fingers hooked around my waist. I didn't know him, his face was an amethyst in the glow of the lights. "Hey," he croaked, dark bruises under his eyes. "I know you, you're Lola."

I said, "Yup." With one hand trapped by my drink, I tried to use the other to pry myself free. The guy, whoever the fuck he was, wouldn't have it.

Yanking me close, his sour breath invaded my nose. "You were amazing up there." His nose touched my forehead, sniffed my hair. "Come on, let's dance, babe." Too fast, his hands ran up my ribs like giant spiders.

No way, not letting this happen. This asshole was sporting a giant grin. Wrenching back my arm, I erased it with a blast of ice and rum. I dropped the glass, the plastic 'clonk' not reaching me over the music.

In disbelief, he wiped his face; his eyes were furious. "You fucking bitch!"

There was a part of me that wanted him to try something. My brain was full of disgust for the other night, when the guards had thrown me down so easily. I wasn't a victim; those days were in my past. I could fight and I *would* fight, if someone gave me a reason.

Let this fucker give me a reason.

It would relieve so much poisonous energy if I could let loose and just go crazy.

The stranger gritted his teeth, but he didn't take a step towards me. His eyes shot up, over my shoulder. In the funny lighting of the club, Drezden was a purple demon. I'd have called him an angel, but I didn't need saving, and there was nothing angelic about him.

"There a problem?" He was looking at me while clearly talking to the guy soaked in my drink. The nameless shithead had to know who my 'hero' was. If he'd recognized me, Drezden Halifax was a given.

The stranger scrubbed his cheek, barely talking over the music. "No problem. Forget it." He faded into the crowd, become another writhing body.

Drezden stared after the man longer than I did. Facing him, I noticed how people had given us some space. No one wanted to accidentally upset this beast of a man by bumping into him. Through my alcohol cloud, I noticed how serious he seemed. "I didn't start that," I said, expecting him to be snippy. "And I could have handled it myself."

"The drink stain on his shirt says you did handle it." Cocking his head like a hawk, a smile tugged at one side of his lips. "If I get too close, will you do the same thing to me?"

Tobacco and salt filled my nose, replacing the sourness of the stranger. I honestly didn't know what I would do if Drez got too close. "Get me a new drink and let's find out."

He threw back his head, laughing. His green eyes became black smoke. "What if I tell you I don't want to get you a drink?"

"You think I've had too much already."
It was a flat statement. I was halfway to drunk,
but not there yet. Things were fuzzy and fun
and my head could have floated away. But I
wasn't smashed.

I ran my eyes over his torso in that tight
fitted ribbed top, a clean replacement after our
show. He was gorgeous; he knew it, everyone
knew it.

I definitely knew it.

The singer was quiet. We stood there in
the middle of a war, fists and knees punching
all around us. Magically, we were untouched.
He and I managed to escape into a bubble no
one dared to break. What did others sense
around us? What kept them at bay?

His fingers glided up the outside of my
left wrist before I thought to stop him. By then,
it was too late. "It's not that," he said. "You can
drink as much as you want. It's just hard to
dance with a glass in your hand."

Heat twinkled like stars in his face. I
wanted to gaze on him forever and vanish into
his galaxy. It was so easy to just fall into him. If
I tumbled headfirst, I'd float forever and never
return. "You want to dance with *me* when every
crazy-hot girl here is clawing her eyes out to get
your attention?"

"Why would that matter?" He tugged my
arm, forcing me closer to his chest. "I want to
spend more time with you."

More? The music rolled in my belly, coaxing me to give in. "We spent the last two days trapped on a bus together. There's not much time that we missed."

"It wasn't enough." Drezden's hands dug into me. It was a beautiful pain, begging me to crush myself against him. "I need more, and I'll find any way to get it. Even if that means not sleeping... or not breathing. I want to devote every second I have to you, Lola."

Fear warned me not to get closer; if we touched our bodies, we'd both burn up. *But would it be the worst way to go?* I looked for my tongue, tried to make it wet my dry mouth. Nothing was in my control anymore. All my pieces wanted to obey the ache Drezden was creating between my thighs. "Suffocating over me sounds ridiculous." *When did my hips start rocking to the beat?* "Normal people just cut out activities they can afford to stop."

He made a path up to my shoulders, tracing the outside edge of my sleeves. "Advise me."

Boldly, I reached for his ass. His nostrils flared wide. The spike of pleasure I got from surprising him was... thrilling. Especially when I squeezed his back pocket; the empty pack of cigarettes crinkled under my grip.

"This," I said softly. We were close enough that the music didn't blur me out. "How about you try smoking less? Earlier today, all the time you wasted when you

221

stormed off to—"

Drezden's expression darkened. "I know." His palm closed over my fingers, trapping my hand against his lower back. "It's just something I do when I'm stressed."

"Why not just quit?"

His thumb squeezed, I worried he'd leave his fingerprints on my flesh. "Withdrawal is soul sucking." In his pause, there was something unsaid. Watching me with a dangerously vivid hunger, he bent down. His whisper clenched around my lungs. "When did you become my drug?"

There were so many words I wanted to say.

Too bad he'd stolen them all.

I keep trying to tell him no. My mouth says one thing, while the rest of me gets hot and wet. My brother had told me to get closer to Drezden. There was no way he meant I should get *this* close to him.

Together we started to weave. I didn't struggle; when he released my hand, I kept it on his ass. There was a pulsing in me, in us. It went beyond the rapid music.

We didn't dance like strangers. I expected more mistakes, more fumbles. Drezden held my spine, coaxing me to roll my hips. Before, I'd been lacking air. Now, I was a balloon, waiting for Drezden to pop me.

How could my fragile existence stand up to his sharp appetite?

222

Taking my waist, he brushed his pelvis—
himself—against me. The stiff resistance of his
hard-on brought a whimper from my lips. My
knees melted like ice cream on the summer
pavement. I felt the dampness of my pussy
ruining my panties and worried my jeans
would be next.

I leaned my weight on him, rubbing over
every single fucking muscle he had... and he
had a lot of them. What remained of my
resistance was flying away. I was up against an
enemy I'd never faced. Here I was, falling apart
at the hands of a man I'd glorified over the
years as I listened to his music late into the
night. He was dancing with *me*, he wanted *me*.

I couldn't recall why I'd been rejecting
him.

His lips came for mine. I beat him there,
linking my arms around his thick neck to keep
him in place. I tasted the sweetness of rum, but
his flavor was stronger in the end. It left hooks
in my brain, implanting a gluttony for him.

Nothing would ever be the same
between us.

When had I stopped caring?

****

The elevator dinged.

Drezden pressed me on the mirror,
holding my chin so he could take his time with

my throat. I didn't remember getting into the hotel, there was just a vague fog made from purple lights, crisp air and the crunching of tires. A part of me knew we'd climbed into a taxi, ignoring the personal car. The rest was all teeth and seeking tongues.

He kissed better than anyone could have —should have—been able to. The last time we'd been in this elevator had been this morning. Then, when he'd shoved me on the wall and tried to convince me to give him a chance... I'd almost done it.

Performing in front of thousands had filled me with courage. Was that what had changed? Was I no longer scared? *I'm unbreakable. Nothing can ruin this. I'm a rock star.*

The world had welcomed me. I wanted to swallow it whole.

The elevator doors started to close, the machine having no clue that we'd reached our floor, but had decided to stay inside and keep making out. I put out a foot, stopping the doors, yanking Drezden out into the hall and towards my room.

He stopped us and banged his keycard on the door next to mine; the one that belonged to him. Together we fell through the doorway, the lights automatically flicking on when they sensed our movement.

Behind me, the door crashed shut heavily. Drez was kissing me, as if he couldn't stop. Through my fluttering lashes, I caught glimpses of his room. It was big, wide—a copy of mine with its white walls and large screen TV.

A ripple of fear surfaced at the sight of his bed.

Wait. What am I doing?

His hands pushed my hair off my neck from behind. My worries went with it. "I can't believe you're here." He grazed the curve of my jaw with his teeth. Hard fingertips moved down my back, tugging the hem of my shirt up.

Swallowing didn't help me find a response. I tried again, but only a quick gasp escaped. He'd discovered my skin, exploring my spine. Drezden bumped my bra strap; without asking, he unclasped it.

The black lingerie whispered when it hit the floor; he was too fast. On reflex, I crossed my arms over my chest. Drez spun me, eyes eagerly raking over my pale flesh. Nerves were erasing my confidence. I reached for the light; his body blocked me. "No," he growled, scooping up my chin. I froze under the need in his stare. "I want to see you, all of you."

It's too much. This is too much. I'd forgotten who he really was. Drezden Halifax had let me see some of the darkness inside of him before. But now, I'd walked into his lair.

In private, he could be himself. He could let go. I'd stumbled into a whirlpool when I'd thought it was a basic jacuzzi. He kissed me violently, tugging my lower lip with his teeth.

I felt myself falling, thought it was vertigo until I actually hit the bed. Drezden went down with me. He pounced, tangling fingers in my hair.

He's going to destroy me.

And yet, the more he touched me, the less I fucking cared. His warmth settled over me on the mattress, shadows cloaking his eyes. Leaning away, he flashed me a quick smirk. It stole more of my resistance.

Palms dragged down, scratching my ribs. I wriggled, openly whining as he explored me. Drezden was skirting around my breasts. I was initially thankful, terrified to let him touch me there when I was already losing my mind in less tender places.

Soon enough, the throbbing in my lower belly grew disappointed. The smirk he'd given me made sense. *The bastard, he's teasing me. How can he have the strength to tease when he acts like he wants me so badly?*

He looked down, green eyes contaminated with lust. "Something wrong, Lola?"

My poor lower lip was getting chewed up. "Why are you—why go so slow?"

His index finger brushed down my middle, just between my breasts. "You want me to speed up?"

Narrowing my eyes, I tried to look fierce. A gentle caress from his hand near my hip changed that. "I just... no. Fine. Do what you want."

There, a flash of the rabid animal living in his soul. "I plan to."

The muscles in my legs squeezed, toes pointing in my boots. A hollowness was forming in my pussy. Drezden made me want things I couldn't say out loud.

Inch by inch, he twirled his fingers closer to my chest. I was breathing heavily, my cheeks pure fire as my breasts shook with my strain. It was impossible to hold anything back. With him sitting on me, knees on either side of my thighs, I was trapped. I knew he felt every tiny twitch of my hips grinding.

I willed my body to calm down. I wasn't surprised it didn't listen. *At this rate, my brain will just crumple like tissue paper.*

Looking over him, the light behind his head made his features sharp as daggers. The indents along his bare shoulders hinted at his strength, his complete restraint in being patient with me.

Drezden flinched as I gripped his shirt, trying to lift it over his head. I thought he'd help me; his hands imprisoned my wrists. "No," he said sternly. "It stays on."

"That's not fair." *I want to see you, too.* Trying again was futile, he just crushed my wrists until I squeaked.

Shoving my arms down onto the mattress, he pressed his nose to mine. The gold

227

flecks I'd loved in his eyes now reminded me of jagged glass. "You want to see more of me? You're so sure?"

My voice was a mere croak. "Of course I'm sure." *I think I am, I think...*

Considering me for a long minute, Drezden let my hands go. He straightened up, then stepped off the bed. I was paralyzed as he unbuckled his belt. The leather fell to the floor, my heart jumping.

"I'll show you more." His meaning had a razor edge. He wasn't removing his shirt, he was unbuttoning his jeans. The sound of the zipper reverberated in my atoms.

In spite of my uneasiness, I sat up on my elbows. I was transfixed on his thumbs guiding his pants downwards. Drezden kicked his shoes off, they joined his jeans in a forgotten pile.

He was clad in tight, charcoal grey briefs. The material left little to my imagination. The shape of his cock was obvious as day, tenting out from his stomach and making my pussy throb.

When I finally lifted my eyes away from it, I found Drezden grinning. "I guess you did want to see, then."

Blushing redder than ever, I looked at the ceiling. My escape was too brief; he climbed back over me. Expecting him to say something, to maybe kiss me, I cried out as he buried his hands on my breasts.

His erection bumped my thigh, driving

tremors to my swelling clit. How the hell could I have prepared for this? *I couldn't have. I don't think anyone could be ready for someone like Drezden.*

His mouth secured mine. In the dizzying heat of his lips, I lost track of time. Fingers wrapped my hardening nipples, tugging them gently. Each pull woke more of me, prodded at my own inner animal.

Sliding down, the singer kissed my nipples, one at a time. Then he licked his fingers, the sight scalding my blood. Staring right at me, Drez teased one rosebud. Simultaneously, he suckled the other.

Colors bloomed in my mind. I was blind and deaf and made of nothing. When I came back, I honed in on the ball of slippery pleasure growing between my thighs. I *wanted*—no, needed—Drezden to fuck me.

It wasn't something I could voice.

Rocking my hips, I whimpered pathetically. With my breast still in his warm mouth, he chuckled. The sound he made when he let go was obscenely liquid. "Your heart sounds like it's going to explode."

It's going to break. Opening my eyes, forgetting when I had shut them, I saw the glow in his face. He was barely controlling his lust. "You're fucking cruel," I mumbled. Reaching between us, I unzipped my pants. His look of surprise was almost as good as when I'd grabbed his ass in the club.

He moved, helping me shimmy the jeans and boots off. We both saw how soaked my blue panties were. His chuckle was galling. He didn't mock me, though; he leaned down and *inhaled* my scent as deeply as he could. His cheek, rough with stubble, scraped on my leg.

"Fuck," he said against my dampness. "You smell so fucking good."

I was mortified and turned on all at once. "Stop, come up here." One look from him said he wasn't going to listen to me.

Tugging my panties down, he revealed my pink lower lips. Strands of my juice went with the cloth, and we both knew how much I wanted him. Drezden adjusted himself in his briefs with a grunt. "I wanted to draw this out longer, fuck."

My head was shaking side to side. Speaking was hard, each of his words was a breath of air on my eager pussy. Every time it throbbed I lost the ability to use my tongue.

Luckily for us both, Drezden had full control of his.

His first lick made me gasp, the second made me squeal. I covered my mouth to stifle the rest, trying to roll away from him. He wouldn't have it, not him. Coiling his arms around my thighs, he spread me open and trapped me in place.

I was strong for my size, I wasn't some shrinking violet. But in that moment, I lost every fiber that said 'get away' each time he dipped his tongue onto my pussy. He ate me through my first helpless spasms. Drezden had me in his grips, and I was fading fast.

Greedily he buried his mouth between my thighs. Being a virgin was one thing, I still had a healthy appetite for masturbation. But this was *nothing* like that. His determination and skill drove me to submit.

Teasing my clit gently, he groaned with his thirst. My fingers went down, guiding his head and feeling his soft hair. The pressure in me was electric; it frightened me. I couldn't bear to let myself come, not on his face like this.

"Drezden," I blurted, tugging at his hair. "You need to—ah! Stop, come on, come up!"

In argument, he nibbled just on the edge of my clit. My scream was wild, back arching on the bed. A ripple of tension stretched, an elastic that connected me from my scalp to my pussy. "W—wait, wait...!"

The singer for Headstones wasn't listening to me. In a funny moment of clarity, I didn't think he ever had. He'd forced me to show him my bitten tongue, insisted he treat my wounds, kissed me and touched me and chased me down all after I'd told him we couldn't happen.

And here I was. The result of all his pressing.

Letting him eat me out.

My elastic snapped, tingles shooting

through and centering on my lower belly. I came hard, screaming and biting down on my wrist. The noise still reached my ears, another thing to imprint and associate with Drezden Halifax.

He was taking hold of me in every possible way.

Gasping, I didn't notice he moved until he tangled his tongue with mine. Cupping my cheeks, he kissed me until my heart came back down from the clouds. But he wasn't done, there was no stopping him.

Sliding his briefs down, he exposed his thick cock. It bounced off of me, pressing warmly on my belly. I caught a glimpse of it, the fat head an angry purple from how he'd held back. If what I'd experienced was a controlled Drezden, the unrestricted version could only spell doom.

"Lola," he said, his voice labored. I heard him reach for something on the edge of the bed. From his crumpled jeans, he slipped out a foil packet. Expertly, he rolled the condom over his engorged prick.

Our foreheads touched, his shirt rubbing over my sensitive nipples. I think he expected me to say something—but I couldn't. My throat was tight, useless.

The tip of his cock brushed my wet entrance. My lungs, my insides, everything became cement. This was it; the moment I'd been waiting for. Movies and books had warned me over and over that sex would hurt the first time.

Drezden bit down on my shoulder, spreading me open inch by inch. There was a sense of being filled, one that continued on as he kept entering me. I didn't know how big he should feel. What was normal? How could I know? My brain kept warning me that it was too much. He was stretching me, surely I would break in two.

Against my temple, he groaned. He had my hips in a vice grip, keeping me still as he kept sliding in. It took forever; I existed in an eternity with the man who seemed keen to rip me apart.

With a long sigh, he sank in to the root of his dick. My eyes snapped open, confused. *Where was the pain? Shouldn't that have hurt?* It wasn't a peaceful moment to wonder. Drezden was withdrawing, taking my sanity with him.

The ridge of his cock-head came to the edge of my pussy. In a deliberately slow thrust, he sank back in. The pattern started that way, calm and collected. Each pump of his hips drove Drezden further to the brink; I heard it in his breathing.

"You're so tight," he gasped. It was amazing I heard him at all, I was sinking in a sea of warmth and cotton. Everything he did felt astounding. Why the hell had I fought him off?

Waiting was a mistake.

Two days wasted. I could have just kissed him from the onset and begun this wonderfully insane ride. I'd chided Drezden over two days being plenty of time, but now, I was a hypocrite—I wanted more.

He swelled inside of me, his length pulsing. Slamming into me faster, Drezden held me down like I would try to escape. *Doesn't he know by now?* I wondered. *I'm stuck.* He was everything I wanted, a creature made up from the songs he sang. Songs that had healed me.

In the black, you walk with me...

Yes. I'd walked with him in my head for years. He was a voice that rang with understanding. Someone who seemed to get what it meant to suffer and fight and be alone.

But I wasn't alone... not right now.

I'll walk in the black with him, if he'll let me.

Our cries were melting together. We rocked our bodies and surged with mounting passion. I wanted him, wanted him so much, and nothing would take that away. I could have whatever I wanted... that was the dream, right?

I was a rock star.

Nothing could stop me.

There was a tide of pleasure growing in me. I let it dash me on the rocks, I didn't try to fight as a second orgasm approached. He was insistent in his pace, driving rough and fast without a hint of slowing. We were in sync, my hips meeting his with constant liquid-sounding contact.

"Come for me," he demanded in my ear. "I need to feel your pussy milking me."

That was it, I was done. "Drezden! I'm—ah!" Trembling, I shut my eyes and endured the hot flash of delight. My muscles tensed and released, toes cramping as I came.

With a throttled snarl, Drezden buried his face in my neck and climaxed, too. He was quaking in me, stirring me up while he filled the condom. A part of me felt denied, as if his seed belonged to me, not some rubber tube.

This wasn't a true silence. Our breathing had merged, raspy and wet. He laid on me fully, the flutter of his heart knocking on my ribs. For some time, we just stayed like that. I didn't know who moved first, only that we disengaged with mutual winces.

Sitting back, Drezden sat on the bed. He was quick to unroll the condom; precise.

He didn't ask me if it was my first time. But how could he even guess?

My eyes ate him up, watching him toss the condom in the trash. He still wore his shirt. I felt a little... robbed. Why had he refused to take it off?

"Are you alright?" he asked, concern warming his emerald eyes.

Sitting up, I searched for my clothes. "I'm fine, just stunned, I guess."

Moving close, he stopped me from getting changed. Pushing me back on the blankets, he kissed me so long I went dizzy. "Lola, you're—fuck. You were amazing."

"Yeah?" Blushing, I snuggled closer to him. I couldn't tell him that he was my first. Maybe he didn't need to know, why would it matter?

The mattress springs squeaked when he settled next to me. Gently, he urged me up onto the pillows so we were both more comfortable. I didn't struggle, I was happy to let him pull me against his body.

Drez was a wall of scorching heat. His cock was still mostly hard, thudding against my ass cheek as we spooned. But if I expected him to go for round two, I was wrong; the strain of the long day was taking its toll. Drezden yawned, his breathing transforming into the gentle sway of sleep.

I stayed there in his arms, my joy shifting into discomfort. The light was still on, the glow impossible to ignore. If I didn't turn it off, I'd never rest.

With care, I extracted myself. On bare feet I padded to the light switch... then I stopped. Turning, I stared at Drez, counting the seconds. Had my movement woken him? The lift and fall of his shoulders said no.

He was curled on his side, back facing me where I stood. The idea that arose gave me chills.

I shouldn't.

But I was already tip-toeing to his side of the bed.

Crouching low, I faced his shoulder blades. Under the cloth, his muscles flexed even in sleep. Trembling fingers inches through the air towards him. I had to stop, restarting twice before I felt calm enough to try.

Edging up his shirt, I listened to the blood slam in my skull. *Slow, slow, go slow.* Drezden had worked so hard to make sure I didn't get his shirt off. There had to be a reason, I was too curious not to take the chance and see what it was.

I didn't need to lift much of the fabric to understand.

There, glossy and old on his lower back, was a scar as long as my hand. Releasing the shirt quickly, I covered my mouth. *What is that, what's that from?* It wasn't a small wound. Whatever had happened to Drezden had been painful.

For a long while, I just crouched there. I watched him sleep, staring a hole through the shirt where the scar was. There were knots in my calves when I finally stood up to turn the light off.

Sinking down beside him, I gazed into the darkness where the ceiling was. It didn't matter if my eyes were open or shut, blackness became my world, cursing me with a paranoia that grew like weeds. *Why would he hide that?*

237

Absently, I traced the inside of my right arm where my own old scars were. *Did he think he couldn't trust me not to pry?*

Guilt coiled, sharp and jagged. *He'd have been right; I would have asked.*

Something, or someone, had hurt Drezden Halifax. I didn't blame him for wanting to avoid explaining, but relating didn't soothe my worries. Curling on my side, I buried my cheek in the pillow. His sounds, his smell, it smothered the air. He was close to capturing every part of me, and yet, I still knew so little about him.

Tomorrow, will we both be different people?

What will he act like? What about me?

Sleep would not come easy for me tonight.

But that was fine.

I needed every bit of time I could salvage so I could think.

- Chapter Fifteen -
Drezden

"What do you think is the most important thing you need to be a good guitarist?"

I lifted my head. My father watched me, his fingers perched like sparrows on the strings of his guitar. *What did you need to be a good guitarist?* It was a weird question. Somehow, I knew it was the most important thing he would ask me.

My lips peeled back to speak. Around me, the world shimmered. My father looked down with a grin so sweet it caused me pain. Above him, the sun burned until sweat ruined my vision.

Then he reached out, bringing horror and the cold reality of existence.

Inhaling sharply, I sat up on the bed. The room was quick to solidify; white walls, the vague hint of the sun through the covered hotel windows. My fingers scraped across my damp forehead.

I hadn't had a dream about my father in some time.

Why now? I wondered, the tickle of his question still rattling my skull. The bed springs squeaked, reminding me of something far more pressing than my haunting memories. Right

239

next to me was the pale shape of another ghost.

Lola breathed peacefully, blanket discarded like she was too warm. The dip of her waist tugged me in, leading me on a journey from her neck to her thighs. *Fucking hell, she's beautiful when she's so vulnerable.* She faced away, showing me her spine, elegant fingers twitching. *I bet she's dreaming of playing her guitar.*

A crude buzzing noise started up. It cut into my moment, infuriating me further when Lola mumbled and shifted. In only my wrinkled shirt, I slid from the mattress just enough to find my discarded jeans. Crushing the source of the awful noise, my phone, I recognized the missed calls from Brenda.

It wouldn't be the first time I'd hung up on her. It would, however, be the first time I'd so easily decided to ignore my responsibilities.

The first time I'm choosing something—someone—over my career.

The implications of that tightened my guts. In an attempt to not dwell, I buried the silent phone deep in my pile of denim. There would be time for introspection later.

Rolling back, I gazed into the bleary blue-eyes of one very naked Lola Cooper. Her hair was tangled over her shoulders, partially hiding the tips of her impossibly perfect breasts. "What is it?" she yawned, still half-asleep.

The second I buried my mouth on hers she woke fully.

"Nothing important," I whispered. Speaking was a waste of air, of time. I needed every bit of existence I had to be spent on Lola. I wanted to taste her again; to claim her, remind her where she was and who *I* was.

Who we both were, now.

It made no fucking sense. I was sure if I tried to explain it, I'd just sound insane. My fingers dragged across her ribs, crushing her deeper into the rumpled blankets. They would have to speak for me.

The knock on the door doused me with ice. Who the hell would dare interrupt me?

"Drez." Lola tightened, paralyzed by... what? The knocking? That did nothing to help my mood. "Go see who it is," she urged me.

I ignored her suggestion to answer the door. I had a pretty good idea what it was about, I just didn't want to acknowledge it.

When the knock came again, followed by the recognizable—and pissed off—voice of Brenda, Lola gave me a hard shove. I sat up enough to stare at her sobering glare. "Go talk to her. It's obviously important."

"Alright, I'm going. Fuck." There was no disguising my disappointment. Peeling off of Lola, I jammed my legs into my briefs and jeans. My cock argued with me the whole time, not wanting to fit into the tight confines of my clothing.

Gripping the door knob, wishing I could snap it off, I yanked it open. Brenda stood there in all her frazzled glory. Her crimson strands were knotted in a messy bun. In spite of all the signs she'd rushed over to my room, she *still* had thrown on some shiny black heels.

She reached out, fingers wrapping in the front of my shirt like she was some tough thug. It would have been funny if her face wasn't twisted in disgust. "What the hell is wrong with you?"

If vipers could talk. I closed my hand over hers pointedly. I was bigger, stronger, and didn't like anyone trying to man-handle me; managers not excepted. "Morning to you, too."

"Don't 'morning' me, you giant dick-hole!" It took everything she had, but she managed to move me a foot forward out into the hall with a solid twist of her body. If being my manager didn't work out, she should consider wrestling. "Ignoring my calls? Are you fucking insane? What were you—" She never finished. I knew what she was seeing around me, or rather, *who* she was seeing. Lola was easy to spot in my bed.

Pushing her further into the hall, I shut the door behind me. "Yeah. She's in there."

For uncounted seconds, Brenda just stared at me. Pulling her arm back, she wiped her palm on the front of her blouse like she'd been touching something slimy. "You aren't

even ashamed about it, are you? Jesus—
Drezden, what were you *thinking?*"

I was thinking that I wanted Lola.
Nothing close to that rolled off my tongue.
Instead, I squinted down at Brenda
thoughtfully. This situation, it almost made me
crave a smoke. Almost. With Lola in my
system, I didn't want for much.

"Brenda," I said slowly, "Sorry about
ignoring your calls. I'll get our stuff and get
down to the bus in five minutes, tops."

Her laugh was crisp and cynical. "Oh no.
You don't get to just walk away from this.
Drezden, *everyone* saw you two grinding
together like horny teens at the club last night!
It's all over the fucking internet, my phone is
blowing up, it's ridiculous! Were you drunk?
Was *she* drunk?"

Prickles went up my neck. "We knew
what we were doing." I wouldn't allow myself
to think otherwise.

"How the hell am I going to hide this?"
She was watching me with... pity? Her
emotions were all over the place. The lack of
lipstick she wore hinted more at her distress
than anything she'd said.

My arms bundled over my chest. "You
aren't going to."

"You're saying you don't think I can?"
she scoffed.

"No. I'm telling you not to bother."

With her hands falling to her sides, my manager froze. "I *have* to hide this. We all have to!"

The vein in her forehead is going to split wide open. There was no room for argument in my tone. "I want the whole damn world to know about Lola and me." *Let them see she's mine.*

Groaning openly, Brenda rubbed at her cheeks until they went raw. "You're joking! Drezden, if I bury this now, people will forget about it in a few days. Maybe less if we give them something else to gossip over. What would make you want to risk losing fans, gaining jealous stalkers, and—and just what are you after here?"

There were a few things that floated up in my mind. *I was the one who told Lola to take the risk. I was the one who wanted this.*

My answer was both frightening and enticing.

"I'm after her." Showing Brenda my back, I twisted the door knob. "We'll be down in five." Without another word, I closed myself away from the world.

Closed myself off from everything but Lola Cooper.

- Chapter Sixteen -
Lola

The instant Drezden left, I was out of the bed. Sitting there nude was too much for me. The shock on Brenda's face when she'd spotted me left me cold with guilt. *I shouldn't feel bad. I didn't do anything wrong.* My confidence was shaken beyond any rationalizing.

The clothes from last night felt itchy and out of place as I slid them on. They smelled entirely like Drezden Halifax. Everything about me did.

Running my fingers down my stomach, I glimpsed myself in the mirror across the room. *I look the same. I just don't feel the same.* Frankly, it baffled me that I didn't feel *more* different than I did.

It was a new day, but I wasn't a new person.

Outside, a single raised voice pricked my ears. Brenda was shouting without bothering to stifle herself. Whatever she was saying was too garbled to discern. I didn't need to hear the details.

Pulling my phone from my pocket, I stared at the missed calls and text messages. My battery was over halfway drained, the time flashing at me, warning me how late in the morning it was. *No wonder she's so pissed. We should have been on the road an hour ago.* Scrolling through my voicemail showed Brenda had called me eleven times.

My brother had texted me just once: 'We need to talk.'

That message tightened my throat. *He knows what Drezden and I did.* Imagining how obvious we'd been at the club, how we'd danced —how we'd kissed—in front of so many people... *If I thought no one would find out, I'm a moron.* A part of me had suspected, maybe even hoped, the world would recognize the pull between the singer and myself.

Faced with the reality in my head-throbbing state was different.

There really is no way to turn the clock back.

Drezden couldn't hide what had happened, either. The lack of options was... freeing. In the world of facts, there was comfort.

The sound of the door opening made me spin around. He entered, seeking me out like a lion on the hunt. Green irises rolled over me, intangible, yet still lifting goosebumps. "Is everything alright?" I croaked, wishing for some water. "Brenda sounded really pissed."

Drezden pounced. The blankets tangled around me, far less constraining than his fingers in my hair. He tasted stale when we

246

kissed, I didn't care about that... he was
intoxicating any time of the day.

But I did care about what my manager
had been upset about.

My limbs felt far away as I nudged them
onto his shoulders. I succeeded in forcing his
lips off of mine. "Drez, what did she say to
you?" The breathy way I spoke wasn't
intimidating. He indulged me, sitting back and
straddling my hips. I was glad I'd dressed. It
would have been astronomical to deny him
anything with only skin between us.

"Take a guess," he said. There was a
strange smile dancing on the corner of his
mouth. I ached to kiss it away, but resisted.

"She's angry about us not being ready
and on the tour bus by now. That," I sighed,
"Or about how I'm in your bed right now."

His fingers crawled down, playing with
the top button of his jeans. Just seeing that had
my heart jumping, wishing he wouldn't go
further while praying otherwise. "Try both."

Both. Of course it's both. Shimmying up
the mattress, I balanced my hands on his
thighs. My goal was to detach, to scramble and
hurry so we could get downstairs and appease
Brenda. I didn't want her mad, I didn't want
anyone mad, I didn't want—

Firm hands closed over mine, pressing
them like flowers meant to dry in a book.
Drezden stopped my struggle. In an instant, he
made me freeze where I was and stare up at

him. *What's that expression he's wearing?* His forehead was scrunched, but his mouth was relaxed. Drez's tone didn't match those tempting lips one bit. "You're upset about this, aren't you?" he asked.

It was such an obvious observation. I had to bite back the laugh of disbelief. "You may be used to Brenda getting mad at you, but I'm not. I don't think I really want to *get* used to it, either."

The tips of his thumbs crept up to caress my earlobes. He waited until I hissed outward; only then did he speak again. "Tell me why this is bothering you, Lola."

"I—what?" *Isn't it clear?*

The turmoil growing in his unfairly handsome face told me it wasn't. "Are you regretting what we did? Regretting last night?"

Last night. Just the words turned my face hot. A thickness overtook my throat, everything numb but my ears under his touch. The power Drezden was so eager to use over me. I didn't care, not right then. What he'd said... *Now I understand what his expression means.*

Drezden thought that *I* thought what we'd done was a mistake.

I couldn't move my arms. With Drezden so near, I didn't need to. The tension in his face melted when I bent forward, closing the gap and kissing him fiercely.

I didn't regret last night.

I *couldn't* regret it.

If I even considered it a mistake, in any capacity, I'd fall too far into brutal shame. My right forearm throbbed at the thought, the tattoo of a castle writhing in my mind.

"Lola," he gasped, releasing me only to trap me again as he gripped my cheeks. The heat in his eyes boiled over. On the edge of the world, I waited to hear what he would say. My heart tangled with my tongue, abandoning me to breathless silence. "I told Brenda we'd be down in five minutes."

It took me a second to devour the words and make sense of them. I was laughing before I knew it. *Of all the things to say in this moment.* Wiping the corner of my eye, my smile stretched wider. "Think she'd mind waiting fifteen?"

"Of course she will." He scratched a nail down my long neck, a path to my collar bone. "She'll hate twenty even more."

My body remembered everything he'd done to me last night. It had done a wonderful job burying the one incident marring the event. When I arched into him, hands trailing down his back, it was the hem of his shirt that reminded me.

That scar. His scar that he hid from me while we were having sex. I'd spotted it without his knowledge while he slept. Confusion raked at my heart; Drez's teeth on my jaw smoothed it all away. His talent in singing warred with his skill in melting my brain.

Beneath us, the springs squealed with his weight on me. Drezden had teased me last night, spoiled me by taking his time. Now, he yanked free the shirt I'd put on only minutes ago. It left my hair tangled, worsened what sleep had done to my brunette strands.

I was battling with the side of me that wanted to just *forget*. Why did I care so much about that stupid scar? Drezden was promising me with his deft fingers, his warm lips, that he could take me away from my paranoid worry. If I just let him break down the shards of concern that warned me he was hiding himself, I could liquefy under his muscles and thrumming chest.

A single hand, reaching between us to stroke the outside of my jeans, won the fight.

I stopped holding on to that one worry.

Metallic teeth vibrated apart, Drez tugging my pants down my thighs. He didn't remove them all the way, just enough to reveal my panties between us. The front of his denim was unyielding with his swelling hard-on. Crushing against me, he ground his hips in gentle waves. If the fabric of my underwear hadn't been ruined last night, it was now.

Circling my arms around his shoulders, I kissed his neck, muted my gasp. I'd craved him after our dance in the club. I thought I couldn't have wanted him more than that. *But then I actually had him. It's worse, knowing what waits.* It was like tasting air, learning to breathe for the first time.

His hand guided to my lower back, forced me to curve my chest against him. With his free fingers, he unbuttoned himself, slipped his pants out of the way. Though it was the texture of his soft briefs and not the roughness of jeans, Drez's erection wasn't gentle.

"Shit," he grunted, hoarse with his need. "We have a problem."

Heat stung my cheeks; he'd stopped moving, but my own hips were bucking against the shape of his cock. The fact there was only thin fabric between us was driving me mad. "What, what's wrong?" *Is it the time, has it already been twenty minutes somehow?*

Drezden paused, caught up as he stared down at me. His inhale was a whistle, and I thrilled knowing I was making him lose control. "Fucking fuck," he said, clenching his jaw. "We used up the only condom I had."

A metallic taste flooded my mouth; disappointment. *How many does he go through if that was his last?* It was a stark reminder of how different our lives were. I didn't carry condoms on me, I'd never thought about needing them on the tour. My expectation of the journey had been hard work and potential opportunities. *All of which have come true, to varying degrees.*

Scrunching his forehead, Drezden dug his palm into my spine. The motion coaxed me to rub my damp panties on his swollen member, both of us moaning in response. "This is damn awful." Laughing as hollow as a drum, Drez shook his head. "How terrible is it that I don't want to stop?" Seemingly goaded on by my whimper, he rocked against me firmly.

Sparks went off in my brain. The pressure inside of me, just from his sliding against the outside of my covered slit, was maddening. "I—then don't." *Don't stop,* I thought selfishly. I knew I was giving him permission to do something dangerous. If I'd made bad choices before in my life, this one trumped them all.

The very last thing I needed was to end up pregnant.

Encouraged by how I was helplessly rubbing against him, legs trembling, Drezden bent low and stole a kiss. The discussion was over; perhaps there was no reason to have one. If he had been giving me an out, I'd missed it. *Was he going to just fuck me anyway?* I wondered in a daze.

Teeth cut against my earlobe. "You really want this, don't you?" he whispered.

All I could manage was a tiny squeak.

His chuckle was sinful, driving my senses higher. Easily, he hooked his fingers into the top of my underwear. The air was cool against my melting pussy.

I couldn't see anything but Drez's temple, his hair tickling my nose. He must have pushed his briefs out of the way, for the smooth, decadent weight of his cock bounced against my belly. "Tell me you want me to fuck you," he taunted, speaking against my throat.

Holy shit. My heart swelled, matching his shaft's reaction. "I want—"

"Say my name when you beg me." Rolling his thighs, he bumped my twitching clit.

Digging my nails into his hips, I tried to force him into me. I was distantly aware of him stiffening at where I touched, but I'd let myself forget why that could even be. "Drezden, just fuck me! Please!"

Groaning long and low, the singer shoved himself inside. There was a hint of soreness in me; I hadn't recovered since he'd stolen my virginity last night. But like then, whatever sharp pain existed was muted by my slippery bundle of desperation. Drezden *owned* my senses.

And, hell, I wanted him to.

Drez held me steady while he pounded into my convulsing pussy. It was lightning, *I* was lightning. The orgasm struck me so fast I didn't know what it was at first. I thought I was having a stroke, my eyes rolling, my bones as stiff as his cock inside of me. "Nngh—that—fuck, I'm coming!"

"Go for it, baby doll," he groaned, shivering over me.

I'd never finished as fast as that, not on my own, not otherwise. Whining with the overwhelming pleasure, I cried out harder as Drez abruptly pulled free. My muscles grabbed for him, tried to trap him inside, but he was too strong. In the fog of my mind, I didn't grasp why he'd abandoned me.

Hot, sticky seed spilled on my navel. Drezden growled during his release. I caught a glimpse of his cock, angry and red, his fist holding it tight over my skin. Fear and delirious excitement flooded my acutely-aware body.

He almost came inside of me. Too many thoughts slammed into my skull, sobering me by the end. *I shouldn't have let that happen, fuck. Did I want him that bad, that I'd risk that?*

I knew the answer.

Sitting up, Drez looked me in the eye. There was no glimmer of fear there. "You're thinking that was stupid, aren't you?"

Biting my lip, I gave a steady nod. "It *was* stupid, Drezden."

Considering me seriously, I watched his half-smile return. "I guess it was. You're just— never mind."

I'm just what? I wished he'd finished his thought.

Standing, he brought me some tissues from the small side table. "I'll make sure not to be caught without protection next time."

A syrup of pure adrenaline settled into my veins. *Next time*.

I loved the sound of that.

****

We'd struggled—or perhaps it was just me—for two days. I'd pushed back on every single craving Drezden caused. I'd worked so *fucking* hard to not buckle at his voice, his smell, or his touch.

Now, I couldn't keep my hands off of him.

In the elevator, we kissed with furious passion around our pile of luggage. If I thought I was addicted, Drezden was truly obsessed. Even when I was gathering my items from my room, he'd been unable to stop touching me.

His mouth moved down to my shoulder. In the mirrors, I saw my snowy neck was red and purple. This man, this impossible man, he wanted to mark me from head to toe.

But I want that. I want him to brand me.

The knowledge of my desire rippled down to my pussy. The world would see me and know I belonged to Drezden Halifax. *Yes. I think I'm pretty damn okay with that*.

255

We stumbled out of the elevator, the air in the lobby fresh, bursting with the promise of a wonderful day. Standing in the white light, Brenda looked like a glowing phantasm. Her features were bound tight as a sausage in its casing.

Drezden was right. She didn't like that twenty minutes we stole.

Marching up to us, our manager jerked her head towards the door. "Hurry up and get in the bus, Drez." It was a simple command. Looking upwards, I spotted the casual shrug Drezden gave her. It was quick, his long legs pacing him out of the hotel.

"Brenda," I started, fingers crushing my guitar case. *What do I even say?*

She was already walking away. "We'll talk in the car."

"I—the car?" My feet quit on me, leaving me standing in the lobby. I was alone for a brief moment before I hurried out into the parking lot with my bag bouncing behind me.

The whole lot had been blocked off by cars and orange cones, my tour bus waiting by the curb. Security had created a wall across the pavement, keeping the milling crowd at bay.

We'd clearly caused a hiccup in the schedule. Otherwise, they'd never have brought the bus to the hotel. This was an easy target for fans to swarm us.

Brenda was hovering near the bus steps, I jogged towards her with my bag dragging behind me. "Hey! What do you mean we'll talk in the car?"

She peeked up at me from her phone. "You're riding with me for a bit."

"No, she isn't," Drez said. He was standing in the bus, staring down on us. I saw the look in his eyes I knew all too well. It was the same look he'd given Brenda when she'd pleaded with him to let me get promo photos taken.

He doesn't like hiccups in his plans, and his plan was to ride with me.

Snatching up my bag, Brenda laughed. "Oh yes, she is." I covered my mouth, amazed at the way she shoved the luggage into him hard enough to make him stumble back on the stairs. Behind him, I spotted Porter and Colt. Their faces shifted from amusement to discomfort when they saw me.

What are they thinking? Chewing my bottom lip just made it rawer. *They know about last night, about Drez and me. Are they angry, disgusted? What?*

Drezden pushed the bag behind him, moving to follow after Brenda as she returned to my side. "I said she isn't! Why does she need to go with you?"

"Drez, man, calm down," Colt muttered. The lanky man gripped Drez's upper arm, but the singer shoved him off.

Like a wall, Brenda blocked me from the group's eyes. "One, you guys keep complaining

257

about food on the bus. I'm going to get some shopping done. And two..." She never blinked as she stared me down, even if her words were meant for all of us. "Lola and I need to talk."

Warily, I fiddled with my messy hair under all the attention. She made me cringe, made me shrink. Brenda was too much like an intimidating mother. I'd left home to get *away* from tactics like this.

Swallowing down the acid that rose, I reminded myself that Brenda was *not* one of my parents. "What if I don't want to go with you?"

She only gripped her hips at my question, but it was a silent snarl in my ears. "Believe me," she said, and amazingly, I noticed something akin to sympathy in her soft brown eyes, "You *want* to come with me, Lola."

It wasn't much of a stand-off. Brushing past her, I walked towards the bus. Drez's green eyes welled with satisfaction the closer I got to him. It pained me to destroy his assumption that he'd won. Standing on the bottom step, I handed him my guitar, whispering into his ear. "I'm riding with her, Drez. I think it might smooth over some of what we've done if I can talk to her privately."

His grimace was as chilling as arctic snow. Wordlessly, he curled his warmth around me, lips connecting with mine and flooding my brain with whiteout.

Thumbing my chin, Drezden stared at me with mild frustration. My ears were still ringing when he sighed. "Fine. Give me your phone."

Everything moved sluggishly. I saw the way Colt and Porter were staring at us, saw how Drez pointedly ignored them. Somehow my phone was in my palm, then in Drez's fingers. "Are you giving me your number?" I asked, blushing over such a normal thing. *It's because it's so normal. People usually do that before they—well.*

His nod was quick. "Call me if anything happens."

"Like what?" Taking back my phone, I held it tight and enjoyed the warmth he'd left on its surface.

He squeezed the edge of the door. Every tendon in his arm flexed beautifully. "It doesn't matter what. If you need to call me, for any reason you can come up with, just do it."

I didn't notice I was smiling until my face ached. The moment was shattered by Colt, his shaved head pressing in close beside Drez's. "Hey, you want my number too? I might not get *as* lonely as Drez, but I do love hearing a woman's voice."

"Hey, whoa," Porter scoffed. His beefy shoulders squeezed into the doorway of the bus, shoving the singer out further. "I thought you only liked when *I* called you, man! Fuck this, you trying to make me jealous?"

"Who'd try to make *you* jealous?" Colt snapped, waving a hand side to side. He hit Drez's nose in the process, ignoring the man's grunt as he kept talking over him and at Porter. "Have you even brushed your teeth yet this morning?"

"That hurts, man." The bassist frowned as deep as he could, eyes shutting. "Right in the heart. Damn."

The ball of fear that had been hatching in me like a rotten egg... it dissipated. *They're trying to make me laugh, aren't they?* These guys, these ridiculously talented guys, they wanted me to see they weren't angry at me. Whatever had happened last night, they were doing their best to show me nothing had changed between all of us.

Brenda tugged me backwards, clearly exasperated. "Could you guys not make us even more late? Get on the bus, get going. We'll meet up with you later."

Shrugging her off, I flashed my band a smile and waved. "See you all after!"

"Make sure she buys some fruit!" Porter shouted, so close to Drez's ear that the singer grimaced.

In a smooth motion, Drez knocked the bassist back into the bus. Then he nodded at me. "Remember what I said." His hand reached down, patting his pocket.

In answer, I tapped where my phone was tucked away. Did he think it was possible for me to forget what he'd said? As far as I was concerned, I'd never forget a single word Drezden Halifax told me.

Not now.

Not ever.

****

The wind felt wonderful as we sped down the highway. The silence in the car, however, did not. Brenda had commandeered a hatchback. I didn't ask her who she'd taken it from, and she didn't offer the info.

Now, as we tore down the asphalt with every window open and the breeze screaming in our ears, I waited for her to say... something. *For someone so insistent on getting me alone to talk, she's been patiently biting her tongue.*

Abruptly, the windows went up. The noise was suctioned away; I missed it dearly. It was all that had been keeping things from becoming fully awkward.

Not looking at me, she said, "So. What the hell were you thinking last night?"

"Excuse me?" I squinted at her stoic profile as she watched the road. *Alright. No warm-up. She wants to jump right in.*

"You know what I'm talking about, Lola."

Of course I knew. But with such a blunt question, how could I answer? I'd been running through the steps all day. I barely understood my decision myself, how could I explain it to her?

I opened my mouth, then closed it. Licking my lips didn't make speaking any easier. "I don't know if 'thinking' is the right word."

"Well, at least *you* said it first."

I tightened my lips. "I mean; I *did* think about it. For a while I thought about it. I didn't... last night didn't happen because I wasn't thinking. It happened because I let out my—" *My what? Urges? Desires?* My tongue stuck to the roof of my mouth.

Brenda was keen to assist me. "Hormones?"

Every bit of skin welled up and became pink. "No! Would you give me a break?"

"I *am* giving you a break." She changed lanes fast, pushing me deeper into my seat. "It might not seem like it, but this whole thing— Lola, I'm going easy on you."

"This is you being easy?" Scratching my scalp, I forced a tiny smile. "Tell me why you're so pissed off."

"I'm sorry, was it not obvious?" Brenda sped up, making me expect police sirens any second. "I thought you were smart. Did you not think for one minute about how badly this could go? About how easy it would be for you two to mess up and tear this band apart?"

My brows merged together. "That's all I've thought about since the start." She shot me a sideways look, then eyed the road again. "Brenda, I really did consider all of that. Yeah, I'm not stupid, I *know* bands get ruined by members dating."

"Dating!" Her burst of laughter was acrid. "You guys aren't even—are you serious? You and Drez had a drunken fling, that's all it was."

Squirming in my seat, I folded my arms. *No. It was more than that. He kissed me this morning in front of everyone. He wants more than a one-night stand.*

And so do I.

My brooding silence stretched until Brenda cracked first. I finally caught a hint of her exhaustion. "Sorry. That came out wrong. Let me ask you this. Knowing how this could freak out the fans, how it could make crazy people crazier, would you consider letting me hide this?"

The question burned down into my belly. It made me forget I hadn't eaten that morning. In the side-mirror, I rubbed my neck where the soft bruises left by Drezden still lingered. *Could* this be hidden? Did I want it to be?

My hand fell from my throat. "I won't pretend nothing happened."

Her huff of air was full of bitter amusement. "I suspected as much. He said something similar this morning."

"Wait, he? Drezden?" Blinking, I watched as she pulled off the highway and down a curved exit ramp. The large, white Super Mart building rose up before us.

Gliding into a parking space, Brenda pulled two pairs of sunglasses from her fat purse. One of them was offered my way as she said, "I think you're both going to regret this. But at least you're in agreement about wanting the same thing. That's something. Put these on."

The dark glasses hid away the puffy skin under my eyes. "Drezden really said he didn't want to hide us away?" The knowledge pushed my heart into my ribs.

"He told me he wanted the whole world to know." She must have seen my smile, because she met it with a worried frown. "I'm not going to lie. I think this whole thing between you two is going to go badly." Shaking her head, she slid her glasses into place. Her voice was soft as she exited the car, talking more to herself than me. "I swear, this band gives me nothing but trouble. I should never have taken them on."

I wasn't listening. I was busy wandering in my head, relishing what Brenda had told me.

Drezden Halifax wanted the *world* to know about us.

My heart was racing to prove it could beat faster, harder, and longer than any other heart in existence. I wanted everyone to know about me and the singer. In the grocery store, I fought off the insane desire to run up to a counter and scream about it through the intercom. Drezden was mine, mine, mine.

And I was his.

Most of the shopping went by in a daze. Brenda, ever the organizer, had a list. We filled a cart to the brim with everything from coffee to cereal to the fruit Porter had demanded. It seemed like a lot of stuff, but thinking about the three men, it might have been too little.

With our sunglasses on and being just the two of us, Brenda was convinced no one would recognize me; I was too new to the band, she was just the manager. Without a tour bus in the parking lot or security swarming, no one batted an eye our way.

A familiar voice crackled out of a television stuck in the far wall of the store. I knew those gritty lyrics too well to ignore them. On the screen, a news channel was playing shots from Four and a Half Headstones and the tour. At first, my reaction was blushing glee. There I was—on stage!

Then the feed switched, showing police on another scene. I stopped in my tracks to stare. There, split lipped and haggard, was a man I'd managed to forget existed.

Johnny Muse.

He was being led away in cuffs, his teeth stained red as he shouted. I'd never seen him so upset, so... broken. The time between being kicked out of the band and now, a time that felt so short to me, had left a lifetime of ruin on the former guitar player's face.

He glared at the camera as he was shoved into a police car. It was a split second, his green eyes burning into me. They were *seeing me,* even if I knew that was impossible. I started to shiver.

"Lola?" Brenda stood next to me, sunglasses hiding her expression. I didn't need to respond, she'd seen the television. Even in my grim fog, I could feel the distress wafting from her. "Oh, son of a—is he really getting air time over this?" The phone was in her hand, long nails stabbing the buttons.

My fingers ached when I squeezed them together. Something about being confronted with Johnny's sky-dive into destruction was scaring me. *This is what's happened to him since Drezden kicked him out.* I swallowed around the sand in my throat. *I've replaced him. Does he know that, has he seen me on stage, playing with his former friends?*

I was being worshiped in the media. He was being destroyed.

In my soul, I was sure Johnny Muse loathed me.

"Hey." Brenda flicked her cellphone shut. "Hey, Lola. Snap out of it. You okay?"

266

My head moved neither up or down. I didn't know if I was okay or not. "It's weird to see him like that. Why did he get arrested? What happened, when was that?"

We both heard her phone buzzing in her purse; she didn't move to retrieve it. "I'd say you should check the internet for once, but honestly? I'd rather you didn't see what people were saying about you and Drezden." My mouth twisted at her comment, but she only pressed on with a groan. "This band is going to kill me from stress. Johnny sort of... after he got kicked out so unceremoniously, he tried to get in touch with me. He called me from prison —"

"*Prison?*"

She hushed me, looking around at the milling, mostly empty store. "Jesus, not so loud. It's not as bad as it sounds. That time it wasn't, I mean. The night Drez hit him, he was wasted and going insane so the cops just put him in a cell to sober up. He called me around six in the morning the next day. Of course, I already knew about the whole situation by then."

Everything I'd heard about Johnny and Drezden had been in regards to the fight. The aftermath had escaped my mind. "What did he say to you?"

"Just tried to talk me into overruling Drez." Those strawberry lips quirked. "I knew better than that. Drez formed the band,

267

keeping Johnny in would have just made it all fall apart permanently." Her tiny smile faded. "I sent someone to bail him out after we signed your contract. There was never any clause saying we couldn't kick him—or anyone—out."

My fingers curled, recalling how the pen had felt when it ran over those crisp white papers. "You waited to bail him out until our bus had left."

Thin eyebrows flitted over the rims of her glasses. "I knew he was angry. Figured it was safe to get out of there. But honestly, I never thought Johnny would do anything. He's immature, not dangerous."

"You thought he would cause *some* trouble, though."

"Trouble as in causing a scene." Brenda pushed the cart of groceries towards the front of the store. I followed behind, bending in to hear her low grumble. "Which he did last night."

Last night. Those words didn't give me the same warm thrill they had before. No, now they sent tremors down my spine. "Tell me what he did."

Her jaw, normally such an elegant curve, hardened. "The idiot got drunk, no surprise there, and caused a brawl trying to get into the club he knew you and Drez were at. It's lucky that you two left before he arrived or he might have punched one of you, instead."

268

I covered my mouth, my eyeballs straining. "He *what?*"

"Got drunk. Punched a security officer." The cart bumped into the check-out counter. Brenda turned one sharp heel, leaning in so close I could smell her minty breath. "When I told Drezden I could smooth over the gossip about you and him, I meant it. Johnny's insanity will be just as much of a headline, or even bigger. He's sitting in jail right now, he can't give his side of the story, we can cause a real fuss."

"How do you know all this?" I gripped the cart tighter. "Fuck, did he ask you to bail him out a second time?"

Digging her phone from her purse, Brenda sighed. "Nope. He didn't bother to call me. I was trying to find out more details about the mess, if the guard is pressing charges or what." She waved the phone at me, the screen glowing. "So far, no one can tell me what's up. I hate not knowing the details."

The slim shot that Johnny Muse wasn't in jail, that no one could tell us where he was... it was as good as a punch to the gut. "Should we call Drezden and warn him?" I was already retrieving my cell phone.

She dropped a bag of apples onto the conveyor belt. The fruit made a heavy sound, rolling toward the bored cashier. "By now, the guys have told him everything. They were both at the club when Johnny showed up."

I wanted to ask more, but my manager had turned towards the abruptly cheerful face of the cashier. They both wore false smiles, chattering away with pointless pleasantries as the numbers on the register stacked up.

Reaching down, I lifted a plastic container of coffee grounds from the cart. My goal was to stay busy. I had to keep myself from dwelling on this foreboding news.

It was no use. I kept picturing Drez's face when he'd told me about Johnny. He'd looked like a bushel of snakes waiting to strike. That had been days ago, what would be his reaction when he learned about the close call between us and Johnny Muse last night?

If we'd been slower... we might have spent our evening in a hospital instead of Drez's hotel room. Pushing back my hair, I inhaled until my stomach swelled. *No. Drezden wouldn't have gone down.* The singer was huge, fast, and I'd experienced his strength.

He'd also promised that he'd *ruin* Johnny if he ever saw him again.

I had no reason to doubt it.

That was the one thing that gave me enough courage to stop fretting over the fact that I might have a violent man coming after me. Even so, as we headed out towards Brenda's car with our purchases rolling in the shopping cart...

I didn't stop looking over my shoulder until I was buckled in.

- Chapter Seventeen -
Drezden

Coffee dripped on my shoes. It stained my jeans, burned where it had soaked through to my skin. Everything screamed for me to find cold water, a towel, anything.

I didn't fucking care.

"Whoa, Drez!" Porter stammered, hands rising while he stood nervously in the middle of the aisle. "Holy shit! Calm down man, let me get you a rag or—or something."

"Tell me again." There was a quiet threat on my tongue. Porter and Colt had heard it before; the wary look in both their faces said enough.

The drummer remained in his seat. I could tell from the tightness around his eyes that he was doing his best to control the adrenaline flooding his veins. "I said you missed the action last night. Yeah, you fucking heard me. Johnny came around looking for you."

Johnny. Johnny Johnny Johnny. The crushed Styrofoam cup fell from my fist. The noise it made when it landed was hollow. "That's what I thought you said." *That piece of shit actually dared to show his face. Did he want to fight, to get back at me for kicking him out?*

Wiping my palms on my shirt, I debated reaching for my cigarettes. It wouldn't have done any good if I had. After last night with Lola I hadn't bothered to replace my empty pack.

Lola.

Imagining her face was enough to turn my rage into something just as heated, yet different. *Johnny thinks he can waltz in after a show as good as last night and—what? Try and change my mind? Get me to take him back?*

The idea was laughable.

Lola is the best replacement I could have dreamed of. I dug my nails into my opposite shoulder. I wanted to pretend they were hers, that she was clawing at me desperately like she had this morning. Knowing the girl wasn't here, on my bus, made my skull pound.

And Johnny would dare fucking show up and interrupt— A sudden wave of paranoia dropped my jaw.

"Drez?" Porter risked coming closer, approaching like I was some rabid animal. "Hey, you alright? Don't worry about anything. They arrested Johnny, he's probably sitting drunk in some cell, his usual motif. You know that."

I'd heard him, but I was too busy working through my nugget of worry. *Johnny might not have been there to talk to me.*

Cramps wormed into my guts. *There's a chance he was looking...*

Looking for Lola.

"Drez, man, snap out of it!" My bassist squeezed my shoulder. The touch sent me reeling, eyes focusing on his furrowed brow. If it weren't for the familiar worry in Porter's eyes, I would have pushed him off of me.

My fingers pinched the bridge of my nose. "I'm fine. Just pissed that Johnny would have the balls to show up like that."

"It's not about balls," Colt snorted. "He's always been a little nuts. I figured that was why you picked him years ago."

The reminder that I'd chosen Johnny to be in my band didn't make me feel any better. I'd been sure he'd work out, he'd played better than anyone else who'd auditioned. That day, listening to the people who'd shown up in Colt's garage, it had been eye opening.

We'd had so few people. Especially compared to the line fighting for a chance at the gas station on this tour.

If only Lola had shown up back then.

Instead, her brother had. Pursing my lips, I brushed Porter off of me. Gripping a handful of napkins from a cupboard, I mopped at the coffee on my skin and clothes. "I was too optimistic back then," I mumbled.

That had both of the boys laughing. "You think you were in a better mood *then?*" Porter

273

asked, sharing a meaningful look with Colt. "Man, your memory is broken or something."

"Yeah?" Throwing the wet paper ball at the bassist, I crossed my arms. "You think I'd bring on Johnny today with how he is?"

"I'm talking less about Johnny, and more about a certain someone bringing out a side of you I've never seen you show before," Porter said.

With careful patience, I lowered my hands to my hips. "You want to try and fucking lecture me like Brenda did?"

"You could use a lecture." Colt rose up with a grunt. In a smooth motion, he swayed my way without a hint of fear in his eyes. If anything, he looked like he was judging *me*. "Maybe a few, now that I think about it."

In that small corner of the bus, I felt the scrutinizing stares of my band mates. We'd spent so much time together, even before forming Four and a Half Headstones. Rarely did they become so intense with me.

I owed them my ear. "Say what's on your mind," I grunted. "Both of you. Just get it all off your fucking chests."

Palming his skull, Colt grit his teeth in preparation.

Porter spoke first, his hand coming down, landing on the table so hard it reverberated through the bus. "Drez, just tell us the truth. Is this thing—you and Lola—going to mess up the tour?"

"Not just the tour." Colt jutted his chin at me. "Everything. You and her, you going to turn us into some shit show? Tear us apart and leave us like some forgotten group of nobodies?"

"Of course not!" I straightened as disgust rushed up my spine. I wanted to do something with this energy, this angry flood of emotions, but there was no place to channel it. It left me on edge, molars creaking from clenching them. "You're actually worried I'd do something like that?"

Colt hunched his shoulders, reminding me of a vulture. "I don't know. Maybe not intentionally, but come on. She's been with us a few days, played one single damn show!" His voice rose, the skin around his mouth going pale. "You couldn't keep your dick in your pants long enough for her to integrate with us better? What *is* it about her that's turned you so—so..."

"What?" I didn't remember stepping forward. My face was mere inches from Colt's, pressure thrumming in my temples. "Turned me so fucking what? Say it."

He stared me down. I knew Porter was still beside us, but he didn't exist. It was just me and Colt, horns locked on the verge of a fight. One beat, two beats; my heart counted as I waited for him to answer me.

Unblinking, he finally did. "Selfish. You kicked Johnny out because he was putting this

275

band at risk. Now you're willing to be the one who breaks us apart. Why? What changed?"

Even with all my built up rage, I had no answer. I sensed their surprise when I turned away, effectively abandoning the challenge. *He's right. When did I start caring more about getting what I want—no. I always chased what I wanted.*

But when did that turn into Lola Cooper?

Like my bones had melted, I fell into a leather seat. "I don't know what changed. You're right," I said, watching them both in resignation, "Something has. But it doesn't matter. Call it selfish all you want, you'd be spot on. I want to have Lola *and* I want this band to succeed. I want both."

Porter's voice was swimming with sadness. "*Can* you have both?"

It was the question I hadn't wanted to hear. I felt the answer bubble up before I could think on it. "Yeah. I can." There was a certainty in my response that didn't reflect my internal struggle.

Was it possible to have both Lola and my band?

If I had to choose between them—*No. I don't need to choose.*

I don't need to pick one or the other.
I fucking refuse to.

Exhaling loudly, Colt's skinny arms folded behind his head. "As long as I don't need

276

to hear you and her banging at night on this bus, I'll zip my lips."

It was as close to acceptance as I could expect from him right then. Grinning sideways, I helped break the tension. "No promises there."

Porter laughed first. It was contagious, all of us letting the sound escape while tension evaporated from our bodies. It was a reminder that we were all friends. It was a reminder that I needed.

With their worries spoken and the air cleared, we hung out on the bus and reveled in the comfortable quiet. The world rolled past, Colorado looking especially beautiful that sunny day.

Though I smiled at Colt's jokes, or shared eye-rolls with Porter when they fell flat, my mind roamed. The silent cellphone in my pocket began to feel like a throbbing tumor. I touched it, ran my fingers over the shape and waited.

We were an hour out from Aspen, the location of our next show that very night, and I still hadn't heard from Lola. An itch of worry grew, similar to my craving for tobacco. *She hasn't messaged me. Are her and Brenda that busy shopping for food? No, it's more than that. She wanted to get Lola alone.*

I imagined Brenda trying to talk Lola into hiding what had happened, like she'd tried with me this morning. It curdled my blood.

Lola won't agree to that. She couldn't. Honestly, I wouldn't let her try. My mind ran with the idea. I pictured Lola attempting to slink into the shadows. Or worse, turning away as I got close.

But that would be all she could manage, I thought fiercely. My hands squeezed the tops of my thighs. *I'd chase her down, steal her lips, her tongue, in front of every single pair of eyes watching.* I burrowed my nails in further. *If she dared to try and turn herself, us, invisible, I'll just have to expose our relationship to the fucking world.*

Relationship.

Mountains rolled by, but I didn't see them. *That's the word for this, isn't it? I want her—need her—to the point of insanity.*

What else could this be but a relationship?

A smile tugged at the corner of my lips. *So that makes me her boyfriend. I like the sound of that.* Again, I fondled the silent cellphone. *I'd like the sound of her voice more right now.*

Porter dropped down across from me, his dark eyes focusing. "You're worried. What's wrong?"

"Why do you think I'm worried?" My hands loosened on my legs.

Rolling a palm over his faux-hawk, Porter's chuckle was gentle. "It's like you forget

278

how well I know you, man. I know that face you're making."

I glanced at my reflection in the window. *No use arguing.* "Fine, you win." He lifted an eyebrow, silently prompting me to keep talking. "We'll be at the venue in two hours. Show starts at five."

"You're wondering where Brenda and Lola are."

"Yeah. Guess I am." I checked my phone, making sure it wasn't dead.

He spread his fingers on the table, fanned them wide. "Here's an idea. You look like shit, why not go take a shower and take your mind off things?"

"For someone who knows me so well, you're naive to expect some hot water could wash away my thoughts." Some of my teeth flashed. "It's a good idea, still. I should clean up before tonight's show."

"It's a genius idea," Colt added, kicking his feet up where he was lounging. "I've been smelling you all day. Just doing the polite thing and not mentioning it."

"Always so kind," the bassist snorted.

Digging a finger in his ear, Colt knotted his eyebrows. "Just doing my part."

Leaving the pair behind, I strolled down the aisle. Passing by Lola's bunk, my feet stuck on the rug. The curtain hung limp, hiding what I knew was her empty bed. Even with that knowledge, I brushed the cloth aside, confirming the messy blankets were bare. Closing my eyes, I let the curtain fall.

Stepping into the bathroom, I stripped down and ducked under the water-spout. Cranking the knobs, I hung my head and let the steam wash over me. But the shower couldn't get hot enough. I'd turned it on full blast, wishing it would rip the skin from my bones.

The thoughts from my brain.

Lola is fine, everything is fine. Spreading my hands on the wall, I slung my chin low. The drain, swirling with water, was my focus. *She'll be back soon. Then, I can have her to myself.* It was what I was hanging on for.

Wet lashes touched my cheeks, my mind wandering with images of the girl from last night... from this morning. She'd been fucking perfect. A vision of carnal purity that had left me panting, left me groaning for more.

I touched my chest, feeling the dip between my muscles. It was easy to imagine Lola against me. Those pert breasts, tips hard as nails and burying into my skin. *No,* I reminded myself sullenly, *I didn't feel her like that. I kept my shirt on like some shy kid at his first public swimming pool.*

Whipping my hair back, I grabbed for the sponge hanging from the shower spout. It scoured on my flesh, over my stomach and down my thighs. *Did she wonder about that?* Reaching behind, the sodden sponge rolled over my lower back. *Did she think I was being bashful?* The idea was laughable.

Gingerly at first, then with snarling gusto, I scrubbed at the scar.

I wasn't ready to let her see.

I didn't want her questions to ruin the moment.

Turning in place, I looked back at the old wound. It had been over seven years, yet still, the injury haunted me. I hated everything about it; what it represented.

Closing my eyes, I thought about the dream—the nightmare—that had ripped me from sleep this morning. *Will I ever escape that chunk of my life? Escape him?*

Inhaling, choking on wetness, I focused on how amazing my time with Lola had been. Dropping the sponge, I begged for more scalding water; something to blind me from my memories, from everything I didn't want.

The shower handle brought nothing.

- Chapter Eighteen -
Lola

"Maybe I should have tipped him."

Pulled from my stupor, I found Brenda watching me. "Sorry, what?"

The red-head shifted in the driver's seat, fingers drumming the wheel anxiously. "The kid who helped us load everything into the trunk. He looked exhausted, probably working himself to death." Turning in place, she squinted out into the parking lot. "Maybe I can still catch him."

"I—what?" None of this was making sense to me. Maybe it was my distracted brain, still full of Drez's cryptic words and Johnny's intimidating face on the television. "Brenda, wait! Where are you going?"

She didn't look back, her body slipping out the door so she could stomp across the pavement. I leaned over to watch, amazed at the sight of her speeding on her heels after the scrawny teenager in the distance. *She's that worried about someone she doesn't even know?* It was a side of Brenda I hadn't seen before—*No,* I corrected myself mentally. *If I think about it, when I auditioned for Headstones...*

Didn't she show me a similar kindness?

That day, sweltering in the sun, my now-manager had stared at me under her giant hat and told me I'd failed the 'test' Drezden had given her. That damn question, I'd forgotten all about it.

What do you think is the most important thing you need to be a good guitarist?

And I had said honesty.

Brenda was speaking to the boy, shoving something into his hands. From where I was in the car, I could see his confused—if pleased—wide eyes. On her ruby lips, Brenda's smile came and went like a blink. By the time she reached me again, she was all business. "Sorry about that," she said, sliding in and shutting the door gently.

"It's fine." I felt my helpless grin taking hold.

Glancing at me, Brenda froze. "Why are you making that face?"

"No reason," I said, covering my mouth in a poor attempt to hide my amusement. "I'm just... I guess I'm happy to see you being so nice."

Instead of answering right away, the sound of the engine did it for her. The car jerked forward, slamming me into the seat while Brenda roared out of the parking lot. It wasn't until we were on the long, empty swatch of the freeway that she said anything. "There's nothing wrong with helping people."

"No," I agreed softly, "There's not." My heart swelled, driving a glow of warmth to my face. It was a strange revelation, one that I needed. It put a perspective on Brenda's anger, her frustration, with Drez and myself. *She's worried about us.*

How could I ever be mad at anyone for that?

I expected us to drive for some time, so when she guided the car off another exit, I wrinkled my forehead. Soon, a sprawling mall appeared in the distance. "I noticed you were running out of outfits," Brenda said. "Can't have our new star looking so run down."

"Do we have the time for this? The next show is tonight."

The flat look she gave me said volumes. "Lola, take a second and remember who I am. Do you really think your manager would make a stop like this if there wasn't time?" Narrowing her eyes, she pushed my patience with a long pause. "We're only two hours out from the venue. If we take an hour to shop, we'll still roll in with time to spare before sound check."

Fidgeting in my seat, I nodded. "Guess I'm just anxious."

Her smile cut across her face. "Too anxious to let me buy you some new jeans?"

We shared a pointed look down at my dirty, torn denim. "No," I chuckled, "Not too anxious for that at all."

"Good." She pointed at the sunglasses on my head. "Then pop those back into place, and let's do some *extremely* incognito shopping."

****

The mall was huge, packed with people in spite of the afternoon hour. Escalators poured the milling shoppers out on every floor, groups of teenagers huddling in clumps. I'd never been much of a mall-girl. It was the place the 'cool' kids gathered.

That had never been me.

It's so weird, I thought, squinting at everyone from behind my glasses—my mask. *I was always too nervous to come to places like these because I didn't want anyone to see me. Now, I'm hiding for a reason so similar... but so fucking different.*

Way fucking different.

This was nothing like being a scared kid, wary of the judging looks.

Lola Cooper wasn't weak or ashamed.

She—I—was a damn rock god now.

"In here," Brenda said, cutting through my swelling, confusing pride. She led the way into a busy store, the sign reading 'Glam Grime' in giant jagged letters.

Inside, the walls were coated with denim everything. Pants, skirts, even leggings. Colors of ebony and gold dust; the grungy, intentional style of people who made real money and could afford the perks.

It was the sort of place I'd always ached to shop at.

Turning in place, I lost sight of Brenda. Glam Grime was big, a second floor climbing above on twisting stairs. *When she said we'd go shopping, I imagined just some new jeans and a tank-top or two. Can I afford this?* The reminder that, yes, of course I could—I was hiding for a reason—came in the form of an approaching clerk.

The woman had on giant, dangling earrings and a glittery smile. "Hey there! Need help finding anything?"

"Oh, uh." *Shit, should I be speaking to people?* My brain wrapped around itself. The memory of Drezden standing in the hotel and smooth talking the receptionist came forward. He'd worn sunglasses, too, until he wanted to reveal his identity. *Talking is fine, she won't know who I am. I'm still too new, right?* "I was just... looking for jeans."

"Then you want that wall," she said, gesturing over my head. "If you need anything else, just ask."

My hair flopped as I nodded. "Awesome, thanks!" I followed where she pointed, forcing down a wave of nerves. A set of firm fingers closing down on my shoulder just spiraled me back to square one. "Ah! Jesus, Brenda!"

Scowling tightly, she stared over her glasses at me. "Focus, would you? Don't go making chit-chat with strangers in here. We have a job to do."

"Yeah, I know," I mumbled. Shaking her free, I moved to the wall of pants. "I was trying to *do* that job. That woman back there was just showing me where to go."

"I could have shown you if you'd been following me." Smoothing her hair behind her ears, Brenda started picking through the clothing. "Incognito, right?"

Biting the inside of my cheek, I just nodded. I *had* been incognito. There was no way the employee had recognized me. *I don't think so, anyway.* Darting a look over my shoulder, imagining eyes burning into me, I frowned.

The two of us wandered the displays, my fingers drifting over the articles of clothing. Brenda would stop occasionally, forcing something into my arms while pointedly ignoring my dubious stare. Once I was trembling with the weight of it all, I coughed. "This is too much. Let me get a basket to carry it easier."

"Don't waste your time." Leaning over me, she waved at the far wall. "Lug it all back to the changing room. We don't have the luxury of dilly-dallying here. Just try everything on,

287

decide what you want to keep, and then we'll get out of here."

She's so business, even when the topic is playing dress-up. Brenda reminded me of my brother. "Alright. If I don't come back soon, send help," I laughed, grimacing while I walked away. "I've probably been crushed by all of these clothes."

In the far corner of the store, the changing room was easy to miss. There was no one standing around running it. *Hope they don't think I'm trying to steal any of this.* I would have felt more comfortable if someone *had* been around to see me go in, or to count my items and hand me one of those tiny plastic numbered cards.

Inside the hall there were four doors, my only companion was the pop-music piping in through the speakers. It reminded me of the time of day, how most teen-shoppers would be just getting out of school. *This place will be flooded later. Brenda's right, we shouldn't waste time,* I thought grimly. *Even if I'm new to the band, after last night...* The memory of being on stage, basking in the glow of the crowd, sent a rush to the base of my brain. *There's a good chance people might recognize me.*

But could that really be so bad?

In the mirror, I studied myself in a new pair of dark denim jeans. They clung to me fantastically. In my tall boots I looked like a beast from hell, and I thrilled at the idea. *I'm getting addicted to the thought of being noticed, of being out there while thrashing music free from my guitar.*

Goosebumps lifted with my delight. *I'm changing, aren't I?* With no one to answer my silent musing but me, I brushed it away and slid the jeans to my ankles. The sight of my own lower back in the mirror reminded me of the long scar on a certain singer.

Drezden. My eyes fixed on my reflection, but I wasn't really seeing myself. *I wish I could just pretend I never saw that. He clearly didn't want me to see the scar, but why?* Too many questions, too much paranoia, flooded my mind.

The sound of someone knocking on my door turned my heart into an earthquake. "S— sorry! Someone's in this one," I said, quickly bending down to pull my old jeans back on. Below the edge of the door, a pair of white flats waited. Whoever was outside my door wasn't moving or speaking.

Swallowing down a wave of unease, I squinted at those feet. "Hey," I said briskly, "Didn't you hear me? Do you need something?" *Maybe it's the girl who runs the changing rooms.* The thought was a flicker of comfort over my rising tide of warning.

In front of my eyes, the feet shifted until whoever it was stood on the tips of their toes. I knew what I would see even before I tilted back my head. That was, in a way, the worst part of it all.

Gawking at me over the top of the door was a young woman, maybe my age. Her hair was a mess of blonde ringlets, thick eyeliner piled on to match her dramatic crimson lips. The lines on her forehead spoke a weird mixture of shock and disgust. "It *is* you!" she gasped, fingers digging into the wood.

I'd removed my sunglasses in the safety of the room. Now, faced with the seeking stare of a stranger, I wished I hadn't. The girl flicked her accusing look from my pale face, down to my right arm; I knew she was eyeing my tattoo. *I'm an idiot. Of course someone would recognize my tattoo.*

Narrowing my eyes, I blindly felt around for my sneakers. "What the hell are you doing? Get out of here!"

"You're really her," she whispered.

I crouched, shoving my feet into my shoes. *Yes,* I thought while I tangled the laces. *Yes, I'm her. I'm the new guitarist for Four and a Half Headstones, Lola Coop—*

"You're the fucking *bitch* who's trying to steal our Drezden away!"

My world slowed down around me. It took a great effort to raise my chin and gape up at the contorted rage in the blonde's expression. "I don't—what?" *Bitch? Stealing?*

I could see the gums in her mouth; bloodless, drained in tight fury. "Yeah! That's

290

you! It's all over the fan sites, pictures of you throwing yourself at him after the show last night! How dare you try that, isn't it selfish to take our Drezden away? Isn't it?"

My brain was struggling to keep up. When I stood, I did it with such patience I might as well have been facing a rabid dog. This girl had me cornered, she was unpredictable. "Who *are* you?"

Not answering me, the blonde dropped down out of view. I heard the 'beep' of a phone, the tell-tale clicking of someone typing furiously. "I'm letting my friends know I found you."

In a surge of panic, I grappled for the lock on my changing room. The door bent outward, then mashed back into place as the girl shoved it closed. Together, we fought for what we both desperately desired. *I need to get out of here!* I thought wildly. *If this crazy girl gets her crazier friends here, I don't want to imagine what they'll do to me!*

Did they honestly think I had *stolen* Drezden from them?

"Let me out!" I shouted, unable to keep my fear from taking over. It sank like poison into my body, demanding I shove and kick and claw at the door. I was trapped, and every part of me felt the impending danger like it was a slow death. I'd been here before, pinned in a bathroom at school, mocked by girls who delighted in torturing me.

I couldn't do this again.

I wouldn't.

Slamming my shoulder on the door, I heard the girl's surprised squeak. But it wasn't me she was scared of. "Get away from there!" Brenda screamed, filling me with relief.

"You get away, you dumb fucking—hey!"

Instantly the changing room opened. Stumbling out, chest thrumming for air, I saw why. My manager had the blonde by the arms, pinning her on the floor with effort. Those chocolate eyes shot to me, bursting with worry. "Are you hurt, Lola? What did she do to you?"

The stranger bent her neck, glaring at me with unbridled hate. I met that look evenly, fighting to keep the waver out of my voice. "Nothing. She didn't do a thing to me." The blonde struggled until Brenda pushed her back down. "She was calling her friends to tell them I'm here, though. I think we should leave."

Understanding flashed across my manager's face. "Right." Eyeing the empty changing area, she jumped to her feet and scrambled backwards. "Don't follow us, Blondie, or I'll get you charged with stalking. Lucky for you, I'm feeling strangely generous today."

Generous? No, I realized, *Brenda knows we don't have the time to get the police involved, we need to leave, and fast.* It was hard for me to look away from the girl. She sat up, glaring directly at me over her shoulder.

292

The fact she had no parting words left me tipping on the edge of panic. I would have preferred if she'd just said *something* to me.

Gripping my wrist, shoving her own sunglasses onto my face to hide me, Brenda yanked me back into the store. "Come on," she hissed. "If that girl did call her friends, we need to move."

Nodding quickly, I sped up to keep pace. In my skull, the hateful words kept blossoming up. *You're that bitch. You stole him.* My mouth tasted like pennies; I eased my teeth apart, knowing I'd opened the old tongue wound.

Through the mall we moved at one-step slower than a run. Every set of eyes, every face, terrified me. A group of girls by a fountain, a woman standing too near, everyone was a potential danger; a possible enemy out to harm me.

To be recognized in public was one thing, to be a source of disgust...

It wasn't something I had imagined while dreaming of becoming a rock star.

Outside, the cold air was a taste of freedom. I was pulling Brenda now, forcing her towards the car. I didn't let go until I was inside, the slamming of the door a great comfort. In the bubble of the vehicle, I heard my own heavy panting. "You alright?" she asked, keys jingling in the ignition.

My gaze roamed to those fingers of hers, her perfect nails. I'd left indents on the skin of her arm from my grip; it was a cold slap. "Oh no, I'm so sorry, I—"

"Forget it." And she meant it, there was no space to argue. Watching me seriously, free of any smiles, Brenda made it clear she didn't want my apology. In that instant, I respected her, loved her, in a way I never expected. "Let's just get out of here."

"I'd like that, yeah." Brushing my hair back, I felt the oily sweat on my forehead. "Shit. I can't believe that even happened."

"What *exactly* happened? I came to check on you, then I saw that girl blocking you in the stall, but..." Glancing in her mirror, Brenda froze. "Son of a bitch."

Twisting in my seat, I spotted the car that had rolled up behind us. It was full of women, and I didn't need confirmation that they were the ones the blonde had called. They were pointing, yelling behind the windows. *How did they know this was our car?* "Drive, Brenda! Go, just go!"

"You think?" She slammed on the gas, rattling my spine with the inertia. We tore through the parking lot at record speeds, and the entire time, I kept my attention on the girls. It baffled me that they weren't following. I squinted at them until they became shapes that vanished in the distance.

Brenda didn't pull onto the freeway, an action that prompted me to gape at her. "Where are we going?"

She turned down a side road with a quick jerk of the wheel. "Going where they could easily follow us would be idiotic. The highway is a straight shot, too risky."

"Right," I said numbly. "Yeah. Okay." I was faced with my own naivety. Stalkers, escape plans, what was all of this? *Glory and fame, that's what being a rock star should be.* Peering into the side-mirror nervously, I expected headlights to appear behind us any second. *Not running away from people who want to harm you.*

Brenda didn't slow down for a long time. When she did, it felt like the sign that we were out of hot water. "You alright over there?" she asked.

I answered with a dry laugh. "Not exactly."

"Feels weird, doesn't it?"

"What, fleeing from maniacs? That girl back there... she looked at me with such *hate*. How could that be possible? She doesn't even know me."

"She knows the Lola Cooper from last night." Turning our car around the bend of a quiet street surrounded by trees, my manager shot me a look. "Don't be so surprised. Lots of people find it easy to hate a girl who has it all, especially if they think she doesn't deserve it."

Pain stabbed through my chest. *Lots of people find it easy to hate me?* I was close to laughing, closer to crying. "It shouldn't feel so new to me when you put it that way."

The sudden jolt that rocketed through the car interrupted our conversation. "Oh, seriously?" she cried, slamming on the breaks. I braced myself, only bouncing forward slightly.

"What, what is it?" I gasped, darting stares all around, expecting hateful teenagers to descend on us.

Brenda was half-way out of the car. "I think it was—yeah, no, it was. Fucking tire, dammit!"

Following her out, I spotted the source of her anger. The back left tire was shredded, useless. Covering my mouth, I crouched beside her on the empty road. "Did we hit a nail or something?"

Fingering the rubber, Brenda wrinkled her nose. "If 'something' means a knife, then yeah, guess we hit one."

A knife. The implication was horrifying. "You mean someone did this on purpose."

Dusting off her knees, she straightened and dug for her phone. "I'm guessing it was those idiotic girls back there. Are they insane? We could have been seriously hurt!"

It felt impossible to look away from the ruined tire. *Someone—maybe multiple someones—didn't even care if we got killed.* The pattern of my heart was erratic. "They must have been following us from before," I said softly. "All the way from the grocery store."

Turning, cellphone to her ear, my manager leveled a look of disbelief at me. "What?"

"It's the only way they'd have had time," I explained hesitantly.

Her face was stone. Not responding to me, she spoke into the phone. "Hey, it's me. The car just busted a tire. Send someone down Pine Creek, off of—yeah. Yeah, not far from the mall. Just hurry, the show is in a few hours, and... yeah. Mmhmm. Fine, thanks."

Shivering in spite of the warm air, I reached for my phone on reflex. "I should call Drez, let him know what happened."

"No, you should *not* do that." Popping the trunk, Brenda tugged out two bottles of water. "It'll only make him freak out. Last thing I need is him hijacking a car and driving around in a panic looking for us."

"Would he really do that? I could just say we're fine, someone is coming for us."

Lifting an eyebrow, Brenda tossed me a water. "This is Drezden Halifax. He won't trust someone else to handle this. Let him be, it won't take long for someone to reach us and change the tire."

Groaning, stiff like I'd been in a fight, I stood. The water was heavy in my hand. "I kind of hate that you won't let me call him."

Stepping around the car, she settled on the hood. "Just trust that I know best. I swear

I'm suggesting this for a reason, not to be a jerk."

With resignation, I sat beside her on the car. The water was fresh, welcome on my sticky tongue. "I know you aren't being a jerk. I just— I don't know."

"You want to talk to him."

Turning my head, I was faced with her knowing smile. "Yes."

She stretched languidly across the car. "Take a breath. You'll see him tonight, and knowing Drez, when he gets his claws back in you it'll be hard tearing you two apart." Shutting one eye, Brenda grinned at my glowing blush. "Sorry, trying to ease the tension some."

"I know." Fluffing my hair off my neck, I relaxed the tightness in my shoulders. "That whole thing *was* pretty insane."

Brenda considered me for a long moment. "Earlier, you mentioned not being surprised about being hated. What did you mean?"

Ah, shit. Tucking my chin, I hid behind my wall of dark hair. "It was nothing, just something that crossed my mind."

The car creaked, a hand closing on my elbow. Gently, Brenda guided me backwards until I was half-stretched beside her on the hood. "It was more than that. Something happened to you before, similar to this." My muscles became steel, and I knew my wide-eyes gave it all away to her. "Yeah," she said softly, "I'm right, aren't I? Lola, talk to me. Tell me what happened."

Faces.

Everyone laughing.

"It's nothing. Nothing at all," I muttered. Breaking free of her, I crumpled forward with my knees by my ears. I was a stone gargoyle— or I wished I was. If I was perched high on a building, I could protect myself from her prying questions.

Recalling how Brenda had chased down the bag-boy earlier in order to tip him, then how she'd taken me shopping—even *if* it had gone poorly—I let out a tiny puff of air. *Brenda just wants to help. That's who she is, I can't be angry at her for that.*

She was watching me. I appreciated her quiet patience. Brushing my hair from my cheek, I turned just enough to meet her gaze. "You really want to know about this? It's... heavy stuff."

"Of course I want to know," she said firmly. "But only if you want to tell me. Hell, it'll give us something to talk about while we sit here, right?"

Trying to smooth the tension again. I copied her smile, but laughter evaded me. "Alright. But remember, you asked for it." Draping an elbow over my knee, my attention went to the scrawling tattoo across my right forearm. It was there to remind me of who I

299

was. I'd need it, if I was going to talk about who I'd been.

Taking a breath so big it made me woozy, I grasped at that last fragment of ignorance—this little moment where Brenda didn't know a thing about my past. Then, with a simple parting of my lips, my secrets dripped off my tongue. "I was never supposed to be born."

Brenda sat up, unable to hold back her surprise. "Oh, Lola, that..." I could *feel* her struggling to talk to me, to rationalize what I'd said. "I'm sure that isn't right."

Cocking my head sent my hair scrambling down my shoulder like insect legs. "I don't mean I was just an accident. Nothing that simple." The disgust in my voice clearly unsettled Brenda. "My mother cheated on my father. He knew because he'd had a vasectomy after Sean was born. It's how everyone knew."

Everyone.

The word was sharp in my skull.

In front of me, Brenda squirmed. I said, "It wasn't possible to disguise it. Small towns, you know? My parents would have aborted me if they weren't so strongly against it. Instead, they let me become their *shameful* burden." I spat that last word out. "I was living proof of their broken marriage. Of my mother's weakness."

"It wasn't your fault!" she insisted.

300

"That never mattered to anyone." Brenda reached out to brush my hand where it rested on the car. Like she was made of fire, I jerked away. "Like I said, everyone knew about it, even the other kids. It just got worse as I got older. Especially when I entered high school."

"Why would high school—"

"The man my mother had the affair with was the fucking principal." Grimacing, I wrenched my hair off my neck and held it in a painful knot. I imagined every single hair tugging at its root, threatening to rip free. "His daughter, she was the same age as me. She hated me the most. I don't really get why—not exactly. Maybe she was just channeling the rage and humiliation of her own mother. Either way, I suffered for it."

"That's awful!" Brenda gasped. I hadn't noticed her inching closer; a manicured hand suddenly clamped down on my shoulder. Going stiff, I managed not to shove her away. "You did nothing wrong. Someone had to realize a child was being punished for no reason, did no one step in?"

"The town blamed my mother for the scandal, but they all took it out on me—everyone but Sean." My mind's eye flickered with my brother's grin. "He was there to step in when I was being bullied. Sean always came to help me."

No. Not always.

301

That time everything fell to pieces...
when those girls took my guitar and busted
it... In Brenda's grip, my fingers twitched—she
squeezed back sympathetically. My first guitar
had meant so much to me. It had been Sean's
hand-me-down, but it had been *mine*.

And then they broke it.
And then I broke them.

Blood, busted knuckles; my veins raced,
reliving the day I'd finally snapped and fought
back. The day I had stood up for myself and
risked losing everything.

And Sean wasn't there to help at all.
Not then. Where was he that day? Why wasn't
he around when I—when I...

Her hand tightened. "Your face just went
from almost happy to defeated again."

I debated telling her about how I'd
almost gone to juvenile detention, that it had
taken a miracle I still didn't understand to
convince my parents to keep me out of it. They,
of all people, had loved the idea of hiding me
away.

No, she doesn't need that part of my
past. "This conversation started because you
wanted to know why I'd be used to people
hating me." I tugged away from her, hating
how sadness bloomed in her eyes. I didn't want
anyone else to be sad over this. I was plenty sad
enough. "Here's the thing. I'm *not* used to it,
not really. I never magically adjusted to the
hate. I just dove down inside myself, made a

shell, found things to—to distract me from everything."

Shivering, I ran a fingertip over the inside of my right arm. I could feel the slightly raised edges of old scars, pretended they were the texture of my tattoo's castle walls.

Brenda moved her eyes down to my ink. She didn't voice her suspicion, but the flash of pity in her face told me she *knew*. My manager realized I was hinting at how I used to cut myself.

Good, I thought selfishly. *Now I don't need to say it out loud. Yes, Brenda. I was that kind of fucked up person.* My palm crushed over my right wrist until the skin went white. *But not anymore.*

Not anymore.

"What changed?" Brenda asked suddenly. Her voice was hushed, as if I was a deer who'd bolt any second. Realizing that she was actually scared of ruining this raw, honest peek into my personality... I blinked. Then I blinked again.

My laughter began as a chuckle, quickly sending me into shakes that made me hug myself to slow them down. Brenda's mouth contorted in shock. Seeing her make such a hilarious face was too much; tears prickled at the corners of my eyes.

"Lola! Are you okay? What's happening here?"

"Sorry, it's just..." Rubbing at my cheeks, I smiled helplessly. "You asked me what changed." Reaching out, I closed my fingers over her own. "The answer might make you laugh, too."

She took a slow, deep breath. "I'm ready for some laughter, go ahead."

The tattoo on my arm flexed when I made a fist. *What happened that turned my life around? What saved me from falling further into a pit so dark no one could have pulled me out of it?*

With genuine sincerity in my voice, I looked at Brenda and said, "I heard Drezden sing."

- Chapter Nineteen -
Drezden

The venue, a bar known as Belly Up, was surrounded by eager fans. I could see them all from the window of the bus. Though I was sure they couldn't see me, it was clear many of them were trying.

"You want to head out there?"

It was Colt who'd spoke. I didn't spare him a glance. "I want Brenda to answer her damn phone is what I want."

Crouching low, the drummer's ear-gauge swung in my face; it no longer sported a bandage from the bar fight with Johnny. "She isn't answering for a reason."

"No shit," I mumbled. "It's the 'reason' that worries me."

"You try to call Lola?"

My fingers traced the hard lump of my cell phone in my pocket. *Three fucking times. I called her over and over, she didn't pick up once.* "Yes."

Colt tapped his nails to an unheard rhythm. For some time it was the only noise; that, and the muffled roar of the crowd outside. "Listen," he started, speaking more to the window than me, "You can't sit here worrying. They're fine, just running late. Brenda was pissed at you earlier, right? I bet she isn't picking up because of that."

I considered him thoughtfully. "And Lola? What's her reason?"

"I—look, Drez." He sighed heavily. "I don't know. Maybe she's just busy, or maybe Brenda won't let her answer. That's possible, yeah?"

Leaning away from the window, my tiny frown grew. *Could Brenda do that?* This morning, Brenda had made it clear she wanted us to pretend that Lola and I hadn't hooked up. I'd told her I wouldn't. If I knew anything about Brenda, it was that she was stubborn as me.

Fuck. Is she trying to force a wedge between us? Colt might be right about this.

I noticed he was grinning triumphantly, like he'd read my face and realized I agreed with him. Standing with a groan, I said, "Since our *attentive* manager isn't here with those groceries, want to go find something to eat before sound check?"

"Hell yeah!" Laughing openly, Colt stood and cracked his back. "Hey, Porter!" The bassist craned his head out from his room. "Come on, let's go get some grub. I'm starving."

As a group, we stepped out of the bus. The wave of screams welcomed us to the world, security holding back the throngs of attendees with quickly constructed barriers. Girls thrust signs in the air, each proclaiming their love for the band, or for me, specifically.

306

Porter and Colt were more generous with their returned smiles than I was. Even under the energy of our adoring fans, my mind was stuck on where Lola could be. Not knowing was poison in my blood. It gnawed deep and there was no antidote.

Rounding the corner, we vanished behind the building. Trailers and food trucks filled the parking lot; enticing, greasy smells softened my worries. *A hamburger won't make me think about Lola any less.* That didn't stop me from grabbing one from a cart.

Digging into my back pocket for my wallet, I tried to yank it free in between bites of food. A hand, coming down hard on my shoulder, froze me. "Here, I'll get that for you," Sean said.

Lola's brother.

"There." He tossed a five-dollar bill at the vendor while wearing a huge smile. "That should cover it."

I had a strong feeling that he was putting on an act, and I trusted my instincts more than I trusted him. Pushing backwards, not hiding my suspicion, I glared at the guitarist. Sean was shorter than me, but not by much. "I don't need your charity." Hamburger juice dripped down my wrist; I ignored it.

His smile wavered. "No shit. It's called being nice. Familiar with it?"

In my peripheral vision, Colt and Porter appeared. Likewise, the vaguely familiar members of Barbed Fire moved in behind Sean. I didn't know them well, but in the rising static tension, I noted the size of the long-haired blonde on the left. *The drummer, if I'm right.* My eyes moved slowly the other way. *And that skinny-fuck there must be the singer.*

"So you're being nice to me," I said, not tempering my distaste. "Why, what do you want?" *There's no way he doesn't know about what happened last night.* Was Sean the kind of brother that would think I'd corrupted his sister, taken advantage of her or some shit?

Sean lifted his chin, eyes—blue as anything and too similar to Lola's—rolling to Colt, then to Porter, before falling back on me. "You're acting like it's weird for me to be nice to you."

I took another bite of my burger, my silence a good enough answer.

He continued staring me down. I half expected him to throw a punch. This guy, I wasn't convinced he didn't hate my guts. He had a few good reasons to.

I finished my meal before he finally spoke again. That was good; I'd have choked otherwise. "Listen," he mumbled, looking away awkwardly. "Lola won't answer my calls. Okay? I just want to talk to her. Could you get her out of the bus for me?"

The food felt like it was caught low in my throat. "She won't answer your calls, either?"

Sean jerked his head around, shock openly glistening in his eyes. It unnerved me, again, how similar they were to the girl I was obsessed with. "Lola isn't with you?"

"She went with Brenda to grab us some supplies earlier," Porter said, stepping forward. "They probably just got caught up in something. I'm sure they're fine."

Sean coiled his fingers in my bassist's shirt, yanking him so they were nose to nose. It was quick, too quick for anyone to react to. "How the *hell* would you know if they're fine? Tell me where they fucking went!"

The guy had some muscle on him, but I didn't think he was a threat to Porter.

I still didn't like him touching my fucking friend.

Guided by the anxiousness that had plagued me since Lola left this morning, I snatched Sean's wrist, yanking him off the bassist as my fingers dug into his skin. "Back the fuck off, man. You don't want to get physical here."

"Aren't you even worried about her?" he spat, trying to wrench himself free from me. To his credit, Sean was strong.

I was just stronger.

Pulling him towards me in one smooth motion, I shoved him down onto the pavement. He landed hard on his hands and knees. "Of course I'm fucking worried!" Sean had given me a place to aim my rapidly growing delusions

309

about what had happened to Lola. My body heated with the familiar tingle of adrenaline fueled fight-or-flight.

The scar on my lower back burned.

Sean started to get up; the big blonde guy moved closer. I thought he was going to help his band-mate, but instead, he swung one meaty fist at my skull. Desperately, I started to dodge. It wasn't necessary.

Colt slammed into the guy's blindside, his arms tangling around his waist as they hit the rough parking lot. All sinew and grunts, they rolled into a violent knot of punches and kicks.

Sean was still on his knees, his fingers burying in his scalp while he yelled frantically at the wrestling men. "Shark! Back the hell off, man! Stay out of this!"

Both of them ignored the shouts, the big guy—Shark, I guess—pushing his bicep against Colt's throat. I started to close in, unable to resist any longer, especially not when my friend's face was turning purple.

Porter and the last, unnamed member of Barbed Fire beat me. Together, they pulled the guys apart. The fight could have ended there. I *knew* it could be done with.

But I was done standing around.

Reaching down, I grabbed Sean Cooper by the hair and *squeezed*. His hiss of surprised pain was intoxicating. "Listen," I growled into his ear. "If this is your idea of what being nice means, then I can get *right* fucking behind it."

His fingers dug into my forearm; I didn't feel the skin break. "*Let me the fuck go!*"

In my chest, my lungs rattled with my hunger for chaos. I had Sean at my mercy. I knew I could slam him into the ground, break his jaw, make him taste his own rusty blood. My hands became claws, my desire to hear his nose cartilage crumble as I drove it into my knee and—

"*I'm just looking for my sister!*"

Inside, the beast retreated. Crouched there, hovering over Sean with my own heart throbbing in my ears, I felt the eyes on me. Everyone was watching. Waiting. No one had the guts to try and get between me and Sean.

In my skull, his shout bounced around and never ended. *That's right. He's right. He's just trying to find Lola.*

Just like I am.

There was a soreness in my hand when I released his hair. Those muscles felt too tight, like they weren't meant to be opened. We stood up simultaneously, the pressure around us fading. Colt and Shark huddled with Porter and the skinny singer, the four of them looking less like enemies, more like soldiers waiting to be told what to do.

Touching a palm to his skull, Sean glared at me indignantly. There it was; the look he'd given me way back during his audition. I hadn't deserved it, then. *But now, maybe I do.* Inhaling until I felt on the edge of popping, I breathed out through my nose. "That got out of control," I said flatly.

"You think?" Eyeing his hand, as if he expected—and was surprised not to—see blood, Sean snorted. "Your temper is off the wall."

"You were the one who started it," Porter said, his shoulders crawling upwards. "Drez was just reacting."

"Dude's just looking for Lola," Shark replied. He began to say more, but Sean silenced him with a wave of his fingers.

The vibrant battle lust drained from me bit by bit. I felt so fucking tired. "Next time just come out and ask us where she is, like a normal person."

"Normal?" Sean lifted his eyebrows, not elaborating. "Here's the situation. My sister is missing, and she's *your* guitarist. Sound check is in thirty minutes. If she doesn't show soon, what happens? Even if she's fine, you guys can't play without her."

A cold spike trickled down my back. "That's our concern, not yours." *Isn't it?* Peeking at Colt and Porter, I wondered if they had the same suspicion I did. *Why would Sean give a shit about if we were playing or not?*

I battled the urge to probe further. The issue was moot, luckily, when a familiar car roared into the parking lot. As one, we all twisted to follow the vehicle until it halted a

312

few feet away. Before anyone climbed from the car, I was moving.

Lola managed to crack the door, starting to unbuckle. "Drez—" Pushing her in the seat, I ended my name on her tongue with a kiss. Under my touch, she twitched and melted with rising excitement. I could sense her tensing, feel her muscles giving way. It was good that she was sitting.

"That's a nice way to say hello," Brenda said. I didn't bother looking at my manager. I was too eager to fill my vision with this beautiful fucking girl. The burger I'd eaten had done nothing for me. She was the real cause of my famine, and now, I had her to gorge myself on. "Why don't I get greetings like that?" Brenda laughed, shutting the door loudly.

Breaking the kiss, I thrilled at the desperate, sharp inhale Lola made. Leaning back enough to gaze on her blushing cheeks, I also saw her sparkling eyes.

Eyes like her brother's.

I was reminded why I'd been consumed with panic all day. "Where the hell were you?" I asked, crushing the edges of the car seat.

Her delicious lips fell open. "Oh. It's kind of a long story. Mostly, we had a flat tire."

"*Mostly?*"

Rubbing her tattoo, Lola glanced to the side. "Let me tell you about it later. Brenda said as we were pulling in that we need to hurry and do sound check."

I flushed with a million things; frustration, bitterness, and the all too powerful desire to just keep Lola right there and taste her again. *Sound check.* Not backing out of the open car door, I noticed Sean scowling at me from the corner of my eye. "Fine. Later. But I want to know everything."

Stiffening, Lola squeezed her arm again. "Sure. Okay."

Whatever she was worrying about, I wanted to erase it. Thumbing her lower lip, I buried my mouth on hers once more. Our tongues glided together, her moan soft, for my ears only. I *felt* it more than I heard it. With as much control as I could muster, I released her and backed away.

Sliding free, Lola smoothed her hair. The glow on her skin was from me, and I reveled in it. The young woman froze, spotting her brother where he hovered nearby. "Sean?" she asked, taking a single step out of the car. "What's going on, why are you hanging out here?"

I knew what 'here' meant; why was he hanging out with *me?*

"You wouldn't answer your phone," Sean said, palming his neck. "I got worried, thought you were avoiding me."

Brenda cleared her throat. "Blame me. I didn't want us worrying anyone, or for people to try and come help us despite us not needing it." Her eyes shot to me pointedly. "We got a busted tire, took a bit for someone to come out and fix it, that's all."

"You couldn't have just texted me to say that's what was up?" Sean asked, wearing his hurt on his sleeve.

"Not just that." Shaking her head violently, Lola lifted her phone and opened it. The black screen gazed back at us. "It died early on, I forgot to charge it last night. I couldn't have said anything if I had wanted to."

Her phone died? The knowledge left me nervous. *What if this had been an actual emergency?* Reaching out, I took Lola by the wrist. "Come on, let's go."

"Slow down," Sean said through gritted teeth. "I need to talk to her first!"

"I thought you just wanted to make sure she was okay?" I asked. Keeping my hold on Lola, I peered at Sean over my shoulder. I didn't see Lola's irritation until she pulled free from me with a grunt.

Rubbing her wrist gingerly, she frowned my way. "Let me talk to him, we can all walk over to sound check together. It won't mess up the schedule."

It'll take away from the time I want with just you, I thought darkly. I was being greedy, but I chose not to voice it. *I'll have her to myself soon enough.* "Fine." Ruffling my hair, I glanced sideways at Sean. "Let's walk and talk, then."

315

My manager, phone to her ear, waved someone down. "In the trunk," she said to the young man, "There's a bunch of food. Hopefully nothing went bad, it's been a bit since the store. Load it onto the bus—and you." Those chocolate eyes stabbed at me. "We need to hurry, so less 'walk' and more 'jog' to the building."

Taking my eyes off of Lola and her brother, the two of them strolling with their heads together in front of me, I wrinkled my nose. "It's not my fault you're so late. Speaking of which, what the hell was that bullshit about not calling me to tell me what was wrong?"

She tucked a loose strand of hair behind her ear. Speaking softly, Brenda leaned towards me as we walked. "Be angry at me if you want, but with all the alone time I got with Lola, she finally opened up to me. I learned... some hard stuff. I think it really helped her to get it off her chest."

My mind was floored. Watching the siblings, I saw how hunched Sean's shoulders were. The guy looked *pissed*. Abruptly, Sean broke away. The guitarist stomped off to the side, no longer heading towards the back door of Belly Up.

"Uh oh," Brenda mumbled next to me.

We came to a halt beside the girl, her sapphire eyes fixed on the fleeing back of her brother. The hurt in her face was tangible. "What happened? Why'd he leave like that?" I asked, curling an arm around her waist in an attempt to comfort—or claim—her.

"It's stupid," she said quickly, features smoothing to hide any emotion. "He's just being a jerk. He wanted to know what went down, and I said I'd talk to him about it another time."

Colt, who had followed us as we moved, bent down to grab Lola's shoulder gently. "Don't let it get to you. Siblings can be real assholes to each other, take it from me." The wink he offered softened the teasing.

Lifting her head, Lola broke into a weak smile. "You said before that you had a brother. I remember that now. Does he get like this sometimes?"

The lanky guy waved a hand, displaying three fingers. "I have three brothers, *and* two sisters." He chuckled at Lola's amazed gawking. "And do they get like what, immature stuck up babies? Yeah, every single one of them has at some point. It's normal."

"Hey," I said, breaking into the discussion. "Let's just get set for the show tonight, we can worry about family dynamics when things aren't so time sensitive."

Covering her mouth, Brenda gasped dramatically. "Holy shit, has the real Drezden Halifax returned to us? I thought you'd been replaced by a selfish prick who didn't *care* about schedules anymore!"

My eyes became slits. "I always cared."

317

Lifting her hands, she spun on a heel and opened the back door. "I could have sworn that the man I had to drag out of the hotel this morning didn't care about leaving on time. That's all I'm saying."

Lola and I shared a look. Her face was pink, a rose in bloom; I was sure she was thinking about what we'd done. Any anger at Brenda for busting my balls dissipated at the tiny, private smile the girl sent me.

There were many thoughts roaming my skull that evening. Most of them suspicious, dark things that traveled from the root of my past to the dawn of my problems cropping up on this tour.

Gripping Lola's hip, guiding her into Belly Up, I made a decision.

She was my main thought.

For that evening.

And for as long as I could keep her *at my side*.

- Chapter Twenty -
Lola

Sean wouldn't look at me during sound check.

Every lick of music I made was haphazard, my eyes trying to force my brother's attention towards me. By the time the set was done, all I had to show for my effort was a massive migraine.

I should have just told him. The guitar felt heavier than usual; a reminder that it, like my first, had been a gift from Sean. *Should have just taken five minutes to tell him I'd gotten stalked at the mall, had a tire sabotaged, and then spilled my guts to Brenda.*

Hanging my head, I snapped the instrument's case shut. I barely got off the stage before Drezden moved beside me. His words, his heat, clung to me. "Everything alright? You seemed distracted up there."

Tossing a quick look at Sean across the room, I noticed Drez following my eyes. "I'm stressing over him ignoring me," I said.

"I could drag him over here for you," the singer said casually. I wrenched my head around to stare at him; he was smirking like a champ. "Or... you could give him some time alone to think."

Chuckling, I let my shoulders slide down. "Does that mean your offer isn't really on the table?"

Bending low, Drezden traced his fingers along the nape of my neck. Knowing everyone could see, that Drezden didn't give a shit, set my senses on hyper-aware. "I'll do anything you ask me to, Lola. Want me to drag him here kicking and screaming? Just say the words."

A tremble shook me to my knees. *How do words work?* He was too talented at stealing my control. "No," I rasped. "Giving him some time is fine."

He kissed me once, teasing with his teeth. "You know," he whispered, dragging a thumb-pad over my jugular, "They might need to put makeup on your neck tonight. You're covered in my hickies."

I clasped a palm over my throat. "Shit, that's right." *I forgot about the bruises!*

Straightening, his hands let me go... but his stare kept me ensnared. Tucking his fingers into his pockets, Drezden didn't hide the smoldering hunger in his angular face. "If they try, don't let them."

"What?"

"Don't let them hide my marks." Wild fire flickered in his green eyes. "I want the world to see what I did to you."

One beat, four beats, a million beats; my heart couldn't take it. Unable to articulate my thoughts, I gave him a tiny nod. His instant, sly grin made my mouth feel fuzzy.

"Fuck," he growled, "I want to get alone with you."

"No. No no no." Brenda strolled forward, a clipboard in her hand. She wielded it like a giant hammer, smacking Drez on the top of his head—lightly, but he still winced. "No one runs off. This place is going to get packed in less than an hour. I need you all to stick around."

Drez lifted his eyebrows at her. Grabbing my wrist, the singer pulled me towards the rear exit of the bar. I let him take me, I didn't even struggle.

"Hey!" Our manager waved her arms, shouting at us, drawing every eye in the room. "What did I just say?"

"I'm not sure," Drez said. "I think that clipboard gave me a concussion."

"I said *get back here!*" she shouted. "You heard me the first time!"

Chuckling, he kept on walking. "Okay, I heard you. I still need a smoke break." He spared only a second to glance down at me, mystery leaking from his muted smile. "I always smoke before a show."

Behind us, Brenda was still yelling. It wasn't even words; just frustrated groans. We stepped through a door and into the parking lot. It was chilly, the air waking up the parts of my brain that Drez had managed to weaken.

I asked, "Are you really going out for a smoke?" In my heart, I knew he wasn't.

I just wanted to hear the truth out loud.

Peering around, taking in the fading light above, he answered me with a voice crafted from honey. "No. Of course not." In the growing shadows, his face was a puzzle. "It's you I want. Lola Cooper... my new addiction."

****

My question about where we would go was cleared up before I voiced it.

The inside of the trailer was empty. I figured it must have been meant for some of the crew, all of which were now inside Belly Up. There was little to see but some fold-up chairs, a small card table, and leftover coffee and snacks on the counter.

The sharp 'click' behind me was a warning. Twisting, I saw Drezden's fingers leave the locking bolt. No one could get inside anymore.

I was trapped with Drezden Halifax.

He's going to wreck me before the show! The realization was chilling. *There's no way I can play after he's through with me, he'll rip me to shreds, I'll forget the songs!*

The word 'wait' was on my tongue.

The answer of 'no' poured from his eyes.

322

He shoved me against the trailer wall, the building vibrated from impact; *I* vibrated. The marrow in my bones shook with my fear, but also my anticipation. Even if I knew it was a bad idea to do this, I still *wanted* him.

Where the kiss started, I couldn't say. The ending was what mattered; it was what allowed me to finally breathe. "Drez," I said weakly, searching his face for clarity. "Wait, hold on, we can't—the show will start soon!"

"They don't need us for the start."

"But I want to see my brother play!"

"And I," the singer murmured, "Want you." Gripping my middle, he slid his palms down until they met the top of my jeans. His thumbs hooked in, sandwiching between the denim and my skin.

I endured a flutter of pleasure. It forced my head back, my eyes shutting. *If he keeps going, I won't be able to resist him. And then I'll miss Barbed Fire.* Suddenly, I understood what was happening.

It hit me hard, left me cold under Drezden's expert fingers.

He's making me choose between him... and Sean. Since my brother had played his first show at school, I'd watched every single one of his performances. When he started bringing me along to help at shows, I'd jumped in whole-hog.

That was how I'd gotten my first taste of Four and a Half Headstones. Their music had turned my life around; Drezden's lyrics had soothed my soul.

And now, the man who crafted that music? Lifting my chin, I stared into his acid-green eyes. *He's right here, making me pick between him—the guy I'm falling for—or the brother who's supported me from the start.*

My lips spread, preparing to say something—anything—that would free me from Drezden's spell. His fingers closed on my bottom lip, peeled it down, exposed the sensitive inside. His agile tongue slid side to side, tasting the soft flesh until I forgot what I was even doing.

He has me, I thought in the distant ocean of my mind. *He has me, and he knows it.* There was a hint of something wicked and cruel in how Drezden was kissing me. If it was possible to taste triumph, it was leaking from him.

"Take off your bra," he said against my temple. Reaching behind, I fumbled until I'd done so. He didn't ask me to remove my shirt, but I reached down to do it anyway. "No, don't." One firm palm on my elbow halted me. "Leave it on, just slide your bra out."

Baffled by his insistence, I tugged the straps down my arms, the piece of lingerie tumbling to the floor. He coiled his grip in my thin shirt, tightening it until it strained over my breasts. My already aching nipples were outlined like perfect, tiny pieces of candy.

Drez's hungry mouth descended, rubbing over the cloth, sending convulsions straight down to my calves.

It should have been impossible; he'd managed to make my skin *more* sensitive by not exposing it. Closing my eyes, my head tilted back against the wall. Open mouthed, panting, my tongue went dry as my pussy dripped.

Abruptly, he stepped away from me. It took me some time before I could collect myself enough to look at him, painfully aware of my rock-hard nipples, how flushed my face must be. Drez wore a hard smirk, his fingers offering something small and square to me.

A condom, I realized. "Where did you get it? I thought you were out?" Taking it, my eyes fixed on how casually he unzipped the front of his jeans. The material was tenting from his swollen cock.

"I keep them on the bus. Come here," he said. Motioning me forward, Drez reached for my wrist. I let him guide me, my heart thumping with uncertainty. "No risks this time, not like this morning. Put it on me."

Every hair of mine prickled. *Oh, fuck.* I'd never even opened a condom wrapper before. At Drez's light prompting, his hands on my shoulders, I dropped to my knees in front of him. Eye level with his hard-on, I licked my lips once; twice. *I'm going to mess this up. He's going to realize I don't know what I'm doing.*

I'd been avoiding the fact that I hadn't yet told Drezden I was a virgin—that he'd been my first. Now, kneeling with a condom in hand, his eager face above, I faced a hard reality. *I was never going to tell him, was I?* The guilt wormed into my blood. *I was going to just let it go and hope it never came up.*

An impatient hand came down, stroking the top of my scalp. Closing my eyes, I squeezed the foil packet. "Drez?"

"Hm?" He was watching me, and from my angle, he looked like a beautiful angel. An angel who'd fallen so far from heaven he was swimming in liquid black sin.

"I—there's something I need to tell you." My throat closed on my words, trying to keep them at bay. *No, I can't avoid this. If anything is going to happen between Drez and me— anything meaningful—I have to tell him.*

The hand on my head trailed down, sliding along the back of my ear. "I'm listening, Lola."

Unable to meet his curious gaze, I focused on the condom in my hand. It was strangely heavy, I wanted to drop it and forget it. "I've never... well. I've never opened a condom before."

Laughing, but not unkindly, Drez played with my hair. "Just tear it open."

"No—I mean, I've never held one." Heat built behind my eye sockets. Everything wobbled, congesting as I fought back humiliated tears. "Never touched one. Never had to even think about putting one on—on anyone." I swallowed, tasting sour regret. "Ever. Until... you."

Drezden went still, fingers locking in place on my head. His silence was torture, and if I wasn't such a coward, I would have looked up to see what he was doing. I was freed of the choice; he grabbed my chin while he simultaneously crouched in front of me. In his perfect green-mirror eyes, I saw my own pale sadness. "Lola," he said flatly, "Are you trying to tell me I was the first guy you ever slept with?"

I swallowed loudly. "That's exactly what I mean. I'm so sorry, I should have said something before."

"Why *didn't* you?"

Reaching up, I wiped at the corners of my eyes. "Fuck, I don't know. I was just nervous, and it happened so fast, and then I just... I just—" A hiccup interrupted me.

Pulling me close, Drezden crushed me against his chest, nose going into my hair. "Idiot. Why would I care if you were a virgin or not?"

Trying to control myself, I didn't hug him back. The hiccups jolted me, preventing me from fully calming down. "I don't know, Drez! I was just... just so fucking terrified that you'd want to stop because I didn't know how to do anything. You've been with more people

327

than me, you're experienced, if I said you were my first maybe the pressure would have been too much and..."

Gruffly, he held me by my shoulders at a distance. The shock in his face scared off my hiccups. "How would you know how many people I've slept with?"

"I don't! You just—this morning—the whole running out of condoms thing." I couldn't handle his staring anymore; I looked away. "If you ran out, it's because you use the damn things, right?"

"Shit. Lola," he sighed, thumbing away a leftover tear from my cheek. "You're acting like I finished a whole box in the week before we met or something. It was *one* condom, because who doesn't want to be safe? You never know who you'll meet."

He said that last part seriously. Lifting my eyes, I caught his meaning. *He's talking about me.* If he hadn't had that condom on him, would we have gone as far after our first show? Had he kept it in his wallet because he'd hoped... or planned... to sleep with me?

My laughter broke free, escaping my palm as I covered my mouth. It was ridiculous, I'd been so worked up over nothing. "I'm sorry, I really thought—"

"That I was some kind of man-whore," he said, cutting me off. Arching one eyebrow, Drez ruffled my hair. "I don't even know if I'm insulted."

I smiled weakly. *It doesn't matter what he's done before, what matters is what he's doing now. WHO he's doing it with.* And that was me. "Sorry if I ruined the mood."

Plucking the condom from my fingers, he slid it into his pocket and zipped his pants. "You didn't." His lips pressed on my forehead; it was the most tender kiss he'd given me. Stunned, I stayed on my knees, my mouth hanging open. Squinting, Drezden adjusted himself in his pants with a grunt. "If you stay down there like that, I'll be tempted to continue."

Grinning wide, I sat on my calves. "What's stopping you?"

Scratching at his hair, the singer lifted his phone free. "Barbed Fire is finishing up their show, Brenda will kill me if you don't at least get into a clean outfit for our set."

Like that, my heart shrank. *Oh no. Oh no oh no.*

Standing in a whirl, I scrambled to find my bra. I took even longer to get it back on, finally just yanking my shirt over my shoulders to ease the process. Drez stared appreciatively, but I was in too much of a panic to care.

Yanking at the trailer door, I breathed faster—harder. In my distress, it took me a second to remember I had to unlock it.

I missed Sean's show.

Drezden had done it. He'd made me forget, and I could only blame myself.

329

And blaming myself...

Well.

That was the easy part.

Cold evening air assaulted me. I barely felt it, legs pumping, carrying me back into Belly Up's. The backdoor had security floating around, but they took one look at me, who I was, and didn't slow me down.

It was sort of strange. Not so long ago, guards like that had thrown me to the ground outside the Headstones' bus. They'd stomped on my morale, all because they didn't know who I was.

Now they knew.

"Sean!" My shoes pounded backstage, my attention flying around as I tried to spot my brother among the crew tearing the set down. Through the walls, the screaming tsunami of the crowd was deafening. "Sean! Sean, where— Sean!"

I spotted him a few feet away. The only hint that he'd heard me shouting his name was a quick, dismissive glance over one shoulder. Then he walked away, following the rest of his band to the rear of the building.

I wasn't going to give up, though. The fear that was swelling in me threatened that if I didn't explain myself to Sean *now*...

There would never be another chance.

Panting, I chased him out a side door and back into the low-lit parking lot of Belly Up. "Wait, hey, just hold up!" My voice was ragged; I was glad it wasn't my job to sing tonight.

Sean didn't stop until I grabbed his shoulder. Finally, he spun around, the other Barbed Fire members slowing to see what was going on. "What the hell do you want, Lola?" he snapped.

Pulling up short, I held a hand to my burning chest. "I need to talk to you!"

"Yeah?" Shooting a glare at the sky, he avoided my pleading eyes. "Maybe I don't have the time, maybe you'll just need to talk to me later."

"Don't pull that shit!" Through my guilt, a tumor of frustration was bloating. "Earlier was different, you know I had no time, but I *was* going to talk to you!"

"Just like how you were going to answer your phone one of the fucking times I called?"

"*It was fucking dead!*"

Wiping his nose, my brother shrugged to his ears. "For all I knew, so were you."

Wind fled my lungs. What could I say to that? "It—I was fine." *But he didn't know that.* "Sean, please—"

"Why don't you just go hang out with your fuck-buddy, Drezden?" Pointing, I followed his finger, spotting the singer where he was leaning nearby on the outside wall of the bar. "That's all you care about. Doesn't matter what I've done for you, you don't give a

331

shit about any of it now that you're the 'famous' one."

It was like he'd stabbed me between my ribs. I grabbed for him, but Sean easily stepped away. The cold indifference in his eyes reminded me terribly of our father. How he would look at me with contempt, the constant reminder of his wife's infidelity. "Sean... please... it isn't like that."

"We both know why you missed my show just now." Turning away, his scowling profile belonged to someone I didn't know. This bitter person wasn't my brother.

He couldn't be.

Did he change... or was it me? Staring after his vanishing form, I lifted a hand. It was all I could do, all I had. Sean was right—he was fucking *right*. I'd been distracted by Drezden, and today, I hadn't once called my brother when I could have.

I brushed him off earlier.

Now he's showing me how it feels.

Drezden appeared beside me, a ghost in the night. When he touched my shoulder, I pushed away. "Come on," I mumbled, "We need to get ready. We've got a show tonight."

A show I know Sean won't be watching.

- Chapter Twenty-One -
Drezden

I couldn't sit still backstage.

My eyes hadn't moved from the doorway, waiting to swallow Lola up once more. She'd been whisked off for makeup and wardrobe as soon as Brenda had found us. The scathing look she'd narrowed my way couldn't affect me.

The despair in Lola's beautiful blue centers did.

All because of her fucking brother. My boot tapped the ground over and over. *That piece of shit really messes with her head.* I'd watched it all go down, and when he'd stormed off, it had taken strict control not to chase after Sean and yank him back to Lola by his hair.

Honestly, it was my fault. I'd been the one who'd delayed her and made her miss Barbed Fire's show. I'd wanted to make her forget about everything—everyone—else. *And I did that,* I thought triumphantly. *The only thing that existed for her in that trailer was me.* Lola had crumbled at my feet. She'd gazed up at me, lips parted, chest rising rapidly.

Breathing in sharply, I adjusted my swelling cock in my jeans.

I was surprised when she told me she'd been a virgin. Not angry, not even suspicious;

just surprised. I hadn't even suspected I'd been her first. *That slice of her is mine now.* Smiling to myself, I ran fingers over my forearms. It wouldn't have mattered to me if she'd been innocent or if I'd been her hundredth fuck.

But knowing I'd claimed that side of her?

It fucking thrilled me in a perverse way.

The door opened, Lola striding into view with Brenda at her heels. Her hair was hanging in wild waves, her eyes rimmed dark as tar and lips shiny like blood. She was stunning.

Her old clothes were replaced by skin-tight grey denim. Hard, angular spikes coated her ankle-high boots. In a thin purple and black tank-top, she was a walking vision of sex and power.

I took note of the most important detail; her long, elegant neck was still dappled in my bruises.

Brenda spotted me, her shoes pounding my way audibly as she left Lola in her dust. "I guess I have *you* to thank, huh?" she said when she was out of earshot of the guitarist. "She refused to let them hide those damn hickies."

My smirk was a razor. "They look fantastic on her."

"It's just going to make the fans crazier, even worse than earlier," Brenda hissed.

A ripple rushed through my chest. With a plastic mask of calmness, I pushed off the wall and stood in front of my manager. *"Earlier?"*

Skepticism swam across her face. Together, we watched Lola approaching. In the seconds before the guitarist could hear, Brenda whispered, "She didn't tell you yet? Then what were you doing with her that whole time you two were alone—no, don't tell me." Her voice fell lower. "Some girls messed with Lola today. Messed with her bad. You've got some pissed off, jealous, *dangerous* fans on your hands, Drez."

Dangerous. The word lifted the hairs on my neck. *Dangerous in what way?*

There wasn't time to pry. Lola smoothed the front of her shirt, glancing between us. "Guess we're up soon. Where's my guitar?"

"Here." Grabbing the case from the wall, Brenda handed it over. I watched how Lola's fingers squeezed the container with fierce protectiveness. "I need to go find Colt and Porter, please don't vanish on me again, okay?"

A roar went up from the stage, drowning out whatever Lola said next. Shaking her head warily, Brenda hurried out of view. In her wake, the screams died enough for Lola and me to finally speak.

Neither of us did.

Looking her guitar case over, Lola kept her eyes down. I didn't understand the awkward air around us; I just knew I loathed it.

Whatever happened when they were out was worse than I thought.

Dangerous, Brenda had said. The word rattled me.

Clearing my throat, I slid my fingers under the top of my belt. "You feeling alright?"

"Sure," she answered too quickly. "Just ready to play. The set for tonight, any changes I should know about?"

Her tone was emotionless. Reaching out, I held her shoulders. "Don't lie to me."

A hint of something furious swam in her crystal eyes. "I'm not lying, I'm really fine."

"Your brother tells you to fuck off, and you want me to believe you're fine?"

She tried to shove my hands away; I just squeezed tighter. "What am I supposed to say to you? We're going on stage, I don't have time to fucking open up about all of this!"

No matter how tough she acted, I knew she was hurting. "Tell me what happened earlier today."

Inhaling through her nose, Lola closed her eyes. "When I can, I will."

"That's exactly what you did with Sean," I said softly. "You keep finding excuses not to tell anyone what happened."

Curling back her lips like a wild animal, she slammed her hands into my chest. It surprised me enough that I released her, stumbling back an inch. "I didn't—I really

336

haven't had time to talk about it! It's too complicated!"

"My fans tried to hurt you. That isn't that complicated."

Lola's eyebrows shot up, then knotted so ferociously she hardly looked like herself. "Brenda told you?"

"Yeah. In ten seconds, she told me more than you even *tried* to."

Her expression fell, vulnerability skipping across her slack mouth to her shining eyes. "It's not because I didn't want to tell you. Drez, there's just... so much we need to talk about, and all of it terrifies me."

More secrets. What else has she kept hidden from me?

The heavy silence choked us, creating a limbo where neither of us dared to speak first. Nearby the crowd cheered, their jubilee floating backstage and into our bitter world. The band before us had finished. It was our turn, but...

How could we play in unison when our hearts were battling to find any harmony at all?

****

In spite of what plagued her, Lola didn't hold back on stage. She smoked through Tuesday Left Behind, smashed expectations

337

with No More Stars, and dared her strings to rupture during an encore of Black Grit.

Her guitar thundered while the crowd strained to be heard over the music. Every flick of sound she created made my heart twitch. She forced me to remember one crucial thing among all the shit we were tangled in:

Lola was perfect.

Several times, I looked right at her, but she never looked back. She didn't *need* to; her music was inside of me.

Porter hit a heavy, shuddering note. The bass moved like a train that had gone off its tracks, slamming around the venue. I let it guide me towards our final song, Velvet Lost. "Sticky sweetness," I sang, "Burning fast. My love, my dear, this will be your last..."

And that was when I saw it.

Over the sea of waving arms and gnashing teeth, a stark white poster drew my attention. The garish words read a simple phrase: 'Lola is a Slut.'

Air caught in my throat. Twisting my head, I gaped at Lola, wondering if she'd noticed. Suddenly, the way she'd been keeping her eyes down during our set made sense. Sweat burned down my collar bone; now that I'd noticed one sign, I couldn't stop seeing them.

'Go Home Lola.'
'Drezden Isn't Yours.'
'Bring Back Johnny Muse.'

'Kill Yourself.'

My lungs shriveled, then flared with my rage. *Who the hell are these people?* Everyone I looked at became a potential enemy. *Get rid of Lola, bring back Johnny?*

He wasn't even there, but I hated him more than ever.

It was a testament to my ability that I finished out the song. My skull was bloating with images of people who would *dare* insult the woman I had found fit to let into my life. Looking across at Lola, I studied the lonely corner of her frown. I felt incredibly stupid, my brain just now putting the pieces together. This amazing woman, she'd handled so much today, and I was just beginning to glean some of it.

Brenda said crazy fans messed with Lola earlier. That had cut me to my core just to hear. The signs in the crowd, displaying jealousy fueled disgust for the girl I adored, were the last wounds I could handle.

Crushing the mic, I spoke over the echoing clapping hands and shouts. "I know we're finished, but I have an announcement." From the side-lines, I caught a glimpse of Brenda's face; she was whiter than normal. I was going off script and it terrified her. "I have something to say, and all of you better be listening."

Porter was mouthing something at me, Colt was fidgeting with his sticks.

It was Lola who held me.

Finally, after the whole set, she was looking my way. "You all know that we've got a new member here." Winding the mic-wire around my wrist, I spoke louder. "And you all know she's the best fucking thing to happen to this band in a long time."

A mixture of cheers and confusion erupted. I was glad they were listening. It was the least they all could do.

I said, "So, here it is." My tongue wet my lips, prepping me for my own spontaneous decision. "Lola and I will be writing a new song together, a song we'll be performing at the final show on this tour." My body swelled with indignant pride. "It's going to be the best fucking thing you've ever heard. I can't wait to share it."

Dropping the mic, I stormed backstage with a wall of squeals buffeting me. I hadn't known what I was going to say when I began my speech, but it felt so *right*. I hadn't created a new song in some time. I'd definitely never co-written one.

This would be beautiful. Lola and I were going to break the damn world into pieces. I didn't care if we left it burnt and barren. If I had her, the rest could fade away for good.

"Drez!"

Breathing heavily, Colt stopped beside me. "Holy shit, man! Were you serious out there?"

"Of course I was." Reaching back, I felt my empty pocket, reminding myself I had no cigarettes. Old habits were hard to break. "I want to write a song with her."

"Why didn't you warn us you were going to announce that?" he asked.

Tilting my head, I considered my explanation. Talking about Lola's enemies came too close to legitimizing them, so I held my tongue. "Guess I didn't think I had to," I said.

The drummer reached for me, then pulled up short. Maybe he sensed the seething anger that still boiled in me, maybe it was something else, but Colt was acting like I was poisonous. "Fine," he sighed. "It doesn't matter."

"It *does* matter," Brenda snapped, hands choking her hips as she walked up. "Drezden! Did Lola even know about your plan?"

"No," a dazed, distant voice said. "I didn't know." Standing tall, Lola pushed Colt and Brenda aside. She was hugging her purple Stratocaster, the color merging with her shirt, as if the two could finally become one. "You really want to write a song with me?"

Locking my knees, I grit my teeth to keep my voice steady. "I meant everything I said out there." I wished I could read her mind. Instead, I endured a long minute of her unblinking silence.

Finally, in a great slump of her muscles, Lola melted. "Oh, Drezden. That's—I just…" No tears escaped, but a wet-warmth twinkled in her blue eyes. The skin on her cheeks and nose flushed, redness brought on by her delight.

Ignoring all the eyes on us, I pulled her against me. I'd have crushed her, but I was too aware of her guitar between us. If I damaged it, she'd never forgive me. "That means you want to do it?" I asked.

"Yes!" Laughing, shaking against my ribs, Lola stood on her toes and kissed me like she'd never get to again. "Writing a song with Drezden Halifax is a dream come true."

My arms wound around her shoulders possessively. *I want all her dreams to be about me.* Her dreams… and her reality.

Someone coughed politely; Brenda, trying to be subtle. When I did nothing but tangle my tongue with Lola's again, Brenda groaned. "Okay you two, break it up." She clapped her hands like we were pigeons she could scare off. We didn't budge. "Or don't, whatever, I've got a whiskey-sour with my name on it waiting at the bar."

"I'll join you," Colt said, faking the sound of throwing up. "Porter, don't gawk! You're just encouraging them."

Their laughter faded as they left the backstage. That was when I finally leaned away from Lola. It was a mere few inches; it felt like a chasm. "You want to get out of here?" I asked, my throat thick with desire.

Whatever heat that had been building in Lola evaporated. From her depths, a ghostly sadness came to the surface. It twisted in her wide eyes and tugged at my center. "Yes, but not for anything fun. What I want... is to tell you everything. All the things I should have, and didn't."

My hands rested on her wrists. "Then let's go. I want to hear all of it."

Linking our fingers, she led me out into the night.

****

We could hear the sounds of people partying. The noise sank through the walls of the tour bus, a cruel reminder that out there, the world was full of joy.

Sitting on Lola's bunk, we were coated in black soberness.

"So those girls slashed your tire," I whispered, fighting down the waves of resentment. "Some insane stalkers think they own me, and that if you were gone, I'd waste my time with *them?*"

Sitting in my lap, her head on my chest, Lola stroked my palm. "Shh. I don't know what they think. Just that they don't want me around you."

Burying my nose in the top of her hair, my eyes fell shut. "Too bad for them that I always get what I want." Feeling Lola burrow against my warmth was pure joy. However, I wasn't naive. I knew she had wanted to talk to me about more than what had happened on the road. "There's something else," I said.

She went lifeless in my arms; only the gentle thumping of her heart near mine reassured me she wasn't a corpse. "Yeah. It's something—I don't know how to start."

Reaching down, I brushed her bangs from her forehead. "Start where it makes the most sense."

When her arm lifted, I thought she was reaching for me. In the low-light of the bunk, Lola's tattoo was a smear of black and grey; the castle hardly visible. "You asked me about this." Her voice sounded far away. "You wanted to know what it meant."

That's right. I remembered that night in great detail. "You told me it meant nothing."

"I lied."

"I know," I responded gently.

Spreading her fingers, Lola touched the tattoo with reverence. Twisting it, she showed me the underside. Then, gripping my hand, led me to feel her skin. It was like brail in places; the scars told me what she was going to say. "In high school, I was bullied. It pushed me over the edge, tempted me to... to cut myself. Pain was the only thing that gave me control."

344

The image of how I'd caught her biting her own tongue flashed in my head. *Pain for control. Pain so she could play her music with me near her.*

She whispered, "It was a hard time."

"School?" I was thinking of my own teen years.

"Living," she said flatly. Meeting my eyes, Lola dropped her arm. "People were awful to me from the start. I had a shitty life. This tattoo represents that."

Bile crawled up my esophagus, scalding as much as the hate I felt for the people who had made this girl's life hell. "Who was so cruel to you?"

She didn't pause to think. "My teachers. The people in school, the town. And mostly... my parents."

There was an echo inside of me, a chunk of my being that felt the utmost empathy. I knew what having an awful parent was like. Fuck, I knew it more than anything.

An idea occurred to me. "When you said your parents wouldn't come to your show, it had nothing to do with flying, did it?"

Lola's snort was unadulterated disgust. "They never gave a shit about my music. I don't think they care what I'm doing right now. If you called them, asking about me? I bet they'd just hang up."

Too many sharp, jagged feelings were consuming me. *If her parents never cared*

*about her, then... her relationship with Sean...
the pain and hurt she felt when he shrugged
her off and walked away must have been
immense.*

It clicked, I got where her attachment
came from. The brother who had taught her
guitar, who'd pushed her to audition for my
band—he was the only person she'd had before
me.

"Why do that?" I asked. The thoughts in
my skull were fragmented. "Why get a tattoo
that reminds yourself of such an awful time in
your life?" *Who would choose to make it so
easy to remember the bad moments?* My scar
itched; toxic, mocking me.

"It's there to keep me from falling back
into being that person." Pulling her knees to
her chest, Lola snuggled against me ever
harder. "Running from the past is cowardly."

Now it was my turn to go stiff. "There's
no good in embracing the bad parts of the
past."

Shifting in my lap, Lola faced me fully. I
expected her to tell me more, but the question
in her expression was... out of place. Her plump
lips parted, no sound falling free.

What does she want to ask me?

"Drez," she said quietly, "I was really
messed up before. I got this tattoo to remind
me of my past... and of my decision to change.
But that's not what *made* me change." She
breathed deep. "When I was helping Sean out

346

at this tiny little hole of a club, I found a CD. And the singer on it was... breathtaking." A shy smile grew on her face.

Tingles of disbelief ran down my spine as I suspected what she was saying. *Is she serious?* I didn't want to believe our connection ran the length of time, it was too fucking good to be true. The quaking of my heart made my voice hoarse. "My music?"

Her nod was deliberate. "Your first CD."

My nostrils flared, hands dragging her to me so I could taste that plump little mouth of hers. *She found my first CD,* I thought in quiet shock. *She heard my lyrics and they changed her life. This amazing, insanely wonderful girl...*

She's been meant for me from the start.

There was so much in my heart and head. I was linking her hard past with my own; we were so similar. At the same time, I was struggling with her decision to bravely display her wounds, while I'd done my best to bury mine. Our souls were so similar; our beliefs were not.

I couldn't be like Lola and wear my damage on my sleeve.

That wasn't the path for me.

Nuzzling her throat, thrilling with her beating pulse, I sighed. "Lola, you didn't need to tell me all of this. What made you do it?"

Suddenly, she couldn't look me in the eye. "I just—I think it's important to share this

347

stuff. We should know what's made us who we are. We should... talk about it."

'We' she says. "I thought about this earlier," I said. My stubble traced along her jaw; I spoke against her skull, as if I could penetrate her brain. "There's a better word for us than *we*. Let's call it like it is, we're a couple, right?"

In my embrace, she shuddered. "Boyfriend and girlfriend... it's more than I ever imagined." Around my middle, her limbs stitched into place. "I want that. I want everything that comes with actually dating you —dating Drezden Halifax. I want to know everything about you."

A wriggling line of paranoia crawled in my guts. Was I crazy, or was Lola hinting that she knew I was keeping something from her? *No. She doesn't know about that. I've been careful. She couldn't have seen.* But she was going to learn eventually.

Wasn't she?

I hadn't fully thought it through. If I wanted Lola as completely as I did, it was inevitable that she'd see my scar, that she'd ask about it.

I'll have to explain it to her.

Lola's teeth gnawed at her own lower lip. I kissed her, gave her a new thing to chew on.

But not yet.

Not just yet.

348

Buried in her smell, her flavor, I begged for more time. *Please, just let me have this for a little longer. Don't make me have to tell this wonderful woman what I went through.*

What my father did to me and my mother.

It was as close to a prayer as I'd ever made.

****

Lola's breathing was steady in her sleep. It hadn't taken her long to drift off, but my own unconsciousness alluded me.

We were curled in the small bed, her head under my chin, her scent invading my senses. I'd have blamed her nearness for keeping me awake if I hadn't known better.

I was swamped in the tepid images of my past, Lola exposing herself to me, and the events of the day. In her dream, Lola whimpered. The noise jolted from my scalp to my prick. She trembled against me, flesh smooth and hot. It took a massive effort not to wake her up with my hands down her panties.

Even in sleep, she draws me in.

Her next soft, sad mumble deflated my arousal. She jerked violently, her muscles exerting energy, her eyelids fluttering as the nightmare took her. When her lips parted, I realized she was talking to herself. I strained my ears in the almost-darkness.

"No," she pleaded, "Don't leave me. Please."

Narrowing my eyes, I gripped her hips. *I won't ever leave you. Never.*

Those beautiful lips twisted again. "Please stay... Sean."

I stopped breathing.

In this late hour, the girl I loved—*loved*—was fighting devils in her mind. This wasn't about me, but the strife she was having with her brother. For a long while she shivered on my chest, the air shaking with her gut-wrenching mumbles. Staring at the ceiling, haunted by those sorrowful whispers, I debated what to do.

Craning my neck, my probing gaze fell on Lola's bed-side table. There, calling to me with a solution, sat her cellphone on its charger. The decision I was about to make was a heavy one—but for her, I'd do anything.

Carefully, I guided Lola off of me. She looked peaceful, and still, it killed me to leave her alone. Even so, gathered up her phone in one hand, my jeans in the other. A shadow, I pushed her curtain aside, moving deeper into the bus. No one waited for me in the aisle; I'd heard both Colt and Porter return to their rooms over an hour ago.

Ducking into my room, I zipped my pants on, then shoved my head through the neck-hole of a hooded sweatshirt. In the darkness, I flipped Lola's phone open.

It wasn't hard to find Sean's number.

I typed fast, just my thumb doing the work. It was after two in the morning, there was a strong chance the guy was asleep. Lola's message—my message—was sent. It said 'Meet me outside Belly Up. We need to talk.'

Clicking the device shut, I shoved it deep in my pocket. Yanking the hood over my head, I drifted out of the bus. There were a few security guards loitering outside, and to their credit, they were still awake. I nodded at them; they let me be. They were there to keep stalkers and groupies out, not to keep me in.

The Colorado breeze was crisp. I was grateful for my sweatshirt. Hunkering down against the furthest darkened wall of the bar, I looked out on the lot and waited.

I didn't have to wait long.

Sean walked my way like a phantom. He must have been awake when I'd sent the text, there was no way he'd have come outside so fast otherwise. The dark grey jacket he wore came into focus. "Lola?" he hissed. "Lola, are you out here?"

He couldn't see me in the shadows, the street lights were too far away. I curled my fist in his jacket and ripped him closer. He stumbled, struggling against me with a surprised shout. "What the—what the fuck?

Who the hell—" My wide hand covered his mouth.

Wrenching him around, my muscles worked to slam his back against the cold wall.

Here, no one would see us.

I knew his eyes had adjusted to the dark when they finally went wide, recognizing who had attacked him. "Shh," I growled. "Not so loud. Calm down."

There was still stiffness in his body when Sean released my forearms. With one more pointed glare, I removed my hand. "What the shit, man?" he asked. "Where's Lola?" His eyebrows went up. "Fuck, did you use her phone to message me? You've got some balls."

Ignoring his obvious distress, I said, "You wouldn't have come if you knew it was me. I need to talk to you."

"About *what?*" Scoffing, he buried his hands in his pockets.

His attitude sent an anxious buzzing down my fingers. I wanted to shove him against the wall again, just to make him realize how serious I was. "About you and Lola, what the hell else?"

"What's going on between her and me isn't your problem." Sean's chin bent low, his blue eyes that looked more like ebony narrowing at me.

"*Everything* that has to do with her is my problem." Snarling, I slammed a palm flat on the wall beside his head. His flinch was glorious, goading me on. "And right now, she's miserable because of how you've been treating her."

"How *I've* been treating her?" He shoved my shoulders, the impact solid enough that my heel slid back an inch. "She's the one who's been ignoring me, treating *me* like shit!"

Our voices were rising. Someone might hear us, our secret meeting could be ruined, but I'd stopped caring. He thought Lola was the one treating him badly? *Her?* "You're overreacting," I warned. "She cares about you. She's just been busy getting into the swing of being in a real band."

Madness—disgust —bloomed across Sean's features. "I don't know if that was a fucking dig at Barbed Fire or not, but she's in your 'real' band because I'm the one who pushed her to audition. Getting into the swing of things? That's bullshit. She was just as busy before and she always told me what was going on."

"Talk to her." It was less of a request, more a demand. "You *make* the time to talk to her and clear this up. She's dealt with too much already. Lola doesn't deserve the tension between you two bringing her down."

Out of the blue his anger deflated. Folding his arms, he leaned against the wall and scanned me closely. "She told you, didn't she? About our parents and how those shitty kids in school bullied her. She told you everything."

"Yeah, she told me."

Laughing bitterly, he ruffled his own hair. "Well, good. So you know I'm the only one who ever gave a shit about her, that helped her out." He gazed up at me from under his crinkled eyebrows. "You must think it's easy for me to go talk to her, to clear all of this up."

"It *is* easy, Sean." I softened the razor on my tongue. "If I could be the only person she needed, I would be." *I'd be everything if she let me.* "But she's torn up because you're pissed at her. I can't fix that. Just—man, just fucking talk to her."

The guitarist cocked his head like a bird. "And if I don't?"

Clenching my hands into fists, I took a deep breath. Sean watched me closely, I made sure he could see my gigantic smile; how hollow it was. "Then I'll break your fucking jaw. I've wanted to since you kicked my amp over years back, anyway."

He didn't laugh or squirm. His expression was purely blank. "Guess we are similar after all."

In the chilly air, the two of us waited. I couldn't have said for what; perhaps just the chance one of us would strike first, that there'd be someone to blame for ruining this fragile attempt at an 'agreement' so the other could get violent without repercussion.

354

Sean's exhale broke the moment. Pushing off the wall, he strolled around me, speaking as he went. "I'll talk to her. But don't you dare tell her we had this chat."

I won't, I thought privately. When Sean vanished from sight, I finally uncurled my fists. The tendons throbbed. The discomfort was good, it helped to center me so I could wonder if I was crazy.

Messaging Sean... making him promise to talk to his sister... Who *was* I?

I'd never worked so hard at making someone else happy.

Lola really had changed me.

She didn't wake up when I crept back into her room, or when I set her cellphone back down, the message to Sean long erased. Not until I invaded her bed, my jeans scratching along her bare thighs, did her eyelashes flicker. "Drez?" she mumbled, rubbing at her cheek.

Coiling around her, my tongue explored the side of her ear. "It's just me, yeah."

Every goosebump on her body rose to its peak. "I could have sworn I was alone in here." Her chuckle was frail as new snow.

"It was just a dream." My lips made a trail down her neck; her gasp was sweet candy to me. "I'd never leave you, Lola. Never."

"I know." She kissed my chin, her mouth warm and wet. "Like you said, it was a dream."

My thumb glided over the back of her ear. "When you fall asleep, don't dream that you're alone. Always try to dream of me. *Just me.*"

Heat grew in her cheeks, the shadows not capable of hiding it. "That sounds easy enough."

Soon, we were swirling tongues. It was my brain that felt twisted, though. *If it's so easy, why do you have nightmares about your brother, your pain, your torture?* Closing my eyes, I fought down a twinge of hard guilt.

This night, I'd created another secret for myself. Another lie to hide from Lola.

With her resting on my chest, I luxuriated in her warmth through my shirt and wished I was brave enough to expose my skin. Lola was breathing gently within minutes, returning to her dreams. I hoped they'd be pleasant this time—and I wondered what I'd dream about.

I would have prayed for it to be pleasant...

But I was sure I'd already spent all the prayers I was allowed.

- Chapter Twenty-Two -
Lola

Teeth glided down the inside of my thigh. In the cocoon of my bed, my blankets, only one thing burned warmer than me.

Drezden.

I was still shaking off the mask of sleep, trying to make sense of why I'd gone from dreaming about the man to waking up to something even sweeter. Curled between my legs, he revealed the danger of lying beside him in the late hours wearing nothing but some silky blue panties.

I could hardly see him under the covers. Squinting down, I was rewarded with a flare of green eyes—a beast on the hunt—and a rough squeeze of my ass. Gasping, I arched with my cheek in the pillow.

"Eyes up," was his single command. That whisper burned like pure vodka.

For a man who demanded so much, he had acquired a terrible patience in how he teased me. Gently, he rolled his mouth up my smooth skin. On each inch he left a simple kiss. The distance felt like miles by the time he got to my knee. *Wrong direction,* I thought in a haze.

No. Drezden knew what he was doing.

Back down he went, slower than before. His casual control tugged at my center. My clit

357

was throbbing already. In the blackness of my room, I heard my frantic breathing. Could someone go insane from being tormented like this?

He was on my opposite leg, licking the top of my calf, when I broke. "Stop teasing me," I sobbed.

Stubble raked my skin, his chin dragging down until he hovered just over my shaking pussy. I was hyper aware; his words could have been fingers on my slit. "Stop?" He inhaled; sharp, precise. "Lola, I haven't even started."

Biting my lip didn't stifle my whimper.

His hands came down hard on the insides of my legs. He spread them until I was taut, a violin string he could easily snap. The tip of his nose brushed deliberately down the front of my soaked panties, nudging the swelling node of my clit.

Maybe I'm still asleep. My lashes fluttered, nails curling in the sheets. *Maybe this is a dream.*

Kissing my stomach, he glided the hard muscles of his torso across mine. Climbing upwards, his weight settled, the bed creaking. His jaw angled down to kiss me; I met him halfway.

My tongue danced with his. His hips crushed on mine, making the firm shape of his engorged cock plain as day. The heat of it seared my lower belly. "Fuck," I whispered. I couldn't keep myself from bucking up against him.

Drezden played his long fingers under me. My spine led the way until he had the globes of my ass in his grip, kneading me, shaping me. I'd lost control already, but the carnal hunger in me became all I knew.

I rocked hard against him, tried to pull him towards me with my dripping pussy. The wetness down my thighs was audible, every movement of Drezden's stiff cock increasing the volume. Still, he didn't give in, didn't slide aside my panties or his briefs, nothing.

Couldn't he tell how much I needed him? Didn't he understand my desperation?

When I reached down, trying to yank his underwear off, he just chuckled. "In a rush?"

"You keep doing this," I said, working at the cloth. "Teasing me, making me crazy! Isn't it hard to hold back? Is it just me that feels so—so unhinged?"

My arms were crushed over my head. I couldn't recover before he bent low, kissing me until my mouth was numb. Everything that helped me make sense of my existence fled. I lost gravity, floating until Drezden let me go.

His green eyes simmered inches from me. "Of course it isn't just you. I fight every minute of every day to keep myself from ripping your panties down to your ankles so I can sink my dick inside of you." I gasped sharply; he'd rubbed his raging erection between my thighs. "I work so hard to control what I do to you, Lola." His voice dropped, a rock that vanished in the sea. "I take my time because anything less... and I'd lose myself. I wouldn't be able to stop."

That honesty should have terrified me.

Hooking my legs around his lower back, I pulled him closer. "Do it," I whispered, nipping his lip before he could lean away. What did he see in my eyes? I could only imagine. "Fucking lose yourself, let go with me."

I saw his teeth in the dark. The next sound was my shout of surprise; he'd torn my panties off in a rush. "You're bold." He cut off any words I had left with a throttling kiss. I dragged in air as he pulled away. "You get under my skin so good. No," he said, winding his hand in my hair. "*Deeper* than that. You get *inside* of me."

I wanted to touch him, to run my hands over his shirt, under it, mauling his skin. I almost begged him. The words were on my tongue.

The thick head of his dick, rubbing along my puffy lower lips, shut me up. He had himself in his fist, saturating the smooth tip of his cock with my wetness. *No condom,* I thought in distant panic. In one motion, he filled me to the brim.

Biting his shoulder, I knew it wasn't enough to muffle me. Everyone on that tour bus was going to hear me scream. Drezden didn't care... and it made my heart turn as liquid as my pussy.

He was stuffing me deep, thrusting like he could go further each stroke. Groaning in the back of my throat revealed how decadent such a normal sensation could feel. Drezden made every action sexual.

Gasping, I tried to meet his pounding cock. He was primal, seeking to find what *he* wanted. The pressure built in me, hovering on the cusp of exploding. His shaft buried inside of me almost violently.

I was barely fitting his cock inside of me. I thought it should hurt. Instead, I felt a tingle of excitement. We were bound together at the root; twisting, sweating, uncaring.

My mouth numbed as my cells in my lower belly took control. All of my energy was being directed at my twitching clit. "I'm coming! I'm..." It was all I managed to say. He kissed me as I came, holding me while I trembled.

In my ear, his grunt was strained. In my slippery, delicious delirium, I realized he was fighting the urge to come inside of me. The way he wrenched himself out of my flexing pussy left me hollow. Warm, sticky seed spilled over my belly. Drezden gulped for air.

His head hung low, sweat beading on his brow. He reminded me of a great tree after a rain storm. He was strong, but some things could bend him.

Me, I realized in surprise. *I can make him bend.* I pushed the hair from his slick forehead. "I know how it feels," I said softly. "Getting under your skin, I mean." His look of surprise made me kiss his warm cheek.

Right then, things felt so perfect. Just the two of us, sitting together in our salt and silence, enjoying just being alive. It gave me hope that things were finally smoothing into place.

What a world, if everything could always feel so perfect.

If only.

****

The rain was sharp, it cut through my sweater and into my bones. My soaked jeans made every step I took harder. Honestly, I didn't need them to be any harder than they already were.

Three days had passed since we'd left the city of Aspen in Colorado. We'd played every night for different faces, the screams blurring my brain until I recalled nothing but the itch in my fingers and the sweat staining my brow afterward. Each night, after every show, I'd tried to seek out my brother.

And each night he'd been a ghost.

Sean was a master at avoiding me. At the after parties he slipped off to drink or dance or fuck or whatever it was he was doing. I didn't need the details, the writing on the wall was clear.

He wants nothing to do with me.

Too bad for him that I was done being avoided.

Barbed Fire's ratty bus waited in the parking lot. In the rain, it was a hulking elephant close to dying from old age. I didn't knock, didn't take a moment to consider what I was doing. Slowing down increased the risk of backing out.

I knew these doors. I'd shaken them apart so many times. They never locked right, but no one cared. All the gear worth any money was safe in the back of another van. If anyone was going to try and steal something, they wouldn't be coming here.

Not true, I thought as I climbed the short steps. Lifting my head, I stared across the aisle at the bodies slouched in the ripped seats. *I'm here to steal time from my brother.* We saw each other immediately, his eyes reflecting mine. He looked... worn out. As bad as the bus itself.

Other people were moving, grumbling at the intrusion so early in the morning. Both of us ignored them. I'm unsure if we even blinked. "Come outside with me," I said flatly.

"It's pouring out there." Shoving the blanket off of his naked chest, Sean grabbed for a wrinkled shirt. It muffled his voice when he tugged it over his face. "You want us both to get sick?"

"Come outside," I said again.

Beside me, a giant lump shifted. Shark squinted at us both, clearing his throat roughly. Like we hadn't gotten his meaning, he did it again. "It's fuckin' early as shit, you guys. Go somewhere else to talk. My head's about to crack, fuck."

"Go back to bed, Shark." Sean tried to smooth his hair, but it wouldn't obey.

Droplets of rain water, cool on my burning skin, drifted down my neck. "Just come on," I said. Turning in the seat, my brother began digging around on the floor. He had the balls to not even look at me? That pushed me to the edge. "Stop ignoring me! This is why I had to come here in the first—"

"I'm not ignoring you." With an umbrella in hand, Sean stumbled towards me down the aisle. "I'm just making sure neither of us drowns out there."

Thrown off by his sudden compliance, I followed him out into the storm. The parking lot was flooded, puddles forcing us to walk in awkward patterns. He held the umbrella over both our heads, the nearness reminding me of when we'd walk home together from school as kids.

My mind was already in a strange spot. Nostalgia was doing its best to ruin my courage. When Sean spoke, I visibly jumped. "Lola, why are we out here?"

Lifting my eyes, I watched the edge of the umbrella. Rain fell to its death in rivulets. "I needed to corner you. You've been avoiding me ever since... ever since Drez and I..." My cheeks burned so hot I expected to see steam.

"That's not it." He halted in front of the quiet road, the surface shiny from the street lights. I felt him looking at me, but I kept watching the edge of the canopy. "I wasn't avoiding you because you slept with him. I don't care about any of that."

Burying my hands in my pockets, I searched for warmth and found none. "Is it because we haven't been talking as much? I promised to tell you all sorts of things, and then I stopped, I know, but..."

"No. Lola, you don't get it." The edge of the umbrella wavered; rain tumbled in a cascade into the street, melting away. "It's not about any one thing. It's all of it together. It's what it means for *me*."

That threw me off. "What does it mean for you?" *What is he...*

"It means you don't need me anymore."

My eyes were frozen on his, searching the depths of his sapphire-blues to better understand the hurt, the defeat, simmering there. "Of course I need you! Sean, you're my brother. I'm always going to need you."

I despised how sad his smile was. "I guess I just wanted to be the one you always came to for help... for whatever. I don't know. After everything I've done—well." He broke the stare, gazing off at the nothingness of the thunderclouds. "I'm just being selfish. You made it to the top. I wanted to see you get there, but I also wanted to be there with you. I guess I wasn't ready for your success."

Was it possible for my heart to crumble? I grabbed his wrist where it brushed the umbrella handle. "What are you talking about? You're the one who..." *Who I always looked up to. Who is—was—at the top.* All at once, I understood the wall between my brother and I.

His eyes glistened. Sean knew what I'd just grasped. "Yeah," he said. "You're where I always dreamed I'd be. Headlining a tour like this makes you better than me, Lola. Maybe you always were."

"No! No, I wasn't. I'm not." A compliment had never cut so deep. I didn't *want* to be better than Sean. He'd taught me everything and he'd worked so hard. He was the one who should be in my shoes. "Stop acting like your dream is over."

He adjusted his grip on the umbrella, crushing it. I felt it under my fingers. "You don't get it. There's no way to climb past this."

"'This.' What does 'this' mean?" Eyeing the tension in his jaw, I listened to the rain drumming around us. "There has to be a way for Barbed Fire to go further." *Life can't be unfair like that.* "It's all you ever wanted, right? How can you even imagine giving up?"

His frown was soft on the edges. "If I knew of a way to succeed, would you help me?"

I stood straighter with a rush of excitement. I wanted to cling to the tiny speck of hope in his question. "Of course! You know I'll help you anyway I can, Sean."

There was a storm in his eyes, it was far greater than the one that roared around us. The words that left his mouth clawed away the last of my warmth. "I want you to leave Four and a Half Headstones."

My tongue stuck inside my mouth. "W— what?"

Sean curled his palm around my fingers on the handle, trapping me under his pleading stare. "Quit the band and come join Barbed Fire. You can be our second guitarist, do rhythm! I'm an idiot for never suggesting it before. I know you always wanted to join."

My heart was going wild, it had never felt so big and so small all at once. "Wait, Sean..."

"Lola. Please." His grip tightened on me; I struggled to decide if he was begging me or intimidating me. I didn't like either option. "If you do this, we can both make it big. We'll destroy every stage! Sell out shows! We'll be on top, the both of us."

Both of us. "I can't just abandon Drez and the others."

"Relax. They'll find someone to replace you," he said, laughing like I was some delusional child.

My muscles screamed as I ripped my hand away from his. I stumbled backwards into the rain, the cold droplets clearing my head. "They're my friends." Drezden's scent tickled my brain. "And... more than that."

Lifting his chin, Sean held the umbrella steady. "You're actually picking them over me. Over my dream that you act like you care so much about."

"I do care! But you can't expect me to shove them aside like this!"

"What makes them worth more than me?" He was whispering, I was halfway reading his lips. "What makes *him* worth more?"

The pity in my heart bled away. "He isn't making me choose between you two."

Laughing bitterly, Sean tilted the umbrella at an angle. He didn't react to the water that splashed across his shoulders. "No? Think about it, Lola! That asshole makes you choose every second of the day! Did you forget that you missed my show at Belly Up because of him?"

He was right. He was right, and it hurt more than if he'd just knocked my teeth out. "He didn't mean to make that happen!" *Did he?*

368

Sean spat into the street. "You think a guy like him is worth more than your own damn brother?"

"Stop saying that! Stop acting like it's about any of that!"

"He's an entitled piece of shit!"

I threw my arms down, shouting over the thunder that roared. "You're the one acting entitled! I just wanted us to talk again, for things to be normal! Why are you being this way?"

Rain had drenched us both. It felt like we were the only ones alive in the world right then. Sean mumbled, but I heard him clearly. "Because I care about you. Because I want to protect you."

"I'm not in any danger, Sean."

"You really think *he* isn't dangerous?"

My brain was forever spinning. "Drezden wouldn't hurt me."

Sean's brows ducked low. "Are you sure? He's got a hell of a temper. Do you actually know anything about him?"

"Of course I—"

"Anything *real?*"

Gripping my forehead, I focused through my pulsing temples. "What are you talking about?"

The satisfied smile that crawled across my brother's face left my insides twisting. I didn't know this man. "Do you even know his real name?"

Something inside me crackled; exploded. *His real name.* It left my ears ringing, made me wonder if lightning had boomed inches from me. *Drezden isn't his real name.*

How had I not known that?

How did *Sean?*

He offered me the umbrella. When I didn't reach for it, Sean forced it into my hand, curling my fingers around the base like until I held on. "You think you know this guy. You don't know anything about him, not really. He lies and hides from you. He's a deceptive, greedy motherfucker. Okay?"

I stared at my feet.

"Lola. Look at me."

I did as he asked. There were raindrops perched on my eyelashes; when I lifted my head, they rolled down like tears.

Sean said, "Ask him to tell you the truth. When he won't—and he *won't*—come talk to me. I promise I'll bring you the answers you need." For a while we both just watched each other's pale faces. He moved to leave, hesitating. "Unlike him, you can trust me." Then he was gone, jogging back to his bus.

In the early, muted shades of the world, I stood alone. My existence was tip-tapping rain, the whistle of wind, and that was all. The water rushed along the road, carrying trash and vanishing into the sewer grates, never to be seen again.

I wanted to be that trash.
I wanted to wash away.

- Chapter Twenty-Three -
Drezden

"Hey, you alive in there?" I asked.

Lola sat up ram-rod straight. Sunlight, streaming in from the small window in the roof of the bus, made her face glow. "Sorry, I zoned out. What was that?"

She's been zoned out for days. And the reason is fucking obvious. It bothered me constantly how, after I'd confronted him in the dark hours half a week ago, Sean still hadn't reconciled with Lola. *The piece of shit said he'd talk to her. He clearly hasn't. Do I need to corner him a second time?*

"Now you're the one zoning out," she said, perfect lips tilting in a smile.

If there wasn't a table between us, I would have pushed her down right then and kissed her taunting mouth. I settled for reaching across, stealing her fingers and guiding them over the notebook I'd set in front of her. "I asked what you thought of these lyrics so far?"

Like my touch had revitalized her, Lola squeezed my hands. Curls of her thick hair toppled her bare shoulders when she leaned down to read the words. I hadn't had anyone judge my song-writing skills in such a long time. Watching her scrutinize the bits of my brain and soul carved into ratty, lined paper was making my heart jump.

What if she hates it? Blood pounded in my ears. *Fuck, it doesn't matter if she hates it. Why would that make a difference?* I was sure my lungs were going to collapse from holding my breath. *Of course it would make a difference. I want her to be impressed.*

I'd never felt so vulnerable; I regretted handing her the lyrics.

Maybe I could grab them back?

"These are wonderful." The pink blooming on her cheeks made her blue irises sparkle even brighter. "How did you write these so fast?"

Swallowing past the dry patch in my throat was difficult. "It's been almost a week since we decided to collaborate. That's plenty of time." I'd poured over the words hourly between dreaming and waking. Writing a song like this—and did she understand what it was? —took every moment I had.

And Lola said it was wonderful.

The table between us was mattering less and less.

"I have a question, though," she said. Pulling her hands from me, Lola turned the notebook around, brushing her nail down the paper. "Am I insane, or did you mark down a section for a second guitar?"

Now it was my turn to smile. "We'll play together."

She dropped the notebook like it was a bomb. "Both of us?" I didn't understand the tension crawling across her forehead. What was she thinking about that had her so unsteady?

Leaning forward, I tucked her hair behind her ears. The way she bent into my touch made my jeans far too tight. *Fuck, she works me up just by existing.* "Is that a problem?"

Lola didn't relax, I felt her pulse under my palm. "It's fine. I didn't know you could play guitar, is all. It's... kind of weird to not know that about you."

The bus seat rumpled when I fell back into it with my full weight. "I'm nowhere near as good as you, but I'm decent enough to play with if you'll lead."

"How long have you been playing for?"

Grimacing at the memory of large hands guiding my own across the strings of a guitar, I hesitated. *I don't want to go down that road.* "Who knows," I mumbled quickly. "I guess since I was a kid."

"Then you learned from someone, like me. Was it a brother? Do you *have* any siblings at all?" There was an edge in her voice that left me confused.

"What? Why does that matter?"

Furrowing her eyebrows, Lola set her intense stare right on me. It was impossible to break away. "Because it's something about you I don't know. Tell me about your family, about learning to play. Just give me more information about yourself."

"You're acting weird." Lola flinched at my observation, but she didn't look close to backing off. *What's this all about? Why the sudden digging into my life?* "I don't like this inquisition. You're asking me things that don't matter."

"Then what *does* matter?"

Grabbing my notebook, I spun it on the table, jammed my finger onto it. "This! Our final tour performance is tomorrow night. Let's start practicing so we can show everyone out there how serious this is!"

"Maybe you should show me how serious *we* are, first!" Scowling, Lola pushed out of the seat. "You said we were dating, that you're my boyfriend, but I hardly know anything about you!"

We hung on the precipice of destruction. I could see it in her eyes, *knew* she was about to storm off the bus if I didn't do something. Pulling in a lungful of air, I stood up to block the aisle. "Lola, listen. What you're poking at here... maybe there's a reason I don't want to go into it. Okay?"

Holding her ground, she looked into my eyes and didn't waver. "So there *is* something you're hiding from me."

Frost darted through my veins. *What does she know?* "Everyone hides things." Lola's eyes rippled, hinting at a deep guilt. She had hidden things from me, too, until recently. I was sure I could have turned the whole conversation on its head until she felt bad about pressing me.

Instead, I settled for wrapping her hands in mine. Her breath caught as I pulled her against my chest, my voice soft in the silence of the bus. "Lola, listen to me. You want to know more about my past, but it's just not worth knowing. Nothing about who I was before we met is important."

She leaned into me, stiff as old bread. The way she was resisting me, all while her heart thumped along my ribs, just encouraged me to try and break her down. Before I could do anything beyond nuzzling her tender throat, Lola squeezed my fingers and turned away. "Everything about you is important. Past, present, and even future. Isn't it the same for you about me?"

Shit. She had me there. I wanted to know, to have, everything about Lola Cooper. Gingerly, I glided my fingers up her arms, explored her goosebumps. When I reached her shoulders I cupped them. "Trust me. When I say my old life isn't important, I mean it. I don't want you asking me about it. Alright? Lola?"

Her eyelashes hid those blues from my view. "No. It's not alright." Her elegant neck arched back, allowing her to look at me so matter-of-factly. "You told me not to lie, or to act tough when I'm faking it. So I won't. I'm frustrated you won't talk to me. Hell, I'm even mad about it. But I also won't force you to tell me about your past." Untangling herself, she scooped up the notebook from the table. "Come on. You wanted to practice, let's go do it."

The air around me felt... colder. Watching her taut spine, how her shoulders were pulled back sharply enough to treat her shirt like a coat hanger, I regretted my words. *But what else can I do?*

In what world would telling Lola about my fucked up life help either of us?

****

We had the practice room to ourselves for some time. That was good, because I was rusty as hell on guitar, and didn't want Colt and Porter seeing me fumble. *We should have practiced sooner*. It didn't help that I was feeling the pressure from Lola's glum mood.

Tightening my strings, I glanced up at her where she sat close by. We both needed to see the sheet of paper with the music notes, especially as we randomly scribbled changes while we worked.

The song we were creating was coming together. It was a beautiful thing made muddy by the sourness between us both.

"You think this part should be faster?" she asked, tapping the page, adjusting the Stratocaster in her lap. "Where you sing, 'Wrapping, coiling, merging with the world?'"

When she says the lyrics so bluntly, it makes me feel... ashamed? She was missing the whole core of the song. My face was hot; looking at her was difficult. *Shit. I feel like an awkward teen all over again, fuck.* "Yeah. Let's speed that section up."

Lola smudged more pencil down, then plucked a few notes thoughtfully. "I think that'll sound better. More intense."

I drained my water bottle. "You write a lot of music before this?"

"None." At my look of disbelief, Lola shrugged. "Nothing structured, I mean. I just goofed off and made stuff up when it came to me."

Thinking about her audition, I let my stunned smile take over. "A damn prodigy."

She shifted on the stool. I could see the pink blush coating her cheeks. "Says the guy who can play guitar *and* sing."

"I told you." My fingers slid down the neck of the instrument, exploring it as if I'd never held one of its kind. "I'm only okay at guitar. You have ears."

"My ears tell me you're better than you think."

"Guess we're even, then."

Chewing the side of her lip, Lola focused on the floor. "Come on. Let's play this again. Neither of us are where we want to be, yet."

No, I thought sullenly, letting my guitar pick strike the chords. *Right now I want to be on you, wrapped up in your scent and your eager pussy.* My lower belly thrilled with a surge of heat at the image.

I'd have to settle with singing about my desires.

For now.

We practiced until midday, working until we were sounding cohesive. *At this rate, we'll be able to play this tomorrow night just fine.*

We were interrupted by Colt and Porter. The two slid into the room quietly, respecting how caught up we were in our song. They sat on the sidelines, eyes focused, ears straining.

By that time, I was more comfortable with my instrument. Years of playing as a child, into my teens, were coming back with the waking of my muscles. Lola never called me out on my errors; I noticed all of them, though.

I'm still not as good as I wanted to be, growing up. That doesn't matter anymore.

Being a guitarist hadn't been *my* dream, after all.

It had been my father's.

"It's sounding great," Porter said, clapping when Lola and I paused. "You sure you don't want me and Colt to join in on this?"

"Maybe a little 'oomph' from the drums?" Colt added, mimicking playing his sticks in the air. "It'd add some texture to the song."

Setting the guitar aside, I stood and cracked my back. "I appreciate the offer, but I'd like it to be just Lola and me out there for this one."

Colt rubbed at the side of his right eye. "I'll try to hold in my tears of jealousy."

"I won't." Frowning deep, the bassist gave a few hollow sobs. "This is how it begins. Kicked out of the band. I hear guitar only teams are taking over."

Wrapping his arm around Porter's shoulders, Colt nodded sagely. "I told you, we should have just learned guitar."

"Bass is close!"

"Bass is *not* close," Colt snorted.

Digging out another bottle of water, I drained half of it. "Want some, Lola?"

Setting her guitar in its case, she leaned it on the wall and headed for the door. "I'm fine. Think I'll go find some food."

Lola's escape was briefly ruined by Brenda, the red-head bumping into her as she tried to enter. "Oh! Hey, sorry Lola—where are you running off to?" Turning in place to follow the exiting girl, our manager backed into the practice room.

Hardly slowing, Lola's voice faded the further she got into the bus. "Food. I need to eat."

"But I was going to order us lunch! The hotel we're all staying at is ready for us now, it's super nice! We could all use a day to relax—and —hey!" Holding her hands up, Brenda watched in confusion as Lola escaped. "What the hell was that about?" she asked, looking at all of us.

One by one, they all stared at me. *Ah, shit.* "It's nothing," I said. "Don't worry about it."

"Drezden, what did you do this time?" Brenda sighed.

"Nothing!" Throwing up my arms, I tossed the water bottle at the trash can. The sound of it missing was poignant. "Why would you think she's upset because of me?"

"So she *is* upset," Brenda said. Digging into her purse, she lifted out her phone and squinted. "Doesn't matter. There's nothing going on between now and the final show, let her blow off some steam."

Porter brushed a palm over his faux-hawk uneasily. "No, I wanna know what Drez did that made her so tense."

"Nothing! It was nothing, fuck."

My drummer and bassist shared a knowing look. I wanted to bang their skulls together. Brenda, amazingly, came to my rescue; her hands clapped sharply. "I said forget it. Now, who wants to go check out the jacuzzi in the suite I booked for myself at the Hilton? Oh, that's right." She jammed a ruby nail at herself. "Me. This girl. Now come on, I've got a car waiting to take us over there. Everyone needs a break. *Especially* me."

Relaxing was the furthest thing from my mind. But, if it got everyone off my back, then I was glad to follow the path of least resistance. *Lola's fine. She just needs some time. That's all it is.*

I was never great at lying to myself.

****

As we drove to the hotel, I couldn't control how I looked around for Lola at every turn. In the car, I finally gave in and sent her a quick text, asking her to call me if she needed anything.

Brenda handed our keycards off to us in the Hilton lobby. When she gave me mine, she held it tight, not releasing it from her grip. "This time," she whispered, "I didn't put you and Lola in connecting rooms. Get my drift, Mr. Keep Everyone Awake at All Hours?"

382

Yanking the card free, I shoved it deep in my jeans. "It doesn't matter how far apart you put us. If I want to see her, I'll do it."

"I'm just trying to encourage you to get some sleep. You guys have a huge final show, especially with this new song and all. How's that coming, by the way?"

An arm circled my neck to pull me into a rough hug. "I heard it earlier," Colt said, shaking me playfully. "It sounded great. Tell him to add some drums though, would you? Brenda? Please?"

"As if he'd listen to me," she snorted.

Struggling out of the choke-hold—and making Colt grunt from a light rib punch as I went—I said, "Give me a break. I don't want other instruments in this song."

"Man, it's fine." Palming the back of his head, the drummer winked. "I'm kidding around. For real, I guess I just miss jamming with you. Even if you always wrote the songs, you at least listened to my input when we were kids."

I flushed at his honesty. *I guess we did create stuff together when we were younger.* Was I shortchanging my friends by cutting them out of the process? When had I gotten so insulated in my music? Softly, I said, "After the tour, we should work on a new CD. All of us."

Porter joined us, one fist full of hotel mints that occasional dropped to the floor. "Love that idea. But you know what I'd love more?" The hard, white candies crunched like pottery in his teeth. "Some lunch."

Shaking her thick mane of hair, Brenda pushed us towards the elevator. "Agreed. Enough sappy stuff, let's order some room service. You guys are going to lose it when you see the private suite I have."

"Why do you get all the cool stuff?" Porter whined.

"Because I deserve something nice for dealing with you jerks!"

To be fair to Brenda, our rooms were fine. They even had some nice flat screens on the walls. But, in the end, we still gawked at the suite she proudly walked us into.

One section was an open-air patio, a private jacuzzi taking up half of it. Brenda grinned proudly, asking us to get comfortable while she made a phone call. It must have been to the kitchen, because quick as anything, several servers arrived with a selection of cloches on rolling carts. "Gentlemen," she said, waving grandly. "It's now, officially, time to relax."

Food came and went, my band mates chomping away until they couldn't fit anything else in their stomachs. I managed to work down something, but my appetite was poor enough that I didn't even remember what it was.

We really did need to relax together. Granted, *I* wasn't very relaxed, but Porter and

Colt were goofing off with Brenda. Alcohol helped ease the strain of the tour. There was appreciation in Porter's voice when he held a beer can high, saying, "One more show, boys. We killed this fucking tour."

It wasn't over yet... but I suspected he was right.

We'd given a hell of a tour.

The sky above warping from watercolor red to brackish blues, evening sinking upon us. Porter grunted, standing with a mild sway. "I'm burnt, I'm going to sleep."

"I'm not as lame as Grandpa here," Colt said, following him. "But... I think I'll head to my room and test out the mattress. See you two." He waved, so I joined him absently. My mind was elsewhere, and suddenly alone with my rather quiet and slightly drunk manager, I felt the weight of my day.

Lola hasn't called me once.

"She's fine," Brenda said, too good at figuring me out. Standing tall, she stretched her arms over her head and yawned. "Let her have some space, she needs it."

Lifting an eyebrow, I shifted on the edge of the chair. The last of my beer washed over my tongue, giving me time to consider my response. "How would you know?"

"I just do." Without any lead up, she yanked her shirt over her head. I wasn't shocked; she'd been talking about the jacuzzi all day. In a bright green bikini, my manager slipped into the tempting, circular pool. "Here, just come and try to chill out for once."

"I don't really think it'll help."

"Suit yourself." Dipping in the water to her chin, she pointed at the bucket of champagne—the fourth one—that she'd ordered. "Can you get that for me?"

My knees popped as I stood. *I'm feeling like an old man.* I was too young to have so many aches and pains, but the tour had done a number on me. Sliding the bucket and glasses closer to Brenda, I made a snap decision.

Turning so I faced her, I slid my shirt up across my chest. It kept her from seeing my scar, even though I suspected she'd done her research on me before signing the band. *She probably knows about it, but I'm not taking any chances. I don't want to deal with questions right now.*

I wasn't looking for a reaction, but Brenda ran her eyes up and down me without pretense. "I forgot why your fans go so nuts for you. Meow. Coming in after all?"

Rolling my eyes, I said, "For a bit."

She made a face when I unbuckled my belt. "Please keep your boxers on."

"I don't usually hear girls say that." Carefully, I lowered myself into the heated water across from her. The jets began working out the knots that had made a home in me. "Damn, this does feel good."

"Right?" Beaming, she offered me a glass of champagne. I took it and swallowed a healthy mouthful. "Like I said, you need to relax."

The way she stated that made my mouth pucker. "Don't act so all-knowing."

"I *am* all-knowing," she laughed. "I know you're freaking out about Lola, for one." I shot a glare at her, then peered into my drink in silence. The next time Brenda spoke, it was far softer, more kind than usual. "Drez, what's going on? You're obsessing over this girl—and don't get me wrong, she's talented and pretty —"

"Gorgeous."

"—But I've never seen you so... off. What did she do to you?"

Listening to the bubbling water, I shut my eyes. "You actually want to know?"

"Of course I do."

Swirling my drink, I sipped it. The alcohol was like a blanket of cotton on my brain. It wasn't enough to soothe me, but it was a start. "She asked about my past."

She barely reacted, not grasping how serious this was for me. "I take it you don't want to tell her?"

My champagne glass was empty. Drinking it made me think too much of Lola, of the way we'd celebrated her joining the band. "I just want her to want me as I am. Nothing about who I was, what I dealt with, matters now."

Sinking deep into the water, Brenda considered me. Those thin eyebrows moved into her bangs. "Not everyone gets what they want. If anything, you two are stupid lucky."

"What the hell does that mean, how am I lucky?"

Her attention went off to the side, elbows resting on the edge of the jacuzzi. "Sometimes we fall for someone at the wrong time, or someone who just never meshes with us." Her tone was fragile and bitter. "I don't know, some of us get saddled with being attracted to someone that we have to see all the time but can never touch."

Oh, shit. My back went tense against the wall. Had Brenda just admitted to being secretly in love with me? The very concept was awkward as hell. My skin prickled, suddenly I couldn't look her in the eye. *If my manager has had a crush on me this whole time, then...*

"You fucking moron," she snorted, covering her mouth and laughing. Brenda tucked a curl of crimson hair behind her ear, dark eyes watching me with sly amusement. "I can tell what you're thinking. It's not *you* that I'm interested in, asshole."

I was relieved—crazy relieved. But her arrogance didn't sit well with me. Tilting my head, I said, "Yeah, you're incredibly clever for figuring me out. Also? Good job confirming you were talking about yourself."

Her whole face turned redder than her hair. "That—I—just forget it, jeez. We're supposed to be talking about you and Lola, not me and whoever."

My interest was piqued, but ultimately, Lola was my focus. "You really think I can't have what I want?"

Reaching over, she refilled her glass, taking a deep swig. "If you mean having a relationship beyond the surface level with the girl you *love...*"

Alcohol makes her too bold, I thought sourly.

Brenda said, "Then no. Not without telling her about everything you went through, without facing it all over again. Drezden, Lola isn't the kind of person that can ignore your past."

Does Brenda really know a*ll about it?* I wondered. She was talking like she did. "What kind of person is Lola?"

Hesitating, my manager wiped her mouth. "Did she ever tell you what she answered with on the day she auditioned?"

"I—answered?"

"That stupid question you made me ask everyone."

My heart slammed into my ribs. *What does it take to be a good guitarist?* "She never told me, no." *I forgot—no, I guess I didn't even care about that once I met her. I got caught up in how good she was, in all of her.*

"You told me to turn away anyone who answered 'talent' and to let in everyone who said 'patience, hard work, or determination.' Right?"

Those were the answers I'd decided that came closest to defining the difference between those who would make it big, and those who would not. "Right," I finally said.

Brenda shrugged so hard that her bikini strings tickled the back of her neck. "Lola didn't say any of those things. Her answer was... honesty."

"Honesty?" *How the hell does honesty make any sense—oh. Oh, fuck.* So quickly that it left me reeling, I actually understood Lola. Where her talent came from, why I was constantly drawn to her open nature, her genuine reactions.

Honesty.

I wanted to laugh; the answer was so simple. I grasped why she was upset with me earlier, too. This puzzle piece gave me clarity to see the full picture. *She spilled her guts to me about her ugly past. Then, I refused to do the same.*

My chuckle was throaty, cynical. "I'm a real dumbass, aren't I?"

"Yeah." Brenda wore a tiny smile. "I'll say you are." Water ran down my muscles as I stood up. Blinking, she craned her neck. "Hey! Where are you going?"

I shook droplets from my hair. I knew when I turned around that she would see my scar, but I no longer gave a shit. *Honesty*. "I need you to book a private flight for me."

"Excuse me? When—and to *where?*"

I caught my reflection in the side of the tall, aluminum heater that made the patio comfortable. In the light of the evening, my eyes were darker than pitch. "Right now. I have someone I need to visit."

"Drezden, what the hell are you saying?"

My blood was electric; everything in me was buzzing with realization. I finally knew what I had to do to make everything right. "You can book me this flight tonight so that I make it back in time for the final show, or you can accept that I won't be here for it."

It was a standoff, our eyes locked as she tried to will me to back down.

I said, "Brenda. I need to do this."

Lifting the bottle of champagne, Brenda finished off the contents and gasped for air. The glass rattled when she slammed it into the ice bucket. "I really shouldn't have signed you and your fucking band, Drezden. I'm never going to stop regretting that. Pass me my purse and I'll arrange your stupid as hell flight. Dammit, I was *supposed* to be relaxing!"

Without missing a beat, I handed Brenda her purse.

- Chapter Twenty-Four -
Lola

I wandered the parking lot for a long time. Telling Brenda I was going to find food hadn't really been the truth. I *needed* food, yes, but after sitting with Drezden, being forced to avoid talking about his past, I'd lost my appetite.

I want to know what he isn't telling me. Kicking aside a small rock, I looked back at the giant, glossy tour bus. The breeze was light on my face. With very little direction, I dropped down onto the pavement between two cars and just... waited.

I didn't know what I was waiting for.

My mind kept diving back to one thing: Drezden was refusing to tell me the truth. *It's just like Sean said,* I realized grimly. *He won't tell me anything.*

Movement, voices, drew my eye. From my hidden spot I watched Brenda and the rest of the band climb out of the bus. They were laughing; all of them but Drezden. His expression was like old concrete.

Even from here, he makes my pulse jump. Hugging my knees, I watched them all climb into a solid black car. The windows were tinted to hiding them from prying eyes. *Guess that'll take them to the hotel.* With nothing going on between now and the final show, it was nice that Brenda had arranged a hotel for us.

It made me think about that night. About the first time I'd seen Drezden's scar. Shaking my head, I stared after the car until it was guided out of the lot by uniformed security. Seconds later, my phone vibrated, making me squeak. Fumbling it free, I read the message from Drezden:

'Call me if you need anything. I'll be at the Hilton until then.'

The words, so crisp on my screen, took time to sink into my head. I should have felt excited about the message, Drez was so *good* at making my knees weak. But I just wanted to scream at him to explain his scar, his name, his past, everything.

I wanted the truth.

Craning my neck, I gazed at the swirling clouds. Their tranquility didn't fit my mood. *There is someone who can tell me the truth.* In my palm, my phone felt like a weapon. *How does Sean know anything personal about Drez?*

Looking at my fingers, I studied the hard calluses I'd formed over the years of playing. *Drezden was better at guitar than he thought. Or better than he wanted to claim, anyway.* The man I knew had only ever sung for his band. This whole time, as talented on guitar as he was, why had it never come up?

I don't know anything about his life before Four and a Half Headstones.

Lifting my phone, I started to dial.

If Drez wouldn't tell me himself...

There was only one way for me to find out.

****

I was still sitting on the pavement when Sean arrived.

Leaning over, he blocked out most of the late-day sun. "Got your call," he said softly.

"Yeah." I rested my chin on my knees.

As if I might run, Sean settled across from me in slow motion. There was none of the strange righteousness in his eyes that I'd seen on that rainy morning. Now he just looked sad, maybe even empathetic. "How you doing?"

I pulled my ponytail across my cheek, holding it tight. "Pretty shitty."

When we were younger, there were times when I would hide away from my parents, especially after a rough day at school. Sean would always find me and, without speaking, offer comfort with just his presence.

Reaching out, I grasped his hand and linked my fingers. "You said you could give me answers."

His palm was oddly clammy. "Only if you really want them."

My mouth opened, closed, then opened again. "Drezden refused to talk to me. I feel like I need to know, even if he won't be the one telling me."

Sean guided me to stand, my muscles aching from sitting so long. "I figured that would happen. Come on, then." He pulled his phone out, thumb crushing buttons rapidly.

"Where are we going?" I asked, following my brother across the parking lot.

Sean looked at me briefly, then closed his phone. "We're going where the answers are."

"I thought you knew, that you'd just tell me?" This was getting strange.

"I think," he said, opening the door of the equipment van for his band, "That it would be better if you heard everything from the source."

Standing outside the familiar, beaten up vehicle, I sensed my intuition buzzing. Something about this didn't feel right. "Who's the source, Sean?"

Sighing, he climbed into the van, clipping his seat belt down and turning the ignition. The van beeped incessantly, demanding I get in and close the door. "Lola, trust me. Do you, or do you not, want answers?"

Lifting my chin, my gaze shifted from Sean's serious eyes, to the tour bus in the distance. The big, black behemoth reminded me of Drezden. It warned me that if I didn't go now, I was giving up a solid chance at the information I craved.

And if I wanted to stay with Drez... not just as a guitarist, but as so much more...

I needed to know the truth.

Without giving my anxiety any more credit, I slid into the van and shut the door.

****

The drive was brief.

Sean steered us from the highway and into a small plaza full of tiny shops. At his suggestion, we slid on sunglasses, and I pulled my sleeves down to hide my tattoo. I'd had enough drama with the public. I wasn't keen to repeat it.

I could tell this was a very run down section of Seattle. The overhangs sported faded paint and grime, most of them missing letters. There were massage parlors, tattoo shops, drug dens masquerading as pharmacies, and a lone coffee shop in the far plaza corner. Sean led the way towards it.

"Are you going to tell me who we're meeting here?" I whispered. The whole ride I'd run through the possibilities. Would it be Drez's parents, a relative of some kind? Maybe an old music teacher?

The cafe appeared empty, I was surprised the door even opened—I'd thought it must be closed. It was cluttered with tiny, circular tables that had a sticky sheen to them. The floor was covered in the same gunk.

Grunting, I bent over to tug my heel off the tiles. Busy with removing the awful mystery goo, I didn't see him at first. But when Sean nudged me, pointing at a table in the corner... my heart stopped.

Those eyes, hard and cold as green ice, lit up when they saw me. This was a face I recognized most recently from a grainy television news feed.

Johnny Muse.

I crushed Sean's wrist and dug in my heels. My brother made a small noise, trying to pull away. "Sean." To my own ears, my voice was a mere shadow. "Why is he here? What's going on?"

"Relax, Lola." Untangling my grip, Sean motioned with his chin at Johnny. The former guitarist was eyeing us, not moving from his chair or the paper cup he was nursing. "You don't have to worry, he's not dangerous or something. He knows Drezden better than anyone."

There was no way that was true. *Porter. Colt. They both know Drezden, too. Why would I bother with Johnny?* The answer weighed heavy in my guts. *Because neither of them is going to tell me anything. Just like Drezden.*

It was an awful, cold truth... but one that gave me strength. If Johnny had my answers, then fine. Plus, why was I so scared? I darted a look around the shop. *This is a public place. Between Sean and the guy behind the counter, what could Johnny even do?*

Balling my fists at my hips, I walked around my brother. Johnny didn't stand when I reached him. His only movement was a tiny, crooked smile. "So," he said, voice rigid and sandy, "You're her. Lola Cooper, in the flesh."

I stood as tall as I could. "That's right. And you're Johnny Muse."

"Guilty," he said.

That word was a little too appropriate. I'd seen the video of him getting arrested in the supermarket. "My brother says you can tell me about Drezden."

Furrowing his eyebrows, Johnny looked around me at Sean. "Yeah. I called him a week ago. I wanted to get in touch with *you*, but finding your number was much harder."

Nervously, I touched my phone in my pocket. The idea of Johnny reaching out to me was too weird. *Did Sean sit on this information for a whole week?*

My brother was dutifully avoiding looking at anything but the floor. Finally, he grabbed two chairs and set them at the tiny table. "Let's park our asses." He took the one closest to Johnny, situating himself between us. That subtle protection didn't slip past me.

Under the table, I was acutely aware of how near my knees were to the former Headstone's guitarist. "Can we just get down to business?" I asked.

"Business, she says," Johnny chuckled. A dirty fingernail scratched the rim of his coffee cup. "Sure thing, we can get right down to it." I didn't like how he kept smiling. "What would you like to know about our dear friend, Drezden Halifax?"

This was it. This was what I had been waiting for.

So why did I feel so ashamed suddenly?

Glancing at Sean, I tried to gauge what he was thinking. His expression was neutral, lips bloodless as if he were trying not to make a sound.

He wasn't going to interrupt this moment. Whatever Johnny was going to say, Sean wanted me to hear it. Badly.

In my lap, I clenched my hands in a knot. My answer was brisk.

"Tell me everything."

- Chapter Twenty-Five -
Drezden

It had been years since I'd been back to upstate New York.

Home again, home again, I thought with little fondness. Sliding my sunglasses down, I pulled the shiny, pearl colored Corvette out onto the open road. I knew where I was going, even if I'd never been there in person.

The wind fluttered against my scalp, doing its best to clear the fog from my head. I was tempted to take the back roads, to roll down past my old school, my old home. *There'll be time for pleasant memories later.*

I had to finish what I'd set out to do—as spontaneous as it was. If I didn't, there could never be a future for Lola and me. Inhaling the crisp air, I filled myself with that realization.

For Lola.

The building loomed like a squat dragon, its mouth ready to swallow me up. The parking lot was dotted with police vehicles. One of them had an officer sitting in the front seat, the door cracked, his foot out on the cement while he sipped a paper cup of coffee.

He glanced at me when I parked nearby. I hid my chin in the thick top of my navy

400

hoodie, giving the man a quick nod—he tipped his drink my way, going back to playing on his phone.

Go. Don't think.

With one foot in front of the other, I entered the prison.

My steps sounded loud on the concrete, announcing me to the thick, glass-covered front desk. The process of signing my name, of explaining who I was and why I was there, was surreal. It turned out that the warden on patrol was a huge fan of my band. I put on a plastic grin and signed a CD for him—did he carry it with him everywhere? —before taking the visitor pass.

The warden guided me into the halls, pointing out where I wanted to go.

Where I *needed* to go.

Turning the corner, I stared at the grim rods of iron that held the prisoners at bay. My hands were clammy when I reached the one I was looking for. It was stone-colored, featureless as all the others.

On the bunk, a figure in orange shifted around. His haggard features moved to me, green eyes wide in true shock. Of course he wouldn't expect to see me. I'd never even bothered to send a letter.

My voice was a dry husk. "Hey there, Dad."

Nine Years Ago

"Wow!" My face ached from grinning, but I didn't mind. Eagerly running my fingers down the length of the guitar neck, I spoke without looking away from the beautiful instrument. "Did you really make this for me, Dad? Holy shit, you didn't need to do that!"

"Watch your mouth," my mother said, struggling to sound upset over her own glee. My parents were crushed together on the couch, hovering above me where I sat with my new gift; a guitar my dad had carved for me.

I caught him rolling his eyes. "Come on, honey. If he's going to be a famous rock star someday, swearing is just going to happen."

"Well, when he becomes whatever, he can swear all he wants." Pushing off the couch, she gathered up the shreds of wrapping paper. "Under this roof, he watches his mouth." Moving my way, her scowl broke, lips puckering to press a quick kiss to my forehead. There was only joy in her eyes when she stood straight. "Happy birthday, Anthony."

My dad hit me in the back of the head with a ball of wrapping paper. "Yeah, happy birthday, kid."

Scratching at the back of my neck, I turned the guitar around. My father had always been a great guitarist, but he excelled at

402

woodworking—a fact that I knew bothered him, even if he never flat out said it.

He cleared his throat. "Go on, strum a bit."

"Ah, you know I'm not that good still." My neck was hot at his coaxing. Singing was my passion, but I'd never turned away my dad's attempts at teaching me to play. It had to increase my chances at getting into a big band someday if I could do both, didn't it?

His eyes warmed. "Just a bit, for me. I worked hard on that."

Smiling sideways, I set the instrument in my lap. It smelled of sawdust and polish, fresh enough to make me dizzy. Tweaking the pegs, my fingers were shaking. I wanted to impress him so badly. *I'm already thirteen, I should be better than I am.* All the hours of practice, of classes my parents scrimped to save for...

I should be better.

Moving my fingers like a wave, I began to play. My eyes were stuck on my movements, working so hard to make everything perfect. Each mistake screamed at me, gnawing into my teeth like cavities.

Better. I need to get better.

It was all I ever wanted.

Looking up, I spotted the sad smile on my father's face. Then it was gone, and I knew what he was going to ask before his lips started to move. "What's the most important thing you need to be a good guitarist?"

403

As I'd done a hundred times before, I shook my head.

His answer was always the same. "If you ever figure it out, let me in on the secret."

I will, I thought determinedly. *When I find out, I promise I'll tell you first.*

****

Eight Years Ago

"Why doesn't he want to come?" Colton asked, twirling a drumstick lazily. He dropped it twice before I bothered to try speaking.

Looking up, I shrugged into my ears. "Mom says Dad's just really tired. I don't know, you'd think he'd want to see my first show." It had taken Colton and myself weeks of work to feel ready to perform on our high school's stage.

Picking at his ear, the lanky kid studied me. "So, it doesn't bother you?"

"Of course, it bothers me." I fidgeted with my guitar case. "But what the hell can I do about it? It's his life, not mine." *He used to be so involved. What changed?* The days where my dad would practice with me 'til we were drained, would talk to me about music, discuss his own grand wishes and plans and dreams... those had faded soon after my thirteenth birthday.

404

In the wake of that time, my mother had started to pick up his slack. She took me to every practice, drove me to the music store, endured my chatter about what band was up to what.

It wasn't the same, but her support kept me motivated.

I still wish we could have convinced Porter to play with us, I thought grimly. Colton had done his best to talk our friend into it, but he'd dodged the attempts every time. I didn't understand, but I also didn't pry.

Colton said nothing for a while, just poked his nose with his drumstick. We were virtually alone in the hallway; the auditorium was starting to buzz with the growing crowd. Hearing it made my senses flare.

"Well," he coughed, staring at the far wall. "My whole family is going to be in there. They'll cheer hard enough for us both. Okay?"

Grinning wide, I gave him a hard shove. "*Everyone* will be cheering for us, you mean."

"Yeah." Adjusting his shirt, he flashed me a knowing look. "Yeah, that's what I meant."

Inside the auditorium, people were shouting; it was time.

Hoisting my guitar case, I paused with my hand on the knob. I didn't look back as I spoke. "Thanks, Colt."

Together, we pushed into the room.

****
Seven Years Ago

The walls of my bedroom were decorated with trophies in silver or gold.

Mostly gold.

Winning singing contests had become easy for me. It didn't make me try any less; all I ever did was practice. Playing guitar, running through exercises for my vocal cords, I never stopped.

I couldn't.

I'm still not there yet. I still haven't made it.

At age fifteen, I was starting to feel old. Like my road to being a star was beginning to narrow. Seeing the pinched looked on my father's face as the years went by, I feared my future lay where his did now.

Failure.

I have to try harder. I have to be the best.

Dropping my backpack on the kitchen counter, I poured a glass of lemonade from the fridge. I'd downed all but a final swallow when I spotted the envelope. It was a fat, manila thing addressed to me and my mother.

Setting the glass aside, I wiped my hands on my jeans. The mail was heavy; an important kind of weight. Fingering the edge, I saw it had already been opened. I lifted the letter into the air and read it with mounting excitement.

It was an offer letter from Goldman's—an arts school known for its highly skilled students. Many of my favorite musicians had attended. *And they want me to attend.* When had I started shaking?

"Well, what do you think?"

Spinning, I looked into the watery, smiling face of my mother. The look in her eyes said it all—she'd been waiting all day for me to read that letter.

Wordless, I grabbed her in a hug, listening to her delighted laughter and hoping it would never end. I didn't want this feeling to ever go away.

This is the first step. I can really do it. I can be a rock star.

She pried herself out of my arms, taking the letter gingerly. "It came this morning. I couldn't wait to show you."

A thought burrowed in my guts. "Did Dad see it?"

Her small frown muddled the joyous occasion. "Not yet." Smoothing her hair, she put the envelope back on the counter. "I'll tell him about it when he's... in a better mood."

When he isn't drunk. I knew her code. "Can we really do this? It means moving to Colorado. I won't get to graduate with my friends." *Colt and Porter are going to hate me.*

My mother reached out, kind hands holding my cheeks. "Anthony, honey, this is all up to you. If you want to go here, we—you—have to decide."

Leaning in brought us together. I'd gotten taller than my mother—tall as my father—soon after turning fourteen. In my arms, my mother felt... small. Frail. *She hasn't been eating well since Dad started drinking so much.* I was familiar with the strain he brought.

I was also very familiar with the bruises he could leave.

Thinking about his misery made me hold her tighter. "Listen, Mom." The words were escaping faster than my brain could make sense. "Let's just go together. You and me, we'll vanish and Dad can be the depressed fucker he clearly wants to be by himself."

"Language, Anthony." She squeezed me briefly, her voice low. "I can't leave your father like that. Not... without saying something."

"He doesn't say much to me at all these days."

Pulling away, my mom considered my bitter grimace. Her kiss on my cheek nullified some of my distaste. "He has his reasons. Don't take them personally. Now, why don't you go clean up before dinner."

"What?" Grinning, I ruffled my dark hair. "You saying I smell?"

Together we laughed in the kitchen, a moment of peace that would forever remain cemented in my heart. I could never forget how pleased my mom looked, how she playfully swatted me and chased me upstairs to my room.

It was pure bliss.

Of course it had to end.

****

I heard the screams—no, I *felt* them. It's such a primal, protective reaction when you hear your own mother in danger.

My hair was still wet from the shower, steam escaping me and my hastily thrown on jeans. There was no time for anything else; I just ran towards the source of the noise.

Inside my father's workshop, the scent of polish and pine brought confusing nostalgia. As a child, even a young teen, I'd spent so much time watching my dad work on what he loved.

The sight of him working over my mother—someone *I* loved—made me want to retch.

He had her on the floor, blood on his knuckles, blood on her forehead. He was saying something, but my ears were blinded to all but her pleading screams.

"Stop! Donnie, it's not what you think!"

"You're going to run off and abandon me, you little bitch! After *everything!*" He pulled his arm back to swing again. In the whites of his eyes, insanity bloomed.

I didn't remember moving. Circling my forearms around his shoulders, I wrestled my father backwards, down to the sawdust covered floor. "Get off of her! Stop it, Dad!" My skull vibrated, birthing confusion. How could this be real? What had gone so wrong?

He'd hit me before, but never my mother.

Scuffling, he threw me against the legs of a heavy table. "You'd try to fight your own fucking *father!?*" Hands clung to my throat, nails ripping my cheek. "You piece of shit, you fucking piece of shit!"

The back of my head slammed into something solid; the edge of a work bench. Dots of color fizzled inside of my eyelids. I was blacking out—I couldn't hold him, he scrambled free. I thought he'd attack me again, but instead, he swayed towards my mother.

She looked like a terrified animal. Sliding sideways, holding her palm to the crimson seeping from her left temple, my mom sobbed. "Please, please stop! Get away from me!"

"Ungrateful family," he huffed heavily. "Think you'll just go off and become rich and famous, think you're *better* than *me*. After all of the time I put into making that son of yours so fucking talented!" Bending low, his fingers coiled in her hair. The sawdust at his feet had turned into sludge from the blood.

Under his boot, I saw the edge of my admission letter to Goldman's.

I'd started yelling at some point. My throat was ragged from it. Lurching onto his back, I struggled to get him to the floor—to anywhere away from my mother. Together we rolled into a tool bench, metal instruments he'd once used to lovingly carve his guitars showering down on us.

I didn't see the chisel until it was too late. Pure pain radiated from my lower back.

He'd stabbed me. My own father had stabbed me.

I was screaming again, just one long, strained vowel. Would this ruin my vocal cords?

Who cares if I can't sing again? It doesn't matter if I'm dead.

If she's dead.

Ignoring the sickening weight of the chisel in my flesh, I punched down into my dad's jaw. Again and again, the thud of my knuckles bounced off his face. I didn't stop until he went limp, wet bubbles of red hanging on his lips.

Groaning, I made myself stand. Purple and yellow tickled my vision, my insides threatening to come out of my mouth. Determined not to give up—if I stopped now, I was sure I'd never get up again—I stumbled towards the phone on the wall of the workshop. I could tell my mother was breathing, but wasting another second without calling for help was madness.

As I dialed for an ambulance, my bare foot found the ragged letter from Goldman's. Blood from my dad's shoe stained most of it. It was funny, how important that piece of paper had seemed to me just hours ago.

Now, as I looked over my beaten mother, endured the waves of pain from my wound...

I wished it had never arrived.

****

Present Day

There were half-moon cuts in my palms from how hard I had been clenching my fists. For so long, I'd avoided thinking about what had happened that day. How my father had gone so far in his jealousy that he tried to murder my mother, and no doubt, would have killed me as well.

Standing there watching me, he said nothing. I almost preferred it that way, but that wasn't why I was here. I wouldn't waste this trip.

Honesty.

"Why." The word had been on the tip of my tongue for years. "Why would you do it?"

"Listen, kid—"

"Don't!" Curling back my lips, I gripped my own skull. "Never call me that again. I'm not a fucking kid." My guts balled up, thinking about how I'd called Lola 'kid' initially. *I'm nothing like him. I won't be—I can't be.* "Just tell me why."

His mouth fell open, a pathetic expression that I just loathed more. "I've—been seeing someone about that. Therapy, you know? I'm—"

"*Tell me why!*"

Lines grew deep along his forehead, around his eyes; eyes that were so tired and nothing like they used to be when I was just a child. "Did you really come to see me, after all these years, to ask that?"

"No." *The why doesn't even matter.* "I don't need your answer. I figured it out soon after they sentenced you. I wasn't stupid, I fucking got why you turned into such a pathetic, desperate piece of shit over the years."

He crumpled like a dying balloon. "Then, what do you want from me? You want to talk to me, right? You're here for me."

The back of my neck was sweltering. "I'm not here for you, I'm here for *me*." *I'm here so that I can get over my past. I'm here for...*

For Lola.

413

My dad eyed me with new suspicion. "Fine. You came here to mock me. You proud of that? You proud of looking down on your own father, Anthony?" My hackles went up in rows. "You proud of taunting an old man who struggled to give you what you have now?"

"I used to be proud of *you!*" My bottom lip split with my hard growl, the blood a distant note on my tongue. "I was so damn proud of everything you did, I looked up to you!"

Whatever perfect speech I'd written in my brain on the flight here, it was washed over by the one that had been scratching itself into place since the day my dad had started to ignore me. *He erased me. He hated how good I was becoming, how I'd surpassed him, so he turned me invisible.*

Until he couldn't any longer.

"You looked up to a failure like me?" he asked, eyes going dull; doubtful.

"I did." Raising my arm, I wiped at the burning cut on my mouth. "Until the very first time you hit me, I just wanted to be like you." *I wanted to show you I could be the star you wanted me to be.*

Turning away, Donnie closed his eyes and breathed out. "Well, you've made it further than I ever did. I've seen you on television, son. You're famous—like I always wanted to be." There was a hollowness in his gaze as he looked back at me. "Guess we weren't very similar, in the end."

414

"No," I said, feeling my lower back twinge where my scar was. "We're nothing alike." *And we never will be.* "I'm here to remind myself of that. I'm going to make sure I never, ever become anything like you."

In the shadows of the cell, my father didn't flinch.

From the start, I'd demanded perfection from Lola the way my dad had from me. I'd felt the fear when I saw her talent soar, recognizing the world would crave her as much as I did every second. I'd lost my mind at the idea she'd slip away, told myself I would do anything, *anything* to keep her at my side.

But I was not my father.

Even though our blood was the same, our hearts were not. I'd never let myself become the bitter man he was.

His face was a map of misery. I burned the memory deep into my mind. Turning on my heel, I stuck my hands in my pockets. "One more thing before I leave and never waste my time thinking about you again." My lungs fluttered, mouth tasting like rust and satisfaction. "What does it take to be a good guitarist?"

He finally stood to his full height; I had his attention.

I'd never wanted it more.

"Honesty," I whispered. The single word cut through the stagnant air of the prison. "The answer is honesty. That's why you could never make it." *And why she could. That beautiful, genius fucking girl knew the answer from the start.*

His lips moved, mouthing the word softly. "Honesty?" He was rigid and motionless. "You think that's what matters?"

"Yeah." There wasn't a tremor of doubt in my voice. How could there be? "It's what allows people to be themselves, to be free and unconstrained." *It's what will keep Lola and I together.*

My heels sliced down the concrete hall like machines on a war path. I was slashing and burning everything in my past. Not to erase it, but to clear it away so I could see the roots of who I was beneath the blackened char.

I was finally done with my father.

But there was more to do before I could return to Lola.

- Chapter Twenty-Six -
Lola

Johnny took a sip from his coffee. It looked cold, made me curious how long he'd been nursing it. I thought he was nursing the information, too, like he was counting the seconds, enjoying being the center of attention again.

Finally, Johnny bent low in my direction. "I'm only telling you this because you should know the kind of man Drezden is."

The kind of man he is. I reminded myself to breathe.

"His name isn't Drezden Halifax." There were shiny purple circles under his eyes. "It's Anthony Holland."

I was crushing myself, bracing myself, and then the reveal came and I just... deflated. Sean had already warned me that Drezden wasn't really his name. "So what?" I asked. "Lots of rock stars use fake names. Why does it matter?"

Under the table, something poked me; the tip of Sean's shoe. We shared a look, his saying, *Take this seriously!* Mine saying, *This is what you brought me here for?*

"It's not that he has a stage name," Johnny went on. His excitement grew along with his rising volume. "It's the reason."

My heart wouldn't stop racing. "Give me the reason."

His smile was wicked, lacking sympathy in every corner. "Drez uses a fake name so that it can't be traced back to his dad. The bastard put his own fucking *father* in jail."

"I—he what?" *His father? What the hell?*

"Drez beat the shit out of his dad, yeah." Thin fingers ran through his greasy, unkempt hair. "Got him arrested, too. Guess the cops took Drez's side because his dad was known to drink a bit heavy."

When had I started shaking my head? "That doesn't make sense, why would he attack his dad?"

"What does it matter?" Sean snapped, gripping the edge of the tiny table. "If he could do that to his own dad, the guy has fucking issues! I told you he was dangerous."

Johnny snorted, peering at us both. "That's for sure. He cold-cocked me, remember? I didn't do fuck all to him. If he wanted me out, he didn't need to punch me to do it—"

"Stop." *I don't understand.* "Just stop a second." *This makes no sense.* My temples were throbbing. "If his dad went to jail, it means he did something wrong."

Drezden had to have a reason.

The man across from me scowled. "What, you think they needed a reason to put *me* in jail, too? Sometimes people end up behind bars because they're in the wrong place at the wrong time."

"Then you don't even *know* what happened between him and his dad, right?" I asked slowly.

Johnny's forehead wrinkled, his scowl going deeper. "Maybe I don't know the details —"

"And it doesn't matter!" Sean cut in.

"—But I know the important shit. Drezden hates his dad, and if anything, would love to see the guy dead."

Acid bubbled in my stomach. "You know that how?"

"Why change his name, why would he want nothing to do with the guy?" Johnny's voice had a wild edge; I watched the coffee cup shake, ready to topple. "You tell me! You fucking put the pieces together. The night after we officially formed the band..." He stopped, shooting a look at Sean.

Right. Johnny took the spot Sean auditioned for.

It had been easy for me to forget the connection my brother had to all this. I'd only learned about it recently.

In the back of my brain, my intuition buzzed. *Does Sean have some other reason for wanting me to meet Johnny? Something beyond trying to warn me away from Drezden?*

My brother's 'kindness' was suddenly suspicious.

"Anyway," Johnny mumbled, scratching at the side of his neck. "Me and the others—Porter, Colt... We all ended up in this graveyard, and Drezden was drunk as all get out. Guy was nuts!" Johnny was gesticulating, growing more and more manic. "Got angry when I tripped over a headstone. He, like, jammed me hard in the ribs with his fist." For emphasis, he stabbed at the air. "Like that! Fucker hit me so much, just kept pummeling me! Bam! Told me to respect the dead, even as he went on yammering about the dead being forgotten or something."

I was leaning backwards. Johnny was acting unstable.

"It's where the name comes from," he said, blinking like he'd just noticed me. "Four and a Half Headstones, I mean. Drezden figured it fit us—something like, a half headstone exists to remind us we'll be forgotten someday or... I don't know. He was just crazy. Okay? Drez was always a crazy fucking—" A sharp ringing came from my brother's pocket.

Sean fumbled for his phone. "Sorry," he said, doing a double-take at the number. "It's Shark, hang on. I need to take this." Shoving the chair back, Sean stood and cupped the phone to his ear. "Man, hey," he whispered, walking towards the door. "I'm in the middle of a thing—wait, what? Shit!"

420

I jumped, stunned by how Sean was hunched over, grumbling into the phone and walking back and forth. The man behind the coffee counter was staring, too. My brother was acting like a caged lion.

"Fine, yes. I'm on my way." He shut his phone violently. "We need to go back. Caleb's a fucking moron. Shark just called to tell me he got himself drunk in public this morning, now he's in a holding cell." Shaking his head rapidly, my brother laughed. "The asshole started drinking at ten this morning." It was after five now. "I need to go down and break him out."

I was fine with this excuse to cut the meeting short. Johnny had to be exaggerating about Drezden, he just had to be. I stood on eager legs. "Alright. Let's go back."

A hand touched mine, freezing me. "I want to tell you more. Hell," Johnny snorted, "I feel like I *need* to. There's so much shit. Stay and hear me out."

I jerked my arm away; his touch had been so oily. "Maybe another time." I looked to my brother. He was antsy, bouncing on the balls of his feet. I understood his worry; he needed to get his singer out before tomorrow, or his band couldn't play at all. "We're in a hurry." *There's no way I'm hanging around here alone.*

"Oh, okay! I'll just—okay, another time then," Johnny shouted after me. "Nice to finally meet you, Lola!"

I didn't feel the same.

"I'm going to drop you off at your tour bus," Sean said, guiding the van out onto the road.

Eyeing the sky, mulling over Johnny's words, I shook my head. "Actually, could you drop me off at the Hilton?" *I want to talk to Drezden in person.*

The clouds were a foreboding black as we drove. Sean's headlights made the pavement a muddy yellow, the color reminded me of Johnny's skin. Frowning, I wiped at where he'd touched me. "Has Johnny been living in a gutter or what? He looked awful."

My brother's laugh was tight, sour as bad wine. "Close enough. I met up with him this morning at the Greenmill Motel. Guess that's where he's been for a few days."

That sounded strange. *We only rolled into the city last night. Was Johnny here, waiting for us?* He had to know the tour would end in Seattle. Thinking of the guy, gaunt and edgy, hanging around in a filthy motel just waiting for everyone to arrive...

It made my insides queasy.

"Did you believe what he said?" Sean asked casually, not glancing at me.

Fidgeting in the seat, I watched the road. "Not really. Some of it, but—come on. Sean, that guy is losing it. One look at him and you could tell."

"He could be crazy *and* right about Drezden."

Twisting, I narrowed my eyes on my brother. "What was this really about? Do you want to help me learn about my boyfriend, or are you just trying to prove to me that he's some sort of violent psycho?"

Sean just clenched his jaw in silence.

Slumping in the cushion, I pulled my hood over my head. "Guess I already knew the answer to that."

"Lola—"

"You brought me to meet someone like *Johnny Muse* because you wanted me to think Drezden was dangerous."

"He *is* dangerous!" Sean snapped, crushing the steering wheel.

No, I thought morosely, *it's Johnny's who's dangerous. Not the man I—what? Love?* Closing my eyes, I pictured Drezden's face; his hard edges and wild green eyes. All I wanted was to see him, even just to talk to him and confront him with Johnny's accusations. *He might get mad. But let him.*

There were nuggets of truth in Johnny's words. I wasn't sure which parts, but Drez *had* to explain. He just had to tell me what had happened with his father.

The drive to the Hilton couldn't go fast enough.

It was drizzling as we rolled up to the tall building. Even with the surge of bleak weather, people were milling around, covering their heads with jackets to stay as dry as they could.

My seat belt was unlocked; Sean's hand on my shoulder kept me sitting. "Lola, I know you're confused."

"I'm not confused." There were a lot of questions running wild, jabbing at me, but I had come to a conclusion as we drove. There was one person who could tell me the truth, and chasing after other sources had given me nothing but a bitter aftertaste.

Drezden is the only one who can tell me everything.

"I—Lola, just..." Letting me go, Sean leaned back so fast his elbow banged the window. Amazingly, he didn't act like he felt it at all. "You're stuck on wanting to believe that Drezden isn't to blame for any of the crap he's pulled." Though I listened, I never took my attention from my knees. "But even if you imagine he has 'reasons' or whatever, can't you see he's still responsible for the violence? Hitting Johnny, fighting with his father, and... and the bastard even got into a fight with me."

My neck ached from how fast I turned to stare. "He what? When?"

Shame danced on the corners of my brother's lips. "The day you came back late, the

424

night we played in Aspen. It got a little tense in the parking lot."

"A little tense?" *What the hell?* "You and my boyfriend fought and neither of you told me! Why would you hide that?"

Sean flicked his gaze at me, then away, all too fast.

Pinpricks of heat traveled up my neck. "You didn't tell me because you started it, didn't you?" He stared blankly through the windshield. "Sean. Sean, that's it, isn't it? Why else would you not—"

His fist came down, hitting the wheel with a thud. "I thought you were hurt, or worse! I thought he knew where you were. Either way, trust me, your shitty boyfriend was more than happy to be in that scuffle." He was no longer avoiding my glare, but the rage in his face didn't make me shy away.

I was pissed off, too.

"Why are you so obsessed with making Drezden into a monster?" I didn't breathe, I even wondered if my blood had gone still. I wanted Sean to say something—anything—to justify his actions.

A flicker of pain bloomed in his stare. "I need to go pick up Caleb." He reached across me, opening my door.

If I left now, I knew he'd never tell me what was going on. He'd double down and hide it deeper. Gripping the door, I slammed it shut.

"Please, Sean. Why is this all so important to you? It's not even about *me* anymore... is it?"

"Of course, it's about you." His voice was weak, unconvincing. "It's always been about you."

On instinct I jumped at him. It could have been an attack—it wasn't. My body folded across the middle of the van, encasing my brother in a hug before he could fight me off. His claim was a cry for help. "I'm sorry," I mumbled against his shoulder. "Sean, I'm really just—I'm so sorry."

"Lola? What the hell?" His body was tense, but he hugged me back like it was muscle memory. The times he'd protected me flooded back into both of us. I *felt* the barrier cracking in a sudden shatter. "Why are you apologizing?"

"I don't know," I sniffled, wiping at my eyes.

"Why are you *crying?*"

"I don't know!" A hiccup choked me, broke my sudden tears and turned it into uneasy laughter.

Sean's arm crushed me against him, holding the back of my head. Relieved chuckles shook free from him, too. "You're ridiculous."

"You're worse than that."

Rubbing my shoulder blades, he breathed out loudly. "Yeah. I guess I am."

We sat in the car and listened to the rain. It reminded me of the day, so recently, where we'd gotten soaked while Sean warned me about Drezden. Clarity rolled up my spine. "You've been angry at him for so long, haven't you?"

Gingerly, my brother eased me off of him. His blue eyes were rimmed in red; I noticed the spider-veins crawling in the whites. How long had those been there? "Drezden messed with my head—with everything—that day."

That day. He didn't have to say it. Sean was talking about the audition. "Tell me what happened."

"It wasn't even—lord, I don't know. It's hard to explain."

Reaching for his hands, I cupped them. "Just try, I want to know."

His face was pale in the shadows. "I drove all the way upstate when I heard there was an audition." Sean flexed his fingers in mine. "I showed up, and Lola... I played my damn heart out. I was—" He cut himself off with a bark of cold laughter. "I was so sure I had the position. I was so stoked; how could I *not* be picked?"

Thunder rattled the sky outside. "And?"

Closing his fists, my brother gave me a sad smile. "And Drezden told me to leave. Just that, to leave. I asked him *why*. How could I just walk away without understanding why I wasn't good enough?" Gritting his teeth, he resembled a snarling dog. "The asshole told me

427

—get this—he said he *knew my type*. He said some bullshit like, 'Someone who gets angry and bitter when things aren't handed to them... someone like that doesn't have what it takes.'"

My mouth was hanging open. Not because of what Drezden had told my brother, but because Sean remembered every last word of that sentence. *He's been going over that in his head for years. Reliving that day. Holy shit.*

"He asked me something, too," Sean muttered hotly.

My throat was parched. "What?"

His sapphire eyes looked through the window. They stared into the past, seeing that fateful day instead of the grey rain. "He asked me, 'What makes a good guitarist?'"

The hairs on my body stood on end so tight it hurt. "What did you answer?" I asked eagerly, my curiosity turning my stomach in knots.

He fell back in his seat, arching his neck and watching the ceiling. "Talent. I told him that talent was what made a good guitarist."

My heart was stuffing itself into my throat. "What did *he* say?"

There, the crooked, cynical smile I knew so well. "He told me I was wrong. He responded, quite eloquently, 'Fuck off.' So I kicked over his amp and then I left."

The pounding in my skull wouldn't stop. *That's what this was all about. A several years*

428

long grudge. Drezden had called it. I remembered the night we'd had dinner, my first night spending time with Headstones. *Drezden asked me if my brother was still pissed about what had happened. Brenda told him to stop worrying.*

Drezden was right all along.

The revelation was too much for me. "You held onto the hate this entire time. Why would you tell me to audition for Four and a Half Headstones if you hated Drezden so much?"

"Because I care about you more," he said flatly, eyebrows crawling high. "Because I still wanted you to make it big. I guess I just wasn't strong enough to watch it all happen right in my face."

Wiping my nose with my sleeve, I said, "Asking me to join your band the other day, that wasn't about bringing me on so we could play together, it was about watching him lose me."

My brother was shaking his head before I finished. "No, no! Fuck, no, Lola. Yeah, okay, a big part of me wanted Drezden to fall apart after... after what he said to me. After what he made me feel about myself, my skills." His lips pulled back, low and twisted. "But I did want to see us both make it to the top."

"I'm already at the top," I whispered cynically.

"I know." His hand clasped on my shoulder. I expected sarcasm or cruelty, but he clasped me with genuine warmth in his sad smile.

Tears threatened to bubble back up; I pushed them down with a deep breath. "Promise me you won't give up your dream. We can both still be big rock stars... together. Okay?"

That time, it was Sean who started the hug. I wanted it to go on forever, for the two of us to feel the waves of love and joy that had been missing for far too long. This was my big brother, the guy who had taught me everything, been through so much with me—and for me. I wanted him to be happy... I'd thought I'd known where his pain and struggle came from...

But now I actually understood.

"If you want me to make it big," he said gently, "I'll need to go get my singer out of jail. We've kind of been making him sit there this whole time."

Our grins matched as we pulled apart. "Okay. Go get him out of there. I'll talk to you soon." Folding my hood over my skull tightly, I climbed out into the rain. "Good luck!"

"I'll need it," he chuckled, waving at me until I splashed all the way into the main lobby of the hotel. I was in a whirl of good cheer, ignoring the busy crowd flocking the hotel. I bet most were here for the big show tomorrow.

The woman behind the desk handed me the keycard for my room. *I can't wait to see everyone.* I bounced on my toes as I rode the elevator up to my room. *I should have brought my clothes with me, though. I'll need to go back to the bus tonight for something dry... and for my guitar.*

Fiddling with the door in the long, quiet hallway, I hummed to myself. The song I'd been writing with Drezden was catchy, the tune undulating in my chest and traveling to my brain. Stumbling into my room, I slammed the door and gazed on the place that I had to myself.

I wonder where the others are, where their rooms are?

My tangent of a thought was halted by the brisk knock on my door. Startled, I spun around, still caught up in my emotional high. Gripping the handle, I tugged the door open wide, half expecting to see Drezden himself.

Wet, pale and gaunt from hard times, the man outside was not my boyfriend.

"Hey," Johnny Muse said, eyes jittery in the orange lights. "Sorry to bother you so soon, but I just—I was thinking about earlier—about what I had said—and I wanted to clarify a few things."

Gawking openly, paralyzed by surprise, I fought for words. *What the hell is this?* Had Johnny followed me to the hotel? There was no other explanation.

He looked both ways, ducking low and shoving himself into my room. "Hey, wait," I said, backing up to keep space between us. "You shouldn't be—"

"It's just really, *really* important that I explain everything better! You know?" The door clicked behind him, his hoodie casting sharp shadows on his thin face. He no longer stared anywhere but right at me, an awful hunger deep in his faded emerald eyes. "Okay, so yeah, I got the impression you didn't believe everything earlier. I can't—like, handling that is hard for me. Got it?"

The back of my heel hit the edge of the bed. "Johnny, you need to leave."

"I will, I will!" Ruffling his hair, then palming his throat, he frowned. "Just listen. Please. The thing about the graveyard, okay, so I said Drezden went a little nuts. Maybe I said crazy? He *was* over the top, and he *did* push me down, but okay, so he didn't like, pummel me or anything."

Shaking my head slowly, I felt for my phone in my pocket. The budding seed of danger had become a full on rose with thorns. "Sure. Fine. You still need to go."

His face fell limp. "You don't believe me about him, do you?"

"I—it doesn't matter if I do."

"No!" His teeth glinted at me. "I really, really need you to believe me. You've got to see that he's a psycho, you need to—to leave the band. Okay? Okay, got that?"

I worked to keep a smile on my face. "Sure, okay. I'll do that." My legs inched me sideways, trying to get around him towards the exit.

Johnny held his cheeks, pulling his skin down in exasperation. "You really don't believe me! Dammit!" Too fast for me to react, he snatched my shoulders, shaking me until my teeth clicked together. "Why won't you believe me? *You need to believe me!*"

That was it, my self-preservation kicked in. Shoving at his chest, his forearms, I hurried to disengage. Opening my mouth, I got out a partial scream. A single fist to my skull ended it.

Carpet nuzzled my cheek. Had I fallen? Blacked out from the hit? *I need to move!* Above me, through the bells whistling in my ears, I heard Johnny talking. *Run, fight, anything!* His shadow fell over me. I couldn't make sense of his words, but there was a panicked, apologetic smear in them that made me *furious*.

Run. Fight. Save yourself.

The memory of the bullies shattering my first guitar drilled into my head.

Fight.

"Shit, shit, what do I do? I didn't mean —" Johnny's tirade ended, my knuckles scraping along his cheekbone as I bolted upwards. "What the *fuck!*" Cupping his skin, he made a grab for me. That was fine; I let him pull me close, kneeing him in the guts as we made contact.

I won't let anyone bully me again.

My nails cut along his forehead, blood caking underneath.

I'm not a victim anymore.

Never again.

He shoved me away, hugging himself and coughing. Low in my belly I knew this was it—my one chance. I had to get away from the chaos that was happening in my hotel room. Gasping, I stumbled towards the door.

Johnny Muse wasn't ready to release me.

Long fingers tangled in my hair, throwing me backwards. Off balance, I spun sideways, disoriented. *Run run run!* My temple slammed into the wide-screen TV, toppling it—and me—to the ground. Lifting my eyes, I tried to find Johnny. I didn't have to search hard; his fingers wrapped in the front of my shirt.

In one great swing, he threw me. My shoulder made a sickening crunch on the coffee table. The glass center shattered; my strength went along with it.

No, I thought in disbelief. *No, it can't end this way.* Moving was too hard, every twitch of my body made the torturous fire in my right shoulder worse. *What's wrong with my arm?*

Dizzy with pain, I struggled through the blur. Emerald eyes, dragon-fire that wanted to burn me and take me to hell, waited for me. Johnny was crouched above and ready to pounce.

Fight, I told myself. *Run*, I begged. Nothing in me would move.

"I didn't mean to do this." He was breathing heavy, blood sticking to his temple from my shallow scratches. "Fuck. If you'd only believed me. Then I wouldn't... this wouldn't have..." Shaking himself, he aimed his manic eyes over my head. I didn't know what he was looking at. Thinking was a struggle, my vision turning hazy.

Then it was just black.

- Chapter Twenty-Seven -
Drezden

Brenda had called my phone more than once during the trip, each voicemail getting progressively more manic. I'd returned her call once, when my flight was taking off, saying, "I'll need a car when I land."

She hadn't been impressed. "You're really trying my nerves. It's already three, what were you doing all day out in freaking Syracuse? I'm going to have grey hairs before you're through with me, I swear."

The car was waiting for me outside the airport. I figured the driver would be one of the many forgettable men in black hats that matched the paint job, but then the tinted window rolled down. Brenda's eyes were deep, dark things that spoke volumes. "Get in," she muttered.

Yanking the door open, I slid in next to her. "You didn't need to meet me."

"Of course I did." Her fingers were a blur, typing into her phone. "I've been up since eight, wrangling the setup for the venue, all while wondering when *you*," she spared me a glance, "my special star, would come back to me."

"Chill. I'm here." My chuckle was cut short as I leaned back too hard against the seat. My skin there was on fire.

Brenda arched an eyebrow, shutting her phone. "You alright?"

"It's nothing."

"Nothing," she repeated doubtfully. "Fine. Have your secrets. I'm just glad you're back."

Fingering the shape of my phone in my pocket, I nodded. "Me too. Did... anyone wonder where I was?" *Did Lola ask about me at all?* She hadn't taken any of my calls.

Shaking her head, she smoothed her hair over and over. "I left voice mails for everyone today. No one has responded. My guess is everyone is still sleeping at the hotel."

I'd left so late last night. It had taken everything in me to resist knocking on Lola's room. Imagining her tucked under her blankets, all alone, was torture. The part of me that *needed* to see Lola clawed upwards. "Let's get moving."

A slow, suspicious squint inched along Brenda's face. "Oh. I see now. You're not even worrying about the show, you're still thinking about her." Collapsing deep in the seat, my manager groaned. "Nice priorities. But fine, here we go." She turned the key, the car's tires squealing away from the curb.

Buildings rolled by the deeper we got into the city. I tried to calm my beating heart.

437

Soon, I'll see her. Then I can tell her—show her —everything she asked of me.

Brenda had been talking to herself the whole drive. I'd tuned most of it out. "If I have to pull everyone from their beds, I'll do it," she said. "This whole band has been testing my limits." Her phone rang in her purse. She slid it out, thumb flipping the device open. "Weird, it's the hotel." Not slowing down, she answered the call. "Hello, Brenda Westlake speaking."

Right in front of me, Brenda's expression morphed from confusion, to shock, to flat out anger... and then flustered defeat. "What is it?" I asked.

She motioned at me to leave her be. "Uh huh. Uh huh. Yes, I understand—no, that's fine, these things happen. Hm?" Her voice lowered drastically. "I'll want to see proof of that. Yes, I'm on my way. Just—yes, I'll talk to you there. Thanks." She snapped the phone shut and groaned. "This fucking *band!*"

"What did we do now?"

Her eyes flashed at me. "Someone trashed one of the rooms I rented. This is going to cost me a ton of money." She smacked the steering wheel. "Son of a bitch! You guys should know better by now!"

"Don't blame me, I didn't even sleep in my room. You know that."

"I blame you for other things!" Gritting her teeth, Brenda put a heavy foot on the gas. "It had to be Porter or Colt, maybe the both of them. Probably got some girls up into their room and went nuts. Jackasses."

I wrinkled my brow. "They didn't say which room it was?"

"No, they just said they had a bill for the damages waiting for me." The engine revved loudly. "Ten thousand dollars? Are they *joking?*"

We pulled up outside the Hilton. Brenda flew from the car, stopping only to speak to the valet. "Don't go far, I'll be right back and I might have some headless corpses with me."

Smiling tightly, I followed her inside. The last time a room had gotten busted up on our dime had been over six months ago. *And we had Johnny to thank for that one.* The memory soured my stomach.

Brenda regained her composure, approaching the front desk with a sweet smile. She placed her folded hands on top of the counter. "Excuse me," she said softly, "I took a phone call a few minutes ago. I'm Brenda Westlake."

"Ah! Yes, right." The man who'd been waiting there was young, his gelled hair the color of lemonade. "I'm so sorry about this. But, it seems the cleaning lady found one of your rooms... well." He shrugged, lips stuck in a forever-false smile. "Out of sorts. Here, this is the paperwork."

Sliding up to the counter, I watched over Brenda's shoulder. The front desk associate gave me a brief look, but otherwise, he was content to point out the itemized list. I *felt* Brenda's fury growing. "A television?" she scoffed. "*Seriously?*"

The guy—I saw his name tag said Jeremy—raised his hands as if Brenda might strike him. "Yes, everything listed is accurate."

"I want to see proof." Lifting the paper, she waved it side to side. "Nothing is approved to be charged to my card until I see the damages first hand." Glancing back at the bill, she stood straighter. "Wait, is this the right room?"

Warily, Jeremy offered a key card. "Room two-fifty, correct."

My heart worked itself into a ball of elastics. Why was my blood racing? "Whose room was that?" I whispered.

Brenda met my eyes, her skin ashen. "Lola's room."

Snatching the card, I power-walked to the elevator.

"Drez!" she shouted after me.

This is wrong. Why does it feel so wrong?

"Drezden, slow down!"

I didn't. Even in the elevator, I kept pacing. I didn't stop moving until I slammed the key card into the door slot and pushed my way into room two-fifty.

It was worse than I'd imagined.

The floor was coated in broken glass—the remains of a coffee table, I thought, but the flat screen TV was mixed in, making it hard to tell what fragments belonged to what. The perfectly made bed contrasted sharply with the chaotic scene.

Covering her mouth, Brenda turned in place. "Wow. She really *was* mad at you."

"What?" My muscles hardened like steel. "You think she destroyed her own room because of me?"

"I don't know." Sighing, she folded up the paperwork and stuck it in her purse. Gingerly, she touched the top of the broken TV. "Between her running off yesterday and you spilling your heart to me last night..." I bit my tongue at her interpretation. "If she didn't do this to let out some tension, then why? To break her 'Oh look at me, I'm an out of control rocker' cherry?"

There was sweat staining my throat, a sickening warmth turning my belly into a fetid swamp. *This doesn't make sense. Could Lola—would Lola—do this?* "Are you sure it was her?" I asked.

Brenda sat on the edge of the bed. "She didn't answer when I knocked this morning, I guess she could have run away and it was the cleaning lady who went bonkers and smashed everything."

Lowering my brows, I scowled at her. "Take this seriously."

441

"I *am* taking it seriously." She patted her purse emphatically. "Ten grand worth of seriously. Drez, this isn't the first time someone has smashed up a hotel room on tour."

The longer I stood near the mess, the more my paranoia prickled. "I can't see her doing this."

Brenda stood and came my way. Glass crunched under her heels. "You can't imagine breaking things out of anger? You, of all people?"

I wouldn't be blinded by guilt. "This is Lola we're talking about, not me."

"Sure, but she doesn't have a clean history when it comes to violence, either."

Lola's tattoos swam through my memory. "It feels wrong. Can't you see that?" I waved around the room, facing Brenda down. "Even if she was mad at me, this is too much. Something else is going on." I fished my phone out in a hurry. The fact she hadn't called me, texted me, *anything* at all since we'd last spoken... it left me cold. *Everything will be fine.*

As soon as I saw her, it would be fine.

Her voicemail beeped. I didn't leave a message, I just dialed again. And again. Each time, the tendons in my forearm flexed harder. By the time Brenda reached out to touch my elbow, I was aching with pain. "Where is she?" I snapped. "The show's in three hours. She needs to be here."

"Drez—"

"Let's find the guys." My voice cracked, I cleared it with a snarl. "Maybe they know where she is or what happened in here."

Unlike Lola, Porter and Colt were indeed in their own rooms. There's were connected, making it easy to flash the lights on in one while shouting through the open door at the other.

"Ugh," Colt groaned. "What the hell are you doing? Is it time for the show?"

"Lola," I said briskly, trying to get Colt to focus on my eyes. "Have you seen her?"

"What?" Pushing me off of him, he yanked a dirty shirt on over his head. "What time is it, man?"

"*Have you seen Lola?*"

"I—no, not since yesterday." The drummer walked through into Porter's room. The bigger man was sitting up shirtless in bed, his head in his hands. Grabbing a glass, Colt filled it in the bathroom, grimacing as he took a swig of sink water. "Ugh. That tastes awful."

I wasn't listening, I'd followed him into the room, busy with grabbing at Porter's shoulders. "Tell me you've seen Lola."

Porter looked me in the eye. I saw the red veins and yellow tint—they'd drank hard last night. "Something's wrong, isn't it?" he asked.

"Maybe, maybe not," Brenda said, leaning around the corner of the doorway. "You guys have any wild parties last night? Or *hear* anything like a party from Lola's room?"

Coming up behind us, Colt spoke around a toothbrush in his mouth. "We played a drinking game. We both lost—and won—if that gives you an idea of what we heard."

I scraped at my scalp, no longer hiding my nerves. "Her room was wrecked, and she won't answer when I call her."

Rolling her eyes, Brenda studied her phone. "She wouldn't talk to you if she was breaking-televisions-levels-of-pissed." She was acting calmer than she was, I could tell by how her foot was tapping rapidly on the beige rug.

Porter threw the blankets aside, sticking his legs into some jeans and grabbing a jersey off of a chair. "You call her then, Brenda," he said.

Energy flooded me; I gripped my manager by the shoulders, shaking her. "That's perfect! Call her. If she doesn't pick up, then this has to be about more than me."

"Whoa, easy!" Digging her nails into my wrists, Brenda pushed me off. "I'll call her, calm down. I think you're missing the point, though." Lifting her cell, she tapped the buttons. "I left voice mails for *everyone* this morning. Her too. No one called me back."

The boys managed to look the appropriate level of chagrined. "Oh," Porter laughed. "Uh. Guess I slept through those."

444

Brenda gave me a pointed stare. "It's ringing."

Holding my breath, I bent low, trying to hear through the speaker. Each crackle of noise was a stab in my chest, my hope that Lola would pick up and interrupt the ringing ballooning by the second. At the sound of her voicemail, I bared my teeth and punched the wall. "Dammit!"

"Holy shit, calm down!" Colt said, clapping me on the shoulder. "Maybe she lost her phone. She could be at the tour bus, or even the venue. Right?"

Inhaling 'til my ribs hurt, I strode out of the room. "We'll check there next."

I had to move. I had to do something. If I didn't, I was going to explode.

No one else seemed to feel the way I did —this mounting sense of distress, that something was dangerously *wrong*. The last time Lola had gone missing, she'd been with Brenda. That had terrified me, but this...

This left me in ruin.

****

The tour buses had been moved. I spotted ours along the sidewalk in front of the Paramount Theater, orange cones dotting the street to block off other vehicles. People were crowding, taking photos or lining up early.

I slipped from the car as it came to a stop. On long legs, I hurried to the bus. My haste didn't prevent some people from crying out in delight, cameras flashing to get a memento of me.

Crowning the stairs, I looked over the inside of the vehicle.

No Lola.

"Drez," Porter said, coming up behind me. I didn't speak, I just ran down the aisle, shoving aside the curtains of every room. Her bed was empty. What really hit home was seeing her guitar.

In the practice room, it sat alone—abandoned. It hadn't moved since yesterday, when she'd placed it there and fled the room.

Fled from *me*.

The back of my neck was sweltering. All eyes were on me when I turned, my manager and band mates watching me in the aisle. Their empathy—pity—was turning my stomach. "Don't look at me like that," I whispered.

Their unease was unanimous. "Drez," Colt started, but Brenda waved her hand to silence him.

"The show is in..." She checked her phone, frowned. "Shit. Three hours."

I lowered my chin. "Who the hell cares about the show? Lola is *missing*." *Something has happened to her*. It was the only solution that made sense.

"Can I say something?" Colt raised his hand, a perfect school boy impression. "Uh, I sort of care about the show. Is it just me? Maybe? No?" Flicking his eyes at all of us, the drummer sighed. "This sucks. I can't believe Lola would run away."

"She didn't run," I spat.

Colt opened his mouth, then shut his jaw, considering me. "Let's look in the theater. If she's in there, problem solved. I honestly don't know what we'll do otherwise, but we should think of a fall back—hey!"

Shoving past him, I jumped down the stairs. The crowd was bigger now, faceless people screaming for me. I didn't care at all. I pushed through them, cutting a path until I could march into the theater.

It was huge inside, the lobby ceiling arching overhead. I didn't slow my pace until I was gazing on the stage, always scanning for that one pair of beautiful, perfect blue eyes.

Brenda and my band chased me down. "She isn't here," I said, before they could ask. Turning, I gazed over their expressions, judging them. "Lola isn't here. She isn't *fucking* here!" My shoe jammed into a front row seat, the noise echoing around the auditorium. Security, lighting, assistants; they all stared at me.

"What should we do?" Porter asked softly, like I'd fly further into a rage.

"I'm thinking," Brenda said. "We don't have much time. If she doesn't show up, you guys can't go on tonight."

"This is bad. Do we call the cops?" Colt asked. "What if something happened to her?"

His words rang true with the fear that had been coming to life inside of me.

I felt myself floating away, my mind splitting as it imagined all the things that could have happened to Lola. Why was her room so destroyed? Why was she not answering anyone's phone calls? *It isn't because of me. This is more than me.*

"—replacement."

My head jerked up, gawking at Brenda. "What was that?"

She was looking past me, off to the side of the stage where people were entering. There, a pair of blue eyes that sliced at me so fucking *painfully*. Sean Cooper was smiling, saying something to that big drummer of his.

"A replacement," Brenda said again, gently. "If Lola doesn't show... maybe I could convince Sean to play with you guys instead."

"It might work," Porter mumbled.

Sean sensed me. He stopped where he was, studying me. His eyes traveled around, pausing on each of us... and then his face knotted in confusion.

He noticed Lola isn't here.

My intuition was a wild shark in the ocean. It crowned upwards, demanding I confront Sean because he clearly knew what the hell was going on. I stomped his way. Behind me, I heard a distressed groan from Brenda.

I shut the band's conversation down with my approach. Barbed Fire turned as one, no love on their faces. "Lola," I said, and I caught my fear reflecting in Sean's face. "Have you seen her today?"

His jaw straightened. "No. Why, what's wrong?"

Panic boiled through my limbs, making my voice a hiss. "I don't fucking know. Her hotel room was a mess and no one can find her, when did you last see her?"

"Oh," Shark laughed, elbowing Sean. "Shit, isn't *this* familiar? Hey, fucker, how does it feel to wonder where—"

"Shut up, Shark," Sean snapped, not looking away from me. "Have you tried calling her?"

I lifted my phone out, debated throwing it for all the good it had done me. "She won't answer anyone."

Brenda approached us, saying, "Whatever her reasons, she isn't here. Sean, I need to—this is hard to ask." She gathered herself, and I had the funniest idea that she found talking to him a challenge. I'd never known her to waffle with anyone. "This show tonight is *huge*. If Headstones don't play, we'll lose money, fans, respect—you name it. But you know some of their songs."

When she said that, Sean's mouth tensed.

It was almost as tight as my own right then. Of course he knew some of our songs, he'd auditioned for my damn band.

She asked, "Would you—worst case—consider filling in for Lola?"

My neck creaked as if I were fighting through drying concrete just to stare in her direction. There was absolutely no way I would play with Sean. Outside of how I felt towards him, the reality was that Lola was *missing*. If Brenda thought I was capable of playing in any capacity while the girl I loved was missing, she was insane.

"No," Sean said.

I'd have whiplash before the night was over.

Narrowing his eyes, he looked from Brenda to me. "It's not that I wouldn't... fuck. I'd love the chance to headline. Seriously." He gave his head a quick shake. "But no. How can I do anything but help find my sister?"

I fought down an odd swell of pride for the guy. "You'll help me look?" I asked.

Sean closed his eyes, breathing through his nose. "Of course. It doesn't make sense for her to just run off like this."

Righteousness fueled my voice. "I've felt that way since I saw her hotel room this morning. There's no way she did all that damage. Broken television, broken table, stuff I can't picture Lola doing. Something happened to her, I just don't have a clue what!"

"I think I do." He glided his fingers through his hair. Sean began to crumple, and when he spoke, it was like his tongue wasn't working right—like he didn't want to say a word but knew it was necessary. "It had to be Johnny Muse."

Johnny Muse.

My throat was closing.

The ringing in my ears was deafening.

Brenda was speaking frantically beside me. "I'm calling the cops right now."

"Where?" I licked my lips, feeling the dry cracks. "Where are they?"

He never broke eye contact. "He was staying at Greenmill Motel. We'll take my van."

"I said I'm calling the cops!" Brenda shouted, realizing we were planning our own form of attack. "Drez, no, stay here. Both of you stay here."

"Call the police if you want," I said to her. "If you need to, you can even cancel this whole show. I'm not standing around until someone else fixes this for me."

Her eyes were glossy as she watched me pass her by. The phone hung limp at her side. "What are you going to do to him?" she whispered.

In my hands, my joints crunched.

I did Brenda the favor of not answering.

- Chapter Twenty-Eight -
Lola

Drezden's hands slid up my sides, his fingertips taking my resistance away with every inch. "Lift your shirt," he whispered, lips stroking the patch of skin between neck and shoulder. He was the epitome of living seduction, his heat making me drunk and hazy. "You don't look well," he whispered against me.

In the mirror, I saw my milky skin. Bruises that I thought had long healed crawled up my arms, cuts dripping with fresh blood. *Why is this familiar... but off?*

Holding the back of my head, Drezden bit down on my jaw. The roots of my hair tugged, sending sparks to my cells. I was acutely aware of everything and anything.

My tattoo itched. In the flickering lights of the bathroom, the dark castle was a forest of living snakes and green eyes. "What's going on?" I asked, but my voice was too quiet.

No one could hear me.

Holding me still, Drezden peered into my face. His teeth were fangs, lips searing and melting me where he touched. In my ear, he murmured so gently.

"Look out."

The man I loved shoved me backwards. I went tumbling down into the tub.

I never landed.

As I looked up, his face morphed. Green eyes—but not *my* green eyes.

Johnny Muse.

I felt only pain. My eyes were heavy, hesitant to open. The edges of my vision stabbed like serrated knives, cutting into my temples, my brain. *What happened?* Thinking brought more deep aches, hiding my memory from me.

I realized I was sitting. Gingerly I shifted in place, craning my head carefully to study the low-lit room that hadn't seen a clean sponge in forever. Cracked walls, patchy floors, a bed that was piled with wrinkled blankets.

I didn't know this place at all.

Wriggling my wrists, I tugged hard— then harder. They were tied behind me. One movement was too much; my right shoulder screamed in sharp distress. My natural reaction was to gasp, something in my mouth stunted the cry.

"Oh," a voice said beside me. "You're awake."

Wide-eyed, I came awake as if my feet had been put in a fire. Johnny stood next to me, twitching, pacing as he looked on. The scabs across his face blazed, a shiny bruise splashing on the side of his cheek.

All at once, I remembered the fight in my hotel room.

Oh shit.

My belly rippled, adrenaline shooting through my limbs. Reluctantly, the blackness lifted from my mind. After I'd passed out, I'd flitted in and out of consciousness. Parts of that returned to me—the bits where I was jostled in Johnny's arms, half-dragged, my hood pulled low over my face.

Someone had asked if I was alright, but I'd been too groggy to speak. Johnny had answered quickly, something about me drinking too much because I was excited for all the bands in town.

In the bustle of the busy hotel lobby, no one had realized I was Lola Cooper.

That I was being kidnapped in plain sight.

No one knows what happened to me. The revelation turned my blood cold.

My captor bent close, smelling entirely too much of whiskey. "You okay in there? Comfortable?" Biting onto the rag in my mouth, I made a muffled sound of anger. Johnny blinked, standing straight. "Look, you were the one that went nuts last night."

Last night? How long had I been unconscious for?

A vibration rumbled loudly to my left, paralyzing me with new fear. From where I sat, I saw the shiny device and knew it was my phone. Someone was trying to call me! That brought a new, sickening thought with it. *If he*

*took my phone, that means he touched me...
searched me.*

Had he done anything else while I was
so vulnerable?

He said flatly, "I didn't have any choice
but to do this."

My attention jumped up to his stubble
covered jaw. Johnny's eyes were bloodshot, his
lip ticking occasionally. I was in the hands of a
madman. Rocking in my bonds, I tested
everything. What had he tied on my wrists? It
felt sticky, like old candy.

He took a swig from a bottle he'd left
beside my phone. "You were out so long, I
wondered if you had a concussion."

And he didn't take me to a hospital? A
tremble went down my knees. *Fuck fuck fuck.*
Johnny wasn't concerned for my health. If
something went wrong under his control...

I could die here.

His palm touched my forehead,
unnerving me. "You look pale." Scrutinizing me
for a long moment, he hummed. "I'm really
sorry if you don't feel well. Seriously, none of
this—I didn't *plan* to do this."

No, I didn't think it was planned. The
way he'd followed me, then freaked out in my
room, had all been too spontaneous. *I haven't
been captured by some vaudevillian
character. Just a crazy, unhinged, selfish
prick.*

Wonderful.

456

Coughing against my gag, I moaned. Johnny pulled away, his lips pinched. "What is it? That too tight?"

Freezing my muscles, I considered his question. *If I can get him to ungag me, maybe I can find a way out of this.* My nod of agreement was patiently slow.

"Okay. But listen. You make any loud noise, and I'm putting this on even tighter. Okay?" When I nodded again, he reached behind my head, loosening the tie. With the ability to move my mouth again, I noticed how badly my jaw ached. "There. Better?"

My voice cracked. "Can I have a drink?" He edged the open bottle towards me, the strong scent of alcohol burned my nostrils. "Water, do you have water?"

"Oh." Swallowing more of the liquid down, he wiped his mouth with the back of his arm. Moving out of view around a corner, Johnny jostled something; I heard water running, probably a sink. The paper cup he brought back to me smelled like chlorine, but I drank it eagerly while he tilted it to my mouth.

Tossing the cup aside, its purpose done, Johnny dug a pack of cigarettes from his pocket. "You smoke?"

I curled my lips back. "What are you going to do with me?"

"Take that as a no." Cupping his lighter close, the fire turned his lips cherry-red. Smoke billowed, the smell making me think of

Drezden. "Like I said, this wasn't planned." On the table, my phone buzzed again. We both glanced at it; him, with disgust—and me? I couldn't hide the hope in my eyes, he saw it plainly. "Don't get excited," he muttered.

"Johnny, please, just let me go." I leaned towards him as much as I could "You don't need to keep me here."

Waving smoke away, he rolled the cigarette to one side in his mouth and spoke around it. "Yeah, I do. I tried to talk you out of that band. Tried to fucking tell you how awful Drez is. You didn't want to listen." Ash fell to the rug. "This was the only way to keep you from playing."

Shifting in the chair, I winced at the twinge in my shoulder. Was it out of the socket? "Why do you care if I play or not? You aren't in the band anymore, what does it matter to you?"

He turned his head suddenly, listening for... something. Taking another drag, Johnny let the grey haze flow around him. "You talk too much. Want more water?"

Why does he want me to leave the band? I'd figured out why Sean had been struggling with it, but Johnny—there was only one thing he could want

My eyebrows shot up to my scalp. "You wanted me to leave so you could take my spot again!"

"*Again?*" His foot kicked a chair, sending it flying. I ducked my chin, expecting him to swing at me. "Again? *You* took *my* spot, not the other way around!"

My breath rattled in my chest. Johnny looked rabid, on the verge of taking a bite out of me. I could see the raw edges of his gums, the cigarette illuminating everything. He moved, hands coming down on my shoulders. "Don't touch me!" I screamed.

Again, on the table, my phone vibrated.

Johnny moved away, guilt twisting his forehead into long rows. "Lola, I'm not that kind of guy! I don't just hurt people!" Remembering the way he'd slammed me into the coffee table last night, I didn't comment. "Just calm down," he mumbled. Was he talking to himself, or me? Lighting a new cigarette, Johnny dropped onto the bed and stared at the ceiling.

He can't see my hands. Cautiously, I worked my wrists together behind me. As a kid, I'd played games with Sean where we tied each other up, pretending to be cops or robbers. They were silly games, and while they didn't help me with untying my binds, the memory gave me strength.

My phone, buzzing away, gave me even more.

People have to know something is wrong. What time was it? The filthy blinds over the windows hid the info from me. Never letting Johnny out of my sight, I kept tugging at my wrists. Whatever he'd used, it was starting to yield from the friction.

Tape? Is that it? Not even electrical tape, but the cheap, clear stuff. Johnny really *hadn't* thought up some grand scheme. *He just wanted me to quit the band so he could stroll in and save the day. But he can't now. He has to know that.* There was no way anyone would take him back, even if they were desperate.

The tape slid enough for me to inch my fingers out. My blood pumped like gasoline. One wrong move and I'd be set ablaze. Letting Johnny into my hotel room was the last wrong move I planned to make.

My ankles were attached to the chair legs. *Free hands, but nothing to do with them.* If Johnny came close, could I do something? *Punch him in the teeth is what I want to do, but that won't help me escape.*

Looking at my phone, it became clear. *If I can grab it, I can tell someone where I am.* My stomach coiled over and over. *But where am I?* Johnny hadn't said. Looking around, it was clearly a motel room. But which one?

Scanning the floors, the walls, I looked for something iconic. A crumpled pile of towels revealed the name in poor, faded embroidery: Greenmill Motel. It was like a drum had exploded in my brain. *Sean told me that!* My brother had visited Johnny here. He'd know where to find me.

I peeked at Johnny. He was lying on his side on the bed, his back to me. Inching my aching arms around, I reached for my phone. My fingertips hovered just as it vibrated. The noise touched my bones.

"For fuck's sake!" Johnny cried, rolling over on the old springs. "That damn phone of yours needs to shut up and—hey! *Stop!*"

Desperately I snatched my phone, fumbling with sweaty palms to open it, to dial *anything*. Johnny was on me, digging his nails into me, wrenching for the device. *No, no no no!* Inhaling to capacity, I started to scream for help.

His backhand shut me up, but it didn't stop me. Releasing the phone, I rolled forward, knocking the chair over beneath me. Holding onto his legs, I prayed he'd crack his skull on the side-table as I brought him down.

"You little fucking bitch!" He buried his grip in my hair. "I told you to stay quiet, you lying—aahh!" I'd buried my teeth into the meaty part near his thumb. Dug in, and just worked my jaw as hard as I could.

When he hit me that time, I saw spots of white.

My eyes lolled to the side; the phone rested near my face, open so I could read the missed calls. *Drezden. So many calls from him.*

Johnny shoved the gag in my mouth, tying it so tight I struggled to get air. "Shut up."

461

There was no sympathy anymore. "Were you always the sort to betray people, or did you pick that up from Drez?"

I tasted coppery blood—his, not mine. It filled me with glee knowing I'd managed to hurt him. Grunting, Johnny lifted my chair up, forcing my arms back behind me. "You actually got the tape off?"

Yanking at him was pointless, but I tried anyway.

Something made a plastic-squeal. He bound my wrists with more tape, but that wasn't enough, and we both knew it. "You're more trouble than I was ready for," he muttered. Cloth wrapped over my wrists next. Socks? A shirt? I didn't know.

Picking up my phone, Johnny frowned. "You think the cops can trace this?" Glancing at me, he waited, like I could answer. "Guess it doesn't matter." Looking around, he stomped out the smoking remains of his fallen cigarette. "They're going to find me eventually, huh? Fucking fuck."

Watching blood drip down his arm from my bite marks, I shivered. *He really didn't consider what to do next. What would happen to him next.*

For the first time, Johnny was debating what to do with *me*.

- Chapter Twenty-Nine -
Drezden

"Why the hell would you *bring* her to meet Johnny?" I growled.

Sean bent over the steering wheel, one great hump of regret. "I didn't know he would do something like this!"

"How much further?" I'd been digging my fingers into the tops of my thighs the whole ride.

Squinting out at the growing evening sky, Sean sighed. "I'm not sure. Fifteen minutes. The motel is on the edge of the city."

"You better hope she's okay," I whispered. There were shadows on my tongue. "For your sake." I'd burn the whole world to the ground if it meant saving Lola.

"Why the hell are you so pissed at me?" he asked, pulling us sharply around a turn. "It isn't my fault that the crazy motherfucker kidnapped her!"

Scrunching my face, I looked out the window. It was too easy to imagine the scene— Johnny stealing Lola from her hotel room while she fought tooth and nail to escape. The images fueled my rage even more.

"Now you've gone silent on me," Sean muttered. "Seriously. Why are you such an asshole to me?"

The question caught me off guard. "Pretty sure you've been just as big of a thorn in my side."

His eyes darted up, then away. "I had my reasons not to like you."

"Then we're even."

"We're not fucking even!" He punched his fist into the wheel. "You started this shitty thing between us! You had *no reason* to be such a dick to me years ago, what did I do to deserve your shitty treatment?" In the darkness of the vehicle, his eyes were glowing. "What did I do to you that made you want to hate me so *much?*"

Closing my eyes tight, I breathed through my nose. *The entitlement in his stare of disbelief when I rejected him... I can't forget that look.* It had stayed with me for years. I knew why now, though. My recent excavation into my past had helped me understand.

But how could I explain to Sean that he'd reminded me too much of my father?

"Nothing," I said flatly, "You didn't do anything."

"Then why? Was I really so bad at guitar? Was that enough reason to—"

"No, that wasn't the reason." Grabbing my forehead, I dug through the waves of migraines. I was feeling the exhaustion from my overnight trip home, but more so, the emotional drainage from searching for Lola. *Honesty.* "I knew guys like you. Men who couldn't handle the idea they weren't made for greatness." *Men who tried to destroy those better than them.*

Looking over, I saw Sean staring straight ahead. I said, "You're better now than you were when you auditioned." Those blue eyes flicked my way. "But your sister is miles better."

Sean snorted with laughter. He allowed a tiny smile onto his face. "Yeah, I know she is."

"Do you hate her for that?" In my mind, I pictured the rage on my father's features. How his mouth had writhed like a python, his knuckles coated in my mother's blood.

Sean lifted his eyebrows high. "Hate her? *Lola?*" The engine rumbled softly, the van slowing as we crawled up a hill. "She's my little sister. I couldn't hate her if I tried."

Warm compassion filled me as I listened to him speak. *I judged him wrong.*

Sean was nothing like my father.

"There," he whispered, turning the headlights off. I saw the small, barely lit motel sitting in the parking lot below us. It was the color of stained teeth, the flickering sign threatening to die after each burst of light.

All at once, my blood began to stir. "You think they're both here?"

Sean removed his seat belt in a hurry. "If they aren't, I don't know where else to look."

His words were heavy. *If Lola isn't here, then we have no trail.* Pushing the door open, I flared my nostrils in the putrid air. *She has to be here.*

She just had to.

Quietly, we approached the building. All the doors faced out into the parking lot, some missing numbers on their cracked fronts. Sean and I prowled beneath the window sills. Every room looked empty through the drapes; nothing but still shadows.

Are they not here? My heart was crumbling with a wave of distress. *Where do we go next, what do we do?*

What do I do?

Touching my pocket, I felt my phone. The idea came to me like a live battery on my tongue. Squatting down, I began to dial in the dark. I was hoping to hear ringing, any noise at all through the motel walls. For a long time, there was nothing. Crickets sang, and in the far distance, a car honked.

Looking over, I saw Sean had his phone out as well. *He can't be trying Lola, too, can he?* As her number went to voicemail again, I caught a sound that stopped my breath.

"Fuck!" A gritty voice shouted a mere two rooms over. "Shit shit shit, now they're calling me, dammit!"

Sean looked me in the eye. *He had Johnny's number.* Together we moved, uncaring who saw us now in our blooming

466

excitement. *He's here, she has to be, too!* We didn't have a plan, but that was fine. Both of us wanted the same thing.

A shared look was all it took; together, we rammed our shoulders against the motel door. Inside, I heard Johnny cursing—it just fueled me more. The door was made from old wood. In two, three hits, Sean and I took it down.

And then, there she was.

Lola, whose beautiful blue eyes were boggling at me not in disbelief—no, she had *known* I would come for her—but in satisfaction. If it was fate or divinity or some other fucking magical thing that had brought us together in life, I didn't know. I didn't care. All that mattered was that she was mine.

I would never lose her again.

In that tiny room, I froze my acid-green eyes on Johnny and felt the moment for what it was. Here, we both realized... here was where he'd pay his dues.

Lifting his hands to protect himself, he backed into the wall. "Drez! Wait, man! Hold on!"

Distantly, I remembered the day I'd kicked him out of my band. How I'd sucker-punched him, watched him flail and backpedal in an attempt to escape my wrath. That day, I'd only wanted him gone.

I wanted much more from him now.

Lola's scream was muffled scream around her gag. I'd grabbed Johnny up by the front of his shirt without realizing it, and even better, I'd slammed his skull into the wall, making the room—my marrow—quake. Again and again I smashed his body into the hard surface, trying to break him into tiny pieces.

True fear boiled in his eyes. The sight of it brought a smile to my lips. "This is for hurting her," I whispered, but it came out like a snarl. I don't know if he understood me at all, especially with how his eyes were rolling. Was he blacking out?

Someone called out to me. I ignored them. Twisting, feeling Johnny claw at my wrists, I threw him onto the busted linoleum floor. He belonged perfectly on that scuffed, filthy ground. He'd never looked more at home.

"Drez," he coughed, red streaking his nose. The blood rolled down the bruise on his cheek, over the scabs of old cuts. They looked like claw marks; nails. Had Lola done that?

Reaching down, my fingers trapped his jaw. Johnny struggled but a single knee on his chest pinned him in place. He smelled like vomit and whiskey and revenge. Sweet fucking revenge.

"Drezden!" Her voice was pure, I couldn't ignore her. Lola was leaning on Sean—he'd untied her. As always, she wore no mask, her pale skin twisted in a grimace of fear. "What are you going to do?" she asked.

468

Her terror reached into me and plucked at my heart. Johnny was wheezing, gawking up at me. I tried to recall how this husk of a man had once called himself my friend. From the start, there had never been the connection between us that Colt and Porter had. Johnny was a wild card, too wild.

I should have known better.

"Drez," Lola asked again, firmer. "What are you going to do?"

Squeezing Johnny's cheeks, digging in my nails, I ignored him and kept staring at her. I wondered what she saw in my face. Inside, I felt the wretched talons of the monster I knew I could be. It was hungry, and here, now, lay the decadent chance to taste victory. To chew at a sweet piece of vengeance.

Swallowing, I said, "I'm going to do what I promised. I said if I ever saw Johnny's face again... I was going to break his fucking jaw."

Under my grip, Johnny stiffened. Closing her tired eyes, Lola turned away. It was like she was giving me permission to be the brutal beast I knew I could be. But before I could pull back my fist, she said, "Is this the real you?"

My lungs went still. I couldn't move anything, not even an eyelash. Johnny was shivering; no longer fighting back. He had nothing left for me. What had I even wanted from him?

Is this the real me? Hadn't I gone to face my father to prove I was nothing like him?

For a moment, Johnny's horror looked too much like my own mother's.

Flexing my fingers, I turned away from him. I left him whimpering on the floor, his occasional moan punctuated by a curse word.

"Call the police," I said bluntly.

"No need," Sean said. Nodding his head, he drew my attention to the distant sound of sirens. "Brenda must have called them like she said she would. That, or someone else in this motel did when they heard the fight."

My head bobbed, but I wasn't listening. I was fixated on Lola—on her wide eyes, on her bruises and her smile and how her wrists were raw and red. She met me halfway, not caring about the blood I left on her cheek when I cupped her face.

Her mouth opened, but if she'd wanted to speak... I didn't let her. I buried my lips on hers like she was the first sip of water after days in the dessert. Lola, my fucking beautiful, wonderful Lola.

She tasted like victory.

"Drez," she whispered, but I ate my name away.

Cradling her in my arms, inhaling her scent until it made my senses blind, I listened to her heart beat. *Mine. Mine, mine, and mine again.*

Lola is mine.

470

And I finally deserved her.

****

The police arrested Johnny, taking all of our statements down. It was smooth and professional. Well, minus the one guy who asked me for an autograph.

"Do you need to go to the hospital?" I asked Lola, unable to stop touching her for even one second.

Her smile was soft. "I'm fine. My right shoulder hurts a little, but it's nothing. I'm just... I'm just so sorry about all of this."

"Don't be sorry," Sean said, approaching us in the parking lot. "You didn't do any of this. Johnny was the one who went unhinged."

"I still feel awful that the show was ruined," she mumbled.

Grabbing her chin, I made her look at me. "I don't give a shit about the show, okay? I only need you to be safe. The rest is pointless otherwise."

Sean chuckled, eyeing the time on his phone. "Too bad we can't have both. Show should have started an hour ago."

"We should go there anyway," Lola said, staring between us. "Maybe even just to tell the fans we're sorry. Just... something."

471

I guided her towards Sean's van. "You want that to happen? We'll make it happen. Come on, let's move."

Lola was warm on my lap in the car. As far as I was concerned, if we stayed like this, the drive could go on forever. I felt... whole. On reflex, I linked my arms around her waist, whispering in her ear. "I'm the one who needs to apologize. You would never have talked to Johnny if I had just told you what you wanted to know."

Shifting, Lola's hair tickled my cheek. Her lips pressed to my forehead, hands cradling over mine in her lap. "It doesn't matter now."

"It *does* matter now," I declared. *It has to matter.* "I took care of everything. I'll tell you every single thing about me now, Lola. Everything."

Her body knotted up. "Took care of...?"

"*Holy shit!*" Sean shouted, the van turning onto the street where the Paramount theater was. I didn't need to ask what was wrong. The mob outside was massive.

Pressing my phone to my ear, I dialed quickly. "Brenda," I said when she picked up, "What the hell is going on?"

"Drezden! Please tell me you're all okay!"

"We're fine," I said, eyeballing the shouting people outside our windows. "Lola is

472

with us, we're right outside. Tell me what's going on."

The edge of her voice wavered with excitement. "We managed to delay the show. Everyone is super pissed, but we did it. Can you —I mean, *would* you guys still play tonight?"

Lola had been leaning in, listening to the call. Grabbing the phone from me, she shouted into the receiver. "Yes! We'll do it!"

Sean was staring at me, slowly shaking his head in wonder. "Tell me what's happening."

Pulling the phone back from Lola, I allowed myself to smile. "Guess the show must go on."

Rolling down the windows, we parked the van where the security teams guided us. The walls of fans, all screaming a mixture of joy and anger, tried to swallow us as we approached the venue. All we could do was wave, knowing it was impossible for those people to understand what any of us had been through.

It's good we were able to wash all the blood off at the motel.

Wouldn't that have made an interesting photo for the news?

****

473

Porter and Colt smashed me in a hug when we got backstage. With Lola, they were far more gentle, their voices merging as they asked too many questions.

"Are you alright?"

"Did Johnny really do this?"

"Are you sure you want to play?"

"What happened to him, where is he now?"

It was Brenda, slicing between them and shoving them aside, that ended the parade. Turning, she held Lola by the shoulders, stared into her stunned face. "You really want to play tonight?"

Gulping air, Lola narrowed her eyes. "Yeah. I'm ready."

"How did you manage to delay the show for us?" I asked in wonderment.

Her ruby lips coiled upwards. "I promised everyone free tickets to your next show. Better than trying to handle angry refunds on this, trust me."

Out in the auditorium, the roar of the crowd grew. They were savage, starving for what they had longed for. I understood their feelings.

We did a quick wardrobe change; clean clothes for Lola and myself, makeup to hide some of her marks from the tussle with Johnny.

I wanted to know more about what had happened, but really, the details didn't matter.

Lola was safe now.

"Here," Brenda said, offering the girl her purple guitar. "Take it, tune it, do what you need to in ten minutes."

Hoisting the instrument into place, Lola's face twisted in a brief flinch. She saw me looking, then glanced away hurriedly. "Listen, Drez. That new song... can we even perform it?"

"I know all the words by heart." I took a slow step towards her, studying how she held the guitar. "You could probably keep the tune close enough that no one would notice. They haven't heard it before to compare, after all." She was focusing on her fingers, the floor, everywhere but me. "That's not the issue, is it?"

She said nothing.

"Lola... what's wrong?"

Hanging her head, her dark hair covered her face. "I think my shoulder is hurt bad. Holding my guitar, it's painful."

Brushing her tresses aside, I tried to read the pain in her blue gaze. "You still want to do this?"

"Yeah. If I can. After everything, I really want to try."

My lips closed on hers, the kiss a mere blink. "Then let's try."

Voices were calling out around us, people telling us where to go, what to do. For a moment, we stayed there and only existed with each other.

The cheers outside the curtain took it all away.

Together we moved, standing on our marks, straightening up to handle the wave of energy. Behind me, Porter and Colt settled in, their faces all smiles. It was unfair to them to lead with our new song, something they had no part of, but...

Looking over, I saw a bead of sweat on Lola's temple. *If she's in pain, I want to give her this. She wants it so badly.*

Everyone else had to come second to that.

Holding the mic, I spoke into it with a smirk. "Hello, Seattle." The explosion was immense. The room was a powder keg. I was the flint to light it up. "I'm sorry you had to wait so long for us to perform. But it was worth it, right?" I gestured around, roared into the speakers. "Because we're fucking right here! Four and a Half Headstones, and we've got a new song for you!"

I waited until the world stopped screeching. Then, holding up my hand for silence, I whispered into all their ears. "I hope you enjoy it." Reaching down, I lifted the guitar I'd placed at my feet. The audience hadn't seen it; they went crazy all over again.

Hooking it in place, I took the time for them to settle down to tweak the strings. I'd tuned it before, but I wanted to be sure.

I wanted everything to be right.

In the dead silence, Lola began to play. It was a haunting melody, all ghosts and dust dancing from her fingers. It reminded me of our skill difference; commanded me to take hold and play to my best.

Breathing in to control my muscles, I followed her lead. Our notes flowed together, twirling through the air, burning on flesh. She was perfect, ever perfect, and if my fans didn't see it after this...

They never would.

"Beautiful in defiance," I hushed, "Wicked in how you claw. Come to me again, so close... you're mine, don't see these flaws..." From the moment I'd announced creating a song with Lola, I'd been brewing with ideas. I knew exactly the kind of song I wanted to make with her.

Did anyone ever imagine I would write a love song?

Looking over, I glimpsed the focus on Lola's face. Her lower lip was sucked in her teeth, fingers wild, elegant on her strings. She was exerting herself, but the pain she was going through vibrated in waves.

She can't keep this up for long, I thought desperately, singing for all the world like a man with a message. *But what can we do? What other choice is there?* The crowd, our fans, they'd waited so long to hear Four and a Half Headstones.

What could sate them but this?

477

"Wrapping, coiling, merging with the world..." Like she'd suggested, we punched our guitars, jolted the air with wild music. The energy was frantic, my heart rocketing inside my chest with nowhere to land. "Come to me again! Again, you're mine... you're mine..."

Lola's face was bloodless. *This is too much,* I thought in a panic. As the song came to a close, I saw her breathing heavy. Dogs trapped in cars panted less.

Something had to be done.

Off to the side, just backstage, I caught Sean Cooper looking on.

"Thank you," I said into the mic. Wiping sweat from my brow, I smiled over the crowd, forcing myself to hide my anxiety. I'd decided what I had to do, but there was a chance it would blow up in my face.

One more look at Lola cradling her shoulder was all the convincing I needed.

Clearing my throat, I gestured for Lola to come close. "Lola and I wrote that song together. I've never done that with someone before." Warily, she approached. "I've also never done this." Bending forward, I slid the guitar off of her. She was stunned, everyone was, but I looked again backstage. Sean stared right back. "As much as I want Lola to keep playing, she's been injured. She can't." The audience made various sounds, all loud; I talked louder. "Instead, there's someone here who's wanted to play with us for a long time."

Lola was shaking her head, trying to get my attention. Sean's hand on her shoulder startled her.

I said, "Sean Cooper." With purpose, I offer him her guitar. "Lola's brother, and lead guitarist for Barbed Fire."

No one knew what to do. Brenda was waving her arms at me, Porter and Colt were looking ill, and Lola...

She yanked her guitar away from me before I could stop her. "Thanks everyone," she said into my mic, "But my brother has his *own* guitar he can use."

The tension was shattered by their solid embrace. My grin went high as the crowd cheered. Lola exited, but she took a spot backstage where she could watch everything.

Winking at Sean, I asked, "You think you're finally ready for this?"

He strummed a note. "If I'm not, you're the one who'll be paying for it."

Throwing back my head, I laughed at the ceiling. "You said you knew some of our songs." I set my guitar on the floor, out of the way; I felt so much lighter. "Know Black Grit?"

In answer, he plucked the beginning. The fans heard it, screamed wildly in anticipation. Filling my lungs with air, I looked over my shoulder at Colt. He saw my nod, pounding his drums to herald the opening of the song. Twisting back, I glimpsed Lola looking on.

Those wonderful blue eyes were stuck on her brother. They glistened with affection so fierce, it threatened to overflow. Her fond smile was pure gold.

With my chest full of gratification... I opened my mouth and sang.

- Chapter Thirty -
Lola

The sun tickled along Drezden's back, highlighting the deep indent his spine made. It led my eye over his hard muscles, guided my fingers down to the top of his jeans. With loving precision, I skirted over the fresh ink on his skin.

It had been two days since the final show. The second the performance was over, Drezden had taken me to get my shoulder checked out. He'd ignored everyone clamoring for his attention, bulling his way past the crowds. His entire focus was on me.

I'd been fine—the doctor said it was minor muscle strain. Pain killers quickly soothed me. That was great, but the best part came later when we were finally alone.

In his hotel room, he sat me down and told me everything.

His dreams, his fears, his history...

How his father had grown violent. How his mother had sustained enough damage during the attack that she'd become deaf. The woman who had pushed to get him where he was couldn't even hear the powerful music he lived to make.

He told me everything until my heart weighed so much it crushed my lungs, left me breathless and awash in tears. Together we laid there, hands knitted at our hips between us.

Now, days later, lying on his bed in the tour bus, I studied the tattoo Drezden had covered his father's scar with. He'd raked his soul raw under the needle. *Honesty,* I thought, tracing the edges of the curling letters. He'd carved the word right into his skin.

He hadn't needed to go so far, and yet... for Drezden, there was no such thing as too far.

"Done," I whispered, setting the lotion aside. "It's looking good. Very clean."

Propping himself on his elbow, he curled me against him, teeth seeking my bottom lip. "It's not as elaborate as your tattoos."

I smiled around his kiss. "The meaning is just as important."

"You like it, then?"

Wrapping my fingers in his hair, I held him steady. The green of his eyes was like fresh grass, new and alive. "I like *you.*"

Zeroing in on my gaze, Drezden ran a thumb over my cheek. "Stop acting so tough. You don't like me."

My heart hiccuped. In that second of confusion, he took advantage, swallowing my oxygen with a kiss that ate away my understanding of the world. *I don't like him?* I heard him exhale, felt his stubble on my flesh. *No. He's right.*

Pushing him away, I fought for the inch of air between us. It was small, but for what I wanted to say, it was enough. "I love you, Drezden."

"That's better." He covered me like smoke, took me down into the blankets. I was happy to suffocate there, but he wouldn't let me. His tongue found mine, brought fire to my veins. There was no way to die when he gave me such life. "Lola... I love you, too." His teeth flashed. "Fuck, I really do."

Circling my arms around his neck, I held him on top of me. Our chests caressed, hearts throbbing faster and faster. "Of course, you do," I whispered. "Why else write me a love song?"

His body tightened. "You knew when I sang it."

"I knew when I read the lyrics in your notebook."

The edges of his lips shifted between amusement and wickedness. "You're amazing."

The blush ran to my toes and beyond. "Hardly. Couldn't even finish the final show."

"That wasn't your fault." Stroking my hair, Drezden put his chin on my head. "Besides, you'll have plenty of more shows to perform. Plus a new CD to record, we'll want to release one soon with you on it."

He didn't say 'and not Johnny,' but I heard it. The memory of being kidnapped was a wretched thing. But I'd have new memories before everything was done. Leaning up, I sought out Drezden's soft mouth.

When I'd started out weeks ago as a roadie for my brother, I could never have expected that I'd end up here. *Yes,* I thought, shivering under Drezden's expert fingers. *I never expected any of this.*

Lola Cooper.

Fucking rock star.

My world could never be the same...

And I was just fine with that.

Thanks for reading!

Brenda's Story

Looking in the mirror of that questionable quality but oh-so-cheap downtown boutique, I thought two things to myself.

One: When would it be my turn to find love?

And Two: Were my eye-bags *always* this big?

Sighing, I pushed at my skin, making a face. *I look older than I should because of how much stress this industry puts on me.* You would think that, once he'd started seriously dating someone, Drez would have finally alleviated some of the craziness in his lifestyle.

Amazingly, he hadn't.

Between fans, kidnappings, someone hijacking the tour bus, and a party one night that had involved a giraffe and three clowns— life hadn't calmed down at all.

Maybe once he gets married? Fuck, that thought was probably crazier than everything else put together. I was still having trouble wrapping my brain around it. Drezden Halifax, a married man. I'd thought the wedding invitation was a joke until Lola had confirmed it.

Someone knocked loudly on my stall door. "Hey! People are waiting to change! Hurry up!"

Gently, I pushed my forehead onto the mirror. *I'm doing just that: waiting for something to change.* Tightening my jaw, I stood straight. *No, what is this? I'm not sad, things are great for me! I've got money, status, a job the world is jealous of!*

What more could I need?

Ignoring the tiny voice inside of me that said, *"A serious relationship!"* I kicked the door open dramatically. The lady who'd been knocking jumped back, her thin eyebrows shooting to her hairline. "All yours," I said, motioning like she was a damn queen.

Her eyes flicked to the dress hanging in the stall. "Don't you want that?"

I hadn't even tried it on. I hadn't had the courage to bother. "Nope! All yours, and honestly, green is totally your color." Pushing my sunglasses down over my face, I swayed past the gawking customers and out into the hot New York sun. My mental checklist burned as it realized what I was missing:

No dress for the wedding.

No date.

And no clear idea on why I felt so pissed about all of that.

****

I made it back to my hotel, grateful that the bar was open, even if I was the only patron.

The bartender looked up, his smile going

crooked. "Didn't I see you this morning?"

Had he? *Oh, right,* I thought with dry humor. *I had two mimosas before I went on my shopping adventure.* Settling on the stool, I propped my sunglasses on my head. "Good memory."

"Just wait and see." He moved behind the bar, shaking things together until he placed a perfectly iced gin and tonic in front of me. His grin was too proud. "You wouldn't stop drinking these last night."

Hesitating, my fingers paused by the glass. "Huh?" It was all I could say. Was I seriously drinking that much lately? If I thought back, it was obvious I'd been a bit more... loose with my habits since getting the wedding invitation.

Sipping the drink, I gave him a smile. "It's perfect. Thanks." The guy winked, then went about pretending to be busy for the ghosts or whoever that were sitting at the bar, because as far as I saw, I was alone.

Alone alone alone. Ugh. But, it was true. *I guess this wedding is really hammering it home.* Work was my husband, I was married to my job. I'd gone from managing Four and a Half Headstones to consulting for others, as well as playing a minor agent. I was richer than ever and busier than ever, and no one had forced me to slow down enough to realize how unsatisfying it was.

But what could I fucking do? Online

dating terrified me, and the only guys I ever met belonged to the music industry—and they were as messy as I was. Worse, usually.

There'd never been a guy who'd held my attention.

Well, that's not true. What about—I cut my own thoughts off at the stem. I was *not* about to moon over a guy I had no chance with. After all, I'd interacted with him on the sidelines for years. If he hadn't noticed me by now, he never would.

Yup. That's right. I tilted my glass back and swallowed. *Fate doesn't exist.* I started to chuckle, my eyes lifting to scan the lobby. I was in the perfect spot to watch the doors and see everyone entering.

That meant it was easy to spot Sean Cooper.

Spitting gin and tonic onto the bar, I coughed violently. *Holy shit he's here. I summoned him with my mind!* Maybe fate was real, or maybe I'd just taken for granted that Lola's brother would show up for her wedding.

It's fine, who cares if he's here. I cared. A lot. *Shit, maybe I shouldn't let him see me. Wait, who cares if he sees me? Shit. He saw me.* Sitting up on the stool, I dabbed as casually as I could at the gin and tonic spill while smiling at Sean.

He hooked his dufflebag over his shoulder and grinned. "Brenda? That you?"

Did he know my name because I was his

sister's manager, or did he remember it for other reasons? I was normally so cool and calm. Channeling my inner power-bitch, I thrust my hand in his direction. "Hey there, Kiddo!" *Fuck. Kiddo?*

Sean's eyebrow piercing wiggled over his amused grin. "Uh, hey yourself. I'm guessing you're pregaming before the ceremony?"

Of course he'd noticed the glass in my hand. "Well, I've got another hour to kill before they expect us to show up in the ballroom. Who knows what those two will put us through before I can get to the open bar."

Laughing so that I could see his perfect teeth, Sean nodded. His smile warmed me better than the gin did. "I'd better clean up. I'll see you tonight, okay?"

"Yeah. Okay." Waving at his back, I stared for a long while.

The bartender cleared his throat. "Did you want another drink?"

Jumping up in a flurry of limbs, I threw some cash down. "No time! Thank you!"

Sean was going to be at the wedding.

Sean was going to look *hot*.

If I wanted to get through this evening...

I had to go pick out a damn dress. For real, this time.

****

Ever been to a rock star wedding?

Me either.

As I strut my way into the courtyard on my fuck-me-heels balanced out by my brand new and too expensive but demure green cocktail dress, I gazed up at the decorations in wonder. Lola's taste in black and purple was... well, everywhere.

There were dark flowers on every surface, leading the way into the open air garden. Here, things appeared more traditional. White chairs, flower petals on the green grass, and a gigantic archway crafted from fiddlehead ferns, music notes, and woven vine tendrils.

It was pretty and ethereal. I was impressed—they'd planned all this while finishing up a brand new CD? Huh. Maybe my workaholic nature had rubbed off on them.

"Brenda!" a voice shouted.

Colt waved at me from where he was helping an older woman into a chair near the front. Things were about to start, so I hurried to give him a quick hug. I wouldn't get to see much of him later since he was the best man.

"Hey," I said, looking him up and down. "You clean up nice."

He posed in his dark purple three-piece suite, his ear gauges the same color. "Ah, shit, thanks." The older woman smiled up at me—and I froze. "Brenda, you remember Drezden's mother, right?"

"Of course," I said, leaning down so she

492

could see my lips. My belly shrank at the memory of this sweet woman and her deafness. "How are you?"

Beaming, she dabbed at her eyes. "Already crying," she said, a little too loudly. Music piped through the garden; it was time.

She couldn't hear it, so Colt bent down, pointing at the flower arch. "I need to go!" he shouted.

Nodding, she settled in with her mouth thin and tight. The face of a mom who didn't want to lose it before her son even said his vows.

Keeping a happy look on, I backed away —thumping into something solid. "Oh!" I gasped, spinning to face... Sean. He was wearing a silver vest over a black shirt, his slacks darker than his hair. He looked delicious. "Brenda," he said, guiding me up aisle. "Hurry up, it's starting."

"Uh, right." Clearing my throat, I stood under the flower arch with my knees pressed together. I could smell him over the garden flowers—musky and orange citrus.

Lola and Drez weren't exactly traditional. They'd decided to just have people close to them on the day of. There were no bridesmaids or the like—I kind of wish she'd bothered, then I wouldn't have had to pick a dress.

But no, she had to be kind and all, *do what you want!*

There was an inch of existence between my bare knee and Sean's. I started wondering if I'd shaved close enough. Had I used enough lotion? I was more conscious of that inch of air that could have been erased with a simple adjustment of my toes than I was of how the sitting crowd was watching me.

Drezden lined up beneath the arch with Porter and Colt beside him. He was standing still, that seemed... weird. *He isn't nervous?* How could he not be nervous on his wedding day?

And then Lola entered, and I understood.

He looked at her in that gorgeous cream and purple ombre excuse for a wedding gown, and I'd never seen such a pure expression of love.

Cameras flashed, I was sure the media would have their hands on the photos by tonight in spite of how intimate Lola and Drez had tried to keep this event. She swayed up the aisle, her teeth sparkling and her eyes so big I thought they'd fall from her head.

Her tattoo shined under the setting sun. It had been updated recently, the castle added onto. The curling font spelled out *Honesty* along the top. I didn't know what that meant, except my guess was it had to do with Drez's little game back when he'd auditioned her for the band.

"She's so pretty," I whispered to Sean.

He smiled tenderly. "Damn right."

Lola and Drez embraced under the arch. I wasn't shocked at the lack of a priest—they'd arranged for an officiant who worked for the hotel. It was all just to make it official, I knew neither of them cared who married them.

They just wanted to be *married.*

I had to admire that.

And then the officiant passed around instruments to Drez, Lola, and the rest of the band... and it got a little nuts. Sweet, but nuts.

Normal people write vows. Musicians sing their hearts out. But what really impressed me was the paper screen that had been set up for Drez's mom. As she watched the lyrics roll down the board, her eyes never stopped spilling tears.

Even *I* was getting a little watery. Rubbing my eye, I mumbled, "Bunch of cheese, huh?"

Sean smiled down at me. There was no doubting the red tinging his lower lids. Scrubbing at his face, he laughed. "Yeah. Cheesy."

His raw emotion made my heart stutter.

Standing there, I applauded with everyone else, smiling at the pair as they strut down the aisle to the stampeding sound of Colt's drums. Freed from being locked next to Sean, I bolted into the crowd and followed them eagerly into the reception.

That was where the open bar was.

****

When things quieted down, I made sure to give Drezden a good, hard poke in the back. He spun around, grabbing me in a tight hug. "Congrats!" I shouted, hugging him back. I was careful not to spill my second drink onto his nice suit. "How does it feel?"

Grinning, he pulled Lola close to his hip. "Amazing," he said. "I'm the luckiest man alive."

Lola flushed, but her smile was sweet. "Drez, come on."

I waved my glass. "Well, cheers to you both. But you better be ready for work after that honeymoon! We have a tour in Japan next month, remember."

"Yeah, yeah," Drez sighed. "Let me enjoy my wedding, no work talk."

Bowing my head, I winked at Lola. "I adore your dress."

She twirled, holding the long hem so that the purple edges became a blur. "Thank you! The boutique gave me grief over the color."

"They're idiots. No taste," I said, nodding sagely.

More people crowded up, all wanting to congratulate the new Bride and Groom. Not wanting to overstay, I gave them each one more hug and retreated to the bar. The hall was bustling, much busier than the reception—I was sure people had crashed in that weren't invited.

I'd barely dropped onto a stool when Sean put his elbows on the bar beside me. "Hey, there you are."

Smiling, I shrugged. "Here I am. Were you looking for me?" I joked.

His grin was firm, his eyes twinkling. "I was."

Choking on my drink, I barely avoided a repeat of earlier when I'd spit gin and tonic all over. "What for?" *Whoa heart, down boy.*

Facing towards the busy room, he gestured with his chin. "Want to dance?"

Grinning, I tossed back the last of my drink. "Keep my tab open," I said to the bartender. I was living on liquid courage; it was bound to run out, especially after dancing with Sean.

I hopped off the stool. Circling his arm around me, his fingers grazed my lower back. I stood straighter, wishing I had another drink instantly. *No, this is good and fun and calm the fuck down.* It was just dancing. With the guy I had a giant crush on.

Fuck me.

In the center of the hotel's event hall, lights sparkled to form a circle. Sean pulled me there, the other dancers making room for us like they were leaves on a river and we were something much more solid.

Winking, he took my hand. My mouth was tingling, my tongue too heavy, but I smiled anyway. This was exactly what I'd always wanted. Sean Cooper was holding me close, his hips grinding close to my ass, his skilled fingers drifting along my waist.

The music shifted—became faster paced.

We synced up, our energy moving with the rhythm. He cupped my shoulders, pushing me away then pulling me in. His nose brushed by my ear—did he just inhale? Was he smelling me?

Like we were made of static, our torsos stuck together. I was wild with excitement, my toes throbbing in my heels, but I didn't care. I wanted more—more of him.

He spun me until my heart painted the inside of my ribs. My ears rang—not with music, but with the sound of our feet. Sean stopped me on a dime, bending me down so I was lying across his muscular arm and gazing up into his shadowed face.

His smile was gone.

His cockiness had vanished.

Sean stared down at me with uncertainty shining in his black and blue irises. The centers shrank, focusing on me. They twitched—his tongue gliding over his lower lip. I swore he wanted to say something, why else was his chest filling with air?

And then he looked away and the moment died.

Standing me up, he steadied me. "You're a good dancer," I said, panicking as I felt our energy melting into something awful. Regret? Was this fucking regret?

Shrugging, he buried his hands in his slacks. "I guess. Hey, that was fun. I'm going to try and get a second to congratulate my sister before she's mobbed again."

"Oh. Okay." Lifting my fingers, I did a half-wave. He smiled briefly, then I saw his broad back as he faded into the crowd.

Around me, people laughed and spun on the dance floor.

But somehow...

I'd never felt more alone.

****

I hadn't lingered after that. Tired and miserable, I'd dragged myself upstairs to my room. I was determined to take advantage of the one thing I had left on this trip:

A good night's sleep.

So why the hell was that proving so elusive to me?

Grunting, I yanked at my dress's zipper over and over. "Sonofa...!" Lying on the bed I wrenched as far back as I could. My fingertips couldn't get a good enough grip on the impossibly tiny bit of metal. Why had I bought this stupid outfit again?

Rolling on my side I breathed in, grit my teeth, and pushed my shoulders to the absolute limit no human should *ever* have to endure. I was so close, my muscles creaking, my breath expelling from my exhausted lungs.

Almost there. Keep going. Keep... keep...

A knock came at my door. "Brenda?"

Oh fuck. That was Sean. Corkscrewing around to look, I lost my balance and went over the edge of the bed. "Shit!" I groaned, hitting the ground hard enough to rattle my teeth.

"Brenda! You okay in there?"

"Yeah, fine!" Standing quickly, I ran on bare feet to open the door. He was waiting there in the hall, one hand deep in his sweatpants' pocket. Unlike me, he'd managed to change out of his wedding clothes.

When his eyes ran over my body, I imagined they were his nimble fingers. "What was that noise?"

"Rats," I said quickly. "Hotel rats. Big ones." Leaning on the door, I tried to look casual. "You uh, need something?"

Glancing down the hall, he said, "Could I sleep in here tonight?"

My heart popped.

Everything narrowed to a pinprick. I could see nothing but Sean and his curious eyes. "Sleep?" I stated, "In here?" *What is happening? Holy hell, what do I do? What? What? What? This is...* This was too good to be true. And terrifying.

Sheepishly, he cupped his own neck. "My room shares a wall with Lola's. If you get my drift."

Aaaaand my joy was the next thing to pop. "Oh. Right." That made sense; who wanted to hear their own sibling banging on their wedding night? Standing aside, I motioned for him to come in.

"Thanks," he said, studying my room as he turned in place. His eyes tracked to my suitcase, to my bed, then back to me. His frown stretched outwards. "Why are you still in your dress?"

I tugged at the hem. "Oh. I just hadn't finished changing yet."

"Sorry for interrupting. Go ahead and use the bathroom, I'll wait." He perched on the edge of my mattress.

"Sure, sure. Just a minute." I slid into the bathroom with my big, fat, fake grin. Finally alone, I sucked in air through my nose and grabbed the edge of the sink so hard my fingertips went white.

Sean Cooper was going to sleep in my room.

Tonight.

With me.

Staring at myself in the mirror, I smoothed a palm over my damp forehead. *Get it together, Brenda.* I always had it together. Why was this one guy so great at making me fall apart?

Furious, I ripped at the zipper and *seethed*. "Come... off!" My balance went out, I fell backwards against the glass shower door. White fire exploded from my elbow. "Fuck!"

"Brenda?" he shouted, shoving into the bathroom. "Are you okay?"

Whirring, I faced him with my chest thrusting out, hands on my spine. "I'm—fine."

He squinted at me. "Are you stuck in that dress?"

Giving up, I slumped over limply. "Yes. I am. Can you help me?"

He came my way, his sneakers scuffing over the shiny tiles. "Why didn't you say so earlier?"

The small room suddenly became so much smaller. It took all of my bravery to face away from him. Knowing he was about to touch me was hard, but seeing it happening was killing my confidence. "It doesn't matter."

"Were you embarrassed?"

I bit the inside of my cheek. *Too clever. Or I'm too obvious.* I was going to say something—create some lie that explained away my decision to fight with the busted zipper all alone. Before I could, Sean brushed his fingers over the nape of my neck.

My inhale was so loud it echoed on the white porcelain walls.

Freezing, Sean asked, "You okay?"

I was glowing red; I could see it in the mirror. "Just hurry up. This thing is choking me."

Eager to obey, Sean yanked the zipper straight down. It split open, freeing my upper body to the cool air. *All* of my upper body. He'd pulled so hard that the entire dress had split open and fallen to the floor.

Both of us gawked at my exposed breasts. "Oh shit!" Sean exclaimed, his hands held high as if he wanted to help, but had no clue how to. What the shit was with today? Had someone cursed me—was it the woman at the dress shop I'd been rude to?

Wrapping my arms around my chest, I crouched, lifting the dress enough to hide my ass. At least my panties were cute. "Don't look!" I shouted, mortified.

"I'm not!" Sean spun around, deliberately not looking in my direction. That made me feel a little worse. Was I not his type? Shouldn't he be peeking, at least?

His eyes were shut so tight, his forehead was turning a different color. I grabbed the bust of the cocktail dress and shimmied it back over my chest. I was ready to give up on the world and go join some celibate covenant.

Maybe he sensed my mood, because he turned enough to glance my way. "I really didn't look."

"I believe you," I chuckled sourly.

With nothing but awkward air between us, I started to squeeze past him. I misjudged the space, bumping into him roughly while he was hiding his gaze from me. Gasping, I started to stumble, our ankles scissoring.

As if he was worried I was about to fall, Sean threw his hands out to grab me.

His palm landed perfectly on my ass.

On pure instinct, I whirled around and slapped him. The noise shattered the silence, my palm vibrating from the stinging impact. "Fuck!" Sean grunted, cupping his cheek and gawking at me.

Oh, shit. I just slapped my dream guy. I'd thought today couldn't get worse. I'd been wrong.

His eyes were huge; shocked. My face had to be pure white. Impossibly, his stunned look slowly curled into the most adorable smile since the invention of smiles. He laughed and said, "You've got quite an arm there." He rubbed his chin and laughed again.

The sound was as sweet as the music I'd heard him play over the years. No, it was sweeter.

I was too lost to respond. He took my hand, his grip like velvet wrapped around metal. "What's your secret to muscles like these? I didn't think you had time to work out, Brenda."

I gaped down at our linked fingers. "What do you mean?"

Shrugging, he didn't release me. "Whenever I watch you, you're always running around, super busy-like."

504

When he watches me? We'd been around each other many times, but I'd thought it was me who was always watching *him*.

He kept holding my hand. His smile faded just a bit and those eyes fixed on me like they'd finally focused, like I wasn't some background fixture. I saw his throat ripple as he swallowed.

We were standing there in a hotel bathroom—me holding up a busted dress I'd paid too much for, him gripping my hand like I might vanish—and I had a feeling my legs no longer worked. *Is this really happening?* I wondered.

His hand slid off my shoulder and to my collarbone. He was traveling towards my neck, and when he got there, he brushed along my jaw as if my skin was as fragile as powdered sugar.

I wet my lips. Speaking is hard when your mouth is stuck half-open like a fish. "What are you doing?" I asked him.

Sean worked his way behind my ear, winding his steel hold into my hair. "When we were dancing tonight, I wanted to tell you something."

I couldn't fucking blink. "What?"

"Brenda, earlier you were so—no, not just earlier. You've always been..."

What? I asked myself desperately. *Dammit, spit it out! I'm what?*

His grin lifted up high until I could see

505

his upper row of pristine teeth. "You're beautiful."

The dress fell to my ankles. That time, when he didn't look at my chest and kept staring into my wide eyes, I wasn't offended. Lunging forward, I closed my lips on his and tasted what I'd dreamt about for years.

I didn't let go. I didn't withdraw. I refused to stop kissing him because if I did, I might wake up. He settled around me, his arms wrapping over my shoulders as he pulled me in. My sensitive skin scraped over his cotton shirt; I felt every single fiber. He held me close and dammit, no one had ever smelled so perfect.

I opened my eyes, practically drunk on delight. I'd started to smile like a brainless fool.

There was a twinkle of mischief in his smirk. Sean snatched me up, carrying me into the main room and pushing me hard against the wall. The material shook—I wondered if anyone had heard it or my shocked squeal.

His soft, gentle kisses morphed into rougher, needy things. I pushed off the wall and kissed him back, determined to get as much of him as I could. I wanted him to see I could keep up with him. Whatever was going on here, I wasn't going to ruin it by shying away.

Besides... I was as eager as he was.

Grinding his hips on my bare leg, Sean groaned through his teeth. His hard-on burrowed into me, firm enough to leave a bruise. "Do you feel that?" he asked, guiding my hand down to the shape of his cock. "You've got me so damn *hard.*"

Heat jumped between my thighs. I was glad I was wearing black panties—the one bit of clothing I had left on—since my wet spot would be less obvious. "Fuck, you're big," I chuckled nervously. Gliding my palm along his sweatpants, I explored his thick size.

He leaned in and kissed me again, this time on the side of my cheek. He moved down my jaw, curling down my neck, sending electric surges of delight all over my body. A tiny moan escaped me; I slapped a hand over my mouth. He either didn't notice or didn't care because he spent too much time at my neckline, still driving me mad.

I felt his hand on my leg and glanced down. *Sweet mercy, yes.* The visual of his lust-filled eyes gazing up at me from between my thighs caused me to tremble. His teeth raked down my skin to my knee—when I jumped, he grabbed my ankles and spread me wide.

"Stay," he commanded.

As if I could do anything else.

Nuzzling the inside of my knee, he stretched out on the bed and lowered his mouth to my hip. Nipping the black satin, he worked my panties down—the air cool over my hyper-sensitive swollen pussy.

Sean hissed and I felt the air move. "I've

never seen such a perfect little pussy."

Blushing like a virgin, I dug my fingers into the expensive hotel blankets. His tongue flattened over my clit, stroking it lazily. Realizing he was taking his time had the opposite effect on me.

Flaring with sharp arousal, I shuddered. "Sean, that's amazing. I can't... fuck." I was babbling—my calm exterior had been failing me all day but this? I was a frazzled mess. My mouth opened in a silent scream. I started to sit up as my body tightened, my eyes scrunching as my head rolled back. The slightest whimper drifted off my lips.

I was so out of breath I was seeing spots. My entire brain was just nothing but a cloud of lust. His fingers wriggled, spreading my pussy as they reached where his tongue couldn't. I grabbed the comforter with my right hand and slapped frantically with my left. I bet I looked like I was holding my breath, maybe because I was.

With some vigorous strokes, Sean made my pussy tingle. I strangled his fingers, coming violently—my muscle fibers straining to keep me together at the seams. "Ah! Sean, I'm coming! I'm—ah, ah!"

"Wow," he breathed out, his voice shaking. His fingertips caressed my inner roof, his thumb strumming my clit like he was playing guitar. "Don't tell me you're spent," he teased.

Cracking my first smile since he'd kissed me, I laughed weakly. "Not on your life." I reached for him. My palm mauled his shirt, exploring his hard muscles underneath. I couldn't count the times I'd wanted to touch him, to sense the warmth of his body.

Sean took my cue and peeled his shirt away. I'd never seen him shirtless before. His skin was the color of cinnamon sprinkled on a latte, his ink elegant where it splashed color over his body. I didn't see any scars, but there was a mole on his thigh. I wanted to kiss that perfect little jewel.

Burying his thumbs in his pants, he slid the cotton material easily down his legs. His cock sprang out from his red briefs, the thin material showing off his fat tip. The sight of it made my insides thrum. My pussy clenched; painfully empty.

He kissed me again, I tasted my own tang on his lips. His arms braced on either side of my head, two marble columns that stretched up to the heaven that was his handsome face.

Strands of his dark hair fringed his jaw. I brushed them away, lingering on his skin. We watched each other—tried to read each other's thoughts. Thinking about how this was happening made me wonder too much about the *why*.

A dot of sweat fell from his chin. "Brenda? You okay?"

I flicked my eyes to his mouth, then back

509

up. "Is this really alright?"

He didn't make me expand on what *this* was. He already knew. "When is sex ever wrong?"

Smiling softly, I rolled my thumb to his earlobe, then over to his eyebrow piercing. "You never gave me the time of day before."

Sean flinched. "What? I didn't think you wanted me to. You were always so busy, I thought if you were into me you'd show it."

My laugh was strangled. "I thought it was obvious that I liked you!"

"You're joking. How the hell was I supposed to know a hot woman like you with all her shit together liked me? Me, of all people?"

Now, I was really laughing. The noise hurt me when it came up, bitterness coating my mouth. A few tears welled at the corners of my eyes; he wiped them away before I could.

He sat back, asking, "Brenda? What is it?"

"I'm such a moron," I sniffled, my smile hurting my face. "All this time, I thought I'd made it obvious I was into you. And you're saying I didn't. What sort of woman with her "shit together" messes that up?"

Circling my wrist, he pressed my palm back to his jaw. The blue in his eyes was as serious as a hurricane on the loose. I couldn't escape it—my laughter died abruptly. He whispered, "The kind of woman who can reign in a band like the Headstones. That can strut around in heels on the most busted ass stage and never lose her poise. And the kind that after years of working on the edges of my world while I missed every signal, still gives me a chance like this."

His kiss tasted like a promise—like the severity and silliness of a pinky swear. Sean swirled his tongue with mine, making me thrill. My breathing was high in my throat.

Reaching between us, he fiddled with something. The heavy, hot heat of his cock pressed on my belly. "Let me get a condom," he said huskily.

I grabbed for him, guiding him towards my soaked thighs. "I'm on the pill. Don't you dare try to walk away from this."

He bared his teeth and moaned. "Fuck, your hand feels incredible."

Smiling sideways, I jerked at his rigid shaft. Each little desperate sound he made turned me on further. "Yeah? You like that?"

Focusing on me, he flashed a crooked smirk. "You said you're on the pill?"

I nodded.

"Good." He snatched my hands, pushing them into the pillows over my head. "I'm about to fill this cute pussy with so much come you'll be feeling it inside of you for weeks."

Fuck he was filthy—I loved it. He fondled my ass cheeks, spreading me while he fed his cock patiently into me. My pussy hugged him, straining under his girth. It wasn't just that he was massive, it had been forever since I'd gotten laid. I was surprised there weren't cobwebs down there when he was eating me out.

Groaning obscenely, I shut my eyes. On and on he slid into me, scraping the ridge of his cock-head along my walls. Each inch I took, another followed. My clit was engorged; the pressure of his abdominals grinded on the sensitive nub.

An orgasm threatened to shake me to my roots, and he hadn't even finished entering me! Sean grabbed my chin, whispering, "Look at me." I did. I didn't consider disobeying. I was so used to being in control, and here, finally, someone else was happy to take the reins. "Watch me as I fuck you. I want to see you *seeing me* drive you wild."

Swallowing, I wrapped my arms around his neck. His hair was soft; damp from sweat. Sean Cooper had struck me as a man with a hard edge, but this was way beyond even my darkest fantasies.

I fucking loved it.

Together we shuddered—he'd finally sank to the root. His balls tickled my ass cheeks, and I felt them vanish as he withdrew. Hooking his arms under my knees, he changed his angle. I'd never witnessed such a sexy and terrible smile.

Bracing himself, Sean slammed his cock

deep.

"Ah!" I gasped. He didn't let me catch myself, he withdrew again, the meaty sound of his cock filling up my soaked pussy loud in the hotel room. He fucked me like it was his mission. He was wound up in his desire to make me come, or to come in me, or maybe both.

Panting, I held on tight. I wasn't passive, though; I thrust back to meet each of his strokes. The pressure of orgasm was threatening me, and I knew I was going to come, knew it long before it rippled through my core.

Grunting, he stared me down—dared me to blink. Instead, I kissed him hard, letting him feel my tongue as it went numb with the rest of my senses. I came with my knees shaking, embracing him with my arms and my pussy.

He didn't ask me if I was done. He was finished with talking. Sean drove into me frantically, his cock swelling, twitching with warning. Teeth nipped my ear; he froze up, nothing moving but his dick as it jerked in me.

I moaned again, nuzzling his throat as he filled me up. Each pulse moved through me and into my heart. The reverberations calmed until it was just our ribs that swelled. Our breathing joined the same rhythm.

Brushing hair from my forehead, he looked down on me. "Some wedding, huh?" he asked.

I snorted, covering my mouth. That made him laugh, too. "Yeah. Some wedding, alright."

I didn't want him to leave. Deep down, I was worried he would. Sean slid free, taking a moment to clean up. I held my breath until he dropped back beside me on the bed, his arms creating a pillow. "What?" he asked, blinking at me.

"You're staying?"

His eyebrows went up. "You said I could sleep here."

"Oh, right." I'd forgotten all about that. Thrilling with delight, I wiggled under the blankets. He joined me, our legs touching but nothing else. "That was... really good."

Chuckling warmly, he turned so he could watch me. "Worth the wait?"

I got his meaning, blushing furiously. "Did you really have no clue that I liked you?"

"How could I?"

I opened my mouth—shut it, debating my next words. "Want to hear a funny story?" He nodded, motioning at me to go on. I fidgeted, the blanket under my chin. I treated it like it was armor, but my secret came from within where nothing could keep me safe. "Years ago, I saw you playing at some little hole in the wall club."

"Really?" Sitting up, he considered me. "What were you doing, crushing on me at first sight?"

I gave him a little elbow. He wasn't far off, though. "I was a brand new agent. I was looking for talent." His smile faded away. I had to look at the wall, seeing his blue eyes was too much. "That night, I was planning to sign you. But..." *But then I heard Drezden.* "It didn't work out. My company wanted another band, who was I to disagree?"

The bed springs creaked. I still didn't look at him. "You mean you were almost my manager?"

Biting my tongue did little to help my mood. "I was so excited when you auditioned for Four and a Half Headstones. I really pushed for you, Sean. It just wasn't meant to be."

A wall of heavy silence grew. I swear, I felt each stone being stacked.

His hand cradled my shoulder. Startled, I twisted to look at him. I expected sadness, or anger—not his private little smile. "I guess it worked out for the best."

"What?" I asked. "No, if I'd signed you years ago, you'd have gotten as big and famous as Drez and the rest. You'd have—"

"I'd have never ended up like this," he said, gesturing at the two of us. "If you think I was oblivious to your feelings before, I promise that if you were my manager, I'd have *never* taken a chance with you."

Slowly, my heart filled my throat.

His kiss on my cheek was like an electric butterfly. "So it worked out for the best. See?"

515

I did see. I wouldn't have before, but...

Now, it was all I *could* see.

Hugging him so violently he groaned, I buried my nose in the hollow of his neck and shoulder. Sean held me as I laughed, not commenting on when it shifted into emotional tears.

This morning, I'd looked in a mirror and thought, *When will it be my turn to find love?*

And here it was.

Here it *had* been.

It was just waiting for me to step up and grab it.

ABOUT THE AUTHOR

A USA Today Bestselling Author, Nora Flite loves to write dark romance (especially the dramatic, gritty kind!) Her favorite bad boys are the ones with tattoos, the intense alpha types that make you sweat and beg for more!

Inspired by the complicated events and wild experiences of her own life, she wants to share those stories with her audience. Born in the tiniest state, coming from what was essentially dirt, she's learned to embrace and appreciate every opportunity the world gives her.

She's also, possibly, addicted to coffee and sushi. Not at the same time, of course.

Check out her website, noraflite.com, or email her at noraflite@gmail.com if you want to say hello! Hearing from fans is the best!

ROMANCE THAT PUSHES
THE LIMITS

52137675R00295

Made in the USA
Middletown, DE
08 July 2019